About the Authors

Rebecca Winters lives in Salt Lake City, Utah. With canyons and high alpine meadows full of wildflowers, she never runs out of places to explore. They, plus her favourite vacation spots in Europe, often end up as backgrounds for her romance novels because writing is her passion, along with her family and church. Rebecca loves to hear from readers. If you wish to e-mail her, please visit her website at: www.cleanromances.net

City loving, book addict, peony obsessive, **Katrina Cudmore** lives in Cork, Ireland with her husband, four active children and a very daft dog. A psychology graduate with a M.Sc. in Human Resources, Katrina spent many years working in multinational companies and can't believe she is lucky enough now to have a job that involves daydreaming about love and handsome men! You can visit Katrina at www.katrinacudmore.com

Connie Cox used to think authors were sophisticated creatures who lived in NYC, went to glitzy parties and wrote as the muse dictated. Then she met one. The writer looked a lot like her – jeans, a few extra pounds, a love of books and a quirky imagination. With the encouragement of that writer and many like her, Connie now lives the dream, writing big stories from her little desk in her little town. Even as you read this, she is working on a new story and living happily ever after.

The Gorgeous Greeks

COLLECTION

A Greek Romance

REBECCA WINTERS

KATRINA CUDMORE

CONNIE COX

MILLS & BOON

First Published in Great Britain 2020
By Mills & Boon, an imprint of HarperCollins*Publishers*
1 London Bridge Street, London, SE1 9GF

www.harpercollins.co.uk

HarperCollins*Publishers*
1st Floor, Watermarque Building, Ringsend Road
Dublin 4, Ireland

GORGEOUS GREEKS: A GREEK ROMANCE © 2020
Harlequin Books S.A.

Along Came Twins © 2013 Rebecca Winters
The Best Man's Guarded Heart © 2016 Katrina Cudmore
His Hidden American Beauty © 2013 Connie Cox

ISBN: 978-0-263-28210-8

MIX
Paper from
responsible sources
FSC™ C007454

ALONG CAME TWINS

REBECCA WINTERS

CHAPTER ONE

"DR. SAVAKIS? Thank you for seeing me at the end of your busy day. When Dr. Creer, my doctor in Philadelphia, told me I was pregnant with twins, no one could have been more surprised than I was. You wouldn't know that since my last visit to you before I left Athens, I filed for divorce. It will be final in a few days."

Her fertility doctor shook his balding head. "After such a joyous outcome, what a pity, Mrs. Petralia. I remember how excited you both were to know your allergy problem didn't have to interfere with your ability to conceive. Now that you're pregnant, I'm extremely sorry to hear this news."

No one could be sorrier than she was, but she didn't want to discuss it. "I still need to tell my husband, but it isn't the kind of thing he should hear over the phone. That's why I'm here in Greece for a few days."

"I see."

"I wanted to pay you a visit to let you know the procedure worked. After all we went through together, naturally I wanted to give you my personal thanks." Her voice caught. "It's been a dream of mine to have a baby. Despite my failed marriage, I'm ecstatic over this pregnancy. Leandros will be thrilled, too. As you know, his first wife died carrying their unborn child, and he lost them both. Without your help, this miracle would never have happened."

She should have gone to Leandros first with the news, but decided that by coming to their doctor to tell him her marriage was over, it would make the divorce more real somehow and help her to face Leandros.

Dr. Savakis eyed her soberly through his bifocals. "I'm glad for you and pleased you phoned to see me. How are you feeling?"

"Since the doctor prescribed pills that help my nausea, I'm much better."

He smiled. "Good. You'll need to take extra care of yourself now."

"I know. I plan to, believe me."

"As long as you're here, I have information that might interest you at some later date."

"What is it?"

"More medical research has been done on your condition. Did your doctor tell you?"

"No. I've only seen him once."

"He'll no doubt discuss this with you during one of your appointments with him."

Kellie thought about all the anguish she'd been through hoping to get pregnant. "It doesn't matter now. I'm going to have my hands full raising my twins."

"Nothing could make me happier in that regard. But you need to keep in mind what I'm telling you for the future. You're only twenty-eight. In time you could find yourself remarried and wanting another child."

She shook her head. "No, Dr. Savakis. That part of my life is over." Though they hadn't been able to make their marriage work, Leandros had spoiled her for other men. He'd been the great love of her life. There would never be another.

"You say that now, but one never knows what the future will bring."

"I—I appreciate that," she stammered, "but I can't think about anything else except raising my children."

"I understand," he said kindly. "If you have any problems while you're here in Athens, call me. There's a Dr. Hanno on staff here who's an OB and works with high-risk patients. If you're going to be in Greece for any length of time, I'd advise you to call him and make an appointment for a checkup. Tell him I referred you. And don't forget. I'm always at your disposal."

"Thank you, Dr. Savakis. You've been wonderful. I want you to know I'll always be grateful."

Kellie left his office in the medical building attached to the hospital and took a taxi back to the Civitel Olympic Hotel in central Athens. She was exhausted and hungry. Tomorrow morning she'd approach her soon-to-be ex-husband, wherever he happened to be. Her breath caught just thinking about seeing him again. It was better for her mind not to go there.

Once she had dinner in her room, she'd phone her aunt and uncle to let them know she'd arrived safely.

It was after eleven at night when the door connecting Leandros's office with his private secretary's opened. Everyone had gone home six hours go. It was probably one of the security guards, but he still resented the interruption. He looked up to discover his sister-in-law on her way in with a tray of food in hand.

A scowl broke out on his face. "What are you doing here, Karmela?"

"Mrs. Kostas told me you'd be working through the night to get ready for your mysterious trip. Is it true you're leaving in the morning?"

"That's not your concern."

"I thought you'd like a cup of coffee and some sandwiches to help you stay awake." She put it on his desk.

"You should have gone home with everyone else. I'm not hungry and need total quiet to work through these specs."

"Well, I'm here now." She grabbed a sandwich and sank into one of the chairs near his desk to eat. "Don't be grumpy. I worry about you. So do Mom and Dad. They've tried to get you to come to dinner, but you keep turning them down."

"I've been busy."

"Where are you going on your vacation?"

"That's confidential."

"I'm family, remember? I like to do things for you."

"You need to lead your own life. I appreciate the coffee, but now you have to go."

She didn't budge. "You shouldn't have married Kellie. She wasn't good enough for you, you know."

His hands curled into fists. Before Kellie had shut the door on him in Philadelphia, she'd expressed the same sentiment to him. He'd been crushed that she would even think such a thing, let alone say it to his face.

But for Karmela to dare speak her mind like this made him furious. She was never one to worry about boundaries. His first wife, Petra, had warned him about it and had asked him to overlook that flaw in her sister.

Unfortunately, tonight Karmela had stepped over a line he couldn't forgive. Something wasn't right with his sister-in-law. He recalled the times Kellie had made a quiet comment about Karmela's familiarity with him. *And how many times did you brush it off as unimportant, Petralia?*

He fought to control his temper, but it was wearing thin. "You've said enough."

"Ooh. You really are upset." She got up from the chair. "The only reason I came in here was to help you." Tears filled her eyes. "You used to let me when Petra was alive." *Only because Petra asked me to be kind to you.* "I miss her and know you do, too."

He'd had all he could tolerate. "Leave *now*!"

"Okay. I'm going."

"Take the tray with you." He kept the coffee.

At the door she turned to him. "How long will you be gone?"

"I have no idea. In any event, it's no one's business but mine."

"Why are you being so hurtful?"

"Why do you continually go where angels fear to tread?" he retorted without looking at her. "Good night. Lock the door on your way out."

Relieved when the sound of her footsteps faded, he got back to work. In the morning he'd call Frato and go over the most important items before he took off. His eyes fastened on the picture of Kellie that sat on his desk. He was living to see his golden-blond wife again. Though they'd both hurt each other, he'd do whatever it took to get her back.

When Kellie awakened the next morning, she was so nervous to see Leandros again, she decided it was a mistake to have come to Athens. The talk with Dr. Savakis had opened up thoughts and feelings she'd been trying to suppress.

Soon after their wedding she'd been diagnosed with a semen allergy, but the doctor had said he saw no reason why they couldn't get pregnant. She and Leandros went to their first artificial insemination appointment with such high hopes. Kellie wanted a baby with him desperately. He was eager for it, too, and had made certain his business matters didn't interfere while they went through the steps necessary for conception to work.

Leandros had been so sweet and tender with her about their situation. Like any happily married couple wanting to start a family, they'd waited for the signs that meant she had conceived. Two months into their marriage, her period came. Leandros had kissed her and loved her out of her disappointment.

"Next month," he'd whispered.

Knowing he was disappointed, too, she'd loved him back with all the energy in her, wanting to show him she wouldn't allow this to dampen her spirits. Once again they went back to the hospital, for another try, only to be disappointed the following month.

So many tries full of expectations, but each waiting period had seemed harder than the last, contributing to the problems that had slowly crept into their marriage. What bittersweet irony that now they were divorcing, she was pregnant.

After she showered and got dressed, she phoned for a breakfast tray. Halfway through her meal she panicked. What she ought to do was go right back to Pennsylvania and phone him when there were thousands of miles between them. But it would be the cowardly thing to do. Her aunt and uncle never said as much, but she knew they'd be disappointed in her if she left it to a phone call.

You have to tell him.

You can't leave it up to anyone else.

Whatever is ultimately decided about the children, he has the right to hear it from you in person.

All the voices speaking in Kellie's head finally drove her to follow through with her agenda.

She asked the front desk to phone for a taxi. In a few minutes she found herself being driven along Kifissias Avenue toward the Petralia Corporation office building in downtown Athens. When it pulled up in front, she paid the driver and got out.

After taking a deep breath, she squared her shoulders and opened the doors, where Giorgios, looking like a well-dressed prizefighter, sat at the security desk near the entry. When he saw her, he shot to his feet in surprise.

"*Kyria Petralia—*"

Her chocolate-brown eyes fastened on him. He was one of Leandros's bodyguards and fiercely loyal to him. "Good morning, Giorgios. It's nice to see you. Is my husband on the premises?"

"He arrived an hour ago."

The news relieved her, since she hadn't relished the thought of trying to hunt Leandros down. He could have been out of the city doing business right now. Then again, he could have been at his apartment here in Athens, or at his villa on the family estate on Andros.

"If you still want a job with him, you won't let him or Christos know I'm here," she said in fluent Greek.

His expression turned to shock before Kellie walked

around his desk to the elevator located behind him. Unless Leandros made a helicopter landing on the roof after his flight from Andros Island, the elevator existed for his exclusive use when he entered or left the building from the street. For convenience sake it opened to the foyer of his private inner sanctum on the top floor. Giorgios had orders to guard it with his life.

She pressed her hand to the glass by the door, wondering if it would still recognize her code. For all she knew, Leandros had deleted it. But no, the door opened. She entered, still feeling Giorgios's stunned gaze on her before it closed.

A little over a month ago she'd left Greece, vowing never to return. But a week ago nausea had driven her to make an appointment with her doctor in Philadelphia. When he told her what was wrong with her, a transformation had taken place inside Kellie. It transcended the anguish and pain of the past year and gave her the spine she needed to face Leandros one more time.

Their divorce would soon be final. She intended for nothing to change in that regard, but since this totally unexpected contingency had arisen, it required an alteration in the documents their two lawyers had drawn up. Twenty-four hours should give Leandros's attorney enough time to take care of the necessary changes.

Kellie was desperate to catch her husband off guard; it was the only way to get through this final ordeal with him. She dreaded it, knew it would hurt, but had no other choice. For that reason she hadn't even told her best friend, Fran Meyers, she was coming.

Fran was now married to Nikolos Angelis, a good friend of Leandros's. They lived here in Athens with Nik's baby niece, Demi, soon-to-be their adopted daughter. If Nik knew of her arrival, he'd have phoned Leandros. Among the legal papers in her purse was evidence of the restraining order she'd placed on Leandros to call off her bodyguard. Yannis had been her shadow for the two years she'd been married to Leandros. But when she'd demanded a divorce, she'd drawn the line at the retired secret service agent following her to the States. Leandros had been forced to comply, with the result that he had no prior knowledge she'd flown to Athens yesterday.

As the elevator carried her skyward, Kellie planned to take care of business as quickly as possible. She knew she'd soon be on her way back home to Philadelphia, where she'd been living with her aunt and uncle for the last month. But that was about to change.

By next week she'd move her aunt and uncle from their small apartment into a lovely four-bedroom brick row home in Parkwood with her. It was a charming residential neighborhood in the far northeast corner of Philadelphia, perfect for children. She'd already put down a deposit. A new life awaited her, but first things first.

When the elevator stopped and the door opened, Kellie took a deep breath and headed through the foyer. She walked past Christos, her husband's chief bodyguard. He started to reach for his phone to warn Leandros, but she put a finger to her lips and smiled. He nodded and sat down again.

A few more steps and she reached the entrance to her husband's private suite, which was also protected by a security code. As CEO of the Petralia Corporation, which built resorts all over Greece, he was one of the most successful businessmen in the country and had been a target for crazies long before Kellie had met him.

She had no idea what she might be interrupting, but that wasn't her concern anymore. It had been on her wedding day, two years ago, when Kellie realized she had an enemy in Karmela Paulos. Karmela was the sister of Petra, Leandros's first wife, who'd been pregnant when she'd died in a plane crash. At Kellie's wedding to Leandros, the beautiful, fashionable Karmela would willingly have scratched Kellie's eyes out if she could have gotten away with it.

Fran had been Kellie's matron of honor and had witnessed the obvious fact that Karmela had hoped to become the next Mrs. Leandros Petralia. But it didn't happen, so his sister-in-law had done the next best thing by becoming indispensable to Leandros, first as a confidante to the grieving widower, who was family, and later as a secretary in his inner office, under Mrs. Kostas. With cunning, Karmela had worked her way to the top floor, where she had daily contact with him.

Combined with the stress Kellie had been under because she couldn't conceive, plus her struggle with feelings of inadequacy, the situation had grown intolerable for her. After much thought and soul-searching, she'd told Leandros she wanted a separation, and had left on a trip with Fran. But because of disastrous circumstances, it came to an abrupt end, with her friend staying in Athens to be with Nik. At that point Kellie had left for Philadelphia.

On the night before she was due to fly back, she'd had a fainting spell and Leandros had taken her to the ER. When the doctor could find nothing wrong, she was sent home with the warning to eat, so it wouldn't happen again. They'd just returned when Karmela, whose hand was obviously recognized by the security entry, slipped into their apartment, as she'd done when Petra still lived there.

The fact that Leandros said nothing about his sister-in-law letting herself in unannounced had led Kellie to worry that he had more than brotherly feelings for Karmela. After all, she did resemble Petra. Perhaps, as Kellie had confided to Fran earlier, Karmela had become his pillow friend?

Evidently his brazen sister-in-law figured she had free reign with Leandros now that Kellie was leaving him. Her smiling, catlike eyes stared boldly at Kellie as she explained she'd brought some work for Leandros that needed his attention. Before she slipped out the door again, she'd wished Kellie a safe flight back to the States. No doubt she thought she'd seen the last of her. Kellie knew that her presence would knock the daylights out of Karmela, but this wasn't about her. It was about them—Leandros and Kellie—and their babies.

She put her palm against the glass next to the door. She suspected Karmela's manipulative smile would falter when Kellie walked into the office and word eventually circulated about the miraculous news. Everyone close to Leandros knew he'd mourned the loss of his first wife and unborn child, who would have been a girl.

Despite Kellie's impending divorce from Leandros, for him to learn he was going to be a father again would come as a tremendous thrill. But it would deal a near fatal blow to his sister-in-law's plans to have him for her own.

Kellie knew in her heart that Karmela was waiting for her chance to provide him with a living heir. At least that's what Frato Petralia had confided to Kellie at the wedding, after having too much to drink.

Frato was Leandros's good-looking first cousin and closest friend in the family. Still single, he was one of the vice presidents of the corporation, and enjoyed the company of several beautiful women, which didn't surprise Kellie at all. That evening he'd said quite a few things she didn't take seriously in the beginning, but over time she realized he'd spoken the truth.

On the day Leandros mentioned in passing about hiring Karmela to work under Mrs. Kostas, she'd tried not to let it affect her. But her first impression of Petra's sister at the wedding wouldn't leave her alone. She'd seen the way Karmela had behaved and talked to him. Karmela was no impartial bystander. Two years later the younger woman had insinuated herself into Leandros's office life, and who knew how much more. But it was all history now.

The elevator door opened silently along the wall away from his desk. Leandros sat in his swivel chair, half turned from her while engaged in an intense business discussion with Frato on the speakerphone. She recognized his voice.

At first glance she realized Leandros needed a haircut and a shave. There were wavy tendrils of dark hair, a shade away from being true black, clinging to his bronzed nape. It looked as if he'd been running his hands through it. The sleeves of the white shirt he wore had been pushed up to the elbows. Given his condition, and the accumulation of coffee cups on the desk, she could imagine he might have spent the night here.

She'd never seen him like this before. He was thirty-four, yet he looked five years older right now. Her normally fastidious, temperate husband was nowhere to be found. Kellie had seen him truly out of control only once before. It was the night she'd told him she wanted a divorce. In a way, this was worse—different, even—because there was a savage air about him. For a second she feared she'd done the wrong thing by coming here without his knowledge. But with so much riding on this, she couldn't run from him now. Too much was at stake.

Finding her courage, she called out softly to him. "Leandros?"

She knew he'd heard her voice, because his hard, lean body seemed to freeze in place before he slowly swung around to face her.

He'd lost weight. A pronounced white ring encircled his taut mouth, testifying to his incredulity at seeing her here. It stood out almost as much as his gray eyes, which had gone black as pitch at the moment. Their color reminded her of the dark sky before the tornado had struck the Petralia resort near Thessalonika five weeks ago, killing little Demi's parents.

Frato was on the other end of the phone line, still talking. Leandros muttered something she couldn't understand, before he hung up. His haunted look sent a shiver of alarm through her body. She sensed he was ready to spring from his chair.

"Don't get up," she urged, and walked over to one of the chairs in front of his desk to sit down. Not only had her legs turned to mush at the sight of him, she couldn't handle him touching her. He was still the most gorgeous man she'd ever known. In that regard, nothing had changed.

Kellie heard his sharp intake of breath. "What in the name of all that's holy brings you back to Greece?" His deep voice sounded so shaken, she hardly recognized it. His overarching look of disbelief sent a fresh shock wave of despair through her. The month apart had done the rest of the damage to their marriage, crushing the rubble to microscopic bits.

Suddenly there was a tap on the door and Karmela started to enter. "Not now!" Leandros snapped. Kellie had to admit she'd never seen Leandros this upset with an employee. Maybe he hadn't even realized it was Karmela.

Kellie was shocked by the other woman's sangfroid before she did Leandros's bidding. She was tall enough to wear the attractive black-and-white dress skimming her figure. With her hair falling like a silky black curtain, she was extraordinarily beautiful and would cause a traffic jam when she walked down the street.

Since she and Petra shared such a strong resemblance, Kellie could well imagine how his former wife had turned the sought-after bachelor into a married man. Karmela's hourglass figure was so different from Kellie's rounded curves.

The younger woman closed the door, but not before she shot Kellie a venomous glance. That reaction alone vindicated Kellie's belief that Karmela planned to win Leandros one way or another, if she hadn't already.

"Karmela still works for you, I see. And is still dropping in unannounced. As I recall, the last time we thought we were alone, Karmela dropped by with some papers for you. Though she didn't find us making love, she certainly *could* have if we hadn't been on the verge of divorce."

That was the first time Kellie had truly feared Leandros had been unfaithful to her with Karmela. Before that time, she'd only worried about the other woman's behavior.

"She was wrong to have done that, Kellie."

"It certainly was wrong, but you didn't say so at the time. I was so hurt when you let her come to work for you, and I told you as much, but you kept her on. We're almost divorced, yet she *still* works for you. As I've told you many times, your sister-in-law always had a habit of insinuating herself around you.

"Even a little while ago she walked in without as much as a tap on the door, but it's all right with you because *she's family.*"

Why did she sound so bitter? Kellie wondered. It was no longer her concern what Karmela did with Leandros. They were getting divorced. But the thought that he'd replaced her so soon hurt more than she could ever admit.

His beautiful olive complexion darkened with lines. "It's never been all right with me and I *am* going to do something about it. I'll ask you again. Why are you here?" He seemed to have lost some color.

Clearing her throat, she said, "I have news that demanded I come here in person." She was in possession of certain facts that would alter his world forever.

His hooded gaze pierced hers. "Has something happened to your aunt or uncle?"

Kellie could understand why he'd asked that question. He'd been wonderful to them from the moment he'd first met them. "This has nothing to do with them. They're fine." She moistened her lips nervously. "A week ago I was so nauseated, I went to the doctor in Philadelphia to find out what was wrong. I learned that I'm…pregnant."

His dark head reared back in complete shock. "*What* did you say?" She heard excitement exploding inside him before he'd even had time to assimilate the news. Though he'd never given up hope they would get pregnant, Kellie had stopped believing such a miracle would happen to them.

She breathed in deeply. "I'm more amazed than you. It seems that the last artificial insemination procedure I underwent *worked*. Impossible as it sounds, Dr. Creer says I'm already seven weeks pregnant."

A triumphant cry escaped Leandros. He leaped out of his chair, charged with an energy that transformed him before her eyes. Her pulse raced, because she'd known this would be his reaction. "The doctor said it's the reason I fainted the night before I left Athens. My periods have never been normal, so I never suspected anything."

Leandros came around and hunkered down in front of her, like a knight kneeling before his lady. When he grasped her hands, she could feel him trembling. Emotion had taken the blackness from his eyes, filling the gray irises with pinpoints of light. "We're going to have a baby?" There was awe in his voice as he kissed her fingertips. The news had started to sink in, but he didn't know all of it yet.

"There's more, Leandros."

Fear immediately marred his striking features and his hands gripped hers tighter. "Did the doctor tell you you're a high-risk pregnancy? Is something wrong?"

"No," she rushed to assure him. After he'd lost his first wife and unborn child, she didn't want to put him through such anxiety again. He didn't deserve any more trauma in that regard.

His expressive black brows furrowed. "Then what *do* you mean?"

Averting her eyes, she said, "The doctor ordered an ultrasound."

"And?" His voice shook.

"The technician detected two heartbeats."

"Two?" His explosion of joy reverberated off the walls of his office. "We're going to have twins?"

She nodded. "They're due March 12."

"Kellie—"

The next thing she knew he'd picked her up and wrapped her in his strong arms, burying his face in her neck. She felt moisture against her skin as he crushed her against him. He'd been at the hospital with her to do his part while they'd gone through procedure after procedure. Every time it turned out she hadn't gotten pregnant, he'd been there to comfort her and promise her it would happen next time. He never gave up, and now they were going to be parents. But it was too late for them. The situation had put too much strain on both of them.

His reaction to the news was all she could have wanted if they'd been happily married, but that was the excruciating point. Their marriage was over and had been for months.

Soon they'd be divorced. Having his babies wouldn't solve what was wrong between them. When he lifted his head to kiss her, she put her hands against his chest to separate them, but he wasn't having any of it.

"Don't push me away, *agapi mou*. Not now," he cried. Before she could move, he drew her back into his arms and lowered his mouth to hers, kissing her with startling hunger. She could taste the salt from his tears. Her mind and body reeled from the passion only he could arouse.

For a moment she responded, because it had been so long since she'd known his touch, and because she simply couldn't help herself. But when he moaned and deepened their kiss, she remembered why she was here.

Since he was physically powerful, her only weapon was to refrain from kissing him back until he got the message. He went on kissing every inch of her face and hair till it slowly dawned on him she was no longer participating.

A tremor shook his tall, hard-muscled body before he released her with reluctance. Dazed by his passion, she sank down in the chair behind her. His eyes searched her features, trying to read her. "Are you still suffering from morning sickness?"

"No," she answered honestly. Though she'd love to use it as an excuse, she couldn't. From here on out, everything she told him would be the whole truth and out in the open.

Dr. Creer was very worried about her going through a divorce right now. He'd warned her that since she didn't want to burden her aunt and uncle with her problems, then she needed to find an outlet to deal with all her emotions. Keeping them bottled up inside was the worst thing for her at a time like this. She could tell Dr. Savakis had been worried about her, too.

After being alone with her thoughts for the last month, she realized the doctor was right. She'd gone about things wrong in her marriage. She was sick of trying to protect herself, Leandros and everyone else. But no longer. No more mistakes if she could help it. That's why she'd come all this way. "The doctor has given me medication for it."

His hands went to his hips, as if he needed to do

something with them. Unfortunately, he stood too close to her, affecting her breathing. "This pregnancy puts a different slant on our impending divorce."

"I know. That's one of the reasons I'm here."

"You do realize that a great deal of our pain came from trying to get pregnant without results," he reminded her grimly.

"So now that I'm carrying your child, you think that erases everything?"

"No," he murmured, "but you've just brought me news I'm still trying to assimilate. One moonlit night on the sailboat, after we'd been disappointed a second time, you lifted tear-filled eyes to me and asked me if it was asking too much to reach for the stars. I told you we'd keep reaching for the stars and the moon. Now you've just told me we've been given *both*!"

"I remember." She averted her eyes. "Please sit down so we can talk."

Studying her through veiled eyes, he hitched himself on a corner of his desk. It still wasn't far enough away from her, but that was as much room as he was willing to give her. "I have a better idea. We'll go to our suite at the hotel, where we won't be disturbed."

He was referring to the Cassandra, the main Petralia five-star hotel in Athens, where he kept an elegant, permanent suite. It was like a small house, really, with three bedrooms, a dining and living room and kitchen facilities.

When she'd stayed at the hotel with her aunt and uncle on their first trip to Greece, that's where she'd met him. Some of her happiest memories of their life together were associated with the Cassandra before they were married. It would be painful to go there.

"Why do we have to go to the hotel? Why not the apartment?"

He moved off the corner of the desk. "We can't go to the apartment because I sold it to Frato three weeks ago. I'm living at the hotel."

CHAPTER TWO

LEANDROS HAD SOLD his fabulous penthouse to his cousin? Kellie couldn't believe it. Stunned by the news, she said, "What's to stop Karmela from hurrying over to the hotel with something important for you before the day is out?"

He breathed in sharply. "It'll never happen again."

Kellie blinked. "That sounded final. She must have received quite a shock to see me in here with you a few minutes ago, but no worries. I won't be in Athens much longer."

In the tangible silence that followed, Kellie lowered her eyes and opened her purse. Inside was the paper her attorney had drawn up. "If you'll please read through this and consult with your attorney, then we'll sign it and our divorce can go through as scheduled."

Leandros made no move to take it. She should have known this was going to be a battle to the end. "That's all right. I'll read it to you.

"Point One. If and when one or both children are born, the mother will retain custody at her address in Parkwood, Pennsylvania."

"Why *if*?" he demanded in an anxious voice. "Is there something you haven't told me?"

"No. My attorney simply wanted to cover every contingency."

Shadows darkened his features.

"Point Two. Liberal visitation rights will be offered to the father.

"Point Three. Both mother and father will discuss times when the mother will bring said child or children to Athens for visitation, and when the father will travel to Parkwood for visitation.

"Point Four. The mother asks for no additional money. The father can decide what monies he will afford for the child or children's upbringing."

She looked up at him. "It's all very simple and straightforward."

His eyes glittered a frostbite gray. "If you think I'm going to agree to that, then you never knew me." The words seemed to come from a cavern miles underground.

"You're wrong, Leandros. After being married for a while, I discovered the *real* you. That's why we've reached this impasse." Heartbroken, she stood up and left the paper on his desk.

With a grimace, he immediately wadded it in his fist before pocketing it. "When did you fly in?"

"Yesterday morning. I'm staying at the Civitel Olympic near the north park. You can reach me there after you've talked with your attorney."

Leandros moved like lightning, preventing her from leaving the room. Standing in front of the door, he talked into his cell phone and rapped out instructions. When he clicked off, he said, "You won't be going back to the Civitel. I'll send Yannis for your personal belongings and have him bring them to you. We're flying to Andros right now."

Where else would he take her? It was his favorite place on earth. *Hers, too, except...* "You mean where Karmela and her family drop in on a regular basis to visit your family whenever you're in residence there?"

His eyes narrowed to slits. "They come to visit my parents in their villa. As for my family, they've already left for the yearly reunion in Stenies village and will be gone overnight, so no one will be around. In any case, we'll be staying in my villa. Shall we go?"

So much had happened in the last month, Kellie's mind was spinning. Since he'd dictated the location for the conversation they needed to have, she was left with no choice but to go along with him.

After grabbing his briefcase, he opened the door that led to the elevator, and stepped in behind her. Their bodies brushed, sending darts of awareness through her as they rode to the roof, where the helicopter blades were already rotating.

She smiled at his pilot, Stefon, before climbing in the back to join Christos. Kellie had done this so often in the past, she strapped herself in before Leandros could do it. She watched him take the copilot's seat and put on the earphones. Soon they were airborne for the short flight to Andros, an hour and a half from Athens by car and ferry. There was no airport, but with a helicopter, Leandros could be where he wanted in no time at all.

That pang of familiarity attacked her in waves as they left Athens and headed for the fertile green island in the Cyclades that Leandros called home. It was a contrast of craggy mountains, woods, valleys and streams rising out of the blue Aegean.

The Petralia estate was located on the eastern slope of a hillside with its share of vineyards, lemon and walnut groves near Gialia beach. To Kellie, the island was glorious beyond description.

Close by was the picturesque stone village of Stenies, with its paved streets. The cluster of villas on the estate had been built in the same traditional stone architecture of the region. Parents, grandparents, uncles and aunts, cousins...all lived in the vicinity.

Leandros loved it because tourism hadn't been developed in this quieter area, thus preserving the whole place's authentic character. After their wedding, at the church in Chora, Kellie had thought she'd found paradise on her honeymoon here, until she learned the Paulos family, among other wealthy families, lived on the same part of the island. The two families had enjoyed a warm relationship over the last fifty years.

Once she'd realized this was where Leandros had fallen in love with Petra, Kellie never felt as excited when they flew over on the weekends he didn't have a business commitment elsewhere. To her growing discomfort, she'd often discovered Karmela and her parents were there visiting Leandros's family at his parents' villa. They would always call Leandros and ask him to join them. Their presence had to be a reminder of what he'd lost.

Since his feelings for home were intertwined with his memories of Petra, Kellie imagined he was a prisoner of both. To fight her pain, she'd preferred they stay at the apartment in Athens when she wasn't traveling with him on business.

Now there was no apartment, but none of that mattered at this point. Wherever Leandros took her so they could talk, nothing would change the fact that they were getting a divorce, children or no children. There were some things they just couldn't overcome, no matter how much her heart broke at the thought.

She'd done the right thing by coming to him with the news of his impending fatherhood. It was his God-given right. If he found a way to prevent the divorce from happening as soon as she'd anticipated, she would still go back to Pennsylvania day after tomorrow, and let her attorney deal with it.

While she was deep in thought, Stefon flew them over the capital town of Chora, where the tourists came in throngs to see its charming Venetian architecture. Farther on she spotted the seventeenth century tower of Bisti-Mouvela and the nearby church of Agios Georgios. Soon they were passing over the Petralia estate. It was a wonderful place with an old olive press building, all part of Leandros's idyllic childhood and an intrinsic part of who he was.

The first time Kellie ever saw his romantic stone farmhouse with its flat roof, she'd fallen instantly in love with it. When she stayed there with him, she enjoyed the many terraces planted with fruit and nut trees that flourished in the climate, as well as shrubs, flowers and kitchen gardens. Hidden in the foliage was a small swimming pool.

One of her favorite features was the kitchen with its open fireplace. They could eat on two of the terraces, one alcoved between the kitchen and living room, the other above the master bedroom with its own garden and a view of the beach just steps away. Farther along the beach was the private boat dock housing various watercraft, including the sailboat he'd given her. One thing she'd learned early: Leandros loved the water and swam like a fish.

She thought about the babies growing inside her. After they were born, they'd enjoy this legacy from their father. When they came on visitation, they'd become water babies, too. But their roots would be firmly planted in Philadelphia.

There couldn't be two places on earth more unalike. Almost as unalike as the way she and Leandros viewed their marriage and what was wrong with it. Kellie couldn't bear to look back at what had happened to destroy their happiness, and fought tears as Stefon set them down on the east side of his parents' villa.

Leandros was already removing his headset. Now that she was pregnant, she had to expect that he would watch over her with meticulous care for the short time she was back in Greece. He didn't know any other way. That was one of the reasons she loved him so much.

Too much.

As he helped her down from the helicopter, his pulse raced to see moisture glazing those velvety brown eyes that used to beg him to make love to her. Until this minute, Leandros hadn't seen a sign of emotion from his normally loving, vivacious wife.

Since Kellie had first told him she wanted a separation, she'd turned into an ice princess, erecting walls he couldn't penetrate. For the last month they were together, he hadn't been able to get through to her on any level. The hurt he'd felt had turned to anger.

During the months when she'd gone through one procedure after another to get pregnant, and been so brave about it, they'd both felt the strain. Every time her period came, they both suffered depression and had to fight their way out of it.

Sometimes the strain made them short with each other. Other times there were periods of silence over several days. The emotional turmoil took its toll. By the last month, he didn't feel he knew his wife anymore. His disillusionment was so total, he'd been devastated.

Only the pregnancy could have caused her to venture back here. Though he was euphoric to learn he was going to be a father, his world would never be right again if the divorce went through without one more attempt to try and heal their wounds.

That's why he'd planned to leave today, with a proposition to save their marriage before it became final. For her to have flown here with news of their babies had saved him from flying to Philadelphia. Leandros couldn't have asked for a greater gift than her presence right now.

While the men disappeared to the guest cottage, she walked ahead of him, strolling down the flower-lined path to his villa in her pale orange sundress and jacket. His eyes followed the feminine lines of her hips and legs as she moved. In the summery outfit, his wife took his breath away.

Once upon a time they'd paused and kissed as they made their way along the ancient paths. But he had to push those rapturous memories to the background of his mind and start over with her again in a brand-new way.

Kellie waited for him to unlock the door, then stepped past him into the beamed living room with its simple white walls and hand-carved furniture. Her arm brushed against his, triggering a surge of desire for her with an intensity that caught him off guard. They'd been apart too long.

He set down his briefcase. "Why don't you rest on the couch by the window and I'll get us something cold to drink."

"Thank you."

When he returned a minute later with an icy lemon fruit drink for her, he found her seated on one end of the sofa, staring out at the beach. He handed her the glass. "Wouldn't you like to put your legs up? Since we're having twins, I'm sure the doctor told you to stay off your feet after your long flight from Philadelphia."

"You're right, but I had a good night's sleep at the hotel and ate breakfast in bed before I took a taxi to your office." She sipped her drink. "It's a hot day and this tastes wonderful. Thank you." Her controlled civility was anathema to him.

"You're welcome. When you're hungry, I'll fix us some sandwiches."

"I'm fine for now, but you go ahead."

He frowned. "I haven't had an appetite lately, but I can't claim the excuse of pregnancy." It wasn't meant to be a joke and she didn't take it that way. "How are you feeling physically?"

She avoided looking at him. "Dr. Creer says I'm in great shape. No problems in sight so far, but twins require special monitoring and I intend following his advice."

"That's good. Are you taking any other medicine besides your antinausea medication?"

"Just prenatal vitamins."

He drank part of his drink, then got to his feet, too

restless to sit there. "When you walked in my office, I was on the phone with Frato."

"I know. I recognized his voice."

Leandros stared at her moodily. "He's taking over for me while I'm gone."

That statement caused her to lift startled eyes to him. "Where are you going?"

"I told him I needed a vacation, but no one knows my plans."

"You're taking another one?"

It didn't surprise him she'd ask that question. A month ago he'd taken time off to fly her back to Philadelphia. He was pleased to detect a note of concern in her voice before she smoothed her hands over her knees in what he recognized was a nervous gesture. "That's right."

"For how long this time?"

"For as long as it takes."

She stared at him. "I don't understand."

Leandros rubbed the back of his neck. "I was going to take my jet and fly to Philadelphia today to talk to you about giving us another chance. If you hadn't come to the office this morning, we would have missed each other."

Her eyes widened, then grew shuttered, and her lovely features hardened. "It's too late. Our divorce will be final soon. The fact that I'm pregnant changes nothing."

"I get that, Kellie, but I'd like you to hear me out first."

"What more is there to say?" The bleakness in her question crushed him. "I only came to discuss future visitation for our children and get it in writing."

He had to weigh his words carefully. "Our babies haven't arrived yet. Until they do, we have a lot to talk about that impacts our lives right this minute. What I need you to know is that I *did* listen to what you said to me before I flew home from Philadelphia a month ago. To my shame, it took me until last week to come to terms with it. I can't lose you, so I've made a decision that will affect both of us."

A troubled expression entered her eyes. "That sounds ominous."

He sucked in his breath. "I'm willing to do as you asked and go to marriage counseling with you."

Looking dumbstruck, she put her glass on the coffee table. "I thought you didn't believe in it. I brought up the subject a year ago, but you were adamantly against it."

He scowled in self-deprecation. "It's my nature to believe only in myself, but after being apart from you this last month, I recognize how arrogant that was of me. Since you suggested counseling as a last resort, I'm willing to try anything to save our marriage."

Besides her inability to get pregnant, which had tested them to the breaking point, there'd been other side issues throughout their marriage to exacerbate what was already wrong. One of them was Kellie's insistence that Karmela had a crush on him. Whenever she'd brought it up, he'd dismissed it, telling her Petra's sister was simply a clingy girl who needed lots of attention. Her behavior didn't mean anything. In fact, Petra had asked him to be extra kind to her.

But, he remembered, when Karmela had said last night that Kellie wasn't good enough for him, something in him had snapped. Mostly because in trying to do as Petra had asked, he hadn't taken Kellie's concerns seriously enough, he realized.

She got to her feet, as if on the verge of running away.

"I realize it will have to be someone you trust," he added, "so I want you to pick the therapist." Leandros knew this was a drastic departure from his former attitude, but he was desperate. Seeing her again proved to him he couldn't live without her. "We can do it here in Athens, or we can fly to Philadelphia and find someone there. It's your choice."

Without saying anything, she moved over to the French doors and opened them to walk out on the patio. He followed her, inhaling her flowery fragrance and the scent of the lemon trees close by. Incredible to think that inside her beautiful body, their babies were already seven weeks old and growing.

"Are you too embittered at this stage to even consider it, Kellie? I wouldn't blame you if you were…but I'm begging you."

She clung to the railing. Still no words came.

"I've spent the last week doing research on the best therapists in the city and came up with a list of six names recommended to me. Four men and two women. Let me show you."

He went back inside and reached for his briefcase. After pulling out his laptop, he set it up on the coffee table and turned it on. Kellie came back in and watched as he clicked to the file so she could see it.

"I was going to give you this list when I flew over to see you, but you can look at it now if you want. All the information I've gathered is here. But if this doesn't interest you, I'll fly you back to Philadelphia tomorrow and we'll search for a therapist there."

She shot him a startled glance. "You can't just go back and forth from Greece between sessions. Therapy takes time."

"I can do whatever I want. Frato will be running the company for as long as necessary. He knows the business the same as I do. With both our fathers still alive to advise him, along with other family members on the board, the company will function seamlessly. If you and I decide to do therapy in Philadelphia, then I'll live there and do business. With your help, of course."

"*My* help?"

"Yes. You once asked me if you could work for me. I told you I'd rather you didn't, but I was wrong about that and a host of other things. We can be a team and scout out a property for the first Petralia resort in Pennsylvania. But since you're pregnant, we'll have to proceed as your health dictates."

"You're not serious," she whispered.

"Try me and find out." He fired back the response. "We'll buy or build a house in Philadelphia near your aunt and uncle, if that's what you desire."

She shook her head. "And take you away from your family and responsibilities?"

"*You're* my family. No one else is more important. If we decide to live there, I'll step down as CEO."

"I wouldn't want or expect you to do that. Never!"

He stared into her eyes. "Why not? Don't you realize no place is home to me without you? I'll do anything, Kellie," he vowed. "I know we can make this work. It's not too late. For the sake of our unborn babies, I'm pleading with you to reconsider. If counseling will help us, then it will be worth it for all our sakes. We'll postpone our divorce while we're in therapy."

If Leandros had said these things to her a month ago…
But he's saying them to you now, Kellie.

For a proud man like her husband to be willing to undergo therapy told her how far he'd come. She moved closer to the coffee table, where she could see the list of names on his laptop. He'd done all this without prior knowledge that they were expecting twins? She couldn't believe it.

After supplying her this kind of proof that he was serious, she *had* to believe he'd planned to fly to Philadelphia today. But for Leandros to submit to marriage counseling… It just wasn't like him.

He was a dynamic wonder in the business world and a law unto himself. He'd probably last one session and that would be it. She couldn't imagine therapy working on him. But since she'd been the one to suggest it in the first place, how would it look if she told him no?

Kellie knew exactly what he'd think. During one of their arguments he'd told her she was inflexible, unreasonable and didn't really mean what she'd said. He would have every right to accuse her now of not putting their children first.

The more she thought about it, the more she realized the wisest thing to do would be to try out one of these therapists in Athens. When the counseling didn't work, then she'd fly back to Philadelphia and the divorce could go through. She'd have to let her aunt and uncle know. The news would be welcome to them, because they adored Leandros and were crushed by the news that he and Kellie were getting a divorce.

He watched as she sat down and scrolled through the list of names. All seemed to have impressive credentials. She was glad he'd included some women. She preferred their therapist to be a female, who would understand Kellie's point of view about things. Leandros probably wouldn't like it, but he'd said this was her choice.

She looked at their ages. The first woman was forty-eight, younger than Kellie's aunt. The other therapist was seventy-six. That sounded pretty old, but she did have a long record of running a practice. At that age she'd probably seen thousands of couples, with every type of problem, enter her office. To still be in business meant she'd enjoyed a certain amount of success.

"Today is a workday." Leandros's deep male voice permeated to Kellie's insides. "Is there a name on the list you'd like to call now?"

He stood behind the couch, more or less looking over her shoulder. Though he'd sounded in control just now, she sensed his impatience for their therapy to get started. Actually, she was anxious, too. The sooner they met with someone and discovered counseling wouldn't help, the sooner she could go home and start getting over Leandros once and for all.

"I'm rather impressed with this older woman, Olympia Lasko." She glanced back at him. "The notes say she's been in practice forty-five years. That's longer than any of the other therapists' histories. I think it speaks quite highly of her."

"I couldn't agree more. Go ahead and phone her."

Leandros didn't act the least upset with Kellie's choice. If he was, he'd learned how to hide his true feelings. That ability made him the shrewd genius who'd become one of the leading business figures in Greece.

She reached in her purse for her cell phone and made the call. It rang several times before a woman answered. "This is Olympia Lasko."

"Oh—" Kellie's voice caught. "I guess I expected a receptionist." She spoke in Greek.

"I've never used one. Your name, please."

"Kellie Petralia."

"What can I do for you?"

"M-my husband and I are on the verge of getting a divorce and need marriage counseling," she stammered. "Could I see you soon to discuss our situation, or are you too booked up?"

"Both of you come to my house tomorrow morning at ten o'clock."

"Both?" Kellie had planned to talk to her first and explain things.

"I never see you individually. It's together or nothing."

"I see." She bit her lip. "Then we'll both be there."

"What's your husband's name?"

"Leandros Petralia."

"Thank you. When you enter the driveway, keep going until you reach the side door. Just walk in."

The other woman rang off without making a remark about Kellie's husband. Ninety-nine percent of the time, people couldn't refrain from commenting on him and the famous Petralia name. Kellie sat there blinking in surprise.

Leandros walked around to look at her. "When can she see us?"

"Tomorrow at ten. We're to go to her house. She must work out of her home."

"Would that we all could do that," he murmured.

"I can't believe she had an opening this fast."

"My dentist always leaves the first hour free for emergencies. It sounds like she operates the same way. I'm impressed already."

Kellie got up from the couch, unnerved by the prospect of talking to Mrs. Lasko in front of Leandros without any private time first. "She's very different than I'd supposed." No chitchat of any kind.

"Let's keep the appointment. If we decide she's not the one for us, then we'll try someone else."

Leandros was being so supportive, just as he'd always been during their visits to the hospital, that Kellie felt like screaming. But not at him. She was frightened, and nervous of being alone with him. "I think I'm hungry now."

"Why don't we drive to Chora and have an early dinner." He was reading her mind. She needed to be around other people and he knew it. "Do you have any particular cravings at this stage in your pregnancy?"

"Not yet."

"Let's try a restaurant you haven't been to. The Circe is on the far side of Chora. It's cozy and the cuisine is basically traditional Andriot." He'd probably been there with Petra. *Of course he had, you fool.* If the therapy didn't work out, Kellie would have to take part of the blame, because she couldn't rid herself of her demons. "You'll love their seafood mezes and froutalia."

"I've forgotten what froutalia is."

"A sensational omelet with sausage and other kinds of meat."

"Oh, yes. That sounds delicious."

"Good. Why don't you freshen up first. I'll meet you at the car parked around the side of the house."

"I'll hurry."

"There's no need. We have all the time in the world. By the time we get back, Yannis will have arrived with your luggage. You can have an early night in the guest bedroom."

Her heart ached as she realized how far apart they'd grown. No sleeping in the same bed for the past two months. Most likely never again…

When Kellie went outside a few minutes later, he was waiting for her, and helped her in the passenger side. She glanced at his striking profile as he started the engine. Whether immaculately groomed or disheveled with a five-o'clock shadow as he was now, Leandros's male beauty stood apart from other men's.

Her heart thudded ferociously. A month ago she'd never dreamed she'd be on the island with him again, going to a romantic spot for dinner.

During the six-mile drive to town, she stared out the window at the fruit trees dotting the ancient landscape. When she couldn't stand the silence any longer, she turned to him. "Have you seen Fran and Nik?"

He nodded. "They invited me to their apartment last week for dinner. Demi is thriving and has started to say words even I can understand." Kellie smiled. "I've never seen two people so happy."

Guilt washed over Kellie for the part she'd played in trying to influence Fran to stay away from the gorgeous Nik Angelis, Leandros's good friend. The press had labeled him Greece's number one playboy. Like Leandros, Nik was the head of his family's multimillion-dollar business and could have any woman he wanted.

In Kellie's zeal to protect her divorced friend's wounded heart, she'd done everything she could to get her away from Nik. She'd been convinced he would only use Fran. But it turned out Kellie was wrong. Ultimately, he'd proved to be the perfect man for her, and had married her on the spot. Since he couldn't give her children and she couldn't conceive, they were adopting Demi, who'd lost her parents in a tornado. In time they planned to adopt more.

"I'm so happy for them," Kellie said aloud.

"Me, too."

To Leandros's credit, he didn't rub it in about Kellie's behavior with her best friend before they'd flown to Philadelphia on his private jet. "I'll phone her while I'm here."

"She'll be delighted. Being a mother has turned a light on inside her."

You mean unlike me, who's pregnant but still wants the divorce?

Kellie wouldn't blame Leandros for thinking it, but again, he kept his thoughts to himself. That was the trouble between them. They were both festering in their own private way from behaviors that had driven them apart.

The therapist would have to perform a miracle for them to put their marriage back together. How ironic that Kellie had been the one who'd brought up the idea of counseling. Yet now that Leandros had finally agreed to it, she was only going through the motions. Deep inside she had no real hope of success.

There'd been too much damage done during those

months of planning each hospital visit like clockwork. Everything had to be gauged down to the second— the temperature taking, the preparation, Leandros's time off from work.... All of it had affected the natural rhythm of married life.

If he suggested they skip a month of going to the hospital, and give things a rest, she was afraid he was losing interest in her. Maybe he didn't want a baby as badly as she did. When she asked him if he would still love her if she couldn't give him a child, he'd acted incensed, which in turn made her afraid to approach him again about it.

There were times when she'd feared he needed a break from her, and would tell him to enjoy a night out with friends or go visit his family. If he took her up on the suggestion, she cried herself to sleep. If he insisted on staying home with her, she feared it was out of a sense of duty. The spontaneity of their lives had vanished.

Aside from making sure she'd prepared a good meal for him at night, Kellie found herself spending more and more time playing tennis at Leandros's club with friends, or studying Greek with the tutor he'd hired for her at the university.

With the gulf so wide and deep between them because of what they'd gone through to have a baby, they were different people now. Her heart ached, because she couldn't imagine how they could find their way back to the people they'd once been.

CHAPTER THREE

EARLY THE NEXT MORNING Stefon flew the two of them to the Cassandra in Athens. After eating breakfast in their room, Leandros called for his car and drove them to the Pangrati neighborhood, where Olympia Lasko saw her clients.

Silence filled the Mercedes, as it had last evening on their way home from dinner. Kellie had hardly talked to him and went straight to bed once they'd returned to the villa. If she'd gotten on the phone with Fran or her aunt and uncle, he knew nothing about it.

To his relief she'd eaten a healthy meal this morning and shown more appetite than he had. Leandros didn't know about Kellie, but he'd slept poorly. Not only was he concerned over the process they were about to undergo, he feared Kellie's reaction. Though it had been her idea, this was new territory for both of them.

After he'd dismissed the idea of counseling in the beginning, he was thankful that she was still willing to try it. When they'd reached Andros yesterday, he'd been terrified out of his mind she would tell him it was too late, and fly right back to Pennsylvania.

Before long, he turned the corner and spotted the Lasko home. It was a moderate-size, gray-and-white two-story house, typical of the settled, comfortable looking residences along the street in the quiet neighborhood. Leandros pulled in the driveway and stopped at the side entrance.

He eyed his wife, who, thankfully, was still his wife. He'd already contacted his attorney to get in touch with her attorney and put off the divorce. The only thing left was to follow through with counseling and pray for a breakthrough. "Shall we go in?"

She nodded and started to get out of the car. He hurried around to help her. Together they walked beneath the portico to the porch. "Mrs. Lasko said to just go in. She must be a very trusting person," Kellie murmured.

"Even so, she'll have had cameras installed, as well as an electronic lock." He reached past her and opened the door. They stepped right into an office with a desk and several leather chairs placed in front of it. At a glance he saw shelves with family photos, grandchildren. On one wall was a large oil painting of flowers.

As he closed the door, he heard the click. A few moments later a connecting door into the house opened. A small, attractive woman with streaks of silver in her black hair, worn in a bun, entered the room. She looked on the frail side.

"Thank you for being on time. I'm Olympia. Please call me that. You must be Kellie."

"Yes. It's very nice to meet you. Thank you for making time for us so quickly. I'd like to introduce you to my husband, Leandros."

"How do you do." They all shook hands. "Please sit down."

While the therapist took her seat in a comfortable padded chair behind the desk, Leandros helped Kellie.

With her hair falling like spun gold to her shoulders from a side part, she looked particularly stunning. She was wearing an aquamarine, two-piece summer suit with short sleeves he hadn't seen before. He loved the color on her.

"We'll discuss the fee after I've decided I can help you. As I told you on the phone, I only counsel you as a couple, not individually."

"You mean you never have private sessions with your clients?" Kellie asked.

"Never, and I never record conversations. Once you start down that road, it doesn't work. To remove suspicion, everything must be said in front of each other in my hearing. Otherwise we're wasting each other's time."

Kellie's face crumpled. He wasn't too thrilled about the rules himself. This counselor drove a hard bargain, reminding him of his own business practices. But in all honesty it made the most sense, and his regard for the older woman went up several notches.

Olympia put on her bifocals. "How long have you been married?"

Leandros decided to let Kellie do the talking.

"Two years and one month."

"Which one of you felt the need for counseling?"

"I did," his wife answered.

"What matters is that you're both here. I'll go out of the room for a few minutes. If you're in agreement with my method, then let me know when I come back in, and we'll get started." She disappeared, leaving them alone. His wife sat there, hunched over.

"What do you think, Kellie?"

Slowly she lifted her head and glanced at him with

mournful eyes. "She's the most direct woman I ever met. I think this could be very painful."

He inhaled sharply. "More painful than what we've already been through?"

"Yes," she said without hesitation.

He'd had to ask the question, even though he'd known what her answer would be. Yet upon hearing it, he felt as if she'd just delivered a crippling blow to his midsection. Their problems were like the tip of an iceberg, with nine-tenths lying beneath the surface of the water. Without therapy, they'd be left unexplored, and the prognosis for a happy marriage was anything but good.

Unfortunately, he knew that once they got into deep therapy, the things they found out about each other could bring more pain. It would be a treacherous journey, but they had to make it if they hoped for a resolution that would preserve their marriage. No matter what he'd be forced to go through, he'd do it if he could have back the adorable woman he'd married.

"I want to do it, Kellie."

Her brown eyes swam with tears. "If you really mean it."

His temper flared, but he fought to control it. "I wouldn't have said so otherwise."

Olympia came back into the room. This time Leandros spoke first. "We'd like to go ahead with the therapy. Since we're expecting twins next March, any fee you charge will be worth it if we can fix what's wrong."

Her dark eyes studied them without revealing her thoughts. "That's courageous on both your parts." She took her place at the desk and named her fee. "I'd prefer to see you twice a week for the first month. The sessions will last an hour. When the month is out, it might not be necessary to see you more than once a month or even at all. My only opening left is at eleven in the mornings, Tuesdays and Thursdays."

Leandros didn't need to confer with Kellie. They both wanted the same thing. "We'll be here."

"Good. Then let's get started." The older woman sat back in her chair with her palms pressed together in front of her. "We'll begin with you, Kellie. Why did you marry your husband?"

Bands constricted his lungs while Leandros waited for her answer.

Kellie wouldn't look at him. "Because I fell painfully in love with him."

"Why painfully?"

"Because I didn't want to love a man who'd been married before, let alone one who'd been madly in love. Her name was Petra. Everyone told me they had the perfect marriage."

Leandros stifled a groan. She couldn't have been more wrong.

"Who's everyone?"

"All the people I met before our wedding. His family and friends. I was terrified I would never measure up to the woman who'd died."

"Why would you want to do that? He married *you*."

Kellie looked confounded. "I—I don't know," she stammered.

"Think about that and we'll discuss it at one of your next sessions. For the moment I'd like to know if you had been in love before you met your husband."

"Not like that. Never like that," she whispered.

Her fervency thrilled Leandros.

"But there was someone else?"

"Yes. One of my college friends had wealthy parents who belonged to a club where there was a tennis pro named Rod Silvers. Since I'd played tennis since my junior high days, she often invited me to play with her. That's where I met Rod, and we started dating.

"He was from a prominent Philadelphia family. I was attracted and flattered. But after a month of seeing each other pretty constantly, he stopped calling me. When I broke down and told my friend, she said his family already had someone from the Philadelphia society register picked out for him to marry."

Kellie had mentioned she'd once dated a tennis pro, but this was the first Leandros knew about his background.

"I see," Mrs. Lasko said. "Now I'd like hear when you first suspected all was not well in your marriage."

A few seconds passed before Kellie said, "At our wedding."

"Our *wedding*?" Leandros blurted. Her quiet response stunned him, because he'd noticed a difference in her after they'd gone to his villa to begin their honeymoon. But he'd never suspected she thought anything was wrong.

"I can see this has surprised your husband, Kellie."

Olympia possessed an unflappable demeanor that reminded him of his maternal grandmother. While his heart thundered in his chest from his wife's revelation, the woman went on talking to Kellie with a calm he could only envy.

"How long did you know him before you were married?"

"Three months."

"Was there an official period of engagement?"

"No."

"What happened at the wedding?"

"That's when I became aware I had competition for my husband's affection."

"You mean besides the memory of his dead wife."

"Yes."

"Did it come from another man? Or was it a woman?"

Leandros shot out of the chair, infuriated by the question. "Neither!"

Olympia glanced at him. "That sounded final. Did you hear him, Kellie?"

"Yes," she answered in a muffled voice.

"Go on."

He sat down again, feeling like a ten-year-old child who'd acted out in class and had just been dismissed by his teacher.

"It was a woman."

"Someone he'd known before he met you?"

"Yes."

"Her name is Karmela Paulos," Leandros broke in, completely frustrated because he'd known Kellie would bring her up. "She's the sister of my deceased wife, Petra."

"Karmela is very beautiful and resembles Petra," Kellie continued. "She's smart like her, too. They were only a year apart."

"What did she do that threatened you?"

Upset and curious to hear what Kellie would tell Olympia, Leandros extended his long legs and folded his arms to hold himself in check while he waited for the answer.

"After our wedding at the church on Andros, his

family held a reception at their nearby villa. Everyone invited came up to congratulate us. When Karmela appeared with her family, she cupped his face in her hands and gave him a long kiss on the lips. As her eyes slid to mine, I saw an angry flash no woman could mistake for anything other than pure jealousy."

Leandros sat there, stunned. He'd been so excited to make Kellie his wife, he didn't remember that moment. In fact, the events of the reception were a big blur.

"After kissing my husband, she kissed me on the cheek and murmured, 'Good luck in holding on to him.'"

He straightened in the chair, aghast by what he'd just heard. Karmela's childish, petulant behavior was out of bounds at times, but he hadn't known she'd subjected Kellie to it as early as their wedding reception.

"My best friend, Fran, was standing a little distance off. When she came over to congratulate us, she whispered that she'd noticed Karmela had fixated on my husband throughout the day. In her words, 'By no stretch of the imagination could that kiss be construed as platonic.'"

While Leandros was still digesting information that stuck in his throat, Kellie said, "My friend isn't the kind of person who looks for trouble or thinks the worst of anyone. Her opinion wasn't the only one I heard that night on the subject of Karmela."

He furrowed his brows, wondering what else in blazes she was about to reveal that he knew nothing about.

"At the wedding, my husband's best man, Frato, took me aside to congratulate me. He happens to be his first cousin and is very close to him. After he kissed my cheek, he said that he had something to tell me in confidence, but didn't want it getting back to Leandros."

What in the hell?

"Frato confided he was worried about me because Karmela had had a thing for Leandros even before her sister's marriage to him. After the plane crash that killed Petra and their unborn baby, Karmela confided to him that she planned to be the next Mrs. Petralia and give him the child he wanted so desperately."

What?

"Frato said that since I'd beaten Karmela to the altar, he wanted to warn me to watch out for her, because she didn't care who she hurt. He was afraid Leandros had a blind spot when it came to Karmela, so I had my work cut out."

Leandros's blood pressure spiked through the ceiling.

"I could smell alcohol on Frato's breath and feared he'd had too much to drink, but on the heels of Karmela's kiss and my friend's observations, I couldn't completely ignore what he'd told me. Especially when I found out that the Paulos family were neighbors of the Petralia family on Andros and the children had grown up together. But considering it was my first day of marriage, I chose to push it all to the back of my mind."

Incredulous over what he'd heard, Leandros clenched his hands into fists. He couldn't sit here much longer without exploding. The news about Frato had knocked him sideways.

"Why did you keep your husband in the dark about this?"

"B-because I was trying to be the kind of wife who trusted my new husband completely. Since it was his good friend and cousin who'd asked me not to say anything, I just couldn't betray his confidence. But a little over two months ago, Leandros brought Karmela into his office to be one his secretaries."

That hadn't been Leandros's doing, but he wanted to hear the rest before he interrupted her again.

"For my husband to do that meant he'd had talks with Karmela I didn't know about."

You're wrong, Kellie. So wrong I'm sickened by what I'm hearing.

"That's when I feared what Frato had told me was coming true. In response to the news, I asked Leandros if he'd let me come to work at his office, find me a position."

Good grief. That's why she'd asked him for a job? The pain in her voice stung him.

"What did you hope to accomplish?"

"In case Karmela was still infatuated with my husband, I wanted to be closer to him, so he wouldn't turn to her. With hindsight I can see it was very childish of me. When I broached the subject of my being at the office, Leandros dismissed the idea. Naturally I thought the reason he wouldn't want me there is because it would interfere with his interactions with Karmela."

Leandros flew out of his chair a second time, hot with rage over these new revelations about Karmela's behavior. "I told you why I didn't want you at work, Kellie. I preferred to get business and everything associated with it out of the way, so I could come home to my loving wife every night."

Kellie gave him a pained look, reminding him that their relationship had deteriorated severely over those last months. "I told him I wanted a divorce," she went on, talking to Olympia. "The night before I was going to leave for the States, Karmela walked into our apartment from the private elevator, *unannounced*, to bring Leandros some papers."

Just as she'd done the night before last!

"The two of them disappeared into his den for a little while. After she left, I asked him if he needed further proof of her infatuation with him. He denied any knowledge of expecting her, and swore he had no feelings for her. But I'm afraid I couldn't believe him this time, not when he hadn't even deleted her code from the elevator entrance."

Leandros was afraid he'd jump out of his skin. "Once you and I were married, I never gave the code a thought, Kellie. Only the night Karmela let herself in did I remember. You have to believe she came uninvited." He could have strangled his sister-in-law that night. As for the other night...

"None of it matters anymore, Leandros. All I knew was that I had to get out of our marriage."

"All right," Olympia stated. "I've heard enough to understand where suspicions of infidelity, whether warranted or not, put a pall over your marriage from day one. Let's turn to you, Leandros." She eyed him directly. "Why don't you sit down and try to relax."

Relax being the operative word.

Wild with fury over Karmela's behavior, he raked a hand through his hair before doing her bidding.

"If I understand correctly, you and your first wife knew each other for years prior to your marriage."

The change of subject threw him off for a minute. "Yes, but I went out with various girlfriends and had no romantic interest in Petra. Not until she was living in an apartment in Athens with her sister, who worked for an accounting firm. Both sets of parents asked me to look in on them as a favor, which I did from time to time.

"Petra was an excellent businesswoman who was hired by a local textile company. I admired her drive and intelligence. One thing led to another."

"Did you have an official engagement?"

"Yes. Six months. We were married a year and a half when she was killed."

"You were a widower how long?"

"Two years before I met Kellie."

"Considering you knew your first wife for years and went through a six-month engagement period, your second marriage happened fast. Twelve small weeks, in fact." Olympia scrutinized him. "Why did you ask her to marry you?"

His gaze swerved to his wife. Her wan countenance put him in fresh turmoil. "She thrilled me from the first moment I met her. With the fire lit, that feeling only grew stronger, and I knew I couldn't let her go back to Pennsylvania."

"Tell me, Leandros. When did *you* first know your marriage to Kellie was in trouble?"

Letting out a sigh of frustration, he clasped his hands between his knees. "On our wedding night." His admission brought Kellie's head around in surprise. "When I took her back to the villa, she went through all the motions of being in love with me, but something had changed. I felt she was holding back from me emotionally somehow, and I couldn't figure it out."

He glanced at Kellie. "Now I know why, but at the time I thought it was because she hadn't been married before and everything was still new. I believed that by the time morning came, she'd be the Kellie I'd fallen in love with, but that woman didn't emerge. She was sweet and affectionate as always, but the passion I'd felt from her before the marriage wasn't the same.

"To make things even more complicated, she came down with a rash and hives so severe on the second day of our honeymoon, we had to go to the doctor. We learned she had an allergy to me. Since that meant using protection all the time, it made it impossible for us to get pregnant by normal means."

"How did that make you feel?"

"I won't pretend. It was hard for both of us to hear. We spent the rest of our honeymoon discussing options, and decided we'd try artificial insemination. After the first procedure was done, I took her traveling with me while I looked for new properties. I loved being with her.

"In the beginning, we went everywhere together and spent the odd weekend on Andros. But over the last eight months, she preferred to stay at the apartment in Athens if we weren't going out of town. I assumed maybe she was worrying too much, and wanted to stay close to her doctor. When I asked her about it, she told me nothing was wrong. I could tell she didn't want to discuss it, but I knew the stress of waiting to see if we were pregnant seemed to overtake our lives.

"Two months ago I asked her to go to Rhodes with me. She told me no, that she wanted a separation."

Kellie jerked around, white faced, to look at him. "At the family dinner party a few nights before, Dionne mentioned that Karmela would be accompanying you there on business."

"Then my cousin lied to you, Kellie! I would never

take Karmela with me anywhere under any circumstances."

"Why would Dionne do that?"

Leandros studied her pinched features. "I don't know, but I'm going to find out."

Olympia sat forward. "Let's leave the subject of your cousins and sister-in-law for our session on Thursday. Did you go to Rhodes without your wife?"

"I had no choice, because of business arrangements that couldn't be changed. Then unbeknownst to me, I found out she'd made plans for her best friend, Fran, to come to Greece."

"Best friend, as in Frato has been *your* best friend?"

"Yes." Kellie spoke up before he could. "She's been like the sister I never had."

A grimace marred his features. "They were going to take a two-week trip together while I was away on business. After making that announcement, she moved to the guest bedroom. It meant we'd be missing our next appointment with the doctor."

"Since our marriage had failed, I couldn't see the point."

Olympia eyed the two of them. "Artificial insemination is an arduous process even when a couple is totally committed."

"I was prepared to do anything to have a baby," Kellie cried softly.

"No more than I." And now, miracle of miracles, they were expecting twins just before their divorce.

Kellie glanced at him briefly, then turned away. He drew in a fortifying breath. "Even though things were bad between us, when I flew Kellie back to Philadelphia, I told her I didn't want a divorce. That's when she challenged me to go to counseling with her.

"In my anger and bewilderment, I told her I didn't believe in it, and I returned to Athens. But after our separation, I realized I couldn't bear to lose her, so I agreed to it."

"Did you fly back to Pennsylvania to tell her that in person?"

"I didn't have to. She flew here two days ago with the news that she was pregnant. That's when I told her I'd been doing research to find some good therapists here in Athens. If she didn't want to get therapy here, then we'd do it in Philadelphia. After thinking about it, she chose you to help us because of your long record."

That brought the first sign of mirth from Olympia. "I'm an old fossil, all right. When did the subject of getting pregnant first come up?"

"Before we married, I told her I'd love to have children with her. She told me she couldn't wait to have a baby. Unless I'm wrong, it was a mutual decision before we took our vows."

"You aren't wrong," Kellie blurted in a wounded voice.

Olympia's gaze fell on both of them. "I'd say on that score you've communicated brilliantly. Artificial insemination is not an easy route to go, but you did it— otherwise you wouldn't be expecting twins in the near future. As for the rest, you can see you're poles apart for a married couple who hope to stay together.

"Surely today's revelations have given you your first inkling of where to dig to start finding understanding. You'll have to be brutally honest, open up and listen to each other. You'll be forced to wade through perceptions, whether false or accurate, and no matter how painful, arrive at the truth. I'll see you on Thursday."

Kellie nodded, filling him with relief that she was in agreement. He'd been afraid that when they got out to the car, she would tell him she'd changed her mind, and would refuse to go through with this after all.

While his mind was on the conversation he intended to have with Frato, whether his cousin wanted it or not, Leandros watched Olympia get up from her desk and enter her house through the connecting door. Kellie beat him to the outside door and hurried out to the car, strapping herself in.

He got behind the wheel and backed out to the street. A disturbing silence enveloped them. After heading for the main artery, he turned to her, anxious to fill the rest of their day with something constructive. "Where would you like to go for lunch? Or would you rather eat back at the hotel?"

"The hotel, if that's all right with you."

"Of course. You can rest there for a while."

She recrossed her shapely legs, a sign she was agitated. "Please don't assume I'm always tired."

"I'm sorry."

A heavy sigh escaped her lips. "Forgive me for being cranky."

"After that session, neither of us is at our best." He put on his sunglasses. "You're restless, Kellie. Instead of keeping it all inside until you reach the breaking point, let's take Olympia's advice and start really talking to each other."

"I—I'm afraid...." Her voice faltered.

"Of me?" he demanded.

"Yes—no—I don't know."

"Try me. I swear I won't erupt like I did in her office."

After a long pause, Kellie said, "I have a lot of questions. For one, I don't understand why you sold the penthouse."

Olympia's words still rang in his ears. *Surely today has given you your first inkling of where to dig to start finding understanding. You'll have to be brutally honest, open up and listen to each other. You'll be forced to wade through perceptions, whether false or accurate, and no matter how painful, to arrive at the truth.*

He cast his wife a covert glance before throwing the truth at her. "Pure and simple, I couldn't stand living there without you. That was the only reason. When I got back from Pennsylvania and walked into the living room, it hit me you wouldn't be coming home again. I couldn't take it, and phoned Frato. He'd coveted the penthouse and had said as much many times."

Through the gold curtain of hair, her lovely profile was partially visible, yet her expression hidden. "But I know you missed Petra horribly after she died. Why didn't you sell it then?"

If they hadn't been in therapy today, Leandros could see Kellie would never have had the temerity to ask that question. Now that she had, she deserved all the honesty he could give her.

"As you know, I'd rather live on Andros, and would have always lived there and commuted. But Petra wanted to live in Athens, and kept looking for a place for us. She met with a Realtor who knew the penthouse and its furnishings were up for sale if someone could pay the right price for it. She fell in love with it and wanted nothing else.

"To be honest, I didn't want to move in there, but I bought it to please her. Only two things about it appealed to me. The private elevator and the helicopter landing pad. I figured I could wing back to Andros without fuss when I wanted, but the penthouse never felt like home.

"Petra was a working woman who traveled a lot and kept late hours, like me. She wasn't there that much and hated to cook. That's because she threw all her creativity into her job. We ate out ninety percent of the time. When we entertained, she had the food catered. Once we found out she was expecting, it didn't stop her from working. When the plane went down, she'd been returning from a business trip."

"How awful that period was for you." Kellie's voice shook.

"It was, but you need to understand she never turned the apartment into a haven. *You're* the one who did that for us. Every day I found myself watching the clock, waiting to get home to you and make love. Half the time I cut my work short so we could have more time together in the evenings.

"Without you there, the memories tortured me. You know how it was with us. When I traveled, I had to have you with me—otherwise I couldn't have stood the separations. When you stopped going with me, it was torture."

She'd gone stone-cold quiet.

"Are you upset I sold it?"

He heard a sharp intake of breath. "If you'd asked me that question before we got married, I would have told you I was overjoyed."

CHAPTER FOUR

"WHAT?" LEANDROS'S THOUGHTS reeled, trying to keep up with Kellie.

"Since I'd never been married before, I wanted to start out our life together without memories of Petra. In my mind, that penthouse was her home with you. On our honeymoon, when you told me you had a special wedding present for me, I assumed you were selling it and had plans to find a place in Athens for the two of us.

"Truthfully, I never liked the penthouse. I guess I wanted a real home on the ground, one you and I picked out together."

Leandros groaned. "That small sailboat I bought you hardly qualified, did it?"

"I *love* that boat. It's been one of my great joys."

His hand tightened on the steering wheel. "Why in heaven's name didn't you tell me you didn't want to live at the penthouse?"

"And have you think I was a scheming woman who married you for your money and was already rearranging your life and your assets?" she cried out.

Her reaction astonished him. "Where's all this coming from, Kellie?"

"It doesn't matter now."

"The hell it doesn't. Tell me!"

She smoothed some golden strands away from her temple. "When I resigned from my job at the advertising agency, my boss, Brandon Howard, said, 'Now that you're marrying a man as rich as Croesus, you'll be able to buy anything you want, and become the paparazzo's favorite target.

"But if you think you're the only woman in his life, because of all the toys the great Leandros Petralia gives you, you're even more naive than I thought. Have you ever known a wealthy Greek playboy to be faithful to one woman all his life? You can't name one! It's a fairy tale, Kellie. Wake up and get out of it before it's too late.'"

A gush of adrenaline attacked Leandros's body. "Now I'm beginning to understand some of your initial concerns about Fran getting involved with Nik. It's all making sense. But don't you know that was your employer's jealousy talking, because you would never go out with him?"

"I realize that now, but at the time he made it sound so ugly, I determined never to be the creature he was talking about. No matter how much I might have wanted to ask you to sell your penthouse for my sake, it wasn't something I could have found the nerve to do.

"It would have given your family and friends more ammunition to find fault with me, and start saying that I was trying to change you to get more gifts out of you."

"My family loves you!"

"In your eyes, Leandros, because you see what you want to see. But I heard your cousins Dionne and Zera talking with Karmela at your grandmother's birthday six months after we were married. They didn't know

I'd picked up enough Greek to understand what they were saying. It was quite illuminating to learn all the ways I didn't come close to matching Petra's virtues.

"They saw a foreigner who would never fit in, who couldn't speak Greek in the beginning or get pregnant, who put you through one artificial insemination procedure after another."

"But you never heard my parents say such a thing!"

"That's true," she admitted quietly. "I'm sorry. Your parents are wonderful."

"They love you, Kellie. Just remember that Dionne and Zera are close friends with Karmela. That would explain the damaging conversation." His gut twisted. "You should have told me. You've suffered in silence all this time."

"I married you, not them, Leandros. Families will gossip. That I understand and forgive."

"Your generous nature should make them ashamed."

"I wish I hadn't said anything. As for the penthouse, I would hardly call living there a penance."

"But it took an emotional toll," he muttered grimly. Everything had taken a toll....

By this time they'd arrived at the hotel. He drove into his underground parking space and helped her out of the car to the elevator. After they'd reached his suite, he asked her what she'd like to eat, and called for room service. But when they sat down at the table to eat, he wasn't hungry.

"Kellie? Would you answer me something honestly?"

"What else do we have if we don't have that?"

He leaned forward. "The last thing you said to me before I left Philadelphia was that I shouldn't have married you, because you weren't good enough for me. I never understood where that came from until today, when you told Olympia about Rod's background. For you to clump his family with mine is—"

"His rejection made me feel inferior," she interrupted. "It hurt my pride, nothing more."

"Maybe that feeling was linked to Petra," he theorized. "Why didn't you talk to me about it?"

"I suppose I didn't want to bring her up if it would be painful for you. I realize now that isn't the case. I shouldn't have said I wasn't good enough for you. It was a foolish remark. You and your family are nothing like that. In my pain I've said a lot of things I regret."

"That works both ways. I should never have shut you down when you asked if I'd go to counseling with you."

For the next few minutes they ate in silence.

"I have another confession to make, Leandros."

He put down his coffee cup.

"When you wanted to keep trying the procedure—even though we weren't getting along—I couldn't believe you weren't discouraged," Kellie murmured. "I'm afraid I started thinking that the only reason you married me was to replace the child you'd lost."

He eyed her soulfully. "If that were true, I would have suggested we adopt a baby and save ourselves all the angst we went through. But I loved you and knew how much *you* wanted the experience of being pregnant. I'd already been through that part with Petra."

"I know," she whispered, "and I was secretly envious of her. Years ago, when Fran told me she could never have a baby, I felt terrible for her, but I didn't begin to understand the depth of her pain until the doctor explained how hard you and I would have to work to conceive. You just take it for granted that you'll grow up, get married and have a baby. But it doesn't always play out like that."

"I'll admit I wasn't prepared to find out you were allergic to me. If you want to know the truth, I thought your hives were a physical manifestation that you'd regretted marrying me."

Her eyes teared. "You're kidding me."

"No. Not at all. My heart almost failed me to think the woman I'd married was no longer enamored in the same way. It hurt *my* pride. I know there were times when we couldn't communicate because I couldn't handle it. That didn't help us at a time when we needed to be totally supportive and confident of our love."

"Oh, Leandros...I had no idea."

He took a steadying breath. "This morning's session has opened my eyes to many things, not the least of which is the part Frato has played in our lives. Before we do anything else, I want to sit down with him in person."

Kellie rested her fork on the salad plate. "Because you don't believe I told the truth about him?"

Leandros's hurt and anger were simmering beneath the surface. "I believe you, Kellie. What I didn't know until a few hours ago was that he's not the friend I thought he was. Apparently blood *isn't* thicker than water."

Her brown eyes filled with more pain. "Don't say that, Leandros. He's your cousin, and was only trying to put me in the picture."

Leandros wiped the corner of his mouth with the napkin. "I'll reserve judgment until we've talked to him."

"We?"

"Yes. We're going to take a leaf out of Olympia's book and face him together, where there's no squirming room. He'll be at the office. I'm going to call him now and tell him to meet us at the villa on Andros after he's through work today. I'll put it in terms that won't allow him to avoid the summons."

She pushed herself away from the table. "Well, if you're going to do that, I'm going to phone Fran. She's left several messages over the last few days and has no idea I'm in Athens. I need to respond. Excuse me."

Encouraged that, since their therapy session, they weren't at each other's throats, and she felt like talking to Fran, Leandros pulled out his cell to call his cousin on his private line. Frato answered on the third ring.

"Hey, Leandros—missing the job already?" he teased.

His affection for Frato made this difficult for him. "Actually, something of vital importance has come up. No matter what you've got planned for this evening, I need to talk to you in private and want you to fly out to Andros. How soon can I expect you?"

After a period of quiet his cousin said, "This sounds serious."

"Make no mistake. It is."

"I'm in Volos, doing a walk-through of the construction for the new resort. Those specs you worked up really helped. I should be finished by two-thirty at the latest, then I'll fly straight to Andros."

"I'll be waiting."

"Leandros? What's wrong?"

"I can't talk now. See you later." He purposely hung

up, for fear his anger would overtake any good judgment or magnanimity he had left.

Next he phoned Stefon and told him to get the helicopter ready.

"Kellie? I'm so thrilled it's you! I told Nik that if I didn't hear from you soon, I was going to call your aunt."

"Sorry I didn't get back to you before now, but a lot has been going on. Is this a bad time?" She sank onto the edge of the bed in the guest bedroom to talk.

"Not at all. I just put Demi down for her nap. The next time you see her, you won't believe how much she has grown. I sent you pictures, but you have to see her in person. She's so sweet and beautiful, Kellie. Gorgeous like Nik. I love them both so much I can hardly stand it, but forgive me for rattling on."

The happiness in her voice caused Kellie's eyes to fill with tears. "That's the kind of news I long to hear. After warning you against Nik, I feel so terrible."

"You're my best friend. Don't you know I understood why? Please promise me you won't bring it up again. It's all in the past. So how soon do you take possession of the house in Parkwood? We're going to fly over and help you and your aunt and uncle move in."

"I love you for offering, but I've had to put my plans for the house on hold." In fact, she needed to call her Realtor after she hung up with Fran.

"Why? Was there a snag in the negotiations?"

"N-no," she stammered.

"Kellie...I can tell by that hesitant sound in your voice something's wrong. What is it?"

"Are you sitting down?"

"Do I need to?" she cried in alarm.

"No. I'm sorry. It's good news."

"Thank heaven."

"This week I found out I'm seven weeks pregnant with twins."

"Twins?" Fran squealed with joy.

"Can you believe it?" Kellie half laughed through the tears. "After all my angst?"

"It's another miracle! Oh, wait till I tell Nik! How are you feeling?"

"Dr. Creer gave me medicine for the nausea. I'm doing fine."

"Forgive me for the next question, but I have to ask. How soon are you going to tell Leandros? I have to say, he's so devastated by what's happened, I hardly recognize him."

Kellie had hardly recognized him at the office. She'd been waiting for Fran's question. "He already knows. I flew here day before yesterday."

Another cry came over the phone line, almost bursting her eardrum. "You're in Athens?"

"Yes. There's so much to tell you, I hardly know where to start. Unfortunately, I can't stay on the phone right now because we're flying to Andros the minute I get off. But I promise I'll call you tomorrow. Maybe we can meet for a late lunch on Thursday. Leandros and I will be back in town for the next session with our marriage counselor."

She heard another gasp. "Leandros Petralia, *the* Leandros Petralia, finally agreed to go to counseling?"

"Yes. I flew to Athens to tell him I was pregnant. That's when he told me he wants another chance to save our marriage. I don't know if it will work, but I'll tell you all about it tomorrow. Give that baby and Nik a big kiss from me. *Au revoir*, for now," she said. It was a habit she'd picked up since their boarding school days in France. Aware Leandros would be waiting for her, she clicked off before Fran could say anything else.

After leaving a message for her Realtor to call her back, Kellie freshened up. But before she joined her husband, she ran her hands over her stomach.

"My precious little babies," she whispered. "You deserve a mother and father who love each other desperately and have no secrets."

She might have known Leandros would insist on talking to his cousin ASAP. It was his way to swoop in and take care of whatever needed doing, but this wasn't a business transaction. They would need to tread carefully to find common ground, in order to deal with their problems. Today was a start, but what if this didn't work?

Kellie put her head back. Refusing to think negative thoughts at this early stage, she walked through to the sitting room. He'd changed out of his suit into jeans and a burgundy polo shirt. She averted her eyes to keep from staring at his well-defined physique.

Kellie had always been wildly attracted to him, but in the end even such a strong attraction hadn't been able to overcome her distrust and pain. She could scarcely credit that he was willing to go to counseling with her. However, she needed to remember this was only the first day of therapy. A frisson of fear ran through her because she knew anything could go wrong in the weeks ahead.

"Were you able to reach Frato?"

His haunted gray eyes swerved to hers. "He'll be arriving later this afternoon. How's Fran?"

"She sounds happier than I've ever known her to be."

"Did you tell her about the twins?"

"Yes. She's elated for us. I told her I'd see her on Thursday after our therapy session."

"Good." Leandros's gaze swept over Kellie. "Is there anything you'd like to do before we leave for Andros?"

"No."

"Then let's go."

Except for the kiss at his office, they'd had no contact or relations in over two months. He didn't try to touch her again except to help her get in and out of the car or the helicopter. In those early months, they'd never been able to stay out of each other's arms. Even though Leandros had admitted in therapy he'd felt a change in her since the wedding, he seemed to have brushed his fears to the back of his mind, with the result that she was convinced he thought all was well.

Somehow she needed to learn how to shut off her memories of what it used to be like with them. Otherwise she wouldn't be able to get through this experiment. But it was so hard when they slept under the same roof at night. He went to his room, she went to hers, where she died a little each time without him.

Once more Kellie had to fight the desire that shot through her when he grasped her arm to assist her into the helicopter. His touch always played havoc with her senses. Christos couldn't help but notice.

With her heart still pounding, they were carried over the Parthenon of the three-thousand-year-old city to the island where she'd known joy, accompanied by doubts and fears she'd never been able to shake.

Now she was facing a new fear. She'd seen the wintry look in Leandros's eyes when she'd told him what

Frato had said to her at the wedding. Her husband was a wonderful man, but when crossed he made an even more wonderful adversary. Kellie had it in her heart to feel sorry for Frato, who had no idea what was waiting for him.

It wounded her that there might be trouble between the cousins, who'd always been so close. That was one of the reasons she'd never told Leandros anything. But therapy had forced her to open up if they hoped to save their marriage. It was too late to beg her husband to call off this meeting. In any case, she didn't want to.

For Leandros to hear from his cousin's lips that he had a blind spot where Karmela was concerned would give credence to what she'd told him. Her husband would have to take her fears seriously. She was so deep in thought, she didn't realize they'd landed until Leandros called to her.

"Kellie?" He looked worried. "Are you all right?"

"Yes. Of course." She unstrapped herself and got out of the helicopter with his help. This time she felt his hand slide down her arm like a caress, as if reluctant to let her go. Her breath caught before she moved away to thank Stefon for another safe flight.

Leandros was right behind her as she hurried down the path to his villa. With each step she wondered how many times he and his first wife had rushed into his house to be alone and shut out the world.

When Kellie reached the door, she waited for him to unlock it, but he stood there instead, staring at her with penetrating eyes. "After the many revelations during our therapy session, I realize you have more questions about Petra and me. I wish you'd asked me long ago. I would have told you anything."

He seemed to be reading her mind. "I should have, but I wanted to pretend you didn't have a past. That was another mistake on my part."

"Kellie," he said in a tone of exasperation. "Let's not talk about the mistakes we made. Before we go inside, I want you to know something important."

She gripped her handbag a little tighter.

"Petra agreed to our wedding taking place at the church in Stenies, but after the ceremony, we spent the night aboard her father's yacht with all the amenities. It's moored in a bay two miles from here. The next day we flew to New York for our honeymoon."

Kellie couldn't believe they'd chosen New York when they could have stayed here.

"She was never happy on Andros. It was too steeped in the past for her. She craved life in the big city. We rarely spent time here. On the few times we did come, it was to see her parents. At her insistence, we always spent the night at her parents' villa."

"But what about *your* wishes?"

"I came home when she was away overnight on business." Leandros searched Kellie's eyes. "I'm telling you all this to let you know we never slept in my villa. No woman has ever stayed overnight here except you."

While that piece of news sank in, he turned and unlocked the door. After opening it, he suddenly picked her up like a bride. "I want to carry you over the threshold again. This time you can have the sure knowledge that every memory inside these walls since we met is associated with you and no one else."

She didn't doubt he was telling her the truth. His sincerity reached that vulnerable spot inside her.

"Leand—" She'd started to say his name, but it got

muffled as his hungry mouth came down on hers. He began kissing her with growing urgency, as he'd done on their wedding night. For a moment it was déjà vu. Without effort he swung her around and carried her to his bedroom. Before she knew it they were tangled in each other's arms on top of the bed, and she found herself clinging helplessly to him.

"I love you, Kellie. More than you can imagine. Let me love you. I need you, *agapi mou*."

Here she was again, succumbing to her needs and his. Though he'd relieved her of her false assumptions to do with Petra, there was still so much to deal with, she didn't dare let this go any further. She knew herself too well. To allow herself to be blinded by passion and make love with him might satisfy the ache inside her for the moment. But it wouldn't solve the things that were still wrong outside this bed.

When he lifted his head so she could breathe, Kellie took advantage and rolled away. She got to her feet, wobbling horribly. He lay there looking devastated. "Why have you pulled away from me?"

She held on to his dresser for support. "I'm glad you told me about Petra. It has helped a lot. I *do* love you, Leandros. That will never change, but—"

"But Karmela is still the big impediment." His eyes flashed a gunmetal-gray as he got off the bed.

Kellie took a deep breath. "It isn't just Karmela. I think that until we've finished with therapy, we should concentrate on our problems and not sleep together. I can't forget that Frato will be here in a little while, and I have to admit I'm frightened."

"Why?" he demanded. "Because you haven't told me the truth? Or is it because you finally divulged a secret he asked you not to tell me, and you fear repercussions?"

She clasped her hands together. "I would never lie to you. I'm just afraid of what it might do to your friendship after he's confronted. A rift between the two of you could hurt your family in ways that make me ill to contemplate."

"Because you're afraid they'll blame you?"

"Deep down I suppose I am."

Leandros's eyes glittered in pain. "No rift could be more deadly than the one between you and me. I'll go to any lengths to fix it." She believed him—otherwise he wouldn't be going to therapy with her. "If it alienates my cousin and me, or my family, so be it. I'm going down to the beach for a swim. Do you want to come with me?"

"Yes," she said, making a snap decision that seemed to surprise him. "I'll go in the other bedroom and change into my suit."

Over the past few months, before she'd gone back to Philadelphia, he'd become used to her turning him down. But as Olympia had pointed out, there was a lot Kellie had kept from Leandros. She realized now she'd done so out of fear. Unfortunately, it had combined with his hurt pride to help contribute to the serious problems in their marriage. His determination to put it back together at any cost made her cognizant that she needed to play an equal part in this.

Throwing a wrap over the white bikini he'd given her on her twenty-eighth birthday, four months ago, she joined him at the front door and they walked down the steps to the beach.

"Ooh, this sand is almost hot."

Leandros eyed her up and down after she removed her wrap. His gaze focused on her stomach, which was getting thicker, but so far wasn't protruding. "Then let's get you in the water quick."

"Oh no, you don't!" she cried, and started running toward it, barely escaping his arms, which would have picked up her again. Kellie was a good swimmer and took off, not worried about the depth, since it was fairly shallow for about a hundred feet. He came after her like a torpedo and circled her, preventing her from going out any farther.

"You need to be careful now that our little unborn babies are starting to make their presence known."

Kellie treaded water. "You noticed?" she teased, feeling playful in a brand-new way, because therapy had opened up a dialogue, and she no longer felt threatened by Petra's specter.

His white smile turned her heart over. "You're no longer concave. I love your new shape."

"I'll hold you to that when I need to be carted around in a wheelbarrow at seven months." After the words flew out of her mouth, she realized her mistake. They might not be together in seven months, or even in one more month.

He moved closer, catching her around the hips. The next thing she knew he'd turned her body so her back was against his chest. A voluptuous warmth filled her as moved his hands over her stomach, exploring her until her senses leaped. "I've got the world in my arms," he whispered, kissing her on the side of her neck.

Kellie was so filled with chaotic emotions, she couldn't talk.

"When you told me you were expecting twins, you

made me the happiest man alive, not only for me, but for you. I'm here for you in every way."

"I'm happy for you, too, Leandros. No man ever tried harder to become a father. You never let me give up. For that you have my undying gratitude." His touch had reduced her to pulp, so she was slow to realize she could hear a helicopter coming close to the estate. "That will be Frato!"

"So it is, but we'll beat him. Let's keep our personal business to ourselves."

"I agree."

Leandros pulled her with him to shore, then picked her up again and carried her up the steps into the villa, without taking an extra breath. "I'll meet the helicopter and walk him down here. That should give you enough time to change."

He lowered a hard kiss to her mouth before he took off out the front door to greet his cousin. She pressed fingers to her lips, which still tingled as she watched him leave. He wore black swim trunks that rode low on his hips.

He looked magnificent.

CHAPTER FIVE

LEANDROS WANTED A LOT MORE than his wife's gratitude as he approached the pilot's side of the helicopter. He waited until Frato started to climb out before he told Stefon to stay put. "My cousin will be needing a ride back to Athens, but I don't know the time. You go ahead and use the guest cottage. He'll ring you later."

After the pilot nodded, Leandros walked around the other side. Six feet tall, his cousin was still in a business suit. His dark curly hair and brown eyes proclaimed him a Petralia. Leandros's coloring differed because he'd inherited his mother's gray eyes.

"You made good time, Frato. Thanks for dropping everything to get here so fast. As you can see, I was taking a swim."

"Your phone call made me nervous, so I came as soon as I could. I didn't know you were going to vacation at home."

"My plans are subject to change from moment to moment."

Frato stopped walking long enough to look at him. "That sounded cryptic. What's going on?"

"That's what I want to know. But let's go in the house

first. You need to get out of this heat and shed your jacket."

"If I didn't know better, I'd think you were setting me up," he said with a nervous laugh.

His cousin was a quick study. "If I didn't know better, I'd think maybe that was a guilty conscience talking," Leandros replied.

Frato stopped at the front door. "You *are* setting me up!"

When it unexpectedly opened, revealing Kellie, his jaw went slack. She'd arranged her damp, golden hair in a loose knot and changed into jeans and a summery, blouson-type top in a delicious shade of ice-blue. Pregnancy had made her radiant. "Hello, Frato." She kissed him on both cheeks. "Come in and let me fix you something cool while Leandros gets dressed."

"You're back!" His cousin more or less staggered into the living room. "I had no idea."

She nodded. "Do you want a fruit drink or something stronger?"

"Nothing for me." He removed his jacket and tossed it over one of the chairs.

"Then please sit down. It's good to see you."

"I'll be right back." Leandros disappeared to get dressed. In under a minute he returned, wearing shorts and a sport shirt he was still buttoning. "You're sure you won't have a drink?"

Frato shook his head. "I know you when you've got something important on your mind. Why don't we just get to the point."

Leandros stood in front of his cousin, who'd taken a seat on one end of the couch. Kellie sat on the other.

The moisture on Frato's upper lip wasn't all due to the heat. Leandros detected nervous tension.

"Today I learned of a confidence you shared with Kellie at our wedding. You told her not to tell me. Do you recall what I'm talking about?"

His cousin looked mystified. "I'm afraid I don't. If you say this happened the night of your nuptials, I remember doing more drinking than usual."

"I could smell the alcohol." Kellie spoke up. "You took me aside to congratulate me. Then you told me some things that were very disturbing, before you asked me to keep it to myself. I honored your wishes until this morning, Frato, but I have two regrets. One, that you ever told me anything, and two, that I kept it from Leandros for so long."

"Refresh my memory." Frato could be obstinate when he wanted.

Leandros listened as she repeated verbatim what she'd told Olympia. The room went an unearthly quiet after she'd finished. Frato got a sick look and moved off the couch to gaze out the window with his back toward them.

"Has it all jelled yet?" Leandros asked in a quiet voice.

His cousin continued to say nothing. Leandros moved closer. "So it's true what you told Kellie?"

Frato finally wheeled around with a tormented look in his eyes. "I meant no harm, Leandros. I swear it."

Anger raged inside him. "How would you know if Karmela had feelings for me before I married Petra?"

"Because she told me!" he blurted.

"How intriguing. Why would she tell *you*?"

"Because I've always been crazy about Karmela."

That was news to Leandros. "There've been a few things in our lives I haven't told you. Especially after she refused to go out with me. When I pressed her for a reason, she said she'd been in love with you since she was a teenager on the island."

"Then it was a fantasy of her own infantile imagination."

"Several girls had a crush on you. But unlike them, she never got over it."

After Karmela's performance the other night, Leandros knew it was true. "Then what purpose did you think it would serve to run to my brand-new wife and alarm her?"

Frato's head reared back. "Because you were so oblivious. I was in love with her, but it did no good while she had her heart set on you. When she found out you were marrying Kellie, she told me that one way or another, she was going to get pregnant with your baby. In her mind she assumed that when it happened, you'd have to get a divorce and marry her."

"Surely you could see she was delusional then," Leandros exclaimed. After her appearance at the office, he realized Petra's sister had a problem that had needed a psychiatrist a long time ago. He was appalled at his own lack of vision, but Kellie had seen it. *She'd* been the one hurt by Karmela at the very beginning of their marriage.

"All I saw was a woman who'd had to live in Petra's shadow. I figured that if I bided my time, she would eventually turn to me. But when I saw how she kissed you at the wedding, I couldn't take it and started drinking."

So Frato had noticed that kiss, too. Leandros hadn't remembered anything but his love for Kellie.

His cousin turned to her. "I felt I had to warn you about what was going on. It was because I liked you and was afraid for you."

"Afraid for my wife?" Leandros bit out.

"Yes." He turned back to Leandros. "Karmela always seemed to have you wrapped around her little finger. It looked like she could do no wrong in your eyes. From my vantage point you let her get away with whatever she wanted."

"So you assumed I'd welcome my own sister-in-law into my bed?" Leandros was livid.

Frato's brow rose. "I didn't know, did I?"

"Good grief! What's happened to you? Where's the cousin I grew up with?"

"You got the woman you wanted! Life was easier for you."

Leandros couldn't believe what he was hearing. "I was going to wait to tell Kellie everything until I'd talked to you. But now this can't wait. Though you don't deserve an explanation, I'm going to give you one.

"When Petra and I started seeing each other, she asked me to be kind to her sister. She worried that Karmela would start feeling abandoned and alone after we got married. Now that I have certain information I didn't have two years ago, I'm convinced Petra knew her sister was very disturbed, but she was afraid to tell me.

"As a favor to her, because she was so concerned, I agreed we would let Karmela come and go from the penthouse like she was part of the family. But I never liked it."

Frato gesticulated with his arms. "Then you understand it was an act she put on for Petra, to win her sympathy and get closer to you."

"I agree and I'm convinced." It was all making an ugly kind of sense. "Now I need the answer to another question. If you were so worried I might take advantage of the situation, then perhaps you'd like to tell me and Kellie a couple of things. Why did you beg me to let her come to work under Mrs. Kostas? And why didn't you want anyone to know it was your doing?"

Kellie's shocked cry was music to Leandros's ears. He prayed his wife was taking all this in.

"Because that favor was for *me*," his cousin insisted. "Karmela never left me alone about coming to work for the company, but I wanted it to look aboveboard, and that meant the decision had to come from you."

A scowl broke out on Leandros's face. "I thought you said she wasn't interested in you."

"In the beginning that was true. But I'm not a quitter. It had been a long time since your wedding to Kellie. About eight months ago we started seeing each other and one thing led to another. Since she came to work in your office, things have been really good behind the scenes," he admitted.

"What happened to Anya?"

"I only see her from time to time, but that's all over now."

Leandros wondered if he'd ever really known his cousin.

"I have more news and might as well let you in on it, since it's going to get out pretty soon," Frato continued. "Karmela and I are going to get married."

"You *what*?"

"Shocking to you, isn't it," he muttered. "Don't you know that's why I took you up on your offer and bought the penthouse? In five years I'll have it completely paid off. She loves it there because it feels like home to her."

Kellie's stunned gaze flew to Leandros. By now she'd gotten to her feet. "There's something you need to know before you make a mistake that could ruin your life, Frato," she said.

"What do you mean?"

"The night before Leandros flew me back to Philadelphia, a month ago, Karmela came to the penthouse *uninvited*. You see, she'd heard the gossip about us getting a divorce, and thought I'd already left for the States.

"What she didn't know was that I'd been sick that night and had to go to the E.R. Leandros brought me back to the penthouse. While we were there, Karmela walked in as if she lived there. I could tell she was shocked to see me, but she covered it well and said she'd brought papers from the office for Leandros to look over and sign.

"Did she tell you about that visit? I can give you the exact date and time. Before you marry her, you'd better find out the truth!"

Frato got that bewildered look on his face, one Leandros had seen many times in their childhood. "Since Petra died, I've never given Karmela permission to come to the penthouse," Leandros told him. "If I were you, I'd ask her about that night. If she can satisfy you that she had a legitimate right to use my private elevator and walk in on me unannounced and unexpected, then it appears you're the one living in an oblivious state."

His cousin got off the couch again and started pacing.

"Frato," Kellie said in a kindly voice. "I'm very

sorry, but it's clear to me Karmela has been using you all this time to get to Leandros. That's why she wanted to come to work at his office. She hasn't given up on this fantasy of hers, and needs professional help. If you marry her, you're in for so much pain, you can't imagine."

While his cousin digested everything, Leandros made a decision. "Why don't you stay overnight on the island with your family? If Karmela is expecting you at the penthouse, tell her you had business that kept you longer than planned. Tomorrow you need to call her into the office and tell her you have to let her go."

Frato hung his head. "I can't fire her."

"Then you want me to do it? I'd rather it came from you."

His cousin looked terrified. "I can't. Leandros—if you insist on this, I'll lose her!"

"We don't have a choice here. Though this is going to be painful for you, I have more news. Do you know where she was at eleven two nights ago?"

"Yes. She said she had to work late, and didn't get back to the apartment until midnight."

"She told you a lie, Frato. While I was working at my desk, she came into my office with a tray of food."

"I don't understand."

It was now or never if Leandros was going to get through to him. "I have no idea how long she'd been in the building, but everyone else had gone home at quitting time. I asked her to leave, but she seemed to think it was some sort of game."

"What do you mean?"

"She acted like a rebellious teenager, wanting to know my business. First she cast disparaging remarks about Kellie. Then she pulled tears about how much she knew I missed Petra, and that she wanted to help me. I believe she's ill, as ill as she was at my wedding to Kellie, but I didn't realize it then. She's gotten sicker with time. I came close to removing her physically from my office before she finally left."

His cousin paled. Who would have guessed that Karmela would turn out to be Frato's Achilles' heel?

Kellie shook her head. "She needs to be let go, Frato. If you lose her because of it, then it will prove she was never really yours to lose. Don't you see this is the only way, for the good of the company and our personal lives? How could anyone hope to function with all that subterfuge going on?"

Perspiration broke out on his forehead. "She'll turn her family against ours and everyone will blame me."

Leandros's jaw hardened. "That will be nothing compared to the fact that she's already created enough trouble between Kellie and me to bring us to the brink of divorce!"

"But they're your in-laws! Out of respect for Petra, how can you do that?"

With that remark, Leandros realized his cousin wasn't capable of viewing the situation rationally right now. Maybe never.

"How can I not? You've missed the point, Frato. I have no doubt her parents have been worried about Karmela for years. When this gets out, it's possible they'll be able to find her the help she needs. While they're doing that, you can move on. Don't forget I'm on vacation until further notice and need you to run the company."

Frato reached for his jacket and headed for the door. "I've got to get back to Athens, where I can think."

"It's your life. But if you're tempted to tell Karmela anything before we meet tomorrow, at nine in the morning, then word could get back to the board through her. You'll be lucky if they only give you a forced leave of absence from the company until you come to your senses."

His cousin wasn't listening. No sooner had he disappeared than Leandros's cell phone rang. It was his mother, who explained she'd just returned from town, and saw the helicopter. "I didn't know you were here."

"Frato and I were having a meeting, but he's leaving now."

"Then come up for dinner."

"I can't tonight, *Mana*."

"Leandros...your papa and I hardly see you these days."

"I know, but I'll make it up to you." He wanted Kellie with him when they told his parents about the twins, but they needed to have another session of therapy before he felt they could inform his family of what was happening. "Right now I'm in the middle of delicate negotiations and don't have the time." It was the truth.

"I've been concerned about you. The last time I saw you, you looked too thin. Since Kellie left, you haven't been taking good enough care of yourself."

"Don't worry about me. I'll call you very soon, I promise."

He rang off and went in search of his wife, who'd gone into the kitchen. When he found her, she was eating a peach. He'd like to eat one of those and then start on her, but that was an activity he had to put on hold for the time being.

"How's your mother?"

"Being motherish."

Kellie flashed him a sad smile. "My aunt gets like that, too."

"Let's drive somewhere along the coast for dinner. I'm starving, as well."

"That sounds good. I'll grab my purse."

As they walked out the front door, the helicopter flew overhead, taking Frato back to Athens. Leandros was thankful he'd gone.

Once they got in the car and were on the road, she turned to him. "Do you think he'll tell Karmela?"

Leandros slanted her a veiled glance. "There was a time when I thought I knew my cousin, but no longer. It's anyone's guess what we'll find when we arrive at the office tomorrow."

She glanced at the shimmering blue water. "I've always liked Frato. It's so sad that he's been enamored of someone who never loved him. My heart aches for him."

"It's possible this intervention will shake the scales from his eyes. I care deeply for my cousin and would like to see him work this out with as few repercussions as possible."

"Do you know one of your great traits is your charitable attitude about people, even under the worst of circumstances?" Her comment warmed him.

They drove in silence another five miles to a fishing village before she spoke her mind. "I—I wish you'd told me it was Frato's idea to bring her into the office...."

Kellie's voice faltered. "Why didn't you tell me she walked in on you two nights ago?"

"I could have, but I was waiting to hear what Frato had to say first before I laid every card on the table." Leandros flicked her a glance. "For that matter, I wish you'd told me what he'd said the night of our wedding. As we've both found out, my cousin knows how to wear you down until you end up doing what he wants."

"I—I never wanted to believe you were interested in Karmela," she admitted.

"The idea was so ludicrous, I couldn't understand your suspicions. I was blind in the beginning, because I was so in love with you. But between Fran's and Frato's observations, it's no wonder the bloom was off our wedding night. Frato can be a valuable asset to the company when he's out doing business. But in our case, he's helped the enemy within."

"I remember that quote from Marcus Cicero. 'A nation can survive its fools, and even the ambitious. But it can't survive treason from within.'"

"Exactly. Years ago my father made me memorize it when I started working for the company."

"How does the rest of it go? I'm positive you know it."

He flashed her a smile, because for a few minutes it felt as if they were really communicating again. "'An enemy at the gates is less formidable, for he is known and carries his banner openly. But the traitor moves amongst those within the gate freely. He speaks in accents familiar to his victims, but works secretly in the night to undermine the pillars of the city.'"

After he'd spoken, Leandros felt the shudder that ran through her body even though they weren't touching. "He could have been describing what's happened to us," she murmured

"When you think about it, those words could apply to your former boss, too. Once you told him you were getting married, he couldn't leave it alone and planted doubts in your mind, all in the name of wanting to keep you for himself."

"He never had me." Kellie rested her forehead in her hand. "His assumptions were so hurtful and angered me so much, you'll never know. But looking back, I realize I did worse. In my zeal to protect Fran from getting hurt after her painful divorce, I made a lot of assumptions about Nik that weren't the truth. You have no idea how ashamed I am. He must think I'm horrible." Tears ran down her cheeks.

Leandros pulled into the parking area of one of their favorite seaside restaurants. To his sorrow they hadn't been here for at least six months. He shut off the engine and turned to her. "You're wrong, Kellie." He wiped the moisture from her cheeks with his thumb. "Nik wasn't as completely open as he should have been with Fran about the real reasons he'd never married, thus arousing your suspicions. He regrets that."

She looked away from him. "You're just being diplomatic, but that's another thing about you I admire. I happen to know my aspersions about him hurt you. The breakdown of our marriage turned me into someone I didn't like."

"I didn't like myself, either, Kellie. By the end, I was jealous of their ability to get past their fertility issues. With us, it was the other way around. The more we tried to get pregnant, the more we got bogged down in our insecurities and became alienated. My frustration

over not being the man you thought you were marrying turned into anger. You weren't the only one who
threw up a wall between us."

"Leandros..." she said, sounding distressed. "If you
don't mind, let's go inside. One thing I'm noticing about
this pregnancy. I have to eat on time or I get famished."

He kissed the tip of her nose before getting out of
the car to help her. He was famished, too, for *her*. But
for the moment he had to be satisfied with this amount
of detente, including the compliments she'd been paying him. Before she'd shown up in his office two days
ago, he couldn't have imagined this much progress.
Unfortunately, when they faced Karmela in the morning, there could be a setback that might undermine any
progress they'd made.

At ten to nine the next morning, Kellie got out of the
helicopter with Leandros's help and rode the elevator
down to his office suite with him. She hadn't slept well
during the night and had gotten up early to shower and
wash her hair. After blow drying it so it fell in natural
curls around her shoulders, she'd gone into the kitchen
to take her pills and fix breakfast for the two of them.

After the fabulous seafood dinner with him the night
before, she couldn't believe she was hungry again. Eating for three was no joke, but at this rate she'd have to
start watching her weight. Already her clothes were fitting tighter. Pretty soon she'd need maternity outfits.

In order to feel comfortable, she'd put on a cream-
colored blouse with a khaki skirt that tied loosely
around the waist. On her feet she wore bone-colored
leather sandals. The doctor had warned her high heels
weren't a good idea.

The way Leandros's eyes lingered on her while they ate on the terrace raised her temperature. His appeal was so potent, she was in danger of forgetting her own rule to keep her distance with him. But knowing they'd been through only one session of therapy, not to mention that they'd be confronting Karmela in a few hours, Kellie made certain she didn't succumb to him out of weakness. Instead, she got up and did the dishes before announcing she was ready to go.

No one was in Leandros's office when they entered on the dot of nine. She really hadn't thought Frato would be here, and was sure Leandros hadn't counted on it, either.

"Leandros? I'd rather wait outside the door with Christos while you speak to Karmela. I don't want her to feel like she's being attacked."

He caressed her cheek. "You're an amazingly kind person, Kellie. Tell you what. I'll record everything that goes on so you'll know exactly what was said. No more secrets, remember?"

She nodded and sat down next to his bodyguard to wait. Before Leandros disappeared into his office, she noticed how fabulous he looked in a tan suit and tie that accidentally matched her outfit. He was the picture of the successful CEO in charge of his domain.

There were times, like now, when she wondered how she'd been the one to catch his eye after Petra died. No woman was immune to him. Kellie's heart rate sped up as she imagined what was about to happen.

Leandros closed the door and went around his desk to buzz Mrs. Kostas. "Would you please send in Karmela?"

"Mr. Petralia! I thought you'd gone on vacation."

He smiled to himself. "I thought so, too. Where's Frato?"

"I haven't seen him yet. I'll send Karmela right in."

"Thank you." Leandros sat back in the swivel chair. "Good morning, Karmela," he said as she opened the door. "Come all the way in and sit down."

Karmela walked straight up to him. "Frato told me about your conversation at the villa yesterday. I understand you want my resignation. But let me give you warning. So far he thinks he's the father of my baby. I'll go on letting him believe it as long as I can keep my job. If I can't, then we'll see how well you handle public opinion when news leaks to the press that you're the daddy."

What more proof did anyone need to know she was ill?

"If you're putting on this performance for me, it isn't necessary, Karmela. I have no idea if you're pregnant or not, but a pregnancy test demanded by a court order can clear that up in a matter of minutes. If you're pregnant, it couldn't possibly be my baby. A DNA test will provide the evidence, but surely you don't want to put Frato through that."

Leandros had seen that catlike smile on her face before. "Frato's more gullible than you. Why do you think the company made you CEO at your age? I'll tell him you and I were lovers during the times Petra was away on business. My family's yacht provided the perfect place away from everyone.

"Before you went to Rhodes on your new project, we got together. That was the time I conceived our baby.

Three nights ago we were in this office alone for hours. All he has to do is check with Christos to believe me."

Leandros got to his feet. "I feel sorry for you and Frato. You need help to get over this obsession. It's tragic you've dragged my cousin into it. There's no more job for you here. If you'd like, I'll have your belongings sent to your parents' home."

When she made no move to leave, he paged Christos and asked him to come in.

"You wanted me?"

"Yes. Please follow Ms. Paulos to her desk so she can get her purse. Then escort her out of the building and put her in a taxi."

Her cat's eyes glimmered. She glared at Leandros. "You have no idea what you've done."

"On the contrary. It's the best decision for everyone concerned. Goodbye, Karmela."

As if nothing was wrong, she strode to the door and walked out, with Christos trailing her. The minute they left, Leandros rushed out into the hall to get Kellie and lead her inside.

She eyed him as he spoke to Mrs. Kostas over the phone. "I'm officially on vacation, but I'll be staying in Athens at the Cassandra. If you can't reach Frato, feel free to call me. Karmela will no longer be working for us. See that her final paycheck goes to her parents' home on Andros Island. I'll be out of the office for the rest of the day."

"Yes, sir."

He shut off the speakerphone. "Before we leave, I'll play the recording so you'll know exactly what was said."

Kellie sat down to listen. When it ended, she looked

up at him. "I don't believe for a moment she's pregnant with your baby, or even pregnant. She's like a defiant little girl. What a shame."

"I agree. All I can say is, thank heaven this is over." Leandros called for his car to be brought around the side of the building, his eyes blazing a hot silvery gray as they pierced Kellie's. "Let's get out of here. I want to take us for a drive around the residential neighborhoods in Athens. Maybe we'll see the house you'd hoped I would buy for your wedding present."

"Leandros..." Her voice shook. "After this scene with Karmela, how can you even think about anything else?"

"Very easily. Whatever she chooses to do or not do, we're through with her."

"I'd like to go back to the hotel."

His eyes scrutinized her. "I thought this confrontation meant we'd put Karmela to rest forever."

She shook her head. "I'm still reacting to what she said. Don't you understand? Even though it's not true, she has threatened to go to the media."

His mouth thinned to a white line. "*Even?* That means you're still not sure about me."

"Of course I am, but after her threat, I can't concentrate on anything else right now."

Leandros ushered Kellie inside the elevator and pushed the button. "If you can't, *I* can. With the twins coming, I want to get settled in the right place to raise them. If you've made up your mind to leave me no matter what, I still have to provide for them, and don't want them living in a hotel when it's my turn for visitation."

"I didn't say that!" She felt ill, especially after he'd done everything in his power to deal with Karmela and Frato since they'd left Mrs. Lasko's house. "Please give me some time, Leandros. Don't you realize how worried I am about the damage she could do to *you*?"

"That's not what's bothering you. A part of you is still worried about Karmela," he said in a wintry tone.

Silence reigned during their swift descent to the ground floor. He'd turned into his forbidding self, the side of him she'd seen toward the end of their marriage. It made it impossible for her to reach him. They walked to the car and he helped her in. When they drove out to the street, he said, "I'll drop you off at the hotel."

"No, Leandros. I've changed my mind and want to come with you."

"Why, since you won't be living with me? I'm going to use the rest of the day to look at houses with a Realtor. It could get too tiring for you. I may not find what I'm looking for today or tomorrow, but I can begin my search. If nothing suits, I'll buy a piece of property and hire an architect."

The Cassandra wasn't that far from his office. He pulled up in front and got out to help her inside the front doors, where people were coming and going. "I'll see you later." A nerve throbbed at the corner of his hard mouth. "Promise you'll call me if there's any kind of emergency."

"Leandros…"

"You may be carrying our children, but don't forget I helped put them there, and love them as much as you do."

Fighting tears, she grabbed his arm. "As if I could forget."

But he wasn't listening. "You already have a home

picked out in Philadelphia. I need to find one for our children when they're with me."

I know.

His eyes were mere slits as he helped her to the elevator in the hall. He pinned her with an undecipherable glance before wheeling away. There was no extra squeeze or caress on the cheek. Why would there be when she was still behaving like the woman who'd insisted on leaving him?

Once he'd driven off, Kellie went up to their suite with a heart so heavy she wanted to die. Without hesitation she ran to her room and pulled the phone out of her purse to call Fran. It rang four times. *Please pick up.*

"Kellie? I've been hoping you'd call soon."

"Thank goodness you're there!"

"Hey…you sound frantic."

"I am. Nothing changes, does it?"

"Yes, it does. You're pregnant with twins! That makes three miracles for us."

Tears filled Kellie's eyes. "I know, but I'm still the same mess I've been for months. Can you talk?"

"Yes. My little miracle from out of the blue is in her swing, listening to the songs. I won't be feeding her for another half hour. Now's the time to tell me what's going on. You left me hanging yesterday. That wasn't fair."

"I'm sorry." Kellie kicked off her shoes and flung herself across the bed before she remembered she needed to be more careful. Slowly she turned over on her back and tucked a pillow under her head. Once she got started talking with her best friend, everything came tumbling out, until Fran was completely caught up.

"Deep down I always thought she was unstable, but I never dreamed Frato was involved."

"It's very sad."

"Hey, Kellie? What's going on? Please tell me you didn't believe Karmela's claim that she's carrying your husband's child!"

She shuddered. "No, but you never heard such a convincing performance in your life."

"Oh, Kellie... After everything that's happened, did you tell Leandros you still believe her?"

"I told him just the opposite!"

"But you left him in doubt by not going house hunting with him."

"I couldn't right then," she said defensively as tears scalded her cheeks.

"Then it sounds like she's won and you've lost the greatest man you'll ever meet on this earth. They don't come any finer than Leandros. I love you, Kellie, but I'm sorry for you."

Fran's comment was like a stab through the heart. "I'm going to hang up now."

"Don't do that! Talk to me! Surely learning about Frato's involvement with her explains everything. It should have made a new woman out of you! What's going on with you?"

"Honestly, it *has* removed every doubt I ever had, but I'm terrified of what she's going to do to him. The second Karmela left his office with Christos, Leandros acted like nothing traumatic had happened. After what she'd vowed to do, I couldn't imagine going anywhere."

"That's your husband, Kellie. He seizes the moment, then moves on. It's part of his brilliance."

"But Karmela is going to come after him! It will

cause terrible trouble in their families, just as Frato predicted. I know it."

"Obviously Leandros isn't worried about it. I'd say he's much more concerned about where the four of you are going to live."

"We're not officially back together. We still have other issues to work through. After the way I left him earlier, I don't know when he'll speak to me again."

"Just have faith that he will! You're the one who wanted counseling and agreed to do it here in Athens. Since he gave up his apartment, it's only natural he's anxious to find a place for the new family coming. Hotel living gets old in a hurry, even in one as posh as the Cassandra."

"I realize that, but I'm still reeling from what went on his office with Karmela. I don't know how he puts one foot in front of the other. Oh, Fran, I know I've hurt him again. He probably won't come back to the hotel until I'm asleep tonight."

"Maybe that's not a bad thing. It will give him time to cool off. Just remember he's a big boy and will get over it. You can discuss it with him in front of Mrs. Lasko at your session tomorrow. That's what marriage counseling is all about. What time do you have to be there?"

Kellie could hear little Demi making noises in the background. "At eleven. I think your daughter is getting hungry. I'll hang up so you can feed her."

"Okay. But before you go, you have no idea how thrilled I am that you're going to be in Athens for your therapy. I've missed you."

Kellie closed her eyes tightly. "Same here."

"Why don't we leave plans open for tomorrow? I'd

love to have lunch with you, but depending on how things go at therapy, maybe the four of us could get together for a barbecue here at the apartment on the patio toward evening. Nik and I are dying to be with the two of you again. He told me to ask you to come over."

"I'll talk to Leandros and let you know. That is, if he's still speaking to me."

"Don't be ridiculous."

"Give Demi a kiss from me. Goodbye for now."

Kellie clicked off and rolled onto her stomach. The day's events had drained her. Unfortunately, the relief of knowing the truth about Karmela was overshadowed by the ugliness of her threats.

Kellie was afraid Leandros wasn't taking this seriously enough. Tomorrow she'd discuss this latest fear in front of their therapist. He would be forced to listen. If anything happened to him...

Tears crept out of the corners of her eyes before she knew nothing more.

CHAPTER SIX

AFTER SEEING KELLIE safely inside the hotel, Leandros drove over to his former apartment, feeling like a shellshocked victim. If his wife still harbored any doubts about him where Karmela was concerned, then their marriage truly was over. But until he calmed down, he wanted another talk with Frato.

Leandros didn't know what to expect, but he knew his cousin was in deep trouble and needed help. In order not to embarrass Frato further, this was one visit he needed to make without Kellie.

En route, he contacted a Realtor he knew well and asked him to come up with some houses to show him and Kellie later on. After he'd finished that call, Leandros phoned his attorney and brought him up to speed about the situation with Frato and Karmela. "I want you prepared for anything that might happen in the next few hours or days. Let's get some private detectives to put her under surveillance."

With that accomplished, he drove into the underground parking. He spotted Frato's BMW, but it didn't necessarily mean he was there. As for Karmela, she could be anywhere, drumming up trouble. She was impulsive, disturbed and furious. Leandros didn't know what to expect.

The second the elevator door opened to the penthouse, he saw Frato dressed in a robe, sprawled on the couch in the living room. He had one foot on the floor and had been drinking. His cousin had been doing more and more of that over the past few years.

"Frato? Where's Karmela?"

He squinted up at Leandros. "It's a cinch she's not here with me. I haven't seen her since all hell broke loose after I got back from Andros yesterday."

"For your information, more broke loose in the office this morning after I let her go. She threw out some expected and unexpected threats before I asked Christos to escort her off the premises."

At that news, Frato struggled to his feet with a groan. "You went in to work?"

"Someone needs to be running the Petralia Corporation, don't you think? Don't worry. I covered for you and told Mrs. Kostas I was still on vacation. We're family, Frato, and we have to stick together. The last thing I'm going to do is fire you, but I need you sober. Go take a shower and get dressed for work while I fix you some coffee so we can talk."

While he waited, he phoned his electronics technician and asked him to come over and remove all codes except Frato's from the elevator security system. As Leandros clicked off, Frato reappeared. His cousin had done his best to disguise the fact that he was hungover.

"Who was that?"

"Not Karmela." After telling him he'd called the security technician to come, Leandros handed him a mug of coffee. "I'll explain why in a minute. Tell me the truth. Is Karmela pregnant with your baby? Is that why the rush to get married?"

The shocked look on Frato's face was all the explanation Leandros needed. With that question answered, he pulled out his cell phone. "I recorded everything the second Karmela walked through the door to my office." He turned it on and they both listened.

By the time they'd heard the door close behind Christos, Frato's tanned complexion had faded several degrees. With a trembling hand, he set down his empty mug.

Leandros switched off the recording. "I'm sorry you had to hear that, but it was necessary. She's got a serious problem, Frato. For a long time she's been using our weaknesses to play all of us against each other.

"You need to know I've already alerted my attorney. If you and I join forces, then whatever she tries to do to discredit us to the media or the families, we'll be a step ahead of her until she gets the help she needs."

He had never seen his cousin's brown eyes water like that before. "I can't believe what I just heard." Frato sank down on one of the bar stools. "What a damn fool I've been all these years."

Leandros patted him on the shoulder. "You don't want to hear what a damn fool I've been since I listened to Petra and gave Karmela carte blanche to do what she wanted. In my desire to placate Petra, I enabled Karmela in a way that has brought my marriage to Kellie to the brink of disaster. But we've started marriage counseling to try to save us."

"You're kidding...."

"No. Naturally it was Kellie's idea, because I've been too impossible to deal with."

"So that's what brought her back?"

Leandros shook his head. "She flew here to tell me in person that we're expecting twins next March."

Frato let out a long whistle that reverberated throughout the penthouse. "Twins? I'm beyond happy for you, Leandros."

His cousin sounded so genuine, it brought a lump to Leandros's throat. "I'm ecstatic myself. Kellie said I deserved to hear the news in person, but she still expected the divorce to go through. I told her I'd just made arrangements with you so I could fly to Pennsylvania, where we could go to counseling. After talking it over, we decided to do our counseling here. We've had one session already, with another one scheduled for tomorrow."

Frato's head jerked back. "Does Karmela know about this?"

"Not her or anyone. I want to keep it that way for the time being."

"Understood. Do you want the penthouse back?"

"It's yours, Frato, with my blessing. I found out Kellie never wanted to live here."

"Why not?"

"Because Petra lived here with me. Kellie wanted a place of our own, but I was too caught up in my desires to ask her what she wanted. Right now we're looking for a house."

"Incredible."

"Are you with me?"

"Yes!"

"Good. Together we can withstand any storm. When the families start calling you, pretend you know nothing. I suggest you get to the office so no one will suspect anything's wrong. Mrs. Kostas knows Karmela has been fired. She'll send her final check to her parents. While you dig into work, I'm going to enjoy my vacation."

Frato nodded. "I'm leaving now."

"One more thing. The technician is on his way over to delete Karmela's code from the elevator. When she calls because it's on the blink, tell her to find herself a good attorney, and assure her you'll have her things shipped to her parents."

As Leandros started to leave, Frato grabbed him and gave him a bear hug, the kind they used to share before their lives got complicated. "I swear I'm going to do better."

"I'll make you the same promise." He knew his cousin would hurt for a long time, but at least Frato's blinders had come off for good.

With everything taken care of for the time being, Leandros felt an enormous weight had been lifted. He left for the hotel, eager to talk to Kellie and explain why he'd thought it was wise she remain there until he got back. His Realtor had called and left the message that he had some wonderful prospects for them, whenever they wanted to see them.

It was midafternoon when Leandros found her in her bedroom, sound asleep on top of the bed, resting on her side. She was still dressed in the skirt and top she'd worn to the office. Her shimmering gold hair was splayed across the pillow. There was no sign that she'd eaten lunch.

He stood in the doorway while his eyes devoured the sight lying before him. She was his whole world. Inside her delectable body their children were growing.

They had a glorious future ahead of them. As badly as he wanted to lie down on that bed with her, he didn't dare. For once in his life he needed to practice patience and restraint in order to win back her trust.

"Leandros?" she murmured, after he'd turned to walk down the hall. "Is that you?"

He came back. "Who else?"

She sat up, trying to arrange her disheveled hair. His wife reminded him of a tantalizing mermaid. "When did you get back?"

"Just now."

"It's four o'clock. I can't believe I slept this long."

"Jet lag has finally caught up with you. Did you eat in the restaurant?"

"No." She slid off the bed, causing her skirt to ride up her thighs before she stood. Kellie had no idea how desirable she was to him. "After I got off the phone with Fran, I fell asleep. Have you eaten?"

"Not yet."

"Then you must be starving, too. I'll order something from the kitchen for both of us."

"While you do that, I'll check my voice mail." He went into the sitting room, curious to see if there were any developments that needed immediate attention.

Dionne and Zera had both called. No surprise there. They wanted to know why Karmela had been fired. He moved on to the next call, from his Realtor.

"I've got a property in Mets. It's a taste of old Athens, with a tiled roof and a charming courtyard. Lots of flowering trees and shrubs of jasmine and bougainvillea. It's in one of the most beautiful neighborhoods and won't stay on the market long. If you're interested,

I'll show it to you this evening, along with a couple of others."

Nothing could have pleased Leandros more. The last message came from his father, asking him to call him as soon as possible. As he clicked off, Kellie joined him. "Anything important?"

"I'll let you be the judge. From here on out, you and I are going to do everything together, so there won't be any more misunderstandings that could start another war." He replayed the messages for her.

Kellie looked shattered by his cousins' calls. "Karmela didn't waste any time, did she? It appears her family has already gotten to your father."

"I'll call him back after I've heard from my attorney. That might not be for another day or two. I want to be in possession of more facts before I touch base with him. He'll know how to calm down my mother."

"He's good at that."

A knock on the door alerted them that their dinner had arrived. Once the waiter had come and gone, they sat down to eat. "Shall I let the Realtor know we'd like to see those houses he phoned about?"

"Yes," she said unexpectedly. "This is a lovely hotel, but it's not a home. I'm sure you're anxious to get settled in something permanent."

Meaning she wasn't?

Her response left him feeling raw, but for once he wasn't going to erupt. Instead, he pulled out his phone and made arrangements with the Realtor that would keep them occupied for the evening.

Tomorrow would be their second therapy session. It couldn't come soon enough for him.

* * *

Olympia was already in her chair when Kellie walked into the room with Leandros at eleven. "Good morning, Mrs. Lasko."

"Good morning to you. Thank you for being on time."

Kellie gave the credit to Leandros, who had seemed equally anxious to get on with the therapy once breakfast was over. After they'd looked at four different houses the evening before—all of which she found had something wrong with them—he was up early on the phone with the Realtor, getting another list of houses for them to look at after their session.

"Please sit down."

Leandros helped her into the chair before he took his seat.

"Anything to report since our last session, before we get started?"

"Quite a lot, actually," Kellie blurted. She looked at Leandros. "Shall I tell her?"

"Go ahead."

Kellie explained about their meetings with Karmela and Frato. When she'd finished, Olympia eyed her in surprise. "I had no idea the results of our first session would produce anything as dramatic as what you've just described. Indeed, Karmela Paulos needs professional help.

"What's more important is that you've taken steps to remove the hornets' nest from your lives. It's an impressive start. I wish all my clients had results like yours within a forty-eight-hour period. Are you prepared to face what might come if she goes to the media in her rage?"

"My attorney is already working on it," Leandros stated with his usual confidence.

"In that case, why don't we begin with you. I'd like you to give me a picture of your life growing up on Andros. The mention of cousins came up in the last session. What part do they play in the family dynamic that has brought grief and makes them stand out?"

Since Olympia wrote no notes and didn't use a tape recorder, Kellie marveled at her photographic memory.

"We're a big family and all work in the Petralia Corporation. I have two living grandparents, but they've long since retired. My parents are semiretired. Though I'm an only child, I have five uncles and aunts, all married with children. I also have two great-uncles and aunts still alive with family.

"Of all the cousins, I'm closest to Frato. He's acting as CEO in my place while I'm on vacation right now. I have five boy cousins and six girl cousins, some older, some younger, two of whom have always been friendly with Karmela Paulos."

"So the joining of the Petralia and Paulos families at the time of your first wedding brought you all together even more intimately."

"Yes."

"All are well married, wealthy?"

"Yes."

"Including the Paulos family?"

"Yes."

"Except for Karmela, who's still single and delusional."

"Yes."

The older woman's gaze swerved to Kellie. "Now I want to hear about *your* upbringing." Olympia moved from subject to subject with a swiftness that made it hard to keep up.

Kellie cleared her throat. "My parents died when I was a baby, so I was raised by my mother's sister and her husband in Philadelphia. They weren't blessed with children, so it was the three of us. They're still alive."

"What does your uncle do for a living?"

"Before retirement, he was an insurance salesman who worked very hard. My aunt helped him. They were wonderful to me. As soon as I could, I got jobs while I went to school. My last year of high school, Fran and I went to school in France for an adventure. I paid for half of it, my uncle the other half.

"With student loans I made it through college, and continued to live with them in order to help them out. That's because my uncle suffered a stroke that put him in a wheelchair. It affected his legs, but not his mind. Once I graduated, I obtained a good position at an advertising agency. After working there for a year, the three of us decided to take our first trip to Europe.

"That was about two and a half years ago. When we flew here to Athens, we stayed at the Cassandra. One day while I was trying to get his wheelchair into the elevator, Leandros happened to be walking by, and helped me. That accidental meeting changed my life." Kellie couldn't prevent her voice from trembling.

"It changed both our lives," he declared with unmistakable fervency.

Olympia put her palms on the table. "I hope you've been listening to each other, really listening, because I want both of you to put yourselves in my role as a therapist. Imagine you're sitting in front of this husband and wife who've come to you. Their nationality, upbringing, social, economic and emotional standings are entirely different.

"The husband's parents are living. He comes from a big family with many tentacles, whose name is known throughout Greece. He's been married before to a socialite, but lost her and their unborn child in a tragic accident.

"The second wife has never been married, has never known her own parents and has committed herself to helping the aunt and uncle who raised her on a modest income without any other family around. She's in a country whose language and customs are unfamiliar to her.

"Kellie? Look at your husband and tell him the second emotion that came to mind when you told him you'd marry him. We already know the first one, that you were painfully in love with him."

Her mouth went dry, and her heart was thudding so hard she didn't know if she could get the words out. She turned and lifted her eyes to him. "I was terrified because I felt so completely inadequate in every way."

Leandros started to say something, but Olympia waved her thin index finger at him. "Your wife has just given you the key to understanding her. Do you remember the statement she made on Tuesday, about fearing she would never measure up to your first wife?"

"Yes."

"Now you can understand it was her feelings of inadequacy that made her feel intimidated. Before you override her comment with your well-meaning protests, sit back for a minute and let it sink in while I ask you a question."

His expression sobered.

"After she said yes to your proposal, what emotion drove you?"

In the quiet that followed, Kellie couldn't imagine what his answer would be.

"It's hard to put into words," his deep voice grated.

"Why?"

His gray eyes sought Kellie's. "Because I felt so many things."

"Name the dominant one."

She heard him take a fortifying breath. "Joy."

Kellie had felt joy, too. In fact, it had been overpowering.

"What manner did it take?"

His black brows furrowed. "I'm not sure I understand."

Olympia sat forward. "How did you manifest your joy?"

"I guess I wanted to give her the world."

Following his answer, Kellie started to tell him the world was the last thing she wanted, but Olympia stopped her with another warning finger. "It's your turn to sit back and think about what he just said, because it's the key to *his* personality."

Silence filled the room once more. Olympia eyed both of them. "There's no wrong or right here. What I see before me are two perfectly wonderful people who want the same thing. But you must follow what I'm saying.

"Leandros? Your problem is that you *can* give her the world, financially. You want to remove every obstacle from your wife's path and make her life easier. Being the confident male you are, with few insecurities, you sweep in and take over for the worthiest of reasons. But it makes you a poor listener and blind to certain facts sitting in front of you. In the end you come off seeming cold and insensitive."

He looked thunderstruck.

"Kellie? You have a different problem. You never knew your mother and father and had no siblings. Strictly speaking, Leandros was Petra's husband before he was yours. You couldn't get pregnant in what we consider the normal way. You're tired of not being able to claim anything of your very own. Not even the children growing inside you are strictly yours. All this has made you angry, with the result that your insecurity makes you distrustful and less than sympathetic."

A gasp escaped Kellie's throat. Olympia had hit the nail so squarely on the head, she was astounded.

"It's no wonder that when insensitivity met up with distrust, you two reached an impasse in your marriage."

Kellie darted Leandros a glance and discovered him studying her intently through shuttered eyes. With Mrs. Lasko's help, it all seemed so clear what was wrong.

"Now let's analyze the positive. Though Kellie's insecurity caused her to ask for a divorce, Leandros, she threw you a lifeline by suggesting you go to marriage counseling. That's because she's a problem solver. She's had to be to make it through life this far. Consider that when she found out Karmela was working in your office, she asked if she could work there, too."

"In all honesty, my friend Fran gave me the idea," Kellie exclaimed.

Leandros darted her a shocked glance. "I didn't know that."

Olympia's brows rose. "The point is, you acted on it."

He got up from the chair with a bleak expression on

his hard-boned features. "But I was too blind to understand what was happening, and turned you down."

"Your blindness was temporary," Olympia asserted. "You've been a winner all your life and aren't used to losing. Once separated from your wife without being able to do anything about it, you were humbled enough to realize that money and power couldn't help you obtain the one thing you wanted above all else. In your vulnerable state—a condition in which you've rarely found yourself—you grabbed the lifeline she tossed you, and agreed to go to counseling."

Kellie felt his penetrating gaze before he said, "It's a miracle you didn't tell me it was too late."

While a flood of emotions swept through her, Mrs. Lasko got to her feet, signaling the end of the session. "Before you leave, I have homework for you. Leandros? I want you to explore how you really feel about Kellie's best friend, Fran. I sensed resentment of her at our first session, but I want you to consider the fact that resentment masks jealousy."

"Jealousy?" he exclaimed.

"That's right. Why does she bring out that emotion in you?"

Kellie was so surprised by Olympia's comment, she didn't realize the therapist was now addressing her.

"As for you, Kellie, you not only feel guilt over your aunt and uncle's sacrifice, you feel as if you abandoned them when you married your husband, and are torn between two worlds. These issues need to be resolved in order to stabilize your marriage."

Hearing those words, Kellie bowed her head. How did Olympia understand so much?

"The more you dig, the more you'll begin to achieve

that joy you first felt when you decided to make a life together. I'll see you on Tuesday. Goodbye."

On unsteady legs, Kellie got up from the chair and headed for the door. Leandros reached it first and opened it for her. He must have noticed she was shaken, because he cupped her elbow as he walked her out to the car, parked in the hot sun.

Before he put the key in the ignition he turned to her with a grim look on his striking Greek features. "Would you find me too insensitive if I told you I'd like to put off our plans for dinner with Fran and Nik this evening?"

Kellie drew in a deep breath. "I would have suggested it if you hadn't. What I'd really like to do is forget everything, including house hunting, and fly to Andros."

A light flashed in the recesses of those somber gray eyes. "You mean it?"

"Yes. We have so much to talk about, I hardly know where to begin. I'll call Fran right now and cancel."

"Do you think she'll be offended?"

"Disappointed, certainly, but not offended. It'll be fine." With Olympia's startling observations still spinning in her head, Kellie needed to show her husband that she put him first.

While he started the engine and they backed out to the street, she reached into her purse for her cell and pressed the speed dial. When Fran answered, Kellie turned on the speakerphone so Leandros could hear their conversation while they drove. *Everything out in the open.* Olympia's mantra.

"Kellie!" Fran sounded excited to hear from her. "How did the therapy go?"

She swallowed hard. "In all honesty, it was so heavy-duty this morning, I'm still reeling. Do you mind terribly if Leandros and I take a rain check for this evening?"

"You know better than to ask me that."

"Thanks for being so understanding." Kellie had almost said *thanks for being my best friend*. It was what she always said to her, oftentimes in Leandros's hearing. When she really thought about it, Kellie realized Fran had figured heavily in her life whether on or off stage. Not until this moment did it occur to her that Leandros needed to know *he* was her best friend.

The therapist had picked up on it, while Kellie had been oblivious. Was it possible that in some nebulous way, Leandros felt he came in second in her affections? Before the four of them spent any more time together, this was an area they needed to talk about.

"Fran? I'll call you on Monday."

"Take all the time you need. I'm not going anywhere. *Au revoir.*"

After she clicked off, Leandros turned to her. "If you're hungry for lunch, we can eat at the hotel before we leave for Andros."

She shook her head. "I'm still full from breakfast, but please don't let that keep you from ordering something."

"I'd rather wait until we reach the villa. I'll alert the housekeeper to get things ready for us."

In truth, Kellie had lost her appetite by the end of the session, and sensed Leandros wasn't any better off.

Without more talk, they returned to the hotel to grab a few things and board the helicopter. The presence of his bodyguard further inhibited conversation.

During the flight her mind kept harking back to the conversation at their first therapy session with Olympia.

"Did you go to Rhodes without your wife?"

"Yes. Unbeknownst to me, she'd made arrangements for her best friend, Fran, to come to Greece."

"Best friend, as in Frato has been your best friend?"

"She's been like the sister I never had."

"They were going to take a two-week trip together while I was away on business. After making that announcement, she moved to the guest bedroom."

Kellie recalled the bleak tone in Leandros's voice, but she'd been too upset at the time to give it any real thought. It had taken this second session with the therapist for her to remember it, and it sent a stabbing pain of guilt through her.

Once they reached the villa and were finally alone, she followed him into the kitchen. He'd gone over to the sink and drank from the tap for a long time.

"Leandros?"

He slowly turned around, revealing a wounded expression. She took a step closer. "I'm so sorry."

Lines bracketed his hard mouth. "For what?"

"For making travel plans with Fran behind your back at the height of our marital troubles. It was cruel of me and made it impossible for you and me to communicate. But at the time I was too consumed with pain to realize what a selfish person I'd turned into."

She could hear her voice throbbing. The tears had started. She couldn't stop them. "I—I wouldn't blame you if you never forgave me for what I've done."

Heartsick, she hurried into the guest bedroom and lay down on her side, clutching one of the pillows to her while she sobbed.

"Kellie?" When she looked up, she saw him standing at the side of the bed. "There's nothing to forgive."

With tears dripping down her cheeks, she raised herself up on one elbow. "How can you say that? I used Fran to put a buffer between you and me."

"That was the only time I've ever been hurt by your friendship with her. Olympia caught it because she's good at what she does."

"You're not just saying that to make me feel better?"

"Why would I do that?"

"Because it's your nature to be kind." Kellie wiped her eyes with the back of her arm. "Olympia's a genius. She has me so figured out it's frightening."

His hands went to his hips. "Frightening?"

"Yes. She was right about my always having wanted something of my very own. When I met you, my heart and soul claimed you on some level I wasn't even aware of. After a lifelong search, finding you answered the question of my existence. But knowing you had a history with Petra tortured me."

"Kellie..."

"It's true," she cried. "I grew too possessive of you. You were my best friend and lover. But instead of running to you with my fears, I held them in and became a shrew of a wife. Olympia's right. I *have* been angry, but the fault has lain with me. I'm so ashamed."

Convulsed in fresh tears, she buried her face in the pillow. Within seconds the mattress dipped and Leandros pulled her into his arms.

"I don't know how you can even stand to touch me," she moaned.

His answer was to pull her close. He felt so wonderful and substantial that she relaxed against him, having no desire to push him away as she'd done a few days ago. While in this halcyon state she heard familiar voices calling to Leandros.

Her eyelids flew open in surprise. "Your parents—"

Leandros kissed her temple before rolling away from her. "For them to walk in without phoning first, it means they're either tired of being ignored or they've heard the news about Karmela." As Kellie slid off the bed, he grabbed her hand. "Come on. Let's go talk to them."

"My skirt and blouse are wrinkled."

"I don't see anything wrong."

"Well, I should at least brush my hair."

"No. I love your mussed look."

Leandros. Her heart skittered all over the place.

They found his parents in the living room. Thea hurried toward Kellie and kissed her on both cheeks. "Forgive us for barging in, but we saw you arrive in the helicopter, and it's been too long," his mother cried. She was a beauty in her own right, a stylish and elegant brunette. "We've missed you, Kellie."

"Indeed we have." Leandros's father, an aristocratic-looking man with salt-and-pepper hair, held out his arms to her.

"Vlassius..." She gave him a hug. "It's so good to see both of you."

He held on to her hands. "We retain Christos and Giorgios to keep our son safe. They were so happy to see you back in Athens, they let us know the moment you arrived at the office. You're a sight for sore eyes."

Kellie laughed. "I might have known they couldn't

keep a secret, but at least they let me surprise Leandros in his own lair."

That brought more laughter.

CHAPTER SEVEN

"MY LAIR?" Leandros teased.

When he thought about it, he realized her remark was entirely apropos. After the desolate month he'd spent alone, her presence had been a surprise, all right. While he'd been hiding out in his office like a wounded animal licking his wounds, he'd suddenly heard her voice and seen his gorgeous blonde wife standing there like a vision. For a moment he'd thought he was hallucinating.

"Why don't you two join us out on the patio? We haven't eaten since breakfast," he said.

"Oh, no!" his mother exclaimed. "Let me help."

"We have it covered, *Mana*. Would you like to eat with us?"

"I don't think so. We only finished lunch a while ago."

In a minute he and Kellie took plates of salad and rolls out to the wrought-iron table. The housekeeper had also prepared iced tea. They could all enjoy that.

After devouring a third roll, Leandros eyed his parents frankly. "Before you explode from curiosity, Kellie and I have a few things to tell you. Our divorce has been put on hold while we undergo marriage counseling."

Their eyes widened, but they didn't comment. He admired their restraint.

"It was Kellie's idea. I fought it at first, because you know me, I think I know everything."

His mother laughed. "I never thought I'd live to see the day when you admitted it."

"It takes a big man," his father interjected.

"Yes, it does," Thea joked, staring at her husband.

Leandros thought Kellie had to be enjoying this.

"As soon as I came back from the States alone, I realized I couldn't live without her, and finally agreed to it. But remember, we're not together." He eyed Kellie. "As our therapist says, we're a work in progress."

"Bravo," his mother exclaimed. But there was no bravo about it if Kellie believed Karmela's lie.

"I apologize for not having returned your phone call yet, but there've been reasons," Leandros went on. "As I informed you a few days ago, I'm on vacation. That's why I asked Frato to take over for me at the office. For your information, Kellie and I had our second session this morning."

Leandros darted his wife a glance. "We probably would have walked up to the villa to visit you later today." Kellie's nod confirmed it.

His mother clasped her hands together and let out a happy cry. His father smiled in obvious satisfaction. Their reactions had to have reassured his wife that they loved her. They'd been crushed when he'd told them Kellie was leaving him.

Leandros sent his wife another glance. If she wanted to tell them their other news, he was leaving it up to her. A hushed silence fell over the room. When it became deafening, he started to bring up another subject, but Kellie suddenly put her glass down and said, "Last week I went to my doctor in Philadelphia for a checkup and found out...we're expecting twins."

"Twins?" His mother was so ecstatic, she jumped up from the table and ran around to hug him and Kellie again.

With tears in his eyes, his father followed suit. "This is a great day, a miraculous day!"

Thea's face was wreathed in a huge smile. "Two grandbabies to love. I can't believe it! Thank heaven for modern medicine."

"I can hardly believe the artificial insemination worked," Kellie admitted. "But the thought of taking care of *two* babies at once is pretty overwhelming."

"We'll all help," his mother assured her. "Your aunt and uncle must be thrilled. When are you due?"

"March seventh. They're nearly eight weeks old. The doctor said they're as big as blueberries, with tiny hands and feet emerging."

His parents laughed and cried. Inside, Leandros was thrilled, but until he knew unequivocally that Kellie believed in him, he couldn't celebrate the way he wanted. As for therapy, they still had a long way to go. The only thing helping him right now was that she'd let him hold her a little while ago. She'd even seemed to welcome his arms around her.

He waited until his parents sat down again before asking if there was another reason they'd walked down to his villa unannounced. They shook their heads, clearly mystified by his question.

It meant Karmela still hadn't played her trump card. That's why he hadn't heard from his attorney. He was hoping that not hearing anything yet meant she might be backing down on her threats. If that was the case, then things couldn't be working out better.

"The therapy we've been undergoing has opened my eyes to a dangerous situation that was brewing long before we took our vows. Though we have other issues to work on, this has been one of the big ones threatening to undermine our marriage."

Both his parents frowned, but it was his father who demanded clarity. "Be explicit."

"As Kellie and I discussed earlier, there's been an enemy within our walls. Not only has she done everything in her power to come between Kellie and me, she's been doing an expert job of destroying Frato in the process."

"She?" his mother questioned, patently bewildered.

Leandros nodded grimly. "My former sister-in-law, Karmela."

The shock on his parents' faces convinced him they would never have suspected Petra's sister of any wrongdoing. They'd been completely in the dark about her.

"Kellie? Tell them what you told the therapist about the night of our wedding reception. My parents need to hear from you to understand what we've been up against. Don't leave anything out."

Once his wife began her tale, he watched their reactions. By the time she'd finished, he knew they were horrified.

"There's more," he said, pulling out his cell phone. "Once you hear this conversation between me and Karmela at my office, you'll realize what our family could be up against. Kellie has already listened to it." He switched on the recording.

While his parents sat there in shock, he eyed Kellie. He could tell she was worried about their reaction. When it had played out, he shut the device off.

"The girl's clearly unwell," his father declared.

His mother nodded. She looked ill. "What are you going to do, Leandros?"

"After I took Kellie back to the Cassandra, I went to the penthouse and had a serious talk with Frato. He's been in love with Karmela for a long time, but when he listened to this recording, it forced him to wake up. Frato's finished with her. If she tries to get into his penthouse, she won't be able to."

"Who would have dreamed she had such problems?"

"Maybe her parents *do* know, but haven't been able to help her. It's anyone's guess how far she's willing to take this. Dionne and Zera phoned to find out why I fired her, so she has revealed that much to those in the family who are sympathetic to her. But at this point, anything could be going on. Rest assured I've got her under surveillance and have alerted my attorney."

That didn't seem to mollify his father. "Has Frato told my brother all this?"

"I don't think so, Papa, but I could be wrong. They've always been close, but this business with Karmela is something Frato has kept hidden for years. I've advised him to go on doing his job at the office and say nothing."

"Well, there's something I can do!" His father pushed himself away from the table and stood up. "Let's go, Thea. We're about to pay a visit to Karmela's family right now. Let me have your phone, Leandros. They need to hear this so they can take their daughter in hand."

Leandros shook his head. "Though you know the

facts, I don't want you getting involved. You've been friends for too many years. I'm the one who fired Karmela, and she knows why. If anyone's going to talk to her parents, I'll be the person to do it. But it may not come to that. Should they contact you about this, then direct them to me. I want your promise on that."

His mother got up. "But if she should call one of the newspapers…"

Kellie darted Leandros a worried glance. "That's what I'm concerned about, Thea. Today's so-called journalists don't check their sources. Even if it's all lies, and your attorney forces them to print a retraction, the public goes on believing the lies. This could destroy your reputation and Frato's. The whole family could be hurt, including Karmela's."

"She's right," his father muttered. "With you two expecting twins, I don't like this at all. Does Karmela know about your miraculous news?"

"No. Besides you and her doctor, the only people aware are Kellie's aunt and uncle, our therapist, Frato, and Nik and Fran. For the time being, we'd prefer the rest of the family doesn't know about this."

"Understood. Come on, Thea. We're going to leave, to give you some privacy."

The four of them gravitated to the front door. After more hugs, his father said, "Even if you've got people watching Karmela, you need the security on you doubled."

"I've already taken care of it." Leandros eyed him solemnly. "I promise to keep you informed."

"See that you do. We're in this together. How long do you think you'll be staying on Andros?"

Leandros glanced at his wife. "We don't know yet."

His mother cupped Kellie's cheeks. "Whatever you do, wherever you go, you have to take extra special care of yourself now."

"I agree."

"I had two miscarriages before Leandros was born," Thea confessed. "After that, I was never able to get pregnant again." Her eyes misted. "Those babies you're carrying are extra precious."

"I know. Thank you for caring so much." Kellie kissed his mother again before his parents started walking away.

When Leandros couldn't see them anymore, he closed the door. Kellie had already gone out to the patio to clear the dishes. He had an idea she was trying to hide her emotions. Once he joined her, they got everything cleaned and put away in no time.

"Leandros?" She turned, resting her back against the kitchen counter. His body was on alert for any change of mood in her.

"What is it?"

"Would you like to go for a walk along the beach with me? I feel like stretching my legs."

This was the first time since she'd flown back from the States that she was the one asking him to do something with her. Excitement flooded through him.

He almost said, "I was about to suggest it, if you weren't too tired." But he'd learned his lesson. Because of therapy, he'd discovered she didn't like him hovering, let alone sweeping in and taking over. "I could use some exercise myself. Give me a minute to put on a pair of shorts."

Kellie didn't want to change out of her wraparound skirt. It was the most comfortable piece of clothing in her wardrobe. First thing tomorrow she would go shopping. She needed some loose fitting tops and maternity jeans. Dr. Creer had warned her she'd grow bigger fast.

She went into the bathroom and brushed her hair before fastening it in a ponytail with one of her bands. Though it was late afternoon, the sun was still hot. After applying sunscreen and lipstick, Kellie went in search of Leandros. She found him in the kitchen on the phone, in his bare feet.

He'd changed into a short-sleeved, white cotton shirt left partially unbuttoned. In it and his navy shorts he looked better than any statue of a Greek god. Without her volition, a surge of desire for him welled up inside her.

Glancing up, he finally noticed her, and turned on the speakerphone so she could hear. The conversation with a man she didn't recognize ended soon enough. "That was the private investigator. Karmela's been staying at the Athenian Inn and hasn't left her room all day. He'll continue to keep me apprised."

"Leandros... Since we started therapy, you've let me listen in on every phone conversation. I know why you've been doing it, and I appreciate it. But it isn't natural or necessary. I trust you, and I believe that when you have something important to share with me, you will."

Some of the worry lines on his arresting face relaxed. "That works both ways." He put a couple of water bottles into a pack he fastened around his hips. "I don't want you to get dehydrated."

"Thank you for being so thoughtful." He was being so polite. *Too polite.* She knew why.

"You're welcome," he answered in his low, vibrant voice.

"Before we go, there's something I need to tell you."

"I know what it is."

"No, you don't," Kellie countered. "Petra was revered by everyone in your family. You wouldn't have fallen in love with her if she hadn't been a wonderful person. Unconsciously, I endowed Karmela with the same qualities.

"When she was in your office and declared she was pregnant with your baby, I honestly didn't believe her, but I was in shock to realize I was looking at a truly disturbed woman who isn't anything like her sister. That's why it took me getting out of there and going back to the hotel to see everything for what it is. I hope you can believe me when I tell you my doubts about her are gone. I do trust you. Completely."

"Thank heaven," he answered emotionally. "What do you say we take advantage of the sun?" Her husband never revisited a problem once it was over. He was such a remarkable man.

They left the villa. When they reached the sand, she removed her sandals and dangled them from her fingers while they walked in the opposite direction from the private pier. Kellie saw several boats in the distance. The light breeze was enough to fill their sails, so they skimmed along the shimmering blue water.

Paradise.

She had a lot on her mind and knew Leandros did, too, but neither of them spoke. Slowly they made their way around an outcropping of rocks. It led to a much smaller, sheltered cove where the hillside was filled with wildflowers. No villas had been built here so there were no people around. They had the thin stretch of beach to themselves.

"Leandros," she said tentatively, "I'd like to talk to you about something important."

"There are things I want to discuss with you, too."

"Then let's sit for a little while."

His brows furrowed. "You don't mind getting sandy in that skirt?"

"Not at all."

After she sank down, Leandros handed her a bottle of water. While she took sips, he put his own bottle to his lips and quenched his thirst. When he'd drained it, he stretched out on the sand and leaned back on his elbows. His dark wavy hair gleamed in the sun while he stared out at the water. Kellie got a suffocating feeling in her chest just looking at him.

"Leandros?" she whispered.

He turned on his side toward her. With his jaw set and his eyes shuttered against the sun's slanting rays, she couldn't read his expression, but sensed his emotions were raw. "What's on your mind?"

"Something Olympia hit on about my guilt over my aunt and uncle really touched a nerve with me. I was the luckiest girl in the world to be raised by them. When I married you, there was a part of me that felt like I was abandoning them. Because of that I suffered guilt, and didn't realize it could do so much damage."

His dark brows furrowed. "What do you mean?"

"If on our honeymoon I wasn't the same woman you'd fallen in love with, I'm afraid it was because I couldn't enjoy it completely, knowing they'd gone back to Philadelphia alone. The business with Frato's and

Fran's observations about Karmela were only a small part of my inability to be myself with you.

"All this time I thought I'd hidden it from you, but when you told Olympia you knew something was wrong on our honeymoon, it really threw me. Hindsight is a wonderful thing, but in our case it has come too late."

Kellie felt his body stiffen. "Go on."

"I just want to explain why I didn't like any of the houses we looked at earlier. I know you liked the one with the tiled roof and the courtyard. I liked it, too, but—"

"But what?" He broke in tersely. "Just say what you have to say, Kellie."

"Do you remember when you were talking to me about the penthouse?"

His eyes, dark with emotion, played over her face. "How could I forget?"

"You said," she stammered, "you said that you would always have lived on Andros and commuted if Petra hadn't wanted to live in Athens."

"That's right," he muttered.

"Do you still feel that way? Please be honest."

"Kellie...I'm discovering we can't always have everything we want."

"In other words, you *would* prefer living on Andros if everything else lined up the right way?"

In a sudden move, he got to his feet and stared down at her with a black expression. "What's this about? Are you trying to work up the courage to tell me you're going back to Philadelphia, so I can do what I want?"

"No!" she cried, and hurriedly stood up, shaking the sand from her skirt. "It's too soon to talk about anything like that. You're deliberately misunderstanding me."

"What else am I supposed to think?"

She put a hand on his arm. His body had gone rigid. "Why did you say we can't always have everything we want? Tell me."

He eased his arm away, as if her touch burned him. "Surely you know why. I'm aware of how crazy you are about Athens."

"I am. With all its history and monuments, it's a magnificent city. But I loved your home on Andros the first time you brought me here. When we were looking at houses with the Realtor, I kept thinking about your villa. No place else in the world could possibly compare. It's no wonder you love it so much. To buy or build a home in Athens is ludicrous when this is the only home where the children should live and be raised."

"You honestly mean that?" She heard a tremor in his voice.

"Yes. Their heritage is here with their grandparents and relatives."

Kellie heard him struggle for breath. "Their heritage is in Pennsylvania, too. Don't think I don't know how torn you've been over being separated from your aunt and uncle. I always wanted them to move to Greece, but you said no. I didn't need to hear Olympia's thoughts on the subject to realize how hard it's been for you."

"That's because I know my aunt. She's afraid my uncle wouldn't want to leave their friends. There's also the issue of his health care companion, and whether my uncle could adapt to a new environment. Unfortunately, my thinking has been foggy because of all my hang-ups. But therapy has made me see I've been a fool. I've missed them terribly and realize they've missed me, too. Naturally, I've been their whole world since my parents died. Nothing else has been as important to them."

"I'm glad you finally understand that."

She nodded. "Leandros…if we make the decision to stay together, I want to live here year-round."

He looked thunderstruck. "You love it that much?"

"I might not have been born here, but I love it probably as much as you do. Olympia was right about me. I do crave something of my very own. Since you told me Petra had never lived in the villa with you, that changed everything for me. I know now there was no third party on our honeymoon. I feel like we could start a new life here, built on a firm foundation. But—"

"But you couldn't do it without your aunt and uncle living here, too," he finished for her.

"Yes."

"I've always been aware of that. We need them with us. So will our children. Otherwise we'll never be completely happy. Come on. On our way back to the villa, we'll take a detour. I want to show you something."

After putting their water bottles in his pack, he grasped her hand and held it tightly. Kellie could feel her husband's excitement. He came alive as they retraced their steps around the point to the next cove. When they reached the path leading away from the beach, she slipped her sandals back on. They followed it until it diverged. He took the trail to the right until they came to a small stone villa.

"Wasn't this your great-uncle Manny's house?"

"That's right. His wife died while I was in college. They never had children. Since his death a year ago, it has stood empty." Leandros reached for a key left above the lintel, and let them in the side door. It led into the kitchen.

"I remember being in here before. It's very cozy and charming."

"With some renovations, I believe your aunt and uncle would be very happy here. It's all on one floor and would accommodate his wheelchair. We'd hire a housekeeper to take care of them so they could maintain their independence."

"Oh, if I thought this were possible…"

"Of course it is. If there's a drawback, it's that they'd be surrounded by my relatives. But we'd provide them with a car, so they could drive to the different villages, or go visiting whenever they wanted company."

Kellie's eyelids prickled with salty tears. "This would be a perfect place, but I'm sure your family would have something to say about it."

Leandros grasped her upper arms, bringing her close to his hard-muscled body. "Dozens of people with a lot of money have coveted this villa, sitting on the most prime property of the island. My father and uncles have had dozens of offers to buy it, for many times what it's worth. But they haven't wanted anyone who wasn't family to live here on the estate."

"I can understand that."

"They'd rejoice if your aunt and uncle made this their home. You're family, after all. My extended family will celebrate, anyway, when they hear we're expecting twins."

"You're g-generous beyond belief, Leandros." Her voice caught. "I've never known anyone like you."

She felt his gaze narrow on her mouth, but he held back from kissing her. For once she wished he would devour her the way he used to do, but she'd changed all the rules when she'd asked for a divorce. He was much more careful now. Kellie sensed he was waiting for her to initiate any intimacy between them, because he didn't want to make more mistakes.

Neither did she.

Afraid she'd killed something inside him, she turned away with an ache in her heart, and started for the door. On the way back to the villa, he suggested they drive to one of the other villages to eat dinner. He said it so airily, the tension-filled moment in the kitchen, when she'd wanted to pull his head down to hers and give in to her desire, might never have happened.

On impulse, she said, "I have another idea. Why don't you start up the grill on the patio and I'll make us some lamb kabobs." He loved them. "I'll be able to marinate them for only a few minutes, but they'll still taste good. We'll finish off the salad and rolls, too."

"You really want to cook tonight?" He sounded eager, yet once again she noticed he was careful not to ask her if she was too tired. What had she done to him?

"Absolutely."

I want to do something for you.

Kellie hadn't made a meal for him in over two months. A Greek man loved his food. Leandros had always liked finding her in the kitchen while she cooked up a storm. When he'd claimed in front of Olympia that he'd loved coming home to Kellie after work, she knew he hadn't been lying about that. Because of therapy, she realized he'd never lied to her about anything.

"Make a lot of them," he called out before disappearing into the house.

She smiled, remembering the dozens of times he'd

said the same thing to her when he'd phoned her from work, telling her he was coming home.

After washing her hands, she got busy. As she assembled the ingredients, it occurred to her she hadn't ever been this happy before. This was her kitchen. She was making dinner for her husband. They were pregnant with twin babies. He'd just told her they would move her aunt and uncle to the estate. Except for news about Karmela's next move still hanging over them, Kellie had more joy than any one woman deserved or could hope for in this life.

She was in the middle of her preparations when Leandros came back into the kitchen with his phone in hand. Judging by the lines bracketing his eyes and mouth, the news was bad.

"Who just called you?"

"The private detective."

"Did Karmela elude him and get to the press, anyway?"

Leandros inhaled sharply. "No. She managed to fix it so they got to *her*."

"What do you mean?"

"She's even more devious than I realized. After overdosing on some pills at the hotel, for the sake of theatrics, she called the police so they'd be certain to find her before she could do any real damage. The private detective was out in the hall when the paramedics arrived. He followed them to the hospital, where her stomach was pumped.

"He spoke to one of the officers who heard her statement. She said I ended our affair after finding out she was pregnant with our baby, and fired her from the Petralia Corporation. The news will leak out. It always does."

Somehow Kellie wasn't surprised. "Even if it makes the ten o'clock news, it won't matter," she declared. "Anyone who knows you will realize she's a very sick girl who needs a psychiatrist. Let's get to the hospital. Call your parents so they can fly to Athens with us. It'll be better if we're all together when we talk to her parents. I'll phone Frato. He'll want to meet us there."

Leandros's eyes pierced hers. "You're willing to come with me?" he asked in a grating voice.

She knew what he was asking. Besides everything else, they might have to face a barrage of reporters. If ever they needed to present a united front, it was now. "Yes. I'm your wife. We do everything together."

"Kellie..." For once he forgot the rules and crushed her in his arms. She clung to him before he was forced to let her go and alert Stefon to get the helicopter ready. While Leandros changed clothes and made the call to his parents, she phoned Frato. To her relief, he picked up fast.

"Kellie?"

"Yes. Please listen. Where are you?"

"I'm at the penthouse."

"Then you don't know about Karmela yet."

"What's happened?"

Once she'd explained, he said, "I'll phone Father, then head on over to the hospital and meet you there."

"Good. If we're all together, it'll be the best statement we could make."

"Agreed."

After they hung up, she made a couple of sandwiches for them to eat on the helicopter and put the uncooked food in the fridge. Leandros appeared in the kitchen wearing a gray suit and tie. "Ready?"

"Almost." She wrapped the sandwiches. "Here, take these." While he found a sack and added some apples, she went to the bathroom to freshen up. Moments later they hurried out of the villa. She didn't worry about the coals in the grill. They would burn down.

Her thoughts were on a real fire burning out of control at the hospital in Athens. Kellie loved her husband desperately, but never more than at this moment, when his life and reputation were at the mercy of Karmela.

CHAPTER EIGHT

LEANDROS TOLD STEFON to land at the hotel. From there, he drove the four of them to the hospital. There was a delivery entrance on the south side of the building. Hoping to avoid the paparazzi, he called for permission to park there, and a security guard allowed them to enter the building.

Frato had just phoned and told Leandros to go to the psychiatric unit on the third floor, west wing. He'd be waiting for them in the lounge off the hallway. To his knowledge, the police had notified Karmela's parents, who were still inside the locked area with the doctor.

Kellie held on to Leandros's arm, the way she'd done in the early days of their marriage. He hardly recognized her as the same woman he'd brought to this hospital five weeks ago, after she'd fainted. That woman wouldn't let him touch her.

He wanted to believe she was aching for the intimacy they'd once shared, and that's why she was clinging to him. If this show of solidarity in front of everyone didn't extend beyond this hour of crisis, he didn't think he could bear it.

"Leandros..."

Frato's parents had just appeared, but he'd been too

deep in his torturous thoughts to realize it. Kellie got up first to greet them. Soon Leandros's parents had gathered around. While they were huddled together discussing Karmela's sorry state, the door opened and her parents emerged, white-faced. Leandros thought they'd aged ten years.

Kellie was right with him as they walked over to embrace them. "How is she, Leda?"

"Sedated. We can't see her again until tomorrow morning." Karmela's mother lifted tear-filled eyes to him. "She's always been crazy about you, Leandros, but we hoped and prayed she'd get over it after you married Kellie. If anything, it made her worse, but we had no idea she would try to kill herself."

Leandros's heart went out to them. "Just remember one thing. She called the police so they'd be sure to find her in time."

Nestor nodded. "The doctor said it was a call for help. She didn't want to die. She did it to get your attention. We're so sorry for the grief she has caused you and Kellie...and Frato." He eyed Leandros's cousin with compassion before looking at Leandros again. "Are you two back together?"

He sucked in his breath. "We're working on it. I can tell you with conviction that with enough love and therapy, she'll get through this."

"You really believe that?" Leda's voice trembled.

"We do," Kellie interjected. "We're going to counseling right now. It's been a liberating experience for both of us. I'm sure it will be for Karmela, too."

Leda hugged Kellie. "You deserve all the happiness in the world."

"So does Karmela."

"You can say that after everything's she's done? What we heard her tell the doctor horrified us. But a pregnancy test was done. She's not pregnant."

"We didn't think she was. From what I've learned, she's been in pain for years, Leda. The doctor will help her understand that pain, and then she'll get well."

"Bless you." Leda hugged Kellie again.

Nestor eyed all of them. "The second the police called, I asked them to do all they could to prevent this from leaking to the press."

Leandros patted him on the shoulder. "Don't worry. If there's fallout, we can handle it. One thing you could do is put the record straight to Dionne and Zera. They love Karmela. She'll need their friendship more than ever now."

Leda nodded. "We'll call them before we go to bed."

In an automatic move, Leandros put his arm around his wife's shoulders. "Since there's nothing more we can do here, we'll go. Keep in close touch with us. You know we'll do whatever we can to help."

After more hugs, they said good-night to Frato and his parents, then the four of them left and drove back to the hotel. It was decided his parents would stay the night. Tomorrow they'd fly back to Andros.

Once ensconced in the suite, Kellie made coffee and ordered more food from the kitchen. They all needed time to settle down and relax before they could think about bed. It was better this way.

Leandros was on fire for his wife, but until she showed him she wanted him, body and soul, he wasn't about to push anything. In fact, this would be a good time to broach the subject foremost on his mind, now that Karmela was finally getting the help she needed.

He sat back in the chair, eyeing his parents over the rim of his coffee cup. "Kellie and I have been doing a lot of talking. Since our wedding, she's suffered over missing her aunt and uncle. We've flown to Philadelphia when we could, but traveling there every few months hasn't been enough. It's been harder for them to come here, because he's in a wheelchair.

"Yesterday, while we were out walking, I made a decision." Kellie's head jerked toward him in surprise. "If we agree to stay together, it will depend on her aunt and uncle where we live permanently."

The room went perfectly still.

"Kellie has been worried, with good reason, about uprooting them to live in Greece. They've built a lifetime of memories and friends in Philadelphia, and the move might be too hard on them. This last month she put down earnest money on a house big enough for them and our children. We would all live there."

His mother shook her head in consternation. "But what would you do?"

"I could still work for the corporation long distance. Naturally, I'd step down as CEO."

"And then you'd come and visit us every few months...." His mother's mournful voice trailed off.

"Nothing's written in stone yet, *Mana*. If Kellie and I decide to stay together, and if by some miracle they'd be willing to move here, then we'd live on Andros permanently."

"Permanently?" A squeal of joy escaped his mother's lips before she got up from the couch. "Then we'll make that miracle happen! Your aunt and uncle will be so welcome here, they won't have time to miss peo-

ple. Think how busy we'll all be when the children are born!"

She flew across the expanse to hug him. "I hated it when you moved to that penthouse in Athens."

"I did it for Petra."

"We know you did, but nothing's been the same since." She moved to Kellie, seated in the other chair. "You really want to live on Andros?"

"It's my favorite place in the world. The children will thrive there." Kellie's heartfelt response made its way inside his heart and convinced his parents. His mother squeezed her.

"Did you hear that, Vlassius?"

His father's eyes had glazed over with happy tears. "I heard. I'm still trying to take it all in."

"So what can we do to get your aunt and uncle to come, Kellie?"

Leandros sat forward. "On our way up from the beach yesterday, we stopped to look at Uncle Manny's villa. How do you think the family would fee—"

"It would be perfect for them!" his mother cried out, before he could finish his thought.

His father nodded. "I go fishing every morning on the boat. Jim will come with me."

"And Sybil will come shopping with me!" his mother exclaimed.

"Family should be together and that place shouldn't go empty any longer," his father declared. "With twins on the way, I think it's the best idea you've ever had."

"You're the most generous people on earth," Kellie declared in a tremulous voice. "I guess you realize your son takes after you."

Leandros liked the sound of that. "Though it seems

like a perfect arrangement to us, everyone in the family would have to be in agreement. The villa needs work. I'd want to make improvements to the bathroom."

"I can tell you right now the family will welcome the idea without reservation."

"Thanks, Papa. However, if there is a problem, then there's still room on my piece of the property to build a new villa for them. But until Kellie talks to them about moving to Greece, it's a moot point, considering we're still in the middle of therapy."

His father stood up. "Come on, Thea. Let's go to bed and plot."

Kellie laughed out loud. It was the full-bodied kind he'd missed hearing all these months.

He eyed his parents. "That's a good idea. I'm suddenly exhausted and crave sleep. Everything you need should be in the guest bedroom. We'll see you at breakfast."

Taking a leaf out of their book, he got up and walked over to Kellie. "Get a good night's sleep." He kissed her on the cheek. "See you in the morning."

His heart leaped to see the look of disappointment in those chocolate eyes before he headed for his room. But he was doing better at disciplining himself where his wife was concerned. He wanted her to come to him, day or night, of her own free will. No holding back.

The apartment had gone quiet. Feeling wide-awake, Kellie carried the coffee mugs to the kitchen. She was still in shock that Leandros had gone to bed so fast. After what had happened today, there was so much she wanted to talk to him about, but by leaving the living room with his parents, he'd made any more conversation tonight impossible.

She knew she could always go to his room, but he would take that to mean she wanted to be with him in every sense of the word. Of course, she wanted that more than anything in the world. But when the moment came that they decided to recommit to each other, she preferred to be strictly alone with him on Andros.

Since arriving in Greece, Kellie had done so much sharing with her husband, she hardly recognized the person she'd become. Without him being available, her normal impulse would have been to phone Fran and talk to her about everything, disregarding the lateness of the hour. But that was before the therapy sessions. The revelations they'd uncovered had changed Kellie's life. She was turning into a different person.

When she really thought about it, her only real concern at this point was her aunt and uncle. If they could have seen and heard the reaction of Leandros's parents tonight, it would have warmed their hearts to know how much they wanted them to move to Greece.

Kellie checked her watch. It would be afternoon in Philadelphia. Now would be the best time to call them and have a long talk. After getting ready for bed, she climbed under the covers and picked up the receiver on the bedside table.

"Aunt Sybil?"

"Honey…"

"Have I caught you at an inconvenient time?"

"Heavens, no! I'm just putting the raspberry jam I made into the freezer. You know how much Jim loves it. We were just talking about you at lunch, wondering how the therapy is coming along. Are you still suffer-ing nausea?"

"No. The medicine Dr. Creer prescribed has really helped. Listen, there's something very important I need to talk to you about."

There was a small silence before she said, "You sound excited."

"It's more than that, Aunt Sybil. Could you get Uncle Jim to pick up the extension in your bedroom?" They were one couple she knew who didn't use cell phones.

"Just a minute. He's out on the terrace. I'll wheel him into the bedroom. Hold on."

Kellie's heart was pounding so hard, she feared it couldn't be good for her, but there wasn't anything she could do to slow it down.

"Is that you, Tink?" Her loving uncle had called her his golden Tinker Bell from her childhood. "How's the therapy going? Are you making any progress with this Mrs. Lasko?"

Tears filled Kellie's eyes. She loved them so much. "To make a long story short, Leandros and I are find-ing our way back to each other."

Sounds of pure joy reached her ears.

"I'm going to tell you everything that's happened. Then I need to ask you a question, and you have to an-swer it honestly, because I love you more than anything in the world and want you to be as happy as you've made me all these years."

The silence that followed let her know she'd captured their attention. Getting in a more comfortable position, she began her tale. Leaving out their biggest problem, which had to do with artificial insemination and their struggle to get pregnant, she got into the ins and outs regarding Karmela and Frato.

Next she told them about Leandros's relationship with his first wife, and the many misconceptions Kellie had drawn throughout their marriage. Finally she explained why Karmela was now in the hospital, hopefully getting the kind of help she needed.

"That brings me to the one of the issues in our marriage we still haven't resolved."

"You mean there's more?" her aunt asked in a quiet voice.

"Yes, and it has to do with the two of you."

"What do you mean?"

"Leandros loves you and wants all of us to be together on a permanent basis. If you feel you could never leave home, then he's ready to step down as CEO of the company and move to Philadelphia."

She heard her aunt's gasp.

"I've told him about the house in Parkwood. I already have earnest money down on it. Since you've seen it, you know the place is big enough to accommodate the six of us after the children are born. We'll turn one of the upstairs rooms into a study for Leandros. He'll do business for the corporation from there."

"But—"

"Don't say anything yet, Uncle Jim. Let me finish. Here goes. We've decided that if you're willing to move to Greece, we'll make our permanent home at his villa on Andros Island and commute to Athens by helicopter."

"Honey—"

"I'm not through yet, Aunt Sybil. There's a small, vacant villa only a two-minute walk from his. It belonged to his uncle Manny until he died last year. Thea and Vlassius live only a three-minute walk from the villa in the other direction. We'd all be together! With the babies coming, it would be heaven."

She heard sniffing, but didn't know if it was a good or bad sign.

"Leandros has already talked to his parents about the renovations we'll have done to make you two as comfortable as possible. It's a darling, cozy house with the most glorious garden and fruit trees. The beach is only steps away."

"Tink—"

"We'll hire a person to help you," she talked over him. "It won't be Frank unless he's willing to relocate with you. If not, we'll find someone equally wonderful. There's a small swimming pool on the side of the villa where you can do therapy. The temperature of the air and the water is perfect. Vlassius will be thrilled to take you fishing every morning on his boat, Uncle Jim. Now he'll have someone to go with him."

Her uncle made a croaking sound.

"You'll have your own car, Aunt Sybil. You and Thea can go shopping all the time. We'll take you to visit all the sites and museums. You can browse to your heart's content in all the little villages. And something else about Thea. She's a homebody like you who loves to cook and have family around. There are a bunch of Petralia family members living on the estate. You'll love all of them.

"In fact, I think you'd be shocked how much you have in common with them. We'll get you started learning Greek. By the time the babies are born, you'll be able to converse and understand almost everything. We'll become a bilingual household."

"Kellie," her aunt interrupted her. "You've convinced us it all sounds like a dream come true, but you don't need to go to these lengths because we're perfectly content here."

That was her aunt's stubborn side talking. "If that's your final answer, then I won't say any more about it. But since I'll never be truly content away from you, then Leandros and I will be moving to Philadelphia."

"Then *his* parents will be alone—" her uncle blurted.

"In terms of his being their only child, that's true. But they have brothers and sisters living on the island. They're not in your situation where you've never had family to call on. Of course, they'll fly to the States to visit us whenever possible. Leandros is determined to make this work, because he loves you."

Kellie heard her uncle clear his throat. "We love him.... Sybil? We can't expect Leandros to move here. He's an important man with a job to do." His words caused Kellie's heart to run away with her again.

"I know. I'm only thinking of you, Jim." Her aunt's voice trembled.

"Fiddle faddle. Moving to Greece will be a new adventure for us. Before my stroke, we'd planned to spend a lot of time traveling."

"You can still travel, Uncle Jim. The helicopter will take us everywhere. You can invite your friends to visit."

"Well, that settles it for me. If you want to know the truth, Sybil, I don't want to miss a day of watching our grandbabies grow up. Do you?"

Her aunt had broken down crying. "No."

By now Kellie was dissolved in tears herself. "You two don't have any idea how happy you've made me. Throughout our marriage, Leandros has worried continually about you, but no longer. I can't wait to tell him."

"Do you have any idea how different you sound?"

"All I know is how I feel, Aunt Sybil. I'm so deeply happy on every level, I'm afraid I'm going to burst."

"We don't want you to do that. It's awfully late for you to still be up, honey. You need to take care of yourself and get to bed."

"I will. The next time I call, I'll put Leandros on the phone and we'll start making moving arrangements. In the meantime, decide what you want to bring to your new house. Love you. Good night."

After hanging up, Kellie turned on her side. Oblivion took over while she was imagining when and how she would tell Leandros. It had to be the perfect time and place.

Leandros had just finished shaving when he had a call from his attorney. "Turn on your TV to the nine o'clock *Athenian Morning Show*. I've heard they're doing the story on you this morning despite my attempt to quash anything about you. Call me when it's over and we'll plan a damage strategy."

There was no such animal. Karmela had always been one step ahead and hadn't missed a trick. On a burst of adrenaline, Leandros reached for the TV remote and got in on the last of the weather forecast. Hot and sunny.

"Welcome, everyone. Thanks for tuning in to the *Athenian Morning Show*. Once again the Petralia Corporation is in the news. Five weeks ago a tornado swept through Greece, taking lives and destroying part of the Persephone, their newest resort outside Thessalonika.

"Today we bring you our top story involving the attractive thirty-five-year-old CEO himself, Leandros Petralia, who's been involved in a scandal that has rocked the country. He's been unavailable for comment since the news broke that his striking sister-in-law, Karmela Paulos of the Paulos Manufacturing Company, and one of the secretaries at the Petralia Corporation, is carrying his child.

"Frato Petralia, a cousin who's vice president of operations, has been installed as acting CEO of the corporation while they attempt to weather this crisis. A reliable source has informed the station that his second marriage, of two years duration to Kellie Petralia, his American-born wife, fell apart because of the affair.

"She's divorcing him for an undisclosed amount of money. If you remember, his first wife, prominent beauty Petra Paulos, who'd been working for Halkias Textiles, died four years ago in a tragic plane accident along with their unborn baby. More on this story and pending lawsuits will be reported in tonight's news.

"Moving on to another scandal involving one of Greece's major banks…"

Furious for what this could do to Kellie, Leandros shut off the TV and got dressed. He was on his way out of the room when his phone rang again. Seeing the caller ID, he picked up eagerly. "Nik?"

"I'm glad you answered. It's good to hear your voice. I'm just sorry to learn about your precarious circumstances. My brothers both phoned to tell me about the horrendous lies put out on the morning news. How can Fran and I help? She's beside herself for the two of you.

Frankly, so am I. You don't need this while you're both still in counseling. Karmela's form of sabotage leaves a taint no matter how you try to squelch it."

"It's ugly, all right, but Kellie and I are far enough along in our therapy to have surmounted most of our difficulties, and we know the truth."

"Thank heaven for that."

"Tell Fran not to worry. My wife will be calling her shortly to explain. I'm afraid we're just going to have to ride this storm out. Talk to you later. Thanks for your support, Nik. It means everything."

Leandros hurried out of the bedroom and down the hall. Kellie's door was still closed. It could mean she was still asleep, or maybe she was already on the phone to Fran. Practicing patience wasn't his forte, but once more he held back from joining her, and headed for the living area. He found his parents enjoying breakfast at the dining room table.

His father looked up. "Did you catch the news on TV this morning?"

"Afraid so."

"It's pure tripe."

Nerves twisted his insides. "Have you seen Kellie yet?"

"I'm right behind you."

He wheeled around to discover his wife dressed in the same blouse and skirt she'd worn here last evening. His heart raced at the sight of her beautiful face and body.

She eyed him intently. "I watched the news, too. You have to hand it to Karmela. With her smarts and energy channeled in the right direction, she could do wonders with anything she set her hand to."

His spirits plunged. "I wish you hadn't seen it."

Her smile disarmed him. "Leandros... We knew she'd do her worst. She wove just enough truth into the lies to make it sound authentic. You and your attorney probably have a plan to deny the allegations. But if you want my opinion, I think we should just leave it alone and go on living our lives."

"Oh, I agree!" his mother declared.

His father followed with a "Bravo!"

Leandros drew in a fortifying breath, relieved by his wife's response. "Then the four of us are on the same page."

Those brown eyes shone with a new light. "I've given up on the news stations doing their research and getting documented proof about anything anymore. People who want to believe the worst always will. If you lose business, you wouldn't want them for clients under any circumstances. In time even *they* will realize the story had no substance to it. Unless you have other plans, I'd like to fly back to Andros."

"Not without breakfast, you don't," his mother exclaimed. "Sit down. There's plenty here for both of you."

Suddenly his appetite had come back. He helped Kellie into the chair, tantalized by her alluring fragrance. "You look rested. I take it you got a good sleep."

"The best I've had in months. How about you?"

As he took his place next to her, a prickling sensation broke out on the back of his neck. Something was different about her. He glanced at his parents. "Do you want to fly back with us?"

"No. We're going to stay here until tomorrow," his

father stated. "We'll be meeting up with some of the family later. You two go on."

Anxious to get away from the paparazzi who'd spring at them at every opportunity, he phoned Stefon to get the helicopter ready. Thankfully, he'd doubled the security on Andros to keep them off his property.

Within ten minutes they'd kissed his parents goodbye and were on their way. En route he phoned his attorney and told him there was nothing to be done for now. After thanking him, he made a call to Frato, who'd insulated himself with extra security so he could get his work done.

His cousin seemed to be in surprisingly good spirits considering his pain over Karmela's betrayal. Frato wasn't taking any calls except from his family and Leandros. He did want to know when Leandros planned to return to work.

There was no way to answer that question. If he and Kellie got back together—and that was still an if—then there was a distinct possibility they'd be living in the States. But he was afraid to speculate that far ahead. Though he knew they were making progress in terms of understanding their conflicts and doing something about them, he didn't know if she could bring herself to live with him again. That's what this was all about.

The history they'd been through might have been too painful for her to allow herself to be open and vulnerable to married life once more. That he'd been too blind in certain areas and too inflexible on occasion had done a lot of damage. To live with him on faith, hoping he'd catch himself when he was in danger of falling into old habits, was a lot to ask of her. Maybe too much.

Until further notice he'd remain on vacation. Next

week was their third counseling session with Mrs. Lasko. A month ago he'd fought the idea of allowing anyone to get into his private thoughts, let alone be willing to listen to any constructive criticism. He found it amazing that in just a few visits, he welcomed any insights their therapist offered that would help in bringing him and Kellie back together.

When the helicopter touched down and they'd made their way to the villa, Kellie turned to him. "Do you think it would be all right if we drove into Chora? I realize there'll be reporters lurking, but I'd like to buy some maternity clothes. This skirt is the only thing that feels comfortable. My jeans are too tight."

Her request sent a burst of excitement through him. For once he'd been caught off guard and ran a possessive eye over her curvaceous figure, when he'd promised himself he wouldn't. As a result he almost didn't answer her question. "I've hired enough extra security to make certain we're not bothered."

"You wouldn't mind going with me?"

It thrilled him, because it sounded as if she really wanted him to come. "To buy some outfits for my expectant wife? I've been looking forward to this moment since the day we married."

She bit her lip. "Me, too. There's a darling maternity shop I remember passing."

If he knew his wife, throughout their marriage she'd probably gone in it to look around while they'd both been waiting for the news that she was pregnant. She'd been so brave over all these months, submitting to the procedure. As disappointed as he was each time they found out she wasn't pregnant, it was her pain that had killed him. He'd felt so helpless knowing there were no words to bring her the comfort she needed.

"Let's do it. We'll eat lunch afterward."

"I was hoping you'd say that. Maybe there's something wrong with me that I'm always so hungry."

He frowned. "I'm sure there isn't, but to be wise, let's make an appointment for you to see your doctor in Athens on Tuesday, after our counseling session. If a problem did come up, he needs to know you are pregnant and living in Greece for an undetermined period."

Leandros was getting good at tempering his words so he wouldn't come across as harassing her for a commitment she wasn't ready to give.

"Actually, I saw him the day I flew in."

That came as a surprise.

"I wanted to thank him and let him know the procedure finally worked. I'm sure it made him happy."

"Did you tell him we were getting divorced?"

"Yes. I heard the sadness when he said he was very sorry. He told me to call him anytime...." Her voice trailed off, as if she had something else on her mind. "Give me a minute to change my blouse and freshen up."

"Take your time. I'll meet you at the car."

CHAPTER NINE

AFTER A SHOPPING SPREE that resulted in taking home a couple of loose fitting sundresses, plus three new tops and jeans that allowed for growth, Leandros put the purchases in the car and treated Kellie to a delicious lunch.

When she couldn't eat another bite, she lifted her eyes to her husband. "I ate too much, but it tasted so good."

His white smile turned her heart over. "Do you know this vacation is putting weight back on me?"

She studied his handsome features. "It's done it to both of us." He'd looked gaunt when she'd surprised him in his office last week, but with regular meals and rest, he'd started filling out. No man was more gorgeous than Leandros.

"Do you want to go home, or would you like to stretch your legs for a while longer?"

"There's a cute children's shop down on the other corner. If you don't mind, I'd like to pick up an outfit for Demi before we go back to the villa. Fran says she's growing fast. I imagine she needs the nine-to-twelve-months' size."

"I'm ready when you are." He put some bills on the table and they left the restaurant.

Kellie walked alongside her husband, realizing she had absolutely nothing to complain about. He was his affable, charming self, and he went along with everything she suggested, but a vital spark was missing from his normally vibrant personality.

Every day since her return to Greece, she'd been more and more aware of it. She felt as if she was living with a whitewashed version of the dynamic lover she'd married. All the color seemed to have gone out of him.

That's your *fault, Kellie.*

Over the last few days she felt as if they'd unearthed every major problem and now possessed the tools to keep the lines of communication open. But somewhere in the process he'd changed.

Fear clutched at her to think that the problems in their marriage had done something irreparable to him. She knew he loved her. She knew he loved their unborn babies. But he might not feel the same desire for her anymore. Except for cupping her elbow, or steadying her as she got out of the car, he didn't try to touch her or make overtures as a prelude to making love.

She thought back to the first time she'd met him. It had taken only twenty-four hours from the time he'd helped her get her uncle wheeled into the elevator before he'd kissed her senseless. Kellie would never forget what he told her after he'd finally lifted his head so they could breathe.

"I want you so much, I wish I could bite the heart out of your body. But then I'd never be able to have that experience again, so we need to get married as soon as possible. Don't tell me you don't want the same thing. I've got you in my arms and can feel your heart leaping to reach mine."

"I'm not denying it." She'd half gasped the words while she tried to catch her breath.

"Not everyone experiences the intense desire we feel for each other. It's a precious gift we don't dare lose, Kellie, or neither of us will ever be happy again."

A tremor shook her body when she remembered that incredible night and her passionate response.

Yet the month before she'd left him, she'd been too distrustful and angry to turn to him for the intimacy she'd always craved. It seemed it had been years since they'd made love. The more he'd tried to love her physically, the more she'd pushed him away.

What if he'd done the same thing to her?

But he hadn't! No matter how bad things had gotten, he'd always reached for her in bed. *She* was the one who'd moved into the guest bedroom and had made plans to vacation with Fran.

Rejection like that could be too painful to forget. Leandros was the total opposite of a spiteful person, but if he didn't crave her affection in the same way anymore, it was because she'd killed something inside him.

Last night he'd gone to bed when his parents did. Their presence had never inhibited him before if he'd wanted to be alone with her. Since her return, he'd had every opportunity to come into her bedroom, whether they were at the Cassandra or on Andros.

All these thoughts were torturing her as they shopped for Demi's gift. The whole time they were in there, he didn't suggest they pick out something for their babies. Her old husband would have bought out the store for them by now.

As the clerk wrapped their gift of an adorable pink top and shorts, Kellie felt a blackness descend. This was how all the pain and suffering had started before. She'd let her fears develop into giant problems without sharing them with Leandros.

What was the expression about not learning lessons from the past, or mankind was destined to repeat the mistakes? Suddenly Mrs. Lasko's warning filled her mind.

"Surely today has given you your first inkling of where to dig to start finding understanding. You'll have to be brutally honest, open up and listen to each other. You'll be forced to wade through perceptions, whether false or accurate, and no matter how painful, arrive at the truth."

It came to Kellie that the problems of trying to get pregnant and the disappointment each time it didn't happen had blown up all the other problems until there was no more communication. Now she was dealing with another inner conflict, one she had to step up and face.

What if she girded up her courage and asked him outright how he felt right now?

Why was it so hard?

What was her greatest fear?

That he'll tell you the truth, that his desire for you has waned.

Was she brave enough to hear the truth from his lips? If she wasn't, then she'd learned nothing from therapy.

They left the shop and went back to the car. As they were leaving the town, they passed the church where they'd been married. On impulse, she turned to him. "Leandros? Would you pull over to the curb for a minute?"

He shot her a concerned glance and immediately

found a parking space. "What's wrong? You went quiet on me in the shop. Aren't you feeling well?"

"That's not it," she assured him. "I feel fine, but I realize I haven't been in the church since we took our vows. I only want to go inside for a moment."

A puzzled look broke out on his face. "Why?"

"It's one of my whims. Will you humor me? I've been getting them a lot lately. Do you know, while we were planning our wedding, one of your family members mentioned you and Petra had been married on Andros and—"

"And you assumed this was the church." He ground out the words.

"Yes. I'm sorry to have to admit it was another one of my false assumptions."

He shut off the engine. "Do you want me to go in with you?"

Yes, yes, yes. "If you'd like to."

"I would have brought you here whenever you wanted, but you never expressed a desire. If I'd had my wits about me, I would have asked you to tell me why."

She shook her head. "I wouldn't have told you the real reason. Not then. As for now, I'd like to see it again, knowing you didn't marry Petra in here. Let's face it. I had more than one veil over my eyes on our wedding day."

"I was blinded by the wonder of you."

Leandros.

He came around and helped her out of the car. They walked across the cobblestones to the entrance. The beautiful white church with the latticelike windows had two of the Cycladic, blue-topped spires.

A few people were inside as they entered the nave.

Kellie looked around, marveling over the paintings on the walls and ceiling. He escorted her past columns to the front, where they'd stood before an icon of the Virgin to become man and wife.

His gray eyes searched hers for a heart stopping moment. "What do you remember about that day?" he whispered.

"Being terrified I'd make a mistake in front of all your family and friends," she whispered back. "What about you?"

His features sobered. "I couldn't believe you'd agreed to become my wife. Throughout the ceremony, which I confess was mostly a blur to me, I prayed you wouldn't back out at the last minute."

"You truly worried about that?" She couldn't fathom it. Not Leandros of all people.

"I chased you from the moment we met. You were such an elusive creature, you'll never know the relief I felt when the priest finally made you mine."

Kellie was bemused by his answer. "So I was yours, eh?" she teased.

"Yes," he declared savagely.

Emotion almost closed her throat. "I was so in love with you, I feared you couldn't possibly love me the same way. What had I done to earn such a man's love?"

"Don't you think I asked the same question about you? How come this wonderful, beautiful American woman had agreed to marry me?"

"All I know is I got my heart's desire." Her pulse rate sped up before she grasped his hands. "Two years have gone by and with them a lot of history. Now it seems the tables have turned and I'm the one chasing you."

At first she didn't think he'd gotten the full import

of her words. Not until she saw his chest rise and fall, and felt his fingers tighten around hers.

"We're standing before God. If you lie to me, He'll know it and so will I. So I'm going to ask you a question. Leandros Roussos Petralia—do you still want me in all the ways a man wants a woman? You know what I mean."

A sound like ripping silk came out of him.

"Cat got your tongue? Remember, you're under oath."

He looked tortured. "Kellie…what's going on?"

"If you think about it hard enough, it should come to you."

Removing her hands gently from his, she walked out of the church to the car without looking back.

Leandros grabbed hold of the last pew to steady himself. He didn't know what to think. Kellie was the kind of passionate lover a man would kill for, but she'd never taken the initiative with him in their marriage, not verbally or physically. It had always rested on him.

Therapy had taught him she'd been too insecure all her life to say the words and reach out to him first, of her own accord. But if he'd read her correctly just now, she'd done something unprecedented by letting him know with words she *wanted* him. They hadn't even been to their next therapy session.

Maybe it had taken being in this holy place, with no associations of Petra, for her to find the courage. He was blown away to realize she wanted to sleep with him again. But this didn't necessarily mean she was ready for the final step to get back together.

In a sense he felt fragmented. Part of him couldn't

wait to get her home alone. Yet another part feared that once he'd made love to her again, and then she decided she couldn't live with him, after all, he wouldn't be able to handle the pain. One night with her would never be enough.

Before he made a fatal mistake and temporarily assuaged his longing, only to find out there would never be another time, they had more talking to do. With a mixture of elation and terror, he left the church and joined her in the car. She didn't look at him as he started the engine.

Once they were on the road, he glanced at her profile. "To answer your question, I want you a hundred times more now than I did on our wedding night. If I haven't touched you, you know the reason why."

"That's all I need to hear."

"Kellie—you could have no comprehension of how I felt in the church just now when you let me know you wanted me. Those are the words I've dreamed of hearing you say, but never expected the moment to happen. You've changed from your former self into a woman I hardly recognize."

That brought her head around, causing the golden strands to swish against her shoulders. "I'm sorry you've had to wait so long for me to say the words in my heart," she said with tears in her voice.

"I'm not," he replied. "The wait has made them all the sweeter. Your bravery has emboldened me to ask the one question still unanswered for me. Do you want to call off the divorce? I never wanted it. When you told me you were leaving me..." He gripped the steering wheel harder.

She reached over to touch his arm. "It sounds like

you expect me to spell it out, so I will. I don't want a divorce."

"Thank God."

"Deep inside, whether I was consciously aware of it or not, I know I flew to Athens to get my marriage back. Our precious babies were an excuse to face you after all the terrible things I'd done to you. But that version of me is gone, Leandros. You're beholding the new me, who's ready to love you like you've never been loved before. How am I doing on answering your question so far?"

He could hardly breathe. "Just keep talking until we reach the villa."

"I adore you, Leandros. I always have. You're my whole world, my whole life! I couldn't bear that we were having problems."

"Tell me about it." He half groaned the words.

"It didn't seem possible to me that you could be such a loving husband, and yet be carrying on behind my back with your sister-in-law. Nothing made sense, but I didn't know how to deal with it."

"You weren't alone."

"I have something else to tell you. I spoke with my aunt and uncle for a long time last night."

The information was coming at him like a meteor shower. He could scarcely take it all in.

"The bottom line is, they're going to move into your uncle Manny's villa just as soon as we can arrange it. As you know, Aunt Sybil was always against relocating to Greece because of her worries for Uncle Jim's health. But I got them both on the phone so she couldn't answer for him.

"It would have warmed your heart to hear him tell

us how much he loves you and how crazy he is about the idea of a new adventure. After I explained that your dad would love a fishing partner to go out with every morning, my uncle got excited. He told my aunt he didn't want to miss out on one day of watching their grandchildren grow up. My aunt broke down in tears of happiness. I think we can get Frank to help them here until we find a permanent replacement for him."

Speechless, Leandros grasped her hand and clung to it.

"I wonder what Olympia will say at our next session."

The blood pounded in his ears. "She'll tell us to go slowly."

"I know. And she'll ask questions we haven't thought of."

"That's good. She's been pivotal in helping us see into ourselves. I'd like to keep going to her so we'll stay on track."

Kellie squeezed Leandros's fingers. "So would I. Later on we'll have to send her the right gift to show our gratitude. I'm going to have to think about it for a while, but I can't think while I'm sitting next to you, dying to be in your arms.

"When we get back home, I want to go out on our cabin cruiser. I'll pack the food we love. We're going to need a couple of days and nights to get reacquainted, without anyone else around."

Leandros was already thinking a month at least.

"Be warned, I plan to ravish you before I grow as big as a house!"

He laughed with joyous abandon.

"Then I plan to love you to death and never let you go back to work, but that would make you unhappy."

"You don't really think that—"

"I really do. So in a few days you should fly to Athens and do what you do best, by running the Petralia Corporation. Frato is trying to pull his weight, bless his heart, but I happen to know every man and woman in the company is holding their collective breath until you're back at the helm."

His natural impulse was to speed the rest of the way home so he could crush her in his arms, but the instinct to protect his family was stronger and had come out in full force. His wife had finally come back to him, and their babies were growing inside her. What more could a man ask for?

The second he pulled up to the villa, he hurried around to Kellie's side of the car. She already had the door open and flew into his arms, almost knocking him over. "Kiss me, darling," she cried, lifting her mouth to find his. "Don't ever stop."

There was no space between them as they tried to assuage their great longing for each other. His wife was vibrantly alive, kissing away the shadows. Every touch and caress, every breath filled his mind and body with indescribable ecstasy.

He carried her into the house and followed her down on the bed with his body. But he was careful with her as they found old ways and new to bring each other the pleasure denied them for so long, while they'd been sorting out their lives.

It was evening before they lay sated for a while, their legs entwined, simply enjoying the luxury of looking at each other and being at peace. "The first time we swam together and made love, you reminded me of a painting of the famous Spanish artist Luis Falero. It was called *A Sea Nymph*. She's appearing above the waves with her body submerged. Very enticing. I was taken with it at first glance."

Her smile lit up his insides. "Why didn't you ever tell me?"

"Because you'd never been intimate with a man before and you were easily embarrassed."

She kissed his lips. "But now that I'm with children— *yours*, as a matter of fact—you think I can handle it."

"I think if you saw it, you'd blush, as you do so charmingly. But that was over two years ago and pregnancy has changed you."

"Is that right."

"In the most incredibly gorgeous ways." He pressed a long, hard kiss to her tempting mouth. "Falero did another painting called *The Planet Venus*. The centerpiece is a goddess with flowing gold tresses, very much like you, in fact. After studying you now, I believe his model was in the early stages of her pregnancy. I was always drawn to it."

"I had no idea you were such a lover of nudes."

"Admirer of many, lover of *one*," he corrected, provoking a gentle laugh from her.

"Well..." she eyed him playfully "...since this is confession time, while you were lounging on the sand after we'd made love, it was like the *Reclining Dionysos* on the Parthenon had come to life before my eyes. He's quite spectacular."

Leandros laughed again. "That's not fair. He's missing some of his parts."

She brushed her hand across his well-defined chest.

"Everything important is still there." Suddenly the teasing was gone. She leaned over him. "I love you so much, Leandros. Make love to me again. I'm on fire for you and am feeling insatiable."

"That makes two of us, *agapa mou*."

CHAPTER TEN

"CONGRATULATIONS, Mrs. Petralia. You've reached your thirty-fifth week and all is well with your little boys. Most patients with twins deliver between now and thirty-seven weeks. Since I can predict your babies are going to come earlier than the desired forty weeks for a single baby, I want you to be especially observant of what's going on with your body."

"What *isn't* going on?" she exclaimed. "Last week, when we told our marriage therapist we wanted another appointment with her, to talk about how to be parents to twins, I told her I was as big as a house. I don't think she believed me until she saw me. Secretly, I'm afraid Leandros compares me to a giant walrus." Dr. Hanno burst into laughter. "It's true. That's exactly how I feel."

"It won't be long now. Those menstrual-like cramps you've experienced are normal. So is the lower back pain and uterine pressure. Sometimes you can't tell if you're having contractions. You'll need to listen to your body very carefully from here on out. My advice is to stay off your feet for a few hours every day to avoid that pressure."

"You mean my swollen stumps?" she quipped. "I can't even bend over to see them."

"Be sure you're still getting the equivalent of four glasses of milk a day. Any questions before you leave?"

"Yes. How do I help my husband to calm down? He's known for being a tour de force in the corporate world, but you wouldn't know it if you lived with him."

The doctor grinned. "There's no cure for what he's got except to have those babies."

"I realize that. Half the time he watches me like a hawk. If I yawn or sigh, he asks me what's wrong. When I get up in the night lately to go to the bathroom, he's pacing on the patio off our bedroom. I'm glad he has to go to work! But throughout his day, he phones every few hours. His parents and my aunt and uncle are a stone's throw away from our villa, but nothing seems to ease his mind. Every night he comes home from work with a new toy or outfit. At this rate we're not going to have room for the babies."

Dr. Hanno eyed her speculatively. "I'm sure you know how lucky you are. Too many women don't have a husband, and even if they do, he's not like yours."

Tears filled her eyes. "I know. I'm very blessed. The hardest thing about the end of this pregnancy is trying to help him not get too worried. His first wife was killed in a plane crash, and she was pregnant. I'm sure those demons are haunting him right now."

"What about your marriage counselor? Maybe the two of you should ask her."

"That's a brilliant idea, but I don't think he'd want to. I'm afraid I'm going to have to talk to him and get him to admit what's driving his heightened anxiety. I'll have to find a creative way to reach him. Thanks for everything, Dr. Hanno."

"I'll see you in three days."

"If not before?" She was so tired of being pregnant, it would be wonderful for it to all be over.

"Maybe."

That *maybe* gave her hope. She left his examination room and walked out to the reception area mentally revitalized.

Her aunt had been reading a magazine. When she saw Kellie, she put it down and got to her feet. "How are you doing?"

"Just great. He wants to see me in three days."

"You'll probably be going into labor soon."

"I think so, too."

"Let's get you back to the hotel and order a meal. Before long Leandros will be through with work and we'll fly back to Andros."

"He'll be waiting to hear how my appointment went. I'll call him from the limo."

When they left the building, the temperature outside was 56 degrees, typical for February. Kellie had been hot for months and loved the cool air. There'd been a little rain on their way to the doctor's office, but it had stopped.

As soon as she got in the back of the car with her aunt, she phoned Leandros. He picked up after the first ring. "Kellie?" On a scale of one to ten, his anxiety was a hundred.

"Hi, darling. The doctor said everything looks great. I have to keep my legs up for a few hours a day, but otherwise we're ready to go."

"That's the news I've been waiting for. I'll be leaving the office in twenty minutes. Where are you right now?"

"In the limo."

"You're going straight to the hotel, right?"

"Yes. We'll be there in a few minutes."

"I love you." The tone of his deep voice permeated to her insides, thrilling her.

"I love you, too."

"I've decided this is going to be my last day of work." *Oh, help!* "I've had Frato here in the office. He's going to take over for me starting tomorrow morning. I can't concentrate anymore. Mrs. Kostas told me to go home and not come back."

No doubt he'd been driving her crazy, too. Kellie laughed, resigned to the fact that she was going to have her nervous husband around day and night until the big event. "That's marvelous news. I'll see you shortly." She hung up.

Her aunt smiled. "What was that laugh about?"

"Leandros informed me he won't be going to work anymore until after the babies are born."

"Oh, dear."

They both laughed. "I've got to come up with a project for him that will keep him busy for hours at a time."

"I know just the thing. I want to have some window boxes built on the east side of the house."

"Perfect! I'll send him with you to pick things out. With Uncle Jim directing traffic, it ought to keep his mind occupied for one day, anyway." More laughter ensued.

The limo pulled to a stop in front of the Cassandra. Kellie thanked the driver and they both got out. She took two steps on the pavement and felt her sandal slide in a tiny pool of water. The next thing she knew, she was sitting on the ground, having landed with a hard thud. Talk about a beached walrus that wasn't going anywhere.

"Are you all right, honey?" her aunt cried.

"I think so. I feel like an idiot, but I'm thankful I didn't take you down with me."

"You're not in pain?"

"No." She started to get up.

"Let me help."

"Thanks," she whispered. But the moment she stood, she felt moisture run down her legs in a gush. It wasn't from the pool. "Aunt Sybil? My water just broke."

"Hang on to me, honey. I'll call the driver and tell him to come back."

Within a minute, the limo returned. Kellie climbed in while her aunt told the driver they needed to get straight to the hospital.

"Tell him not to phone Leandros. I'll do it or he'll freak out completely."

"Agreed."

She was starting to have pains that were different than what she'd experienced now and then. Her stomach grew rock-hard. The contractions were starting. While they drove to the hospital, she reached in her purse for her cell and phoned Leandros.

"Kellie?"

"Hi, darling. There's been a change in plans. My water just broke and I'm in the limo on the way to the hospital. Our babies are coming." Her voice wobbled. "I'll meet you at the hospital."

"I'll be there in five minutes." His line went dead.

* * *

Leandros, masked and gowned, sat next to Kellie while he watched the miracle of their firstborn son's birth. The baby had a tuft of black hair, and according to the pediatrician attending him, he weighed in at six pounds two ounces and was twenty-one inches long.

The excitement in the birthing room was palpable. Leandros didn't know he could be this happy.

"Here comes number two, slick as a whistle." The doctor lifted their second son by the ankles. Again they all heard the healthy infant cry announcing his arrival in the world. Leandros felt pure joy in every atom of his body. "You've got yourselves another beautiful boy. How are you doing, Mom?"

Tears streamed down Kellie's face as she beamed at Leandros. "I'm afraid I might die from so much happiness. Are our babies really all right?"

"They're perfect," he whispered before leaning over to kiss her lips gently.

An army of staff filled the birthing room. The other pediatrician turned his head toward them. "Baby number two weighs in at five pounds fourteen ounces and measures twenty and a half inches. You've given birth to healthy fraternal twins. Congratulations."

In a few minutes they'd been washed and wrapped so Kellie could hold them in her arms. "Oh, darling," she wept. "Our babies..." She kissed their heads. "They're gorgeous, just like you."

Leandros was so full of emotion, he had to wipe his eyes to get a good look. "I can see your beautiful features in both of them. Just think. You and I grew up as only children. They'll always have each other."

"I know. Isn't it wonderful?" But her eyes had closed.

Alarmed, Leandros looked at the doctor. "Is she all right?"

"I've given her a hypo. She'll sleep for several hours. Why don't you go down to the nursery with your sons and get acquainted with them."

After kissing his wife's flushed cheek, he watched the nurses put the babies in carts, and followed them down the hall to the newborn unit. For the next half hour he had the time of his life, examining every finger and toenail. Their sons had made it. His wife had made it. A wave of love for her, for their offspring, swept through him, shaking him to the very foundations.

When he finally went out into the hall, he saw everyone standing at the glass—his parents, her aunt and uncle, Fran and Nik. The celebration could probably be heard throughout the wing. His mother flung herself into his arms and sobbed. As for his father, he was so choked up he couldn't talk.

Leandros leaned down to give Jim a hug, then swept Sybil into his arms. All everyone did was cry. Fran was no different. She gave him a giant hug. "Hallelujah this day has come," she whispered.

Then it was Nik's turn to give him the mother of bear hugs. "Sybil told us you're on vacation now. Believe me, you're going to need it with all those two o'clock feedings. I couldn't be happier for you, Leandros."

"I feel like *I've* given birth. I can't even imagine what Kellie's feeling like."

"She's blissfully knocked out."

"You're right." He chuckled. "Thanks for being here."

"We wouldn't be anywhere else. Have you decided on names?"

"We did as soon as we found out we were having boys. We decided the first one to come out would be Nikolas Vlassius Petralia."

Nik's eyes grew suspiciously bright. "You're kidding me."

"I swear I'm not. Kellie was adamant about it. She loves you like a brother. I think you know that by now."

"I'm honored," he said in a croaky voice. "What will you call your other son?"

"Dimitri Milo Petralia in honor of her uncle Jim, who was the perfect father to her all her life, and of course her birth father."

"Does Jim know that yet?"

"We had dinner for everyone last week and told them."

"The Petralia brothers, Nik and Dimitri. That has a definite ring."

Leandros had to admit that it did. After they were born, he'd told Kellie what it meant to him to have sons. She'd kissed him and said, "Don't you think I know that? Don't you know how I watched you suffer each time we knew we weren't pregnant? It almost killed me to see your pain. After all, you're a proud Greek male. I'm just thankful you finally got your heart's desire."

"One day our children will be playing with your Demi."

"They grow up fast. You've done great work, Leandros."

"I give all the credit to my angel wife. She's the one who got us into counseling and saved our marriage."

Nik shook his head. "I'm convinced you would have made your way back to each other no matter what. I shudder to think that if she hadn't phoned Fran to come to Greece..."

Leandros patted his good friend on the shoulder. "You would have met Fran at a later date. When you consider the if's, it makes you realize it was all meant to be."

At 6:00 p.m. Kellie tiptoed into the nursery to check on the babies one more time. They'd both been fed and burped. Now they were sound asleep. She got a swelling in her chest. They were the dearest babies on earth, and that wasn't just because she was their mother. Their Petralia genes made them beautiful.

She looked down at each one, feasting her eyes on their darling faces and bodies. The sky-blue of their little sleepers with feet brought out their dark hair and olive skin, just a few of Leandros's striking assets. They bore a strong resemblance to each other, but there were distinct differences she was happy about.

Kellie wanted them each to grow up being their own person. Leandros felt the same way. It would be fun to play up the twin thing once in a while, but it was important they had their own identities.

They were seven weeks old today. She remembered back to the time when Dr. Creer had told her she was pregnant and seven weeks along. "Big as blueberries," he'd said. Children had brought a whole new meaning to her life.

Lately she'd found herself thinking a lot about her

parents. Unquestionably, they would have loved Kellie the same way. What a lucky girl she'd been to be raised by her aunt and uncle, whom she looked upon as her heroes. They'd not only raised her, they were now helping her and Leandros raise the children.

With everyone in both families pitching in, the exciting, chaotic and exhausting experience of having twins hadn't been quite as overwhelming as she would have imagined. Fran and Nik had spent several weekends with them. With their precious Demi walking around, getting into everything she could touch, while the babies lay on the floor watching her, they had hilarious times.

"Good night, my darlings," she whispered. "Forgive me if I don't see you for the next twenty-four hours, but I've got special plans for your father he doesn't know about. All these weeks he's been waiting on you and me. Now he needs some personal attention. Both your grandmas will be taking care of you until we come back tomorrow night. Be good for them. I'll miss you." She kissed each one and tiptoed out of the nursery.

Thea and Sybil were settled in the living room watching television. Kellie walked over to give them each a hug. "I'm leaving now. Call us if there's an emergency."

Her aunt nodded. "Of course. Now you go on. If you don't come back for a week, we won't mind, will we, Thea?"

"We wish you *would* stay away more than twenty-four hours."

"I couldn't bear to be separated from them that long. And you know Leandros. He's so crazy about them, I'm not sure he'll last until tomorrow night."

The two women gave each other a knowing smile, causing Kellie's cheeks to go warm. "Thank you from the bottom of my heart." She blew them a kiss, then let herself out the front door into the April evening. The helicopter would be bringing him home from work any minute. Her plan was to be there the moment he jumped out.

She was wearing a new pair of jeans and a short-sleeved, oatmeal-colored cotton sweater he'd never seen before. Though she still had ten pounds to lose, she'd gone down enough sizes to fit into non-maternity clothes. To her satisfaction, she could tuck in the sweater. She wanted to make sure he knew she was getting her shape back. He liked her hair long, so she'd left it loose after blow drying it. A little perfume, lipstick and makeup did wonders for her spirits.

When she heard the helicopter coming, she began to tremble, anticipating the night to come. Two weeks ago she'd had a checkup. The doctor told her she could have relations with her husband at seven weeks. Tonight was the night, only Leandros didn't know it yet.

She hid behind a tree until the helicopter touched down and Leandros got out. He spoke with the pilot for a few minutes, then started down the path to their villa, throwing his suit coat over his shoulder. She sneaked up behind him and wrapped her arms around his waist, clutching him tightly against her.

"Don't turn around if you know what's good for you. Do everything I say, and you won't get hurt."

His shoulders started to shake with silent laughter. "Don't I even get a peek?"

"You talk too much, Mr. Petralia. Just keep walking down to the pier. I'm right behind you."

He went along with her little game and began walking. "What do I do when I get there?"

"We're going sailing. Just you and me."

"It'll be dark soon."

"We don't have to set sail tonight. We can wait until morning."

"That's good, because I'm starving."

"I plan to feed you."

"I'll need a shower first."

"That's all been arranged."

They reached the dock where her sailboat was tied up. She'd spent part of the afternoon making the bed and getting things ready belowdecks. After going to the store, she'd stocked the fridge with his favorite goodies. On her final trip, she'd brought down his toiletries and laid out a new robe for him. He wouldn't want for a thing.

"How soon can I turn around?"

"After you go below."

He stepped into the boat. She stepped where he stepped and trailed him down the stairs.

The lights of several dozen votive candles placed around the ledge beckoned him from the small bedroom. He stopped in place when he saw what she'd created. Suddenly he swung around. His eyes blazed as he took in the sight of her. She felt his desire reach out to her like a living thing.

"Kellie—"

"The doctor gave me the seal of approval. I thought it was about time the man who holds my heart was paid a little attention for a change. Tonight there's no one but you and me. I'm dying to make love to you, Leandros."

"You look so beautiful, I'm staggered."

"Good. Now you know how I feel every time I get near you. What would you like to do first?"

"I want to devour you over and over again," he said in a husky voice. "Come here to me, darling."

Kellie didn't need those words to reach for him. His mouth was life to her. The touch of his hands on her body was a revelation to her. They fell on the bed, desperate for the closeness after having to wait the last two months for this moment.

Hours later they surfaced long enough to eat, then they went back to bed. During the night he pulled her into him. "I think I love you too much," he whispered into her hair. "You have no idea how divine you are."

"You took the words out of my mouth." She kissed his hard jaw. "I got so excited waiting for the helicopter to arrive, I almost had a heart attack."

"I would have come home sooner, but I had three unexpected visitors in my office before I left."

She cupped his face in her hands. "Who?"

"The Paulos family. Karmela has been in therapy for months. She came to apologize."

Kellie sat all the way up. "It must have been so hard for her to face you."

"I'm sure it was, but she did it."

"How is she, darling?"

"There's a definite change in her. She's not on the attack anymore. How much medication plays a role in this new behavior, I don't know, but it's welcome. The day you went to the hospital, she saw the news about our twins on TV. She wanted me to tell you she's very happy for us and sorry for any pain she's caused."

"That's a huge step in the right direction."

"I think so, too."

Kellie nestled against him again. "I'm glad you told me. We can finally leave all that in the past where it belongs, and concentrate on our new lives. I love our boys so much. I love you so much."

"Show me again how much, *agapi mou*. Show me again and again."

* * * * *

THE BEST MAN'S GUARDED HEART

KATRINA CUDMORE

To Fin, your unwavering support and love
has made this book possible.
You are my life.

CHAPTER ONE

SOFIA'S VOICEMAIL. AGAIN. Grace Chapman gave her smartphone's contact photo of her best friend a death stare and muttered, 'You can hide, Sofia, but I'll find you.'

Grace loved Sofia to bits; during the madness of the past few years she'd been her rock of cheerful good sense. But every now and again, when life got too intense, Sofia lost the plot big-time. Like today. Yes, Grace might have missed her flight and ended up arriving in Athens seven hours late. But she'd had everything under control. Until Sofia had obviously panicked and called in the big guns: the Petrakis family. Which meant that instead of catching the last ferry of the day at Piraeus port, as she had hoped, Grace was now stuck in the VIP lounge of Athens airport, awaiting the arrival of Sofia's soon-to-be father-in-law. A man who brought the word *intimidating* to a whole new level of meaning.

Sofia would have thought she was helping; but in truth she had totally messed up Grace's already tight schedule. There was no way, now, that she would make it to Sofia's wedding venue, Kasas Island, in time for the flower delivery in the morning.

She wasn't going to panic.

Okay, she *was* panicking.

Less than three days to prepare and organise the flowers for the Greek society wedding of the year.

Three days that would determine the success or failure of her dream to establish her name as a leading wedding floral designer. Three days to prove that she wasn't *'a clueless dreamer'.*

This morning, full of enthusiasm, she had thought she could take on the world. Now she just felt embarrassed and out of her depth.

She pushed the untouched champagne flute the lounge hostess had presented to her further away. Her stomach felt as though it was off doing a moon walk without her.

The lounge door swept open. And her stomach headed into orbit at the prospect of being at the receiving end of Mr Petrakis's surly manner.

But standing at the far end of the airport lounge was *not* the older man she had expected. Instead, penetrating eyes scanned the room and came to a land on her. Long tanned fingers shot upwards. His eyes continued to bore into hers. With a quick tug, he unravelled his bow tie, leaving it to hang lose.

Her smile wavered. She took in the chiselled bone structure, the confidence of his stride as he walked towards her, the perfection of his tuxedo. The tousled disarray of his dark brown hair that made him look as though he had just climbed out of bed.

'Miss Chapman?'

His voice was smooth and refined. If Central Casting was ever looking for a new Bond he would be a shoo-in. Her already racing heart galloped even faster.

Her seat was low and he seemed impossibly tall and menacing as he stood over her.

Clumsily she clambered out of it and tugged down on the hem of her yellow sundress, which suddenly felt too short and casual in the presence of his designer tux and expensive cologne. She was a low-budget package tourist to his first-class sophistication.

His eyes ran leisurely over the length of her body. Her insides melted. A thick dark eyebrow rose as he waited for her to speak, but for the first time in her life no meaningful words jangled in her brain. Instead it was a wasteland of inappropriate thoughts of lust for the man who stood before her.

Just above his left eyebrow a sickle-shaped scar became more prominent as his frown deepened. She balled her hands, worried that she'd give in to temptation and reach out and run her thumb against it.

After another excruciating few seconds of silence she eventually managed to garble out, 'Yes... Yes, I'm Grace Chapman. I was expecting Mr Petrakis. The airport ground staff told me he had asked that I stay here until he arrived.'

With a quick nod he answered, 'Yes I did.'

'Oh.' It slowly dawned on her who he was. '*Oh!* You must be Andreas... Christos's brother. I thought it was your father who had sent the message. He and I met in London last month, at Christos and Sofia's engagement party.' Grace held out her hand. 'You're the best man, I believe?'

He paused for a second before smooth warm skin enclosed her hand. His handshake was firm, the dominant clasp of a powerful man who liked to get his own way.

In her flat sandals she had to arch her neck to meet his stare. Piercing green eyes framed by long dark eyelashes studied her, and his head was thrown back at an arrogant tilt. The apple really hadn't fallen far from the tree. Dark stubble lined smooth golden skin.

'And I believe *you're* to be the chief bridesmaid?'

She ignored the coolness of his tone and let her enthusiasm for the upcoming wedding take over. 'Yes—and also the wedding floral designer. Sofia and I have been best friends for years. It's a shame you missed the engagement party—we had such fun.'

He gave an indifferent shrug and then his mouth curled derisively. 'You missed your flight.'

Her heart leapt at his reproachful tone. About to explain why, she stopped. He really didn't look as if he was in the mood to hear about delayed trains. Instead she said, 'Yes, unfortunately. Now my priority is to get to Kasas as soon as possible.'

'You've missed the last ferry.'

She forced herself not to say something terse and gave a polite smile. 'Yes, I know.' Her smile wobbled. *Don't say anything. Remain calm. I'm sure he doesn't mean to be so arrogant.* Her good intentions lasted all of one second. 'My flight did arrive in time for me to catch the ferry. I had a taxi waiting.'

His mouth thinned. 'And tomorrow the sun will rise in the west...'

Well, really! Frustration hummed in her ears. 'I had an hour.'

He scowled at her, making no effort to conceal his growing irritation. 'Christos realised you would miss the ferry so he called me and asked that I collect you.'

Her frustration gave way to embarrassment. His superior attitude might be rubbing her up the wrong way, but she had to face the fact that his night had obviously ended abruptly because of her.

She gestured to his tux and said, 'I hope I didn't disturb your night out.'

Something flashed in the depths of his eyes. Was it annoyance or some other memory? Had he been with someone? Sofia had said he had a reputation for being a playboy. Maybe she had been right about that tousled hair. It was still relatively early...but then what did *she* know about the bedroom habits of playboys? None of her exes had ever come close to being as dangerously lethal as the man standing before her.

'No doubt Sofia panicked and got Christos to call you. She's worried I'll get lost. It's my first time in Greece. In fact it's my first time being abroad on my own.'

Those dark eyebrows narrowed. He studied her incredulously. An awkward silence followed.

She said the first thing that came into her head. 'I suppose you spend your days travelling...what with your business and everything?'

He tilted his head and gazed at her suspiciously. 'Have you been doing your homework on me?'

'No!' Her cheeks grew hot and she cringed to think he might assume she was blushing out of guilt. 'Of course not. I only know what Sofia told me...that you are Christos's older brother.'

The eldest son of the wealthy and powerful Petrakis family, in fact, who had gone on to amass his own fortune in construction and property.

As he continued to gaze at her sceptically she added, 'I've only met Christos a few times, but from the moment I met him I knew that he and Sofia were perfect for one another. I'm so happy for Sofia. And her dad is equally thrilled that she's marrying a fellow Greek.'

Uncomfortable at the way he studied her, and trying to ignore just how gauche she felt in front of this much too silent and urbane man, she decided to change the subject to something that puzzled her. She gestured towards the other waiting travellers, and frowned when she saw that the other two women in the room, both much more el-

egantly groomed for the VIP lounge than she was, were
staring at Andreas with obvious appreciation.

'How did you know who I was?'

He reached into the inner pocket of his jacket and
took out a phone. After a few quick swipes he handed
it to her. A photo of her and Sofia pulling silly faces at
the camera popped up on the screen. Christos had taken
the photo last weekend, after Sofia's hen party in London...they'd both had one too many mojitos. Grace gave
a squeal of despair.

For the briefest of moments a faint hint of amusement
lifted his mouth upwards, but it faded and he said with
a note of exasperation, 'Christos is flooding my email
with photos of Sofia.'

Confused by his tone, she decided to ignore it and
handed Andreas back his phone. 'That's so cute. They're
so in love. Sofia tells me that Kasas is incredibly romantic. She truly appreciates you hosting the wedding there.'

He deposited the phone back in his pocket and folded
his arms. The side of his upper lip curled upwards. Lord,
he had a beautiful mouth. Wide, with lips that were much
too full. A mouth that promised endless sleepless nights.

She gave herself a mental shake. She had enough on
her plate with the wedding flowers. Getting distracted
by this Greek god standing in front of her was definitely
not a good idea.

He gestured to her chair. 'Please—take a seat. I think
we should discuss your stay on Kasas.'

Puzzled, she sat back down and wished once again
that she had worn a longer dress as her hem rode up the
length of her legs. When she glanced up, Andreas was
sitting opposite her, his eyes trained on her bare legs.
When their eyes met she saw a hint of appreciation. But
then he inhaled a deep breath and moved forward to lean

his elbows on his thighs, the wool of his trousers stretching over hard muscle.

'I had intended taking you to Kasas tonight—'

She could not help but interrupt as relief flooded her veins. 'That would be *fantastic*. The flowers and all the other supplies are being delivered early tomorrow morning, and I need to be there to—'

His hand slashed down through the air to halt her interruption with his own. 'Yes, but considering that you've never been to Greece before why don't I arrange for the wedding planner to organise the flowers? You can spend the next few days travelling. Kasas is isolated. It would be much more enjoyable for you to explore Greece instead. As I'm returning to the island for the rest of the week, you are welcome to use my apartment and the services of my chauffeur here in Athens.'

Her mouth dropped open. Was he being serious?

'But I'm the florist for the wedding.' Through her confusion a horrible thought occurred. 'Christos *did* tell you that I would be arriving early to create all the floral arrangements, didn't he? This has been planned for weeks.'

'He may have mentioned it…amongst all the chaos of the other wedding plans. I hadn't appreciated that you would be staying for so long.'

Heat flared even more brightly on her cheeks. He clearly wasn't keen on her staying on the island. And he obviously had no idea or appreciation for the work and skill involved in flower design.

Memories of her father's sneering comments about her making a living by *'playing with flowers'* had her saying in the politest voice she could muster, 'I appreciate your offer, but tomorrow morning I have over a thousand flowers being delivered to the island. It's essential that I'm there to coordinate their arrival. I take my job very seriously, Mr Petrakis. That's why I've spent the past month planning the designs, sourcing the flowers and organising support florists from nearby islands. I'm not going to walk away from my commitments now to go on *holiday*.'

His jaw tightened and he fixed her with an intense stare. 'My island is secluded. There is only my villa. No shops or bars to entertain you.'

She could not help but give a light laugh. 'I'm not here for shopping or the nightlife.'

'I'm concerned that you will be bored in the evenings, when the wedding planner and her team have left the island. Apart from my married housekeeper and a gardener, who live in a separate villa, there will be no other people around.'

His eyes, filled with a masculine heat, held hers and a surge of tense energy passed between them.

He came a little closer and in a low growl added, 'It will only be you and me.'

For a crazy moment something primal, something beyond comprehension, crackled in the air between them. Heat flared in every cell of her body. Her breath caught as a wave of longing...of desire...rippled through her.

His eyes grew darker as he held her stare, and a slash of heat appeared on his cheeks.

He looked away abruptly, his jaw tightening as he cleared his throat. 'I'll be working late each evening, so I won't be available to entertain you.'

Grace blinked. And blinked again. She felt dizzy with the desire to move towards him, to inhabit his space, to inhale his scent, to feel the heat of his body. What was happening to her?

For the past month she had been so excited about this trip—at the prospect of finally establishing her name as a florist, of finding her freedom. And now her bubble of happiness had truly burst.

Should she take up his offer? The prospect of spending nights alone with him in the seclusion of his island with virtually no one else around was daunting. A strange tug of war of deep attraction and irritation was raging between them...and she wanted to run away from it. And, after years of dealing with her father's unforgiving attitude, did she honestly want to spend time with a man who would be happier if she wasn't there?

But this wedding was about celebrating Sofia and Christos's love. She wasn't going to let Andreas Petrakis stand in the way of her making sure they had the perfect flowers to represent that love and commitment. There was no way he was stopping her from creating Sofia's bouquet—which she intended to do by weaving all her love for her best friend into the design. And she had to remember the importance of this wedding in establishing her career.

So she gave him a brief smile and tried to inject a brusque, no-argument tone to her voice. 'Thank you, but I'm perfectly fine with my own company. I'm here to ensure that the flowers are spectacular on the wedding day, so I'll be extremely busy and certainly won't get in your way. And please don't worry about me missing out. I plan on touring Greece once the wedding is over.'

With that she stood, lifted her weekend bag up and grabbed her heavy pull-along suitcase.

'Now, if it's okay with you, I would like to leave.'

Grace was standing at the edge of the clifftop path that led from the helipad down to Andreas's villa, her weekend bag at her feet. As he neared her the helicopter lifted off to return to Athens, and her hands rushed down to capture the billowing material of her dress as it rose up to expose even more inches of her legs—legs that he had spent the past hour trying not to stare at.

They weren't the longest legs he had ever seen, but there was something about those toned but full thighs and cute dimpled knees that had him fantasising about her in incredibly inappropriate ways. Even as he had stared out into the night sky as they had been flown here images of his fingers trailing along the smooth creamy skin of her thighs had plagued him.

They had barely spoken on the journey, and her quietness surprised him. At the airport she had seemed such an overexcited chatterbox. Had his welcome been too brusque? After all, it wasn't *her* fault that earlier that night at a charity gala ball in the Hotel Grande Bretagne he had been only too aware of the other guests' deliberate avoidance of discussing Christos's upcoming wedding with him. And then Christos had rung to explain that the chief bridesmaid had missed her flight. Asked would he mind rescuing her.

Why on earth had he agreed to host the wedding in the first place? It was getting more complicated by the day…and bringing back humiliating memories he had spent the past two years burying.

Yes, he had vaguely agreed to Grace Chapman's early arrival, but he hadn't expected her to be so elated about the wedding or so distractingly beautiful. Her excitement had brought home just how much he hated the prospect of this wedding. And, unbelievably, this was her first time abroad on her own. He didn't have time to babysit her—not with the serious issues complicating the construction of his new resort on the Cayman Islands. He urgently needed to resolve them to stop further haemorrhaging of the project's finances. Having her on the island was a headache he didn't need right now.

Unfortunately she had other ideas.

'This view is absolutely stunning.'

She didn't turn to him when she spoke, but continued to gaze towards the lights of Naxos in the distance. The sky was a never-ending celestial ocean of stars. Beneath them, far below the cliff-face, the Aegean Sea crashed onto the shore.

She gave a light shiver and rubbed her hands against her bare arms. A silver bracelet jangled at her wrist. He instinctively shrugged off his jacket. When he held it out for her to put on she jerked back in surprise. In the darkness he could just about see the violet-blue depths of her eyes. Eyes that had swallowed his soul for a foolish few seconds at the airport.

Initially she looked as though she would refuse his offer, but then she gave a nod of acceptance. She turned around and pushed her arms into the sleeves. When he pulled it up to her slim shoulders she moved at the same time to sweep up the long length of her golden blonde hair trapped beneath the jacket. Her hair fell against his hands like the gentle weight of silk, her floral scent carried with it. His gut tightened. And when she turned those huge eyes to him they were full of questions, of awareness of the chemistry sizzling between them. He itched to touch the smooth line of her jaw, to run his thumb over the sensual plumpness of her lips.

He took a step away.

She twisted back towards the sea, her shoulders sagging faintly before she went to pick up her weekend bag, but he whipped it up, along with her suitcase.

'The path down to the villa is well lit, but still be careful—it's steep. *Ela*. Come. I will lead the way.'

On the way down the path he paused a number of times, to allow her to catch up and to ensure that she was following him safely. As they rounded the corner that opened up the villa to their view he heard her gasp. He turned in alarm. Grace stood staring at the villa, its walls bathed in the light from the terraces.

'What a stunning building—it's like a stack of sugar cubes perched on the mountainside! How absolutely beautiful.'

Memories of the last woman he had brought here stirred at her words. He pushed them away. 'Thank you. I'll show you to your room as it's getting late. In the morning you can look around the villa and the gardens.'

Instead of following him Grace moved to the furthest reaches of one of the terraces and leaned on the balustrade.

'Now I understand why Christos was so eager to marry here. It's an idyllic wedding location. Sofia showed me some photos, but I had no idea it was so lovely. I can just imagine how incredible it will look on the night of the wedding, when everyone is dancing out here on the terrace, candles lit...'

It was time to move her on. 'As I said, I'll show you to your bedroom and then you can join me for something to eat.'

She stepped more fully into the light of the terrace, as though she didn't want to speak from the shadows. His jacket hung loose on her, almost reaching down to the hem of her dress.

'Thanks, but I'm not hungry.' She wrapped the jacket around her body, folding her arms over it to secure it closed. 'You're not excited about the wedding?'

He paused as he calculated his best response. Time to put his cards on the table. 'I'm concerned that they are rushing into this. They barely know one another. How long have they been together? Four months? The whole thing is unwise.'

'But they are really happy. I've never seen a couple so in love…so right for one another. It truly was love at first sight for them both.'

The gentle wistfulness in her voice had him clenching his fists.

'Really? Love at first sight?'

'Yes—why not?'

Her idealism made him want to be cruel, to shake her out of her romantic bubble. '*Lust* at first sight, maybe.'

Silence followed his words and they stared at each other, the truth of his words, as applied to them, hanging in the space between them.

He forced himself to continue. 'It takes a long time to get to know another person—if you ever can. People aren't what they seem.'

'I'm not sure what you mean.'

'My brother is an exceptionally wealthy man.'

She studied him with a mixed expression of disappointment and hurt. 'That means nothing to Sofia, trust me.'

For a brief moment he hated himself for his cynicism, for causing that wounded expression. But then he remembered how he had been played for a fool before, and he asked with a bitter laugh, 'Do you seriously believe that?'

Hard resolution entered her eyes. 'Yes. Absolutely.' She walked back to him, anger clear in her quick pace, in the way she glared at him.

Well, tough. He would remain convinced that Sofia was marrying Christos for his name and wealth until it was proved otherwise. And as for Grace Chapman… She seemed to know a lot about him. Was she really here just to organise the wedding flowers? Or did she perhaps hope for romance with the best man?

And that wasn't his vanity speaking. He had a constant stream of women eager to date him—to date a Petrakis, date a billionaire. To date him for all the superficial reasons he hated. But it suited him, because no woman was *ever* getting close to knowing the real him again. And no way was he getting entangled with the chief bridesmaid when tradition dictated that they would see each other in the future.

He picked up her suitcase and said once again, 'I'll show you to your room.'

Her phone rang. She checked the screen and turned away. 'Hi, Matt.' A long giggle followed. 'Of *course* I miss you.'

As he took her bags up into the villa he gritted his teeth at how happy she sounded. When was the last time someone had answered *his* call with such warmth and tenderness? And then anger surged through his veins. Was she already in a relationship? If so, why the hell was she allowing the chemistry between them to smoulder on?

'I love you too.'

Grace hung up from Matt and stretched her neck back, easing the tension in her muscles a fraction.

She rolled her shoulders and took in once again the quiet serenity of her surroundings. Then she steeled herself. She walked into the villa and entered a large living room, seeing walls whitewashed in gentle curves, a recessed fireplace. The stillness of the room and its simple refined beauty, from the huge white sofas on white marble floors to the handcrafted teak furniture, were at odds with the sense of injustice raging in her heart.

Andreas had no right to make such horrible assumptions about Sofia. She closed her eyes and inhaled deeply. Was Andreas just like her father? Cold and cynical? A man so obsessed with becoming wealthy he was blind to the magic of love and loyalty?

Whatever the truth, Sofia and Christos could not arrive to find the best man and chief bridesmaid at loggerheads. She and Andreas would have to learn to get on.

She found him in the kitchen, propped against the countertop, peeling an orange. She placed his jacket on the back of a chair. Unconsciously, she let her hand linger for a few moments on the soft wool, until she realised what she was doing.

Long elegant fingers expertly spiralled the peel off the orange, but he didn't glance downwards once to watch his progress—instead he studied her.

She placed a bottle of champagne on the counter. In response to his frown she explained, 'It's a thank-you for having me to stay.'

She had thought it might be an appropriate gift, given the upcoming celebrations, but was rapidly revising *that* idea. She twisted the bracelet at her wrist, her fingers reaching for the two charms that sat at its centre. The tension in her body eased a fraction when she squeezed the silver metal with her thumb and forefinger.

'I think we need to talk.'

He gave a tight nod and walked over to a cupboard. He opened the door on an array of crystal glasses. 'What can I get you to drink? Wine? Beer?'

Not thirsty, she was about to refuse, but then realised that she should accept his offer as a small step forward towards developing some form of *entente cordiale* between them.

'I have a long day tomorrow, so I'd like fruit juice, if that's okay.'

He gestured for her to sit on one of the stools beneath the counter, but instead she leaned against the wall, next to an old-fashioned dresser filled with colourful ceramics which, though at odds with the sleek lines of Andreas's modern kitchen, grounded the room with their reminder of history and other lives lived.

She jumped when her phone rang again. She grabbed it off the dresser. It was Lizzie. She let the call go to her voicemail, but that didn't stop Andreas giving her a critical stare.

The cold apple juice was sharp and refreshing, and thankfully helped her refocus on the task at hand. 'So, can we talk?'

He lifted his own glass of water and took a drink, his eyes never leaving her. 'What about?'

Butterflies fluttered in her stomach at his icy tone. 'Sofia's my best friend. This wedding means the world to her. I don't want anything…or anybody…to upset her.'

'Meaning me?'

She met his gaze and a wave of protectiveness for her friend had her returning his intimidating stare with conviction. 'Yes. Sofia is marrying Christos because she loves him—not for any other reason.'

'So you said before.'

His flippancy irked her and she asked sharply, 'Why have you agreed to host the wedding here, to be best man, if you don't approve?'

He held her gaze with a steady coolness, but his jaw tightened in irritation. 'When Christos asked me to be his best man I told him my concerns. But I believe in family loyalty, so of course I agreed. It would not have been honourable to do otherwise. And as for this island—we spent our childhood summers here, and we always vowed that we would marry in the island chapel one day. I'm not going to deny Christos that wish, no matter what my misgivings are.'

He stared at her hard, as though defying her to ask any more questions. But there was something in his expression that was puzzling her. Was it a hint of wounded pride? Why did she feel as though she was missing some significant point in this conversation? Sofia had mentioned that Andreas had once been briefly married. Was he remembering his own marriage? Or was she just reading this all wrong? Grace had formed the impression from Sofia that he had easily moved on from that marriage to a string of other relationships.

She walked towards him and stopped a little distance away. She forced herself to look into his eyes. Her heart pounded at the hard cynicism she found there. 'I can understand why you might have some concerns. But Sofia is an incredible person and I truly believe they will be extremely happy together. They were made for one another. For their sake I would like us to get on.'

He moved away from the countertop. Beneath his open-necked shirt, golden skin peppered with dark hair was visible. He took a step closer to her. Her breath caught as she inhaled his scent—a sensual muskiness with hints of spice and lemon. She stared at the broadness of his shoulders beneath the slim-fitting white shirt, the narrowness of his hips in the dark tuxedo trousers, the long length of his legs.

He stepped even closer, towering over her, those light green eyes burnished with gold scorching into hers. He leaned down towards her ear and in a low growl asked, 'Tell me…will your boyfriend be joining you for the wedding?'

His voice rumbled through her body. She didn't know

whether to run away from the dark danger that everything about this man screamed or just give in and lean into the heat and invisible pull of his powerful body.

She stepped back. Again he pinned her to the spot with his demanding stare.

'I don't have a boyfriend.'

His eyes narrowed. 'Then who's Matt?'

'Matt? Matt's my brother.'

For a moment he considered her suspiciously, as though searching for the truth. Then abruptly he turned away.

'I understand from Christos that you wish to use the workshops down by the island jetty to prepare the flowers? Tomorrow my gardener Ioannis will show you the way. If you need to travel to any of the other islands Ioannis will take you. My housekeeper Eleni will take care of your meals. Your bedroom is upstairs—the third room to the right. I have left your luggage there.'

Rebelliousness surged through her at his dismissive tone. 'And what about you, Andreas? Will you have a partner at the wedding this weekend?'

He turned and considered her. 'No. I'll be on my own. The way I like it. And, to answer your earlier question, I can see no reason why we cannot get on with one another. I will go along with Christos's wishes...but please don't expect me to embrace this wedding with the same enthusiasm as you. My days of believing in romance and love are long gone.'

He threw the uneaten orange into the bin, muttered, '*Kalinichta*...goodnight...' and walked out of the room.

Grace collapsed against the wall, suddenly exhausted. She closed her eyes and prayed that tomorrow would go more smoothly. That the deliveries would arrive on time.

That in the cold light of the day her senseless attraction to Andreas would diminish.

Because Andreas Petrakis was as far removed from her ideal man as Attila the Hun.

CHAPTER TWO

ANDREAS SLOWED THE pace of his morning swim for the last hundred metres into the shore and trailed his eye up the cliff-face and the numerous terraces built into it.

In only three days' time the island would be overrun with the hundreds of guests who were to be ferried out to the island from Athens. There would be polite avoiding of his eye, curious studying of him to see if he gave any sign of remembering his own vows of commitment, and how his marriage had ended within twelve short months.

He hoped Christos knew what he was doing. That he knew Sofia as well as he said he did. Andreas did not want to see his brother hurt. Or his family humiliated and disappointed again.

He had spent the past month, since Christos had announced his engagement, avoiding any involvement in the wedding preparations. He would respect his brother's decision and play the dutiful best man. Get along with the chief bridesmaid as best he could. But he'd keep his distance from her. To do otherwise, no matter how tempting, would be foolhardy.

There was undoubtedly a spark of attraction between them, but she was an out-and-out romantic and he had no business getting involved with a woman who believed in fairy-tale endings. Not when he knew that love was nothing but a fantasy. Anyway, the best man should *never* get involved with the chief bridesmaid. It was never a good idea in the long run.

On the warm sand at the base of the cliff he grabbed his towel and made his way back up the steep steps to the villa. He had rushed into marriage, like Christos. In the intense whirlwind of infatuation he had thought he had found love. But through her lies and betrayal his ex-wife had hardened his heart for ever. He would never trust again. He had always believed in marriage, in having children. But now those were the long forgotten dreams of an innocent.

Close to the top of his climb, he came to a stop on the final steps. Laden down with files and paperwork, her hair tied up into a high ponytail, bouncing from side to side, Grace rushed down the path towards him. She was dressed in a white lace blouse, pink shorts and trainers, and the sight of her bare legs had his abdominals tensing with frustration.

She spotted him and slowed, her eyes quickly flicking over him. Heat filled her cheeks before she looked away.

'*Kalimera*—good morning, Grace.'

She ventured another quick gaze at him and nodded. This time her eyes held his.

The morning sun highlighted the honey and caramel tones in her hair, emphasising the mesmerising violet colour of her eyes. Eyes that could do funny things to a man's resolve if he wasn't careful.

Invisible strings of mutual attraction tugged tight. He wanted to step closer, to cradle the delicate exposed lines of her neck, draw her mouth up towards his...

The beads of seawater that had been slowly following a lazy path down his body now felt electrified on his unbearably sensitive skin. He felt alive to a world of sensual possibilities.

She made a few attempts to talk, all the while shuffling the files in her arms, her eyes darting to and from him.

Why was she so jumpy? 'Is everything okay?'

Her head moved almost imperceptibly from side to side, as though she was trying to weigh up how she was going to reply. She bit down on her lip, exposing the not quite perfect alignment of her front teeth, with one tooth slightly overlapping the other. Why did he find that imperfection so appealing?

Eventually she said in a rush, 'Ioannis just called. The flowers are already down at the jetty. Apparently they were delivered before dawn. The delivery company were supposed to call me. I was meant to inspect them before they left… And, worse still, they were supposed to carry them as far as the workshops for me.'

The workshops sat on a steep hill overlooking the cove—she would need some help. 'Ask Ioannis to help you.'

'He had to go to Naxos to collect the caterers and the wedding planner and her team. A florist from Naxos was supposed to be coming with them, to assist me today, but she just called to say that she's sick.'

Thee mou! Did Grace know what she was doing? A missed flight, a missed delivery, and now a sick member of staff. 'Get Ioannis and the wedding planner's team to help you when they arrive.'

'I can't leave the flowers out in this heat. I have to get them into the cool of the workshops straight away.'

Why hadn't he opted to stay in Athens for the duration of the wedding preparations? *Because you love your brother. And as his work in London has prevented him from travelling until Thursday you promised to be here in case there were any issues.*

But he had urgent business to deal with too. He didn't have time for this. His instinct about Grace needing baby-sitting hadn't been far off the mark after all.

'Do you usually face so many problems?'

She considered him for a brief moment, her anxiety fading to be replaced by a sharp intelligence. 'There are always unforeseen problems with the flowers for any wedding. It's my job to deal with them as quickly as I can.' She paused, and although her cheeks grew even more enflamed she considered him with a quiet dignity. 'I'm sure *you* must experience unexpected problems all the time in your work…and will therefore understand why I need to ask for your help.'

'*My* help?' He had a mountain of work to do. He didn't have time to act as some florist's assistant.

She inhaled a deep breath and answered, 'I appreciate you're probably very busy, but if you could give me half an hour I'd be grateful.'

She awaited his response with a spirited stare of defiance, challenging him to say no. Despite himself he admired her feistiness.

Against all logic and his pledges to keep a wide berth around the chief bridesmaid he found himself saying, 'I'll give you half an hour. No more. First I must get changed and reschedule a call.'

Light-headed, Grace turned away as Andreas climbed the path up to the villa, her heart pirouetting with humiliation…and something else she didn't want to think about.

He must think she was completely incompetent.

The ground beneath her no longer felt solid. Had she sat in the sun for too long earlier, whilst finalising her

plans for the reception flowers out on the terrace? She
came to a stop and gulped down some air.

Who was she trying to kid? This had nothing to do
with too much sun. Rather too much of Andreas Petrakis. Too much of his near naked body. Too much of seeing the seawater that had fallen in droplets along the hard
muscles of his chest, down over a perfectly defined six-
pack until they'd reached the turquoise swimming shorts
that sat low on his narrow hips.

She had been right last night. He *was* a Greek god. His
sleeked back hair had emphasised the prominence of his
cheekbones, the arrow-straightness of his nose, the enticing fullness of his mouth. And he had a long-limbed
muscular body the likes of which she had only ever seen
cast in marble whilst on a school tour to the British Museum. Sofia and she had circled those statues, giddy with
teenage fascination.

She would *not* turn around and take one final glimpse.
No way.

Oh, what the heck?

His back was a vast golden expanse of taut muscle,
from broad powerful shoulders down to those narrow
hips. And she could not help but notice the firm muscles
of his bottom and the long, athletic shape of his legs as
he easily climbed the steep path back towards the villa.

The goofy grin on her mouth faded. Okay, so he was
gorgeous, and he did very peculiar things to her heart.
But she had to dig one big hole and bury that attraction.
She was here to do a job. She had to act professionally.
Even if the gods were determinedly working against her
right now in a bid to make her appear completely clueless.

Early this morning she had thrown open her balcony
doors to dazzling sunshine and the stunning vista of far-
away islands floating on the azure Aegean Sea. A light

breeze had curled around her like a welcoming hug to the Cyclades Islands. Only the tinkle of goat bells had been carried on the air.

That paradise she had awoken to had given her a renewed determination that she was going to enjoy every second of this trip, which was to be the start of the life of adventure she had craved for so many years. After years of being held hostage to her father's control and manipulation she was determined to be free. Free to love every second of every day, to fill her life with fun and exhilaration. Free to accomplish all her own ambitions and prove that she *did* have worth.

All of which meant that tangling with her arrogant playboy host was the last thing she should be doing. Her priority had to be the flowers. If this project went wrong she could kiss her fledgling career goodbye. And, God forgive her for her pride, she wanted to prove to Andreas that she wasn't a bumbling idiot—contrary to all current evidence.

Set into the cliff-face above the small harbour, the workshops mirrored the sugar cube style of the main house. Inside, the cool double-height rooms with their exposed roof beams and roughly plastered walls would be perfect for storing and assembling the flowers.

Grace quickly moved about the first workshop on the row, sweeping dust off benches and pulling two into the centre of the room for her to work at. Outside again, she raced down to the harbour jetty, grabbed a stack of flower buckets, and ran back up to the workshops. Within minutes her legs were burning because of the steep incline.

Back inside the workshop, she dropped the buckets to the floor and exhaled heavily. What had she taken on? How on earth was she going to strip and trim over a thousand stems of peonies and lisianthus by herself?

She gave herself a shake and scanned the room. There was no tap. What was she going to do about water? She ran into the adjoining room and almost cried in relief when she saw a sink in the far corner. She twisted the tap. The gush of water restored some calm.

Twice more she ran down to the jetty to collect the remaining buckets, and the box she had packed personally, which contained all her essential tools: knives, scissors, pruners and a vast assortment of tapes, wires and cord twine.

By the time Andreas appeared at the workshop door she was not only hot and sweaty but also covered in wet patches from the sloshing water as she carried endless buckets of water from the adjoining room back into her temporary workshop.

He, in contrast, was his usual effortlessly cool and elegant self, wearing faded denim jeans that hung low on his hips and a slim-fitting sea-green polo shirt. Muscular biceps, washboard abs... How good would it be to walk into his arms and feel the athletic strength of his body?

For a few seconds every ounce of energy drained from her and she wondered how she didn't crumble to the workshop floor in a mess of crushing attraction.

Pointedly he glanced at his exquisite platinum watch.

Inwardly she groaned at her lack of focus.

She rushed to the door and pointed down towards the jetty. The pale wooden structure sitting over the teal-blue sea was the perfect romantic setting for the arrival of the wedding guests on Saturday.

'The flowers are all packed in those large rectangular boxes, stacked together. We need to get those inside now. The other boxes can wait until later.'

She was about to pass him when he placed his hand

on her forearm. 'I'll collect the boxes—you stay here and continue with the work you were doing.'

She swallowed hard, her whole body on alert at the pleasurable sensation of his large hand wrapped around her arm. 'We don't have time.'

His eyes moved downwards and lingered on her chest.

Grace followed his gaze. And almost passed out. Her wet blouse was transparent, and clinging to her crimson-trimmed bra.

His lip curled upwards in one corner and for a moment she got a glimpse of how lethal he would be if he decided to seduce her.

'Perhaps it might be better if you stay inside for a while; Ioannis and the wedding team are due to arrive soon.'

Mortified, she twisted away, grabbed some buckets and pointedly turned and nodded in the direction of his watch. 'You'd better get going as your half an hour is ticking away. I reckon you'll struggle to get all of the boxes in by then.'

A smirk grew on his lips. 'I'll try not to break into too much of a sweat...' He paused as his eyes rested on where her wet blouse was sticking to her skin. 'Although it does have its attractions.'

Lightning bolts of lust fired through her body. He noted her wide-eyed reaction and his smirk grew even larger. She twisted around and fled next door. She could have sworn she heard him chuckle.

When she returned with the filled buckets he was gone.

Andreas returned time and time again with the long rectangular flower boxes, and each time Grace heard his footsteps approach she hightailed it into the adjoining room. Only when she realised that he had moved on to carrying in the assortment of different-sized boxes that contained the other essentials did she speak. But despite her assurances that it wasn't necessary for him to bring them in, he continued to do so.

The buckets filled and flower food added, she went about stripping and trimming the stems. With bated breath she opened the first box of peonies and found light pink Sarah Bernhardt, and in the next box the ivory-white Duchesse de Nemours. Both were as big and utterly beautiful as she had hoped, and on track to open to their full blowsy glory for Saturday.

At last *something* was going right for her.

For a moment she leaned down and inhaled the sweet scent of the flowers, closing her eyes in pleasure. She might have to stay up all night to get the prep work done, but she would manage. The flowers had to be perfect for Sofia.

She had the first box completed when Andreas brought the final boxes in. Unfairly, apart from a faint sheen of perspiration on his tanned skin, he didn't appear the least bit ruffled by all the dragging and hauling.

Hitting the timer on her smartphone, she twisted it around to show him the display. 'Thirty-six minutes, fourteen seconds.'

His mouth twitched for a few seconds before he flashed his watch at her and tapped one of the dials. 'Nineteen minutes and forty-three seconds to carry in the flowers, which was all you specified. So I win.'

'I didn't know we were competing.'

Those green eyes flashed with way too much smugness for her liking. 'Why did you time me then?'

'Oh, just curiosity.' Keen to change the subject, she added, 'I'm really grateful for your help—thank you.'

He shrugged in response and turned his attention to

the remaining stack of flower boxes, and then to the already trimmed peonies, sitting in their buckets of water. 'Why so many roses?'

'They're not roses.'

He contemplated the flowers dubiously.

She twisted the stem she was working on and held it out towards him. 'They're peonies. I thought you would have known, being Greek, as apparently they are called after Paean, who healed Hades's wounds. It's thought that they have healing properties. It's also believed that they represent a happy life...and a happy marriage.'

To that he raised a sceptical eyebrow.

With her floral shears, Grace snipped an inch diagonally off the end of the stem. 'Let me guess...you're not the type to buy flowers?'

'On occasion I have.' A grin tugged at the corner of his mouth in reaction to her quizzical glance. 'Okay, I admit that I let my PA organise the details.'

She tried to ignore how good it was to see those eyes sparkle with humour. 'Now, *that's* just cheating... I hope you at least specify what type of flowers you want to send?'

He seemed baffled at the idea. 'No—why should I?'

'Because each flower represents something. When you send a flower you are sending a message with it.'

He looked horrified at that prospect. 'Like what?'

Amused, she decided to make the most of him being on the back foot in this conversation. 'Well, new beginnings are symbolised by daffodils...a secret love is represented by gardenias...' She paused for effect before continuing, 'True love is shown by forget-me-nots, and sensuality by jasmine.'

Their eyes met and tension pulsed in the air. But then

he broke his gaze away. 'How about, *Thanks for a good night, but this is nothing serious*?'

Her heart sank. 'A yellow rose is used for friendship, if that's what you're trying to say. But maybe it would be better not to send anything on those occasions.'

Unable to bear the way his gaze had fastened on her again, she bent her head and trimmed the foliage on the stem with quick cuts, a constant mantra sounding in her brain: *Stay away from him; he's a sure-fire path to heart-break.*

He eventually spoke. 'Perhaps. But I still don't understand why so many flowers are needed for one wedding.'

So often she had heard the same incredulous question from grooms-to-be, who struggled to understand the volume of flowers needed to create a visual impact and how important flowers were for setting the mood and tone of the wedding day. She was used to talking them through her plans, and always keen to make them comfortable and happy with her designs, but with Andreas she felt even more compelled to spell out the intricacies of wedding floral design and the attention to detail required. She wanted it to be clear to him that she was not *playing with flowers*. That her presence on his island was essential.

'Eight hundred peonies. Two hundred lisianthus, to be precise. Along with the bridal party bouquets, and the flower displays that will be needed outside the chapel and on the terrace, each reception table will have a centrepiece of five vases with five peonies in each, so with twenty tables—'

'That adds up to five hundred flowers.'

'Exactly. Today I have to trim, cut and place all the stems in water. Tomorrow the stems will need to be cut again and placed in fresh water. On Friday fifty potted bay trees and storm lanterns will be delivered, to be placed along the walkway between the jetty and the chapel, and on the main terrace for the reception and the dancing.'

He surveyed the boxes of flowers yet to be opened and then looked over to the large pile of other unopened boxes. His gaze narrowed. 'What's in the other boxes?'

She had gone over her stock list so often she had no problem in recalling all the items she had ordered. 'One hundred glass vases for the centrepieces, two hundred votive candles, fifty lantern candles and thirty pillar candles. Flower foam, more string, wire, ribbon... The list goes on. They all need to be unloaded today, ready to be prepped tomorrow. And I also have to finalise my designs.'

He checked his watch and frowned. 'I have to get back to my conference calls. Is there anyone else who can help you with all this?'

'I'll manage.' Even if it meant she would be working late into the night. 'Two more florists will be joining me tomorrow, but I need to get all the basic prep done today or I'll run out of time.'

His eyes drifted over the now crowded room. 'I have to admit that I hadn't realised the volume of work involved.'

A smile tugged at her lips. 'Perhaps now you understand why I need to be here and not touring the night-clubs of Athens.'

He gave a gracious nod in response, his eyes softening in amusement. 'Yes, but that's not to say that I don't think it's all crazy.'

With that he left the room, and Grace stood stock-still for the longest while, her heart colliding against her chest at being on the receiving end of his beautiful smile.

Six hours later Andreas made his way back down to the workshops. Eleni, although tied up in an argument with the catering team over the use of her beloved pots and pans, had whispered to him that Grace had not appeared for lunch, and gestured in appeal towards a tray of food.

Never able to say no to his indomitable housekeeper, who had him wrapped around her little finger, Andreas approached the workshops now in frustration at yet another disruption to his day. But he had to admit to concern for Grace at the huge amount of work she had to tackle alone, and to a grudging respect for her determination and energy in doing so.

Inside the first workshop the tiled floor was akin to a woodland scene, with green leaves and cuttings scattered everywhere. In the middle, armed with a sweeping brush, Grace was corralling the leaves into one giant pile, her face a cloud of tension.

A quick glance about the room told him she was making slow progress. She needed help. And unfortunately he was the only person available.

'Eleni's concerned that you missed lunch.'

She jerked around at his voice.

He dropped the tray on the edge of a workbench.

'That's very kind of her.' She paused as she grabbed a nearby dustpan and composting bag. 'Please thank her for me but tell her not to worry—I can fend for myself.'

The composting bag full, Grace tied it and placed it in a corner. He, meanwhile, had taken over the scooping of the leaves.

She moved next to him, her bare legs inches from where he crouched down. If he reached out, his fingers could follow a lazy path over her creamy skin. He could learn at what point her eyes would glaze over as his fingers traced her sensitive spots. The desire to pull her down onto the mound of leaves and kiss that beautiful mouth raged inside him.

'There's no need for you to help.'

She sounded weary.

He stood. His gut tightened when he saw the exhaustion in her eyes. 'You need a break. Have some lunch. I'll finish here.'

She hesitated, but then walked over to the tray. The deep aroma of Greek coffee filled the workshop but she immediately went back to work, carrying a fresh box over to the table. In between opening the box and sorting through the flowers she hurriedly gulped down some coffee and took quick, small bites of a triangular-shaped parcel of spinach and feta cheese pie—*spanakopita*.

He gathered up the tray, ignoring her confused expression, and took it to a bench outside. When Grace joined him he said, 'You shouldn't work and eat at the same time.'

'I'm too busy.'

'Let's make a deal. If you agree to take a ten-minute break, I'll stay a while and unpack some of the supplies for you.'

She stared at him suspiciously. 'Are you sure?'

He needed to make clear his reasons for doing this. 'You're my guest—it's my duty to take care of you.'

She paused for a moment and considered his words before giving a faint nod. 'I'd appreciate your help, but I must warn you that it might prove to be a tedious job because the suppliers haven't labelled the boxes. I need you to find the glass vases for me first, as I have to prep them today. There's a box-cutter you can use on the table next to the boxes.'

He went back inside and started opening boxes. She rejoined him within five minutes. A five-minute break that had included her answering a phone call from someone called Lizzie.

A begrudging respect for her work ethic toyed with his annoyance that she hadn't adhered to her side of the bargain. He wasn't used to people going against his orders.

They both worked in silence, but the air was charged with an uncomfortable tension.

Eventually she spoke. 'What were these workshops originally used for?'

Sadness tugged in his chest at her question. He swallowed hard before he spoke. 'My uncle was a ceramicist and he built these workshops for his work.'

She rested her hands on the workbench and leaned forward. 'I noticed some ceramic pieces in your house—are they your uncle's?'

'Yes. He created them in these workshops; there's a kiln in the end room.'

'They're beautiful.'

Thrown by the admiration and excitement in her voice, he pressed his thumb against the sharp blade of the box cutter. 'He died two years ago.'

For a long while the only sound was the whistle of the light sea breeze as it swirled into the workshop.

She walked around the bench to where he was working. 'I'm sorry.'

He glanced away from the tender sincerity in her eyes. It tugged much too painfully at the empty pit in his stomach.

'What was he like?'

The centre of my world.

He went back to work, barely registering the rows of candles inside the box he had just opened.

'He was quiet, thoughtful. He loved this island. When I was a small boy the island belonged to my grandparents. They used it as their summer retreat. My uncle lived here permanently. Christos and I used to spend our summers here, free to explore without anyone telling us what to do and when to be home. That freedom was paradise. We'd swim and climb all day, and at night we'd grill fish on the beach with our uncle. He would tell us stories late into the night, trying his best to scare us with tales of sea monsters.'

'There's a gorgeous ceramic pot in the living room, with images of sea monsters and children...did he create that?'

He was taken aback that she had already noticed his single most treasured possession, and it was a while before he answered. 'Yes, the children are Christos and me.'

'What wonderful memories you both must have.'

He turned away from the beguiling softness in her violet eyes. He closed the lid of the box, still having been unable to locate the vases. It was strange to talk to someone about his uncle. Usually he closed off any conversation about him, but being here, in one of his workshops, with this quietly spoken empathetic woman, had him wanting to speak about him.

'He always encouraged me to follow my dreams, even when they were unconventional or high risk. He even funded my first ever property acquisition when I was nineteen. Thankfully I was able to pay him back with interest within a year. He believed in me, trusted me when others didn't.'

Her thumb rubbed against the corner of a box. He noticed that her nails, cut short, were varnish-free. A plaster was wrapped around her index finger and he had to stop himself from taking it in his hand.

She inhaled before she spoke. 'You were lucky to have someone like that in your life.'

Taken aback by the loneliness in her voice, he could only agree. 'Yes.'

She gave him a sad smile. 'Kasas is a very special place…you're lucky to have a house somewhere so magical.'

Old memories came back with a vengeance. 'Some people would hate it.'

'Hate this island? I think it's the most beautiful place I have ever visited.'

Andreas watched her, disarmed by the passion in her voice. He wanted to believe everything she said was heartfelt and genuine. That he wasn't being manipulated by a woman again. But cold logic told him not to buy any of it.

It was time to move this conversation on. It was getting way too personal.

'The vases aren't here.'

Her mouth dropped open and she visibly paled. 'They *have* to be.'

'I've double-checked each box—they're not.'

She gave a low groan and rushed over to the boxes, while frantically pushing buttons on her phone. As she ransacked the boxes she spoke to someone called Jan.

Andreas walked away and into the adjoining room. Once again he tried to ignore the loneliness crowding his chest at being in these workshops for the first time since his uncle had died.

A few minutes later Grace followed him into the end room, where the kiln was located. She stopped at the doorway and clenched her phone tight in her palm. Her paleness had now been replaced by a slash of red on her cheeks.

She spoke in a low voice, her eyes wary. 'The vases were never despatched by the suppliers in Amsterdam; they won't get here before Saturday.'

He had guessed as much. He gestured to the vast array

of white porcelain pots on the bench beside the kiln. 'You can use these instead.'

Her eyes grew wide and she went and picked one up. And then another. Her fingers traced over the smooth delicate ceramic. 'Are you sure?'

'He had moved back to working predominantly with porcelain in the year before he died. I've never known what to do with all his work, I didn't want to sell it...' Unexpected emotion cut off the rest of what he had been about to say.

Soft violet eyes held his. 'This can't be easy for you.'

He glanced away. 'He would like it that his work is being used for Christos's wedding.'

With that he walked back to the main workshop, wanting to put some distance between him and this woman who kept unbalancing his equilibrium. Frustration rolled through him. What was it about Grace that made him break all his own rules?

He had another ten minutes before he had to leave. There were a few small boxes yet to open.

He unwrapped a small rectangular parcel first, and found inside, wrapped in a soft cloth, a pair of silver sandals. 'These are unusual florist's supplies.'

'My sandals!' She dropped the flowers she was working on and took the slender sexy heels from him.

Imagining Grace's enticing legs in the sandals, he felt his blood pressure skyrocket. In need of distraction, he went back to opening the next box.

'The shop didn't have them in my size so I had them delivered here...' Her voice trailed off and then she said in a low, desperate voice, 'Don't open that box.'

But she was too late. His fingers were already looped around two pale pink silk straps. He lifted the material to reveal a sheer lace bustier.

With an expression of absolute mortification Grace stared at the bustier, and then down at the scrap of erotic pink lace still left in the box, sitting on a bed of black tissue paper. Odds on it was the matching panties. Red-hot blood coursed through his body.

'Yours, I take it?'

For a moment her mouth opened and closed, but then she grabbed the bustier and the box and walked away.

She kept her back to him as she bundled the bustier back into its box. 'It's for the wedding, but I'm not sure I'll wear it.'

Time for him to leave—before he burst a blood vessel. 'I have afternoon calls I have to get back to.' He made it as far as the door before he turned back. 'Grace?'

She turned around towards him.

'Wear it.'

He walked away as her lips parted in surprise. He had never wanted to grab a woman and kiss her senseless more in all his life.

CHAPTER THREE

GRACE REACHED FOR the bell clapper, feeling the ladder wobbling beneath her.

'What in the name of the devil are you doing?'

She jerked at the sound of Andreas's irate voice beneath her and the precarious ladder swayed wildly. A startled yelp from deep within her shot out into the evening air, but mercifully the ladder was steadied before it toppled to the ground.

She dared a quick glance down. A livid Andreas was gripping the side bars, one foot on the bottom rung.

She swallowed hard, uncertain as to what was more daunting: this fury, or the heat in his eyes earlier when he had lifted up her bustier. Heat that had ignited a yearning in her that had left her breathless and just plain exasperated. They didn't even particularly *like* each other. Why, then, did she feel as though she was about to combust any time she came into contact with him?

'I've decided that the chapel needs some extra decoration in addition to what I'd planned, so I'm making a garland that will hang from the bell tower down to the ground. I need to measure the exact length.'

'*Aman!* You are breaking my nerves! You shouldn't be doing this alone; the flagstones are too uneven.'

He was right, but she wasn't going to admit it. 'I'm

fine—it's a quick job.' To prove her point she knotted twine around the bell clapper and then dropped the twine spool to the ground before climbing down the ladder. She avoided looking at him and instead pulled the twine out to the angle she wanted the garland positioned at on the wedding day. Cutting it to the desired length, she ignored his infuriated expression. 'I need to climb back up and untie the other end.'

He gave an exasperated sigh and scaled the ladder himself, dropping the twine when he'd untied it. Back on the ground, he unlocked the extension ladder she had borrowed from Ioannis and collapsed it down.

Then he studied her with incensed eyes, his mouth a thin line. 'Don't try that again.'

Of course she would. But she wasn't going to get into an argument with him. 'Was there something you wanted?'

His gaze narrowed. The uncomfortable sensation that he could see right through her had her grabbing the twine off the ground and asking, 'Is it okay if I use some of the rosemary and bay growing on the terraces for the garland?'

He considered the long length of twine sceptically. 'Is it really necessary? I thought you were under pressure timewise?'

She was, but it was these final touches that would make her work stand apart. 'I'll find the time.' She paused and gestured around her. 'I want the flowers to do justice to this setting.'

Set on a rocky promenade beyond the golden sandy beach, the tiny whitewashed chapel with its blue dome had a dramatic backdrop of endless deep blue seas and skies.

His jaw hardened even more, and she winced to think about the pressure his poor teeth must be under.

'My guess is that Sofia would prefer her bridesmaid *not* to be in a plaster cast on her wedding day for the sake of a few flowers.'

Wow, that was a low blow. 'If you'll excuse me? I need to finalise my plans for the chapel's bespoke floral arrangements—or, as you call them, "a few flowers".'

His mouth twisted at her barbed comment. 'It will be dark soon.'

'I won't be long.' When he didn't move, she added, 'You don't need to wait for me.'

'And have you getting lost on the way back? No, thanks. I don't want to have to spend a second night rescuing you.'

With that he turned and went and sat on the low white-washed wall that surrounded the chapel terrace.

Behind him the deep blue sea met the purple evening sky; it was a postcard-perfect image of the Greek Islands but for the scowling man who dominated the frame.

Grace circled the terrace outside the chapel, all the while taking notes, scribbling into her notebook. Every now and again she would glance in his direction and throw him a dirty glare. Which he was just fine with. Because he was in a pretty dirty mood himself. In every sense.

All afternoon he had been plagued with images of her wearing that sexy lingerie. The bustier hugging her small waist, lifting her breasts to a height and plumpness that demanded a man taste them. Those skimpy panties moulded to her pert bottom... Hell, he couldn't go there again. His call to the Cayman Island planners had been a washout as a result.

She had already put in a twelve-hour day, with less

than five minutes taken for lunch. Did it *really* matter this much what the flowers looked like? Did anyone even *notice* the flowers on a wedding day?

'Why does this wedding mean so much to you?'

She turned to him in surprise, her notebook falling to her side. The long length of her golden ponytail curled over one shoulder and his fingers tingled in remembrance of its softness and her delicate sensual scent last night. His gut tightened. Those legs were once again driving him crazy with images of the chief bridesmaid that he certainly shouldn't be thinking of.

He dated some of the most beautiful women in Athens. Why was he so drawn to this out-of-bounds woman?

Eventually she walked over and sat on the wall beside him. She left a significant gap between them.

'I first met Sofia in our local playground when we were both four. A boy had pushed me off the top of the fire pole. Sofia marched right over and kicked him in the shin before helping me up.' She gave an amused shrug. 'We've never looked back since then. We went to the same primary and secondary school…and we were supposed to go to university together…' She paused and gave a small sigh. 'But that didn't work out for me. After years of coming to school concerts with me, and wet Saturday afternoons standing at the side of a freezing cold soccer pitch, I owe Sofia big-time.'

'I don't understand? Why were you going to school concerts together for years?'

Her lips twisted for a moment before she distractedly rubbed a hand along the smooth skin of her calf. 'My parents weren't always available, so I used to go to Matt's football matches and my younger sister Lizzie's school events. Sofia used to come to keep me company. Even though she could have been off doing something much more entertaining than listening to a school orchestra murdering some piece of music.'

He considered what she'd said. Maybe Christos *was* marrying a good woman.

As though to emphasise that point, Grace studied him coolly. 'Christos is a very lucky man. He's marrying an incredible woman—smart and loving.'

'It sounds like he is.'

A small note of triumph registered in her eyes. 'So, can we agree that we will do everything to make this wedding as special a day as possible for them?'

He wanted to say yes, but the word just wouldn't come. He still feared that Christos might regret his haste in years to come. As he did. So instead he said, 'You're one of life's hopeless romantics, aren't you?'

Those astounding violet eyes narrowed and she leaned away from him as she considered his words. 'Romantic, yes—hopeless, no. I'm not ashamed to admit that I believe in love…in marriage. I see it all the time in my work, and with Sofia and Christos. It's the most wonderful thing that exists.'

'Have *you* ever been in love?'

Her shoulders jerked at his question. 'No.'

'But you want to be?'

An unconscious smile broke on her lips, and her eyes shone with dreams. 'Yes. And I'm greedy… I want it all. I want love at first sight, the whirlwind, the marriage, the children, the growing old together. The perfect man.'

He'd once thought life was that simple. In exasperation, he demanded, 'The perfect man…? What on earth is *that*?'

'A man who will sweep me off my feet, who will make life fun and exciting. A man who believes in love too. In kindness and tenderness.'

For a moment she eyed what must be his appalled expression, given the angry frown that had popped up on her brow. And then, as though his reaction had unlocked something inside of her, she let go with all barrels firing.

'A man who's intelligent, honourable, loyal…and great in bed.'

He tried not to laugh at how disconcerted she seemed by her own last statement. Clearing his throat, he said, 'Wow, that's some guy. But I hate to break it to you… that's not reality. Love is complex and messy and full of disappointment. Not like the fairy tale and the X-rated Prince Charming you've just described. Do you *really* believe someone like that exists?'

Solemn eyes met his. 'I hope so.' Then a hint of fear, maybe doubt, clouded her eyes. For a few moments they sat in silence, until she asked, 'How about you?'

For a while he just stared at her—at the high, slanting cheekbones, the freckle-sized birthmark just below her right ear, surprised by her naivety…by her optimism. In truth, a part of him was wildly envious of that.

'As I said last night, I have no interest in love—in relationships full-stop.'

'Why?'

Even if he'd wanted to, even if he'd trusted Grace he wouldn't be able to find adequate words to describe the mess his marriage had descended into.

'I'd rather not talk about it.'

Disappointment filled her eyes. But then she gave him a sympathetic smile and he instantly realised that she already knew about his marriage. Christos must have said something. Just how much *did* she know? Anger flared inside him. He did not want her sympathy. He did not need the humiliation of her pity.

She shifted on the wall and gazed at him uncertainly. 'Sofia mentioned that you were once married...'

He didn't respond, but raised a questioning eyebrow instead, waiting for her to continue.

She gestured towards the chapel. 'Having the ceremony in the same chapel...' She trailed off.

His heart sank. He really didn't want to talk about this. 'I didn't marry here.'

'Oh.' Clearly flustered by his answer, she muttered, 'Sorry, I assumed you had. After what you said last night about Christos and you always wanting to marry here.'

With an impatient sigh, he answered, 'My ex wanted to get married in Athens.'

She digested this for some time before she asked, 'Did you mind not marrying here?'

At the time he *had* minded. But his ex had been determined from day one that theirs would be *the* society wedding of the year in Athens, and had used his uncle's recent death to persuade him not to marry on the island. She had insisted that he would find it too upsetting to be surrounded by reminders of him on their wedding day.

It had all been lies. In the bitter arguments after he had confronted her with the photos of her with her lover she had admitted as much. His one consolation from the entire debacle was that at least the island wasn't tainted with memories of the worst decision of his life. His biggest failure.

He waited for a few minutes before he spoke, afraid of the anger that might spill out otherwise. 'It doesn't matter; it's in the past.'

'I'm sorry your marriage didn't work out. It must have been a difficult time,' she said quietly.

Disconcerted, Andreas could only stare at her. Was she really the first person who had said such a thing to him? Everyone else had been caught up in outrage at his ex's behaviour, or too embarrassed to say anything. No one—probably in the face of his anger and defiance—had dared to acknowledge just how difficult it had been for him.

His pride demanded that he just shrug off her comments, and he was about to do so when she gave him a glance of understanding that totally disarmed him.

Reluctantly he acknowledged, 'It *was* difficult.'

'You never know—you might find happiness in the future with someone else.'

Not her too. 'Please tell me that you're not one of those women who believe they can change a man…make him fall in love.'

At first she stared at him with a stunned expression, but then her eyes grew hard and cold. 'Andreas, I've had a lifetime's worth of arguments and fights, endless disappointments at failing to get a man to love me. The idea of getting into a relationship with a man who doesn't believe in love or have the capacity to love—for whatever reason—would be my idea of hell. And, trust me, I'm no martyr.'

What was she talking about? Had some guy messed her around?

He tried to remain calm when he spoke again. 'Who were you fighting with?'

Her shoulders dropped and she ran a hand tiredly down over her face. With a heavy sigh, she said, 'How about we get a drink.'

A little while later they sat outside on the main terrace of the villa, with the setting sun disappearing behind the horizon in a blaze of fiery pinks on the purple sky. Along with white wine, Andreas had brought to the table a supper of cheese pie—*tiropita*—freshly baked by Eleni that afternoon, and a bowl of Greek salad.

The filo pastry and salty feta cheese of the *tiropita* melted in her mouth, but she was unable to eat more than a few bites in the silence that had settled between them since returning from the chapel.

Her gaze met his and her stomach clenched at the thought of having to recount her past. She took a sip of wine and pushed back into her chair, squeezing her hands tight in her lap. This trip was supposed to be the start of her new life. She didn't want to remember the past. But she wanted to explain why she would never try to force a man to love her. That despite the attraction between them, and Andreas's obvious thoughts to the contrary, she wanted nothing from him.

'When I was seventeen my mum left us. My brother Matt was twelve, my sister Lizzie fourteen. I was due to go to university that year, but I couldn't leave Matt and Lizzie.'

'Why?'

Memories of standing outside her mother's isolated cottage in Scotland, trying to build up the courage to knock, swamped her. The humiliation of begging her mum to allow Matt and Lizzie to go and live with her only for her to refuse.

'My father...'

This was so hard. Should she say nothing? What *could* she say about her father? Would Andreas even understand? After all he was a driven businessman too. Was he as motivated by money and power as her father? Had that ambition caused his marriage to collapse? Despondency washed over her at the thought that that might have been the case. She suddenly had to know if he was like her father.

'What's the most important thing in your life?'

He considered her warily. 'Why do you ask?'

'I'll explain in a little while.'

For a moment she thought he wouldn't give her an answer. Then, 'Without a doubt my family: Christos, my mother.' He paused before he added, 'My father.'

She searched his eyes but he looked away. Though she had only met his father once, at the engagement party, she had quickly formed the impression that he was impatient and brusque—the type of man who would proudly boast that he didn't suffer fools gladly, with no comprehension of just how foolish and shortsighted that comment was.

In a quiet voice she asked, 'Don't you get on? You and your father?'

'It's not the easiest of relationships.'

Why was he so closed? He told her so little about himself. But then maybe he would understand if he too had a difficult relationship with his father.

'With my father, his business is the only thing that matters. Family never features in his priorities. After my mother left, it was down to me to care for Matt and Lizzie. He didn't care. Though we could barely afford it, he wanted to send them away to boarding school. They were both devastated after my mum left. They needed love and comforting, not some impersonal school.'

Apart from Sofia, she had never confided any of this to another person. Vulnerability and embarrassment sat in her throat like a double-vice grip and she studied the terrace table, bewildered by just how upset she felt. Questioning the sense in telling him all of this. Inadequacy washed over her—so ferocious she thought she might drown.

'Are you okay?'

She peeped up and nodded. Her heart slammed to a stop when she saw the gentleness in his eyes.

'You gave up university to stay with your brother and sister; that's very admirable.'

She swallowed against the emotion lodged in her throat and said, 'I thought that I might be able to get my dad to love Matt and Lizzie, to see how much they needed him. But I just couldn't get through to him. I spent years trying to make things perfect, until I realised that there was no point. After that my objective was to get them to university…away from him. Matt started university this year; Lizzie's in her third year. They're both happy and settled.'

'And what about you?'

'I left home last year, at the same time as Matt. I'm hoping I'll be able to buy an apartment soon—one that can be a home for us all. I've always dreamt of being a florist, and for the past few years, while I've studied floristry at night, I've worked with a wedding floral designer at the weekends. Since I left home I've worked as a florist full-time. After this wedding I'm going freelance as a wedding floral designer, and at some point hopefully I'll be able to open my own flower shop too.'

'Why floristry?'

Was that a note of disapproval in his voice? Compared to his success, her dreams must seem so insignificant.

She glanced at him sharply and asked, 'Why do you ask?'

'Out of curiosity…' He considered her for a while, and then with a grin he added, 'And I reckon the best man and the chief bridesmaid should know a little about each other.'

Grace eyed him suspiciously. 'Have we just taken a step forward in peace negotiations?'

He flashed her a wicked grin that almost had her falling off her chair. 'Perhaps. And, for the record, my question wasn't a criticism.'

'Sorry—it's just that you sounded like my dad. He thinks a career in floristry is a dead end.'

'Why would he say that?'

'Because there's little monetary gain to be made in it as a career—certainly not the sort of wealth *he* admires anyway. I worked in my father's business when I left school. He wanted me to stay and take over the logistics department. He even offered to give me a percentage share in the firm to stay.'

'You weren't tempted by his offer?'

'Not for a minute. It was just his way of trying to keep me in his control.'

He looked into the distance and scowled. 'Emotional blackmail.'

She felt something unlock within her at knowing that he understood. 'Yes.'

He gazed at her for a while and an invisible bond stretched between them.

He broke his gaze. 'So, why floristry?'

'I love everything about flowers—their scent, texture, colours. It's challenging to create a beautiful bouquet or a centrepiece, but so much fun too, especially for weddings, which are such happy affairs.'

'I'm impressed that you've taken on *this* wedding. I'm guessing it's a big project for someone relatively new to the business?'

Her doubts and fears about messing up came charging back and she didn't know how to respond as her heart thudded in her chest. She gave a shrug that belied the butterflies soaring in her belly. 'I'm aiming high…

I just hope I don't crash back down to earth in a blaze of bad publicity.'

'That won't happen—not with the amount of prep and planning you've done.'

'I hope so. It's really important to me that my flowers do justice to Sofia and Christos's love and the vows they will be taking.'

'Why did you choose to specialise in weddings? I would have thought they are particularly demanding?'

'They are—but I love pushing myself to design something new and unique for each couple and the time pressures involved. People in love are full of wonder and optimism, and they are usually thrilled with the work you do… What better clients could anyone wish for? I had years of my father's hardness and cynicism. I want to do something that's fun and positive now. I want to live in a world where people care about one another, where there is kindness and respect. Does that sound crazy to you?'

He contemplated her words thoughtfully before eventually saying, 'Perhaps, but it's a nice dream. And to me it sounds like you already show a lot of kindness and care towards your siblings.'

'I try to be there for them as much as I can.'

'Is that why you've never travelled alone before?'

'Up to now I could never go without them. We couldn't afford to travel much, but when we did it was all three of us together—sometimes Sofia came too.'

'They call and text you a lot. Do you still feel responsible for them?'

It wasn't something she had thought about before. 'I suppose I do.'

'Maybe you need to let them go a little in order to focus on your own future.'

Everything in Grace recoiled at what he said. She didn't want to talk about this. She had a duty to them.

She pushed away the uneasy thought that he was possibly right.

'It's not as easy as that.'

Grace stood quickly and began to clear their plates. She kept her eyes low, refusing to look at him.

'I didn't mean to upset you.'

She studied him cautiously. 'It's okay.' She eyed him again for a moment before giving a heavy sigh. 'Anyway, you're not the only one who might say the wrong thing sometimes. I'm sorry if my enthusiasm for the wedding is over the top at times. I should realise not everyone is a wedding freak like I am.'

For a moment he considered challenging her on the fact that what he'd said might not be the wrong thing to point out, but her guarded expression told him to back off. So instead he said, with a smile, 'Wedding freak— that's a new term for me.'

She lowered the dishes in her hands to the table again. 'Thank you for your help today.'

Genuine gratitude shone from her eyes and he was taken aback at how good it felt to be appreciated, to know that he had helped. When had he stopped helping others? Closed himself off from the world?

He was thankfully pulled out of the uncomfortable realisation when she spoke again. 'I realise you must be very busy with your work. I'm sorry if I caused any disruption.'

He tipped back in his chair and scratched the back of his head ruefully. 'I must admit that the contents of that last box affected my concentration all afternoon.'

She gave a nervous smile and hurriedly picked up the

dishes again. 'I'm going in to get a sweater. Is it okay if I get some coffee at the same time?'

'Use the kitchen as you wish.'

'Would you like one too?'

He nodded his acceptance and as she walked away he turned in his chair, his eyes sweeping over the sway of her hips, the pertness of her bottom. She had changed when they'd got back from the chapel, into jeans and a close-fitting baby blue tee shirt that showed the curves of her full, high breasts to perfection.

Damn it, but he was deeply attracted to her. He wanted to hold her and feel those soft lips under his, to touch the plumpness of her bottom, run his thumb along the outline of her breasts.

Aman! This was madness.

Grace wanted love and fairy-tale endings. He couldn't give her either. Being burnt in love, humiliated, was an experience he was never going to repeat. Anyway, this woman who had selflessly raised her siblings and opened up to him so honestly tonight, exposing her tender and honourable nature, deserved more than a short, superficial affair.

He glanced at his watch. She had been gone for well over ten minutes. Was everything okay? Had he upset her more than he'd thought?

He stood and walked out of the alcove in which the terrace table sat, heading towards the kitchen.

In the shadows of the curve of the alcove wall he ran straight into her, their bodies colliding hard. She jerked backwards and he grabbed hold of her as she stumbled. She trembled beneath his fingers.

Disquiet coursed through him. 'Are you okay? Has something happened?'

'I'm fine. I just can't find my sweater. I thought I'd left it in the kitchen this morning.'

She spoke in a low, breathless whisper, and he stepped even closer to her and lowered his head. This close, he could feel the heat of her body. The darkness enveloped them, heightening his awareness of her, of the heat of her body, her sweet floral scent, the smoothness of her skin beneath his fingers, the delicate curve of her arm. He wanted to pull her towards him, to feel her body crushed against his.

His voice was ragged when he spoke. 'Eleni probably moved it...you can borrow one of mine instead.'

She swayed slightly towards him, as though she too was overwhelmed by the need to get closer. He leaned forward in response, their bodies doing a private dance in which neither of them had any say.

He heard her inhale, quickly and deeply. 'No. It's fine. I should just go to bed. I'm feeling tired.'

The thought of Grace and bed had him closing his eyes in despair. He should step away. Now. But with her hair still swept up in that ponytail the delicate column of her neck proved too much of a temptation, and his fingers moved up to caress her soft exposed skin.

She gave a tiny moan and arched her neck. 'I really should go to bed.'

'Yes, you should.'

But neither of them moved.

This couldn't go on. If they didn't say goodnight soon he was going to kiss her.

Desire clogged his brain, but he managed to force out some words. 'We need to be careful.'

'Yes, of course.' She said the right thing, but her low, breathless whisper spoke of nothing but attraction and yearning.

Regret seeped into his bones but he forced himself to say, 'We need to remember that we have years of meeting again because of our ties with Christos and Sofia.'

There was a pause as she registered what he was saying. 'Okay.' She inhaled a shaky breath and took a slight step backwards. 'All the more reason why we need to learn to get on.'

'Yes, and not complicate things between us.'

She cleared her throat and stepped even further back. 'That's sensible.'

He forced himself to be blunt. 'I'm not interested in a relationship; I can't offer you anything.'

She jerked ever so slightly, and for a moment a wounded expression flickered in her eyes, pulled at her mouth. But it was quickly replaced with a proud anger.

'I don't want anything from you.'

He took a step back himself and inhaled a deep breath. '*Kalinichta*. Goodnight, Grace.'

For a few seconds she didn't move, but then she gave a quick nod and turned away.

He leaned back against the alcove wall with a groan. Yes, it was sensible not to complicate things. But sometimes *sensible* hadn't a hope in hell of stopping things getting out of control.

CHAPTER FOUR

THE FOLLOWING AFTERNOON, alone in the workshop, Grace's back ached and her stomach constantly rumbled in protest at not having been fed since dawn. But at least now she was working in the silence of siesta time, which was a welcome reprieve after the frantic pace of the morning.

She plucked up some more rosemary and bay stems and wrapped florist's wire around their base to form a neat and fragrant bundle.

Footsteps approached, at first faint, but then she heard that distinctive stride, with its quick double heel tap on every second step. For a moment they faltered outside, but then quickly climbed the stone steps up to the workshop.

She ducked her head and busied herself with another bundle of herbs, cross with the giddy anticipation that exploded in every cell of her body. She was *not* going to blush. She was *not* going to remember how close they had come to kissing last night and how she had later tossed and turned, tormented with images of beads of seawater dripping down over his taut golden stomach and disappearing beneath his turquoise shorts as they had yesterday morning.

'You're alone.'

Dressed in slim light grey trousers and an open-neck

white shirt, his suit jacket thrown over one shoulder, Andreas stood in the doorway, a hand on his narrow hip.

Why did her heart have to go bananas every time she saw him?

'The other florists have returned to Naxos with the wedding team for siesta. They'll be back later this afternoon.'

This was a detail she stupidly hadn't factored into her plans.

She inhaled a deep breath and decided to change the subject. 'You look like you're going somewhere.'

'I'm returning, in fact. I had a lunch date on Naxos.'

Her head shot up as Sofia's description of Andreas's busy love-life echoed. She gave a wobbly smile, her chest weighed down with disappointment. 'I hope it was enjoyable.'

His gaze narrowed and he walked towards her bench. She wound wire around a new bunch of herbs but almost strangled them in the process. When he didn't speak she eventually looked up at him, frustration now singing in her veins, along with a stomach-clenching sense of dejection.

Dark, serious eyes met hers. 'It was with my lawyer.'

'Oh.' Heat exploded in her cheeks.

She exhaled in relief when he walked away, but tensed when he went to stand in front of her project plans and designs for the wedding day, which she had hung on the wall earlier in order to brief the other florists. She should have taken them down again.

His back still to her, he asked, 'Aren't you having a break? Lunch? A siesta?'

The idea of lying in a darkened room with him had her glancing away from the messy sexiness of his hair, from the mesmerising triangle of the broad width of his shoulders and his narrow hips. 'I can't. I'm already hours behind with my timetable.'

He continued to stare at the plans and her stomach did a nervous roll. What if he didn't like them? Goosebumps of vulnerability popped up on her skin.

When he moved she quickly gazed back at the sad-looking herbs and began to unwind the wire. Maybe she'd be able to rescue them; it wasn't their fault, after all, that she had no sense.

He placed his jacket down on the end of the bench. 'Show me what to do.'

No! He couldn't stay. Her already shot nerves couldn't take it. Nor her pride. 'There's no need.'

'One thing you need to learn about me Grace, is that I don't say things lightly. And I don't make an offer twice.'

'That's two things.'

At first he frowned, but then a grin broke on his lips. His eyes danced mischievously, defying her to say no again to his offer.

Oh, what the heck? She needed all the help she could get.

She gestured to the bench behind her. 'I'm working on the garland for the chapel that I measured out last night. At this bench I'm assembling bunches of herbs, which I will then attach to the twine roping.'

She cut a length of the wire and showed him the required length, to which he nodded.

Then she picked up the herbs and said, 'Take three stems each of rosemary and bay and create a bunch by wrapping the wire around the bottom of the stem.'

He messed up the first bunch, tying the wire too loosely, but within a short few minutes he had picked up on the technique needed.

They worked in silence and she forced herself to

breathe normally. Well, as normally as her adrenaline-soaked body would allow. This was all so strange. Andreas Petrakis, one of the most powerful men in Greece, was standing before her, tying bunches of herbs.

'Why are you so nervous?'

'I'm not!'

He gave her a lazy, incredulous stare.

'I'm not nervous—why should I be?'

He gave a light shrug and went back to work.

'I want this to be right for Sofia.'

For a moment she paused as anxiety steamrollered up through her body, blocking her lungs and throat. She swallowed hard to push the anxiety back down into her tummy, where it nowadays permanently resided.

'But, let's face it, most of Greek society are coming to this wedding—along with various well-connected friends of Sofia and Christos from England. If I mess this up I can kiss my career ambitions goodbye. I'll never be taken seriously as a floral designer.'

He gestured towards the long line of sketches and plans on the wall. 'You have this under control. Of course you're not going to mess up. You're worrying unnecessarily—relax a little.'

Tiredness and frustration rolled through her. 'That's easy for you to say, with *your* success and *your* background.'

Taken aback by her own words, she inhaled deeply. Andreas stared at her, clearly annoyed.

She closed her eyes for a second, abhorring her own behaviour. 'I'm sorry, that was uncalled for.'

'Then why say it?'

His tone said he wasn't about to accept her apology quickly.

Embarrassment and a growing sense of panic that she

didn't have things under control had her saying in a rush, 'Because sometimes I feel so damn inadequate.'

For the longest while they stood in silence. His eyes fixed on hers until humiliation had her glancing away.

'Why inadequate?'

His tone was gentle and she gazed back in surprise. Something unlocked in her at the concern in his eyes, and she spoke in a rush, with all the insecurities tied down inside her for so long launching out of her like heat-seeking missiles.

'I left school early...didn't go to university. I'm not from a particularly wealthy background... I don't understand a lot of the nuances of social behaviour with those who are. I've probably bitten off more than I can chew with this wedding. And as I'm also the chief bridesmaid I'll hear directly any unpleasant comments people make about the flowers.'

For a moment she paused, and then she threw up her hands. A sprig of rosemary from the bundle in her hand worked loose and arced through the air. 'I've no idea why I just told you all of that...but, trust me, I know just how pathetic it sounds. There's no need for you to say anything.'

'You're wrong. There's a lot I need to say.'

She blanched at his grave tone. What had she done? Why couldn't she have kept her mouth shut?

'You're a talented and committed florist, and a good friend determined to give her best friend an incredible wedding day. So what if you didn't go to university? You were caring for your family. And, believe me, coming from a wealthy background doesn't guarantee any advantage for getting through life.'

He leaned forward on the workbench and moved closer to her, his eyes swallowing her up.

'Why do you think you're inadequate? Why do you think people would pass comment on the flowers?'

His voice was low and calm. Its quiet strength made her feel even more vulnerable and exposed. She was used to arguments and threats. Not this gentleness.

With a flippant shrug she said, 'Maybe I've been hanging around my father too long.'

'Meaning...?'

She gritted her teeth. 'My father trusts no one—including me. At work and at home he questioned everything I did, every decision I took. When I was younger I tried to stand up to him, but he would only take it out on Matt and Lizzie...grounding them, dragging them from their beds late at night because we hadn't tidied the house to his satisfaction. Calling them a useless waste of space.'

Andreas picked up a bunch of herbs from the table and plucked at the leaves. The sweetness of rosemary infused the air. His tone was anything but sweet when he spoke, 'Was there nowhere you could go? Why did you stay?'

She winced at his questions. Anger and guilt had her saying bitterly, 'Do you honestly think I would have stayed if I'd had a choice? I was *seventeen*, Andreas. I had no money... Even when I started working there was no way I was going to be able to support myself and Matt and Lizzie. I only took the job with my dad because he offered the best pay. Of course it was his way of controlling me, but I thought I would be able to save enough to move out. But rental costs just kept increasing. We have an aunt who lives in Newcastle, in the North of England, but she has her own family to care for. Anyway, Matt and Lizzie loved their school and their friends. I couldn't take them away from all that.'

He leaned even further over the workbench, resting his hand lightly on hers. When she started his hand enclosed hers, preventing her from jerking away. 'I wasn't blaming you. And you need to realise that you're *not* inadequate.'

She gave him a weak smile and tried to pull away, but his grip tightened.

He scrutinised her with a playful but determined focus. 'Say it for me—that you're not inadequate.'

'Andreas, please…'

'*Say* it.'

Though she squirmed and shook her head in exasperation she eventually gave in. 'Okay, I'll say it. I'm…' She cleared her throat as her chest tightened painfully, thick with emotions she didn't understand. 'I'm not inadequate.'

He gave a satisfied nod. His eyes, deep green pools, flickered with gold, held hers, and her heart thumped frantically.

'Shall I tell you what you *are*? *Ise poli glikos*. You are very sweet, you're loyal, determined and kind, and… very beautiful. A woman with an incredible future in front of her.'

They were the nicest words anyone had ever said to her. And she was totally unable to handle them. Flummoxed, she blushed deeply and said quietly, 'I hope so.'

'And you don't need any man or romance to complete you.'

He was wrong. She *did* need love and romance. Only love would ease the gut-wrenching loneliness that was slowly eating away at her. But she could never explain that to a man so against everything she craved.

'Perhaps, but even you have to admit that it would make life a lot more fun.'

He gave her a light look of warning. 'Be careful what you wish for.'

They worked in silence for the next half an hour, the

pile of bunched herbs between them growing ever larger. Grace tried to maintain a veneer of outward calm, but inside she was a turmoil of emotions: disbelief yet toe-tingling pleasure that he had called her beautiful, regret that he was so against love.

In the end he downed tools with a heavy sigh. 'I can't stand here listening to your stomach rumble any longer. I'm going to get you some food.' He paused to grab his jacket and muttered, almost to himself, 'And then I must tackle my best man's speech.'

Once he had left she carried the completed bunches to the other table and began attaching them to the doubled-up rope twine, creating lush foliage into which she would later place peonies encased in water tubes.

Her hands trembled. He was right. She needed food. And she needed her head examined for saying what she had. So much for staying away from each other. The man was in charge of a multinational empire. He didn't have time to be listening to her.

And yet, even though it had been hard to say what she had, it had felt right. It had been strangely freeing to see his absolute acceptance of what she'd said. None of the doubtful looks or the disinterest that had greeted her in the past when she tried to speak to other family members about her problems with her dad.

Later that evening, Andreas cursed when he reviewed the most recent budget estimates for his Cayman Islands development. The delay in planning was costing them dearly. He would have to bang some heads together to get the outstanding issues resolved. A conference call was scheduled for tonight, with all the key stakeholders. The call would not end until he was satisfied that every single issue was ironed out.

He'd need to have his wits about him for the meeting; the local contractor they were partnering with had a habit of promising the world but delivering very little substantive progress. But this damn wedding was sucking away all his usual focus. For the past few hours he'd had the distraction of the wedding planner and her team outside his window, arguing about the positioning of the reception tables. Then Grace had arrived and she and the planner had locked horns over where the flower displays would be positioned.

Grace. He had to stop thinking about her. Why was she getting under his skin so much? Earlier, she had spoken with such searing honesty he had wanted to take her in his arms and hold her. He was losing his mind.

He propped his elbows on the desk and with his eyes closed massaged his temples. His neck felt like a steel rod.

He made a low groan at the base of his throat when memories of last night returned. Her light floral scent... her skin soft and inviting when he had cradled her neck... What would it be like to trail his hand down further, unbutton her blouse, touch the enticing swell of her high and rounded breasts?

'Are you meditating or asleep?'

He leapt in his seat and let out a curse.

Grace gave a much too sexy giggle in response to his shock.

His disorientation became even more intense when he realised she was freshly showered, her hair still damp, tied up into a messy knot. She had changed into a short-sleeved denim dress that stopped a few inches above her knee and had enticing buttons running the length of it. The top three buttons were undone to reveal the cleavage he had just been fantasising about.

He had allowed physical attraction to override his common sense once before; he wouldn't let it happen again. He would need to keep this conversation short and snappy.

He leaned back in his chair. 'Neither. I was cursing whoever decided that speeches at weddings were a good idea.'

'Have you finished it?'

To that he gave a light laugh, but inside his stomach recoiled. He gestured to the paperwork piled on his desk. 'I need to deal with this first.' He didn't bother to mention his many failed attempts at writing a speech over the past few weeks.

'The wedding is in two days' time—shouldn't you start?'

'I'll get around to it at some point. If I have to, I'll just wing it on the day.'

'You can't *wing it*!'

'Why not?'

'Are you kidding me? With *your* views on love and marriage, you might well say something totally inappropriate.' She paused and shook her head frantically, her hands flying upwards in disbelief. 'Like offering your condolences rather than congratulations. The best man's speech is too important—you can't just *wing it*.'

'Grace, I've presented to thousands at industry conferences worldwide, in a multitude of languages. I think I can handle a wedding speech.'

'Have you given one before?'

'Several times.'

She eyed him for a few seconds. 'Were they before your divorce?'

'What if they were?'

'Well, I'm guessing that your views might be very different now.'

He knew only too well that they were. 'Look, I'm busy now, but I'll pull something together later tonight or tomorrow.'

At that, Grace walked over to his desk and from behind her back brought forward a book, which she dropped onto a set of architectural drawings for a new office block in Melbourne.

He picked it up. She had to be joking. 'Are you being serious? *The Best Man's Survival Manual.*'

She gave him a triumphant smile. 'The wedding planner gave it to me. Apparently she always carries one for emergencies.'

He threw her a disparaging glance. 'The next time I meet with the team at the disaster recovery charity I sponsor, I'll have to check that they carry one at all times.'

She gave him an even brighter smile. 'Hah, very funny. Now, how about I help you pull it together?'

He gestured once again to his desk. 'I'm busy. And I have an urgent conference call in two hours I need to prepare for.'

'Twenty minutes—no more. I promise.'

'Grace, I have to warn you I'm on to you, I overheard your conversation with the wedding planner earlier. I know your technique. You're not going to wear me down by refusing to go away.'

'I'm not!'

She was, but now was not the time to get into that argument. He wanted to get back to his work. 'Why are you doing this?' he asked.

Her laughter died and she sat down on the seat opposite his desk. The indigo denim made her violet eyes shine brighter than ever. 'You helped me with the flowers—I'd like to help you in return.'

'I don't need help.'

'Fine. Wing your speech for me now, and if it's up to scratch then I'll leave you alone.'

He knew she wasn't going to leave without a fight—and anyway he never had been able to resist a dare.

He flew through his introduction and then launched into some witty anecdotes about Christos, one of which even had Grace snorting with laughter. But then he dried up. And died spectacularly. He didn't know what else to say. How could he celebrate marriage and love when he didn't believe in either?

He glanced at Grace and then away again—away from the sympathy in her eyes.

'I shouldn't have agreed to be best man.'

'I think it's admirable that you did. It means the world to Christos.'

Guilt churned inside him. He couldn't let Christos down. But right now he wanted to forget the speech, in fact forget the whole wedding.

With a raised eyebrow he deftly changed the subject. 'Christos rang earlier. Sofia and he are delighted we're getting on so well.'

To that she gave a guilty smile. 'Sofia rang me last night. What was I going to say? That you're against the wedding…? That I'm way behind with the flowers? That we disagree on just about everything?'

'Not everything. Apparently you think I'm hot.'

It took a few seconds for Grace to compute what Andreas had just said. 'What? *No!* Oh, I'm going to kill Sofia when she gets here. We were just messing around on the phone… She kept asking me what I thought of you. I only said it as a joke, to get her off my back. She's always trying to set me up with unsuitable guys.'

He sat back in his chair and folded his arms. 'So I'm unsuitable now?'

'Of course you are. You don't believe in love, commitment, marriage. Need I go on?'

'Hey, but I'm hot—what more do you need?'

Oh, this was excruciating—especially as part of her agreed with him. But if she was going to remain sane for the next few days she couldn't go there.

'It was a joke.' For a second she pressed the palm of her hand against the raging heat on her cheeks. Time to change the subject. 'Back to the speech. Twenty minutes and we'll pull it together. Are you on?'

He considered her for a while and she willed him not to move the conversation back to whether she thought he was hot or not. At first a grin played at the corners of his mouth, but then he cleared his throat, contemplated the messy pile of paper on his desk and shook his head wryly. 'You've been here ten minutes already—you have ten minutes left.'

'Fine. Okay, it was a great start, but now you need to praise Sofia and then finish on your hopes for them as a couple. Let's focus on the last point first: your hopes for them. What *do* you wish for them?'

'I don't know...to be happy-ever-after?'

'Too much of a cliché. Think harder.'

Andreas gave her an exasperated stare and stood up. He walked to the window overlooking the terrace and the Aegean beyond. He rolled his shoulders before he turned to her.

'I spent my lunchtime with my lawyer, agreeing to pay off my ex who's now claiming rights to this island.'

She fidgeted in her seat when his eyes bored into her.

'I could have fought her in the courts, but that would have stopped me giving Christos his wedding present: ownership of half of this island. So forgive me for being a little cynical about marriage. Right now I'm not in the mood to think of anything other than romantic clichés, even knowing that they are unrealistic and unobtainable and the preserve of dreamers.'

Bewildered by the sudden change in his mood, she stood and walked towards him. 'Is that a dig at me?'

Irritation fired in his eyes. 'No, but you can take it as one if you want.'

They stared at each other, angry and frustrated, breathing heavily...and then their anger turned from annoyance to a simmering heat, and the atmosphere in the room grew thick with want and desire.

He crossed the few steps that separated them and yanked her into his arms, muttering words she didn't understand. Her body collided with his and before she could react his mouth was on hers. A hand on the back of her neck held her prisoner, while the other wrapped tight around her waist. For a brief second she tried to pull away, but then she became lost in the heady sensation of his mouth on hers, the intoxicating sweep of his tongue, the pleasure of his hand caressing her back. She wrapped her arms about his neck, deepening the kiss, her body instinctively moving against his hardness.

But then he suddenly pulled away and stepped back, and she stood there, dazed, her lips bruised, her body aching.

He ran a hand through his hair, his jaw flexed tight. 'I'm sorry. That wasn't a good idea.'

No man should be able to kiss like that. Her thoughts

ran in several directions all at once, bringing little sense. Why had he kissed her? What must he be like in bed if his kisses were so scorching? Why? Why? *Why?*

'Are you still in love with your ex?'

'What?'

He glared at her as though it was the most insane question ever, but to her it was the only thing that made sense of his anger and cynical views.

'Is that why you were so upset about the divorce?'

'No, I'm not still in love with my ex. And I'm not upset about my divorce—I'm angry about it.'

'Why?'

'Because I was blind for much too long as to how incompatible my ex and I were.'

'Incompatible in what way?'

'My ex wanted very different things in life to me. She only pretended to want what I did in order to marry me. She was more attracted to what I had than who I was.'

'You mean she married you for your money?'

'Yes. And I was too foolish to see it. Within weeks she was refusing to live here on the island, to spend time with my family. Her social life in Athens was more important.'

'Did you love her when you got married?'

His jaw worked, and he inhaled a deep breath before meeting her eye. 'At the time I thought it was love, but I came to realise that I'd mistaken physical attraction and passion for love.'

'Oh.' Every square inch of her skin was scarlet at this point. She should leave. 'I'm sorry.'

'Don't be sorry. Just learn from it… Love and marriage can be hell on earth.'

'God, Andreas, don't for one second think that I don't know that. I spent my entire childhood witnessing my dad's toxic take on marriage. I know there are bad marriages. But I also know there are wonderful ones. Sofia's parents' marriage, my grandparents'... Now Christos and Sofia's. Marriages that are loving partnerships of trust and respect. Marriages that aren't about judgement and criticism.'

'How can you be so idealistic?'

'Because I believe in love—that the right man is out there for me.'

'Waiting to whisk you away.'

'Yes. And I don't care if you think it's idealistic. To me it's a very real dream. I want a life partner. I want love. I want a man who thinks I'm the coolest thing ever. And I'm not going to settle for anything else.'

She could see a hundred thoughts flickering in the depths of his eyes: puzzlement, incredulity, a hint of tenderness. But then he walked back to his desk, shaking his head. Once he had sat down, he checked his watch.

'Our twenty minutes is up.' The sternness in his voice was matched by the harsh expression on his face; the faint scar above his eyebrow was once again more visible as he frowned. A scar to match the toughness in his soul...

A toughness she would have to feign herself. 'So it is. If you want any further help let me know. And for what it's worth I think you should remember how you felt about love prior to your marriage and include that in your speech.'

When he gave a noncommittal shrug and turned his attention back to his computer screen, she inhaled a deep breath.

'The pre-wedding dinner tomorrow night in Athens...?' she asked.

'My helicopter will collect us at five.'

Grace left the room and walked back towards the

workshops, her heart thumping in her chest. That kiss…
That kiss had been wonderful and sexy…and it had
landed her in a whole heap of trouble.

CHAPTER FIVE

THE FOLLOWING DAY raucous noise spilt through the villa: shouts from the kitchen, the sound of hammering out on the terrace. Andreas sent a final few emails to his office in Athens and shut down his computer; there was little point in trying to get any work done in this mayhem. Anyway, he had worked until three in the morning, resolving the Cayman Islands issues—he needed a break... And, okay, he'd admit it to himself: he wanted to see Grace.

Outside, a crew were fixing lights on to the temporary stage that had been erected on the terrace the day before. He hadn't seen Grace all day, and knew he had no business going in search of her now. It was asking for trouble. But kissing her last night had been unbelievable. For the first time in ages he had lost himself totally in the physical joy of holding a woman, tasting her rather than mentally working out what it was she wanted from him.

He approached the workshops with an eagerness that confounded but exhilarated him. Inside, he felt his enthusiasm waver when two strangers stared back at him. When they finally found their voices one of the women told him that Grace was down on the jetty, helping with the unloading of more supplies. Frustration that she was not alone had him turning abruptly away.

Back outside, he spotted her—lost amongst the potted trees crowding the jetty, which now resembled a small forest. The delivery boat was out in the harbour, sailing back towards Naxos.

As he neared the jetty Grace came towards him unsteadily, carrying one of the potted trees. He went to take it from her but she drew back.

'It's fine—it's not as heavy as it looks; the planter is made from lightweight fibreglass.'

She kept on walking and he called to her. 'Where are you taking it?'

She stopped at the end of the jetty and dropped the white sugar-cube-shaped planter down. 'I want to place the planters and the storm lamps at intervals between here and the chapel.'

Andreas glanced back at the endless planters and storm lamps crowding the jetty. 'Have you any help?'

She rushed back down the jetty and picked up another planter. 'The other florists are finishing off the final prep work and will come and help in a little while.'

She was all business, and barely gave him a glance. He tried not to let it get to him.

'If you take care of the storm lamps, I'll position the planters,' he said.

For a moment she hesitated, as though she was about to refuse his offer, but then she gave a brief nod.

'Thank you.' Picking up the two nearest storm lanterns, she rushed off the jetty, saying, 'The planters were supposed to be delivered this morning but have only just arrived. The other florists have to leave by five as they have to prepare the flowers for another wedding on Naxos tomorrow.'

In silence they worked together: Grace dropping the

storm lamps ten metres apart and he placing the planters in between.

As they moved up onto the path, where it cut along the cliff towards the chapel, her silence and her habit of rushing away from him at every opportunity put him further and further on edge.

They walked back towards the jetty again and he could take no more. He called to her as she walked in front of him. 'Is everything okay?'

She kept on walking, but through the thin material of her pale pink tee shirt he saw her shoulders tense.

'If it's about last night, I apologise.'

She stopped abruptly and swung around to him. 'Apologise?'

'For kissing you. I didn't mean to upset you.'

'You didn't upset me, but it can't happen again.'

She said it with such certainty he was sorely tempted to take her in his arms and test her resolve. But she was right. They were playing with fire.

For the next trip back up the cliff-face Grace insisted on carrying a planter, as she was now way ahead with laying the lanterns. The other florists had joined them, and it had been agreed that he and Grace would carry the planters out as far as the chapel and work backwards from there.

Again silence fell between them. The planter balanced on her hip, she walked before him. He tried hard not to stare at how her cut-off faded denim shorts showed the perfection of her bottom.

He caught up with her when she stopped to move the planter from one hip to the other. Her eyes scanned along the coastline and then she briefly closed her eyes and lifted her face to the afternoon sun.

When she opened her eyes she said quietly, 'Why have

you decided to give Christos half the island? It's incredibly generous.'

'Not generous; just the right thing to do. My uncle should have left it to us both, but he was too stubborn.'

'What happened?'

He gestured for them to continue walking. For a while he didn't speak as an internal argument raged inside him.

Don't answer. You need to distance yourself from her.

But I want to explain. I want her to understand some of the mess that is my life. Why we will never share the same dreams for the future.

'When my grandfather died the family business was left to my father and this island to my uncle. My father has very traditional ideas and he believed that Kasas should also have been left to him as the eldest son. The two brothers fought and didn't speak for years. My father forbade us ever to speak to our uncle again; he wasn't pleased when I disobeyed him. Christos was about to follow my lead, but he gave in when my mother pleaded with him not to do so. For my loyalty, my uncle decided to leave the island to me.'

'But that wasn't fair on Christos.'

'I know. My uncle, usually calm and logical about everything, simply refused to listen to reason. He was a proud man, and in his eyes Christos had chosen my father over him; chosen to side with my father's greed.'

She shifted the planter back to her other hip before asking, 'And now? How do you get on with your father?'

He gave a chortle at the hint of caution in her voice. 'I take it that he left an impression on you when you met him at the engagement party?'

She shrugged uncertainly. 'He likes to speak his mind.'

That was the understatement of the year. His father was opinionated and brash on a good day. His father's angry words about the dishonour brought to the family name echoed in his mind. His grip on the planter tightened as anger and guilt swirled in his chest.

'It's not the easiest of relationships; we're very different. When I was younger I tried to work in the family business, but my father is almost impossible to work with. He'd refuse to delegate authority, question every decision and often reverse them. When all the issues blew up over the inheritance I left.'

'Do you ever regret that?'

'For the upset it caused my mother? Yes. But otherwise, no. I've succeeded on my own terms. Even if at times I've paid the price.'

Grace slowed her pace. 'What do you mean?'

The turmoil and self-doubt of the past few years came back to him in sharp relief. 'The global recession hit my company hard.'

'And succeeding on your own... Was that to prove to him just how capable you are? That you don't need him to be successful?'

'I guess we have that in common...'

She nodded, and for a moment their eyes connected.

'It's not easy, hating a person you love—is it?' he asked.

She came to a stop and readjusted the planter in her hands. At first she frowned, but then she gave a small exhalation of breath. 'I never thought of it like that; but that's exactly how I feel. There's so much I hate about my father's behaviour, but deep down a part of me—reluctant as it is—loves him. I don't understand it, and it would be so much easier if I didn't... Love is such a strange thing, isn't it?'

'Strange, dangerous and unpredictable.'

Her lips pursed and she shook her head crossly. 'Some-

times, but for most it's the one true wonder of being
alive.'

Aman! Had she no sense? 'Still dreaming of your
prince and happy-ever-after?'

A storm brewed in her violet eyes and her lips drew
into a firm line. She glared at him. 'Yes—and when he
comes along I'll send you a postcard.'

With that she flounced away and he followed, amusement tugging at his lips even while he tried to ignore the
jealousy curling in his stomach at the thought of her with
another man.

The chapel was close now, but the planter was starting to weigh heavily in his arms. In a few long strides he
caught up with her. 'Do you want to stop for a break?'

Despite the sheen of perspiration on her skin, she
shook her head defiantly. 'No.'

'You're persistent, aren't you?'

She stared at him belligerently. 'You sound surprised.
Why wouldn't I be?'

He gave a light shrug. 'Most of the women I know
aren't too keen on hard physical work.'

'From what I hear, you don't hang around long enough
to find out. Maybe those women have a lot more going
for them than you give them credit for.' With that she
stalked away, and dropped the first planter at the bottom
of the chapel terrace.

He dumped his ten metres away. 'So what do you suggest? That I stay and give them all hope of a relationship?'

'No, because you're obviously incapable of having
one. I don't want any women getting hurt. But maybe
you shouldn't make assumptions about them.'

How sheltered a life had she lived? She'd obviously
had the good fortune never to encounter the sycophants
he had. 'Are you *really* that innocent, Grace?'

Those violet eyes flared with anger. 'You know what, Andreas? Maybe I am. But I prefer to see the good in human nature.'

Those photographs he had been sent two years ago had shown him the truth about human nature.

With a bitter taste in his mouth, he answered, 'And *that's* where we will always differ.'

Why had someone so beautiful on the outside but so cynical at heart been sent into her life? The gods were truly having a laugh at her expense.

Grace twisted away from him, her blood boiling. She was tired and hungry, stressed about tomorrow, and plagued with an attraction to the six-foot-two, dark and sexy sceptic walking behind her.

If only it was that straightforward.

Though she hated to admit it, and even though Andreas was so disparaging about love and the motives of women, at his core he was a good man. He'd shown care towards her on numerous occasions; he clearly loved his family despite the differences between him and his father. It was as if he wore his scepticism as an armour.

But she had meant it when she'd said that she would never try to change a man. She wanted a man to fall in love with her with no games involved—no persuasion, no pretending she was something she wasn't. More than anything she wanted a relationship based on honesty and respect.

Her phone rang in her pocket and, pulling it out, she answered Matt's call, glad to have a distraction from the pain lancing through at the memory that her mum hadn't even bothered to leave a note when she had walked out on them.

Though Matt professed that nothing was wrong, and

that he'd just called to say hi, she immediately knew he
was upset. With Matt she always had to draw him out
gradually. They were back at the chapel with the next set
of planters when she finally hung up on the call.

She dropped her planter onto the path and was about
to pass Andreas when he placed a hand on her arm.

His eyes soft and concerned, he stepped closer. His
hand moved up to lie gently on her upper arm. 'Are you
okay? You seem tired?'

She wanted to say no, she wasn't okay. That she wanted
him to hold her. To tell her everything would be okay.
That Matt and Lizzie would do well in life. That tomorrow was going to be okay.

Instead she glanced at the time on her phone and then
towards the jetty and the remaining planters. 'I'm not
going to be able to go to the pre-wedding reception tonight... I still have so much to do.'

'Ioannis will be back from Naxos soon. He can take
over the positioning of the planters.'

'It's not just the planters. I have a lot of other prep
work that needs to be completed. Sofia is arriving here
at eleven tomorrow, and I want to spend time with her.
I need to have all the flowers ready in the workshop by
then, for the local florists to position just before the ceremony begins.'

'I'll stay and help.'

'No! Absolutely not.'

But before she knew what was happening Andreas was
on his phone. He spoke in Greek, but she understood his
greeting to Christos.

Wearing denim jeans and a white polo shirt, now
smeared with earth from the planters, he stood watching her as he spoke, his dark hair glistening under the

sun, his voice a low and rapid flow of passionate sounds incomprehensible to her.

Her insides melted as his eyes roamed up and down her body. Something dark and dangerous was building in them as the call continued.

When he'd hung up, he gestured for them to start walking again. 'I spoke to Christos and explained that you were tied up with preparations. He told Sofia and she asked him to send her love. They both insisted that I should stay and help. And they agreed that I should take you out to dinner later.'

'They did not!'

'Call them if you don't believe me.'

He was calling her bluff. Well, she'd show him. 'Fine— I will.'

A few minutes later she hung up on her call to Sofia. Though disappointed that Grace would miss tonight, Sofia had been more concerned that Grace was putting herself under too much pressure. And, though Sofia had tried her best to disguise it, Grace had heard the fear in her voice that the flowers mightn't be ready for tomorrow.

After spending an age reassuring Sofia that she had everything under control, Grace hadn't even bothered to get into an argument about Andreas staying on with her.

'Apparently dinner was your idea?'

He didn't even have the decency to look abashed. 'You can't visit the Cyclades and not see some of the other islands.'

Dinner was *so* not going to happen. 'I won't be finished until very late.'

'How late?'

She deliberately adopted a look of grave consideration. 'Oh, at least eleven.'

He gave a smile that was much too smug for her liking.

'That's not a problem—we eat late here in Greece.' With that Andreas picked up his phone again and spoke briefly in Greek.

When they got back to the jetty, he steered her away and back towards the villa.

She gestured to the pots still on the jetty. 'We need to finish the planters.'

'You need a break first.'

He led her down onto one of the lower terraces built into the cliff-face, where a tray of food was awaiting them on a rattan dining table. Despite herself, Grace sank down onto the plump cream cushions of a rattan chair with a sigh, welcoming the shade provided by the raised parasol at the centre of the table.

Andreas poured some homemade lemonade for them both and uncovered a basket of bread and a selection of dips. Another basket held a selection of freshly baked pastries.

Grace greedily gulped the lemonade, only now realising just how thirsty she was.

'Why do you push yourself so hard?'

She lowered her glass to the table. 'I don't think I do...but I grew up with my dad's exacting standards. I suppose I'm still trying to meet those in some way. But, also, I want to deliver the best service that I can. I take my commitments and responsibilities very seriously.'

Andreas leaned forward and broke a bread roll in two. He handed a piece to her. 'Including your responsibilities to your brother and sister?'

'Yes.'

He regarded her thoughtfully. 'Why?'

She busied herself with breaking her roll into smaller pieces. 'When my mum left they had no one else. They were children. They needed someone to care for them.'

'How did it affect them?'

'Matt went quiet and barely spoke for a year...'

Grace stopped for a moment as memories caused her throat to thicken painfully. An unaccountable emotional force shifted around in her chest, as though it was searching for a way out. And suddenly she needed to tell him it all, so that he would understand why her heart had broken every single day in the year after her mum left.

'He used to get up early every morning...' She met Andreas's eye and then gazed away. 'He'd get up to wash his sheets. I used to have to pretend that I didn't notice the load in the tumble drier. I thought Lizzie was coping—she seemed her usual bubbly self—but then one day I was cleaning her bedroom and found that she was hoarding food...which accounted for her clothes not fitting any longer.'

'I'm sorry.'

She forced herself to shrug. 'It was tough, but now we're really close because of having gone through it together—so I guess some good has come from it all.'

'Do you miss them?'

Unexpected tears sprang to her eyes at his question and, perplexed by their suddenness and the powerful loneliness rolling through her, she took a while before she managed to speak. 'I miss them terribly. I miss our little family. I miss being loved.'

'They still love you.'

The gaping hole inside her widened at his words. How would he react if she told him just how desperate she was to be in love? To find companionship and security, fun and exhilaration?

'I know...but it's not the same when we're apart. And Lizzie's dating now. They're both moving on.'

'Do you ever see your mum now?'

Her heart lurched at his question. 'No. At first I was mad as hell with her and refused to, but after a while I came to understand why she'd left... After years of putting up with my father, it was kind of understandable. But by then we had drifted apart from her—to have got back in contact would have been like opening an old wound.' She gave him a wobbly smile and stood. 'Anyway, we don't have time for this now. I'd better get back to work.'

Andreas stood and walked towards her. Next thing she knew she was in his arms, being given the biggest bear hug of her life. His arms wrapped around her and he lowered his chin onto the top of her head. His arm blocked her eyes so that she was in a cocoon of darkness. She inhaled his scent, a mixture of lemon and fresh salty perspiration, so earthy and male she felt dizzy with the desire to lift his tee shirt and press her nose against his damp skin.

For a moment every worry, every painful memory disappeared as she was held in his protective embrace. Her rigid body slowly melted against him and she gave a little sigh. He drew back and smiled down at her.

Dazed, she hoped her eyes weren't rolling in her head. 'You give a very good hug.'

His thumb ran the length of her cheek. 'I'm here any time you need one.'

For a moment they both smiled at each other, but then she pulled away. She was in serious danger of feeling things she could not afford to for a man intent on never having love in his life.

As they walked back to the workshops Andreas wondered what was happening to him. He didn't hold women like that, want to protect them, wipe out every painful memory for them.

Beside him, Grace gave a contented sigh. 'I haven't travelled to many countries, but Kasas Island has to be the most beautiful place in the world.'

Something dormant in him stirred at her words. When had he stopped enjoying this island? Stopped taking the time to relax in its simple pleasures? For the past two years he had driven himself relentlessly at work, and the island had become a refuge rather than a place he truly enjoyed.

But then a warning bell sounded in his brain. How often had his ex claimed the same?

'You'd tire of it once the novelty wore off.'

She stopped dead and stared at him. 'No, I wouldn't.' She cocked her head to the side. 'You don't believe me, do you?'

Why was he standing here arguing with her? He started to walk away. 'It doesn't matter.'

She caught up with him and pulled him to a stop. 'It might not matter to you, but I'm fed up with the fact that you don't trust me, Andreas. You constantly pull back from telling me about yourself. You'll go so far and then the shutters go down as though you don't trust me. You look at me as though you don't believe what I say. What have I done that makes you think I'm untrustworthy?'

'Come on, Grace, I barely know you.'

'You know me well enough to kiss me senseless.'

She stared at him so indignantly he could not help but smile. 'I kissed you *senseless*?'

Her eyes narrowed and she stamped a foot on the path. 'Wrong phrase—ignore it. Now, are you going to answer my question?'

He took a step closer, his shadow falling over her. He lowered his head and inhaled her scent, his voice automatically turning into a low baritone. 'I have a question for you first: can I kiss you?'

Her violet eyes shadowed and her cheeks flushed deeply. 'I... Not until you promise me that you're going to start trusting me. That you don't think I'm lying to you or that I want anything from you.'

'You drive a hard bargain.'

'You have to mean it. I'm trusting you not to pretend, not to lie to me.'

He drew back, paralysed with indecision. Could he honestly tell her that he trusted her? His stomach was a knot, his heart a time bomb ready to explode. Others might lie, but that was anathema to him. He could just walk away now—go back to the way his life had been a few short days ago. But, gazing deep into her eyes, he realised that he didn't want to this to end—not yet—and that he believed he *could* trust her.

'I trust you.'

She gave him a solemn smile, and when he ran his hand along her cheek she leaned into it.

And then he walked away.

CHAPTER SIX

GRACE STOOD ON the path, dumbstruck. What had happened to their kiss?

She chased after him. 'Did I just miss something?'

He stopped by the steps up to the workshops, his expression sombre. 'You said you wanted to trust in me. Which means that you'll trust me to look out for you, not to hurt you. With that being the case, there's no way that I can kiss you—because, frankly, I don't know where it could lead.'

He was right. Of course he was. She just wished she didn't feel so upset at the prospect of all this being over so quickly. That their kiss last night had been the end of the line for them.

'My helicopter will be here to collect us at eleven. I'll help Ioannis with the remaining planters. What else can we do to help you?'

His businesslike attitude pulled her up short. She needed to start focusing on the wedding.

'The candles need to be placed inside the lanterns...' She paused and gave him a pleading smile. 'And two white ribbons need to be tied to each of the bay trees.'

He inhaled a deep breath. 'If you *dare* tell Christos that I was tying ribbons you'll be in big trouble.'

He looked so hacked off she couldn't help but giggle. And once she started she couldn't stop, because he was studying her so incredulously. But eventually he too laughed, his laughter coming from deep inside him was highly infectious, which only caused Grace to start her 'hiccupping hyena' impression, as Sofia so charmingly called it. He stopped and stared at her, clearly surprised, but then he laughed even harder.

When their laughter eventually petered out he shook his head and eyed her with amusement. 'You do crazy things to me, Grace Chapman.'

With that he walked away, and she stared after him, knowing, despite their differences, that she had never felt so in tune with another person in all her life.

Later that night Grace ran towards the villa. She had fifteen minutes to get ready. Not enough time to wash her hair. *Just great.* She was going out for dinner with the sexiest man she had ever met with unwashed hair and make-up slapped on. But then maybe it was for the best. Maybe he would take one look at her and the attraction between them would wilt.

She took a quick shower and whilst dragging a towel over her body in order to dry herself hopped from one foot to the other in front of the wardrobe, trying to decide what to wear. Would the cocktail dress she had bought especially for the pre-wedding reception tonight be too over the top? Send the wrong message? But all her other clothes were too casual.

She yanked the dress from the wardrobe and pulled it on. Five minutes to go. Quickly she applied some foundation and cream eyeshadow, a rose-pink gloss on her lips. She tied her hair back into a ponytail. A quick spritz of perfume and she was out through the door.

Andreas was waiting for her by the patio doors in the living room, staring out onto the terrace.

She came to an abrupt stop beside him. 'Ready?'

He stood back and his eyes trailed slowly down over her body. He cleared his throat before he spoke. 'You look incredible.'

All evening she had firmly reminded herself that to get involved with Andreas would be a major mistake. Past experience had taught her the awful pain of having someone walk away from her—which undoubtedly *would* happen should she get entangled with this oh-so-gorgeous playboy. This was just a cordial dinner between...

Between what? She had no idea how to define their relationship, but maybe 'friends' was the most suitable description. But how was she supposed to deal with the heat in his eyes and the pull of desire coiling within her?

She gave him a quick smile. 'Thank you...and you don't look half bad yourself.' Which was the understatement of the year. He was freshly showered, and his damp hair was tamer than usual, which emphasised the impossible height of his cheekbones, the green brilliance of his eyes. His dark navy suit fitted him to perfection, the snow-white shirt open at the neck highlighting the golden tones of his skin. She would never get to touch him, to trace her fingers over his skin, to feel the hard muscle underneath...

'Why are you carrying your sandals?'

She tore her eyes away from him and dangled her stiletto heels to swing between them. 'There's no way I'll climb the hill to the helicopter wearing *these* bad boys.'

His gaze travelled downwards and her French polished toes curled when his gaze remained at her feet. When he eventually looked back up there was a new tension to his jaw.

'Your feet will get dirty. Put them on and you can hold my arm—I'll help you to the helicopter.'

Grace sat on the side of a sofa and bent over to place her feet in the sandals. The sandals were new, and she struggled to fasten the strap, the metal bar refusing to go into the tiny eyelet pierced in the dark navy leather strap. She gritted her teeth and pushed as hard as she could, while her hip bone screamed at the awkward position she was leaning over in.

'Sit back and I'll try.'

Before she had time to protest Andreas was crouched down before her. He gently lifted her foot and balanced it on his thigh. She bit down on the dual temptations fighting within her: to pull away—his touch was way too much for a woman already on a knife-edge of temptation—or sigh so loudly she would be heard over on Naxos.

When he was done, he stood up and held his hand out to her. For a moment she hesitated. More than ever this evening seemed like a thoroughly bad idea.

As though reading her mind, Andreas said, 'We're going out for dinner and a little fun—nothing serious.'

Three days ago she had closed the door to her minuscule apartment in Bristol, full of dreams for the future, hoping for excitement. Well, boy, had she got it—in a bucket full. And although she knew she was dancing with danger maybe, just for tonight, she could embrace this crazy scenario and relish being in the company of this utterly gorgeous man.

He was going to have a heart attack. Grace's dress was too much. A mid-thigh-length navy lace wrap dress, embellished with sequins, it was far too short and far too figure-hugging. Way too much flesh was revealed in the deep scoop that ended at the tip of the valley between her breasts. And what was *really* driving his pulse berserk was the knowledge that with a simple tug of the satin ribbon sitting at her waist it would come undone.

How was he supposed to act like a gentleman tonight when she was wearing that?

Next to him in the helicopter, she folded one leg over the other, and he groaned inwardly at the sight of her toned thighs. Thin straps of dark navy leather crisscrossed her foot, which dangled provocatively in front of him, and a jolt of unwanted desire barged through him. Earlier, as he had buckled her sandal, his fingers had trailed against the smooth skin of her slender ankle and he'd had to battle hard against the urge to keep trailing his fingers upwards.

Her words this afternoon that she wanted to trust in him came back to taunt him. He couldn't abuse that trust. He couldn't seduce her as he so desperately wanted to do. Grace believed in love and romance, in happy-ever-after; he had to respect everything she wanted even if the tension of attraction and desire between them was so thick right now he could almost punch it. He had to keep this light and fun—keep the conversation neutral.

'Did you finish all the prep work?'

She gave him a bright grin of relief. 'Yes. All the major displays are finished. I just have to complete the bouquets in the morning.' She puffed out her cheeks. 'I can't believe Sofia's getting married tomorrow; it's all happened so quickly. I need to start getting my head around my chief bridesmaid's duties. Talking of which—have you completed your speech?'

He shifted in his seat. 'Almost.'

She gave him a knowing look. 'Can I help in any way?'

He didn't want to talk about the speech—his ongoing nemesis for reasons he didn't fully understand. 'No, I plan on finishing it tomorrow morning. Christos and my parents aren't arriving until lunchtime.'

For a moment she paused and worried at her lip, doubt clouding her eyes. 'How do you feel about the wedding now?'

Ambivalent was the word that best summed up how he felt about tomorrow…and it was something he didn't want to overthink. Right now he just wanted to pretend it wasn't happening.

'If you're worried that I might object to the vows, or share my views on relationships in my speech, don't worry. I promise to be the perfect best man tomorrow.'

At first she beamed with relief, but then her face clouded with tension. She glanced at him, and then away, and then her eyes darted back to him. 'Do you think the flowers will be okay?'

The fear in her eyes was so sudden and intense his heart jolted. He twisted fully in his seat and placed a hand on hers. 'Grace, I know nothing about flowers. I've been to endless weddings, even my own, and didn't notice them. But even I can see how spectacular yours are. After tomorrow you'll be turning away bookings.'

Her eyes shone with gratitude. 'Thank you.'

The helicopter began to hover down towards the restaurant, which sat high on a clifftop on Santorini Island. Once it had landed Andreas helped Grace out, and as they neared the building the heavy beat of music greeted them.

Friday night was party night at the Ice Cocktail Bar and Restaurant.

He had to lean low, so that Grace could hear him above the music. 'How about we get a cocktail to start and then eat?'

The bar was busy, and as usual the central floor space

had become a dance floor. The music was a fast constant beat, energetic and sensual.

He glanced down when Grace's hand touched against his arm. She reached up to shout in his ear.

'This bar is amazing... I've never seen so many people enjoying themselves so much.'

Her breath tickled his ear. Desire gripped him hard and he had the sudden urge to turn around and lead her somewhere quiet. He bit down on the temptation and taking her hand in his, led her through the throng.

As usual his friend Georgios, Ice's owner, was sitting in the far corner. When Georgios saw him approach he jumped up and the two men embraced. After Andreas had introduced Grace, Georgios insisted they take his seats and promised to return with two of the house specials.

They attempted to have a conversation, but the music was too loud, so they sat sipping their gin and ginger cocktails, watching the dancers out on the dance floor, their movement so carefree and joyful it was addictive. His heartbeat pounded in time with the music, and when Grace moved beside him, her thigh grazing against his, he turned to her.

Her eyes were bright, her skin flushed, and she leaned towards him, a slow smile breaking on her lips. 'Do you want to dance?'

Sense and caution went out of the window at her question, which had been asked in a low voice, whispered against his ear.

He stood and removed his jacket and led her out on to the dance floor, pulling her into the centre of the action.

Her arms reached upwards and her body swayed to the music, her head thrown back. Strobe lights flashed over her tilted face, highlighting the plumpness of her glossy lips, the sultry look in her eyes. The light danced on the sequins of her sexy dress, and the thought of pulling that ribbon and revealing what lay beneath sent firecrackers of desire through his system.

For a few seconds he watched her, trying to resist the inevitable, but then he reached out and pulled her towards him, his hands on her waist, and together their bodies dipped and swayed, their eyes never leaving one another.

Lithe, and with perfect timing, Andreas held her to him, his body lightly controlling her movements. She was on fire. It was all wrong. But right now she didn't care. It felt too good. She felt alive and young and carefree.

Through his shirt her fingers touched against the taut bulk of his biceps. His hips moved against hers and an ache grew in her belly. His hand moved up from her waist and for a brief moment his thumb ran along the side of her breast. She gave him a brief smile and he smiled back, his eyes darkening.

The ache in her belly spread outwards and her breasts grew tight and sensitive. The hard muscles of his thighs pushed against hers, and then he shifted her so that one of her legs was in between his. The ache spread even further, until all her insides felt hollow.

His hands moved around to her back. One held her at the waist while the other splayed downwards, touching the sensitive point at the bottom of her spine. She arched even further into him, her breath catching as his hip bone pushed against her.

She stared at the smooth line of his freshly shaved jaw, fighting the desire to trace her lips against the warm skin. His hard body and his scent of lemons with an undertone of spice tugged her under, into a world where no one but he existed.

Much too quickly the music came to an end. For a brief moment his lips swooped down and he planted a hot kiss on her exposed collarbone. He led her off the dance floor, dazed, and she was unable to wipe the grin from her mouth.

When they reached their seats she sat down, but Andreas remained standing. He took his phone from his back trouser pocket and his brow furrowed when he checked the screen. He pointed at it, and then out to the outside terrace. She nodded and waved towards him, telling him that it was okay for him to go and make a call.

When he was gone an involuntary shiver ran through her body. She was definitely dancing with danger. And she didn't know if she was going to be able to stop.

Andreas sat at a table out on the terrace to return his missed call from Christos. Unlike the other customers, who were all facing outwards towards the spectacle of the night sky, he faced back into the bar, where he had the perfect view of Grace, sitting in front of a low window.

His fear that something was wrong was immediately put to rest when Christos assured him that he was just calling to check that everything was in place for tomorrow. With a jolt Andreas realised that his usually laid-back brother was nervous—*very* nervous, in fact. Guilt pricked against his skin. Yes, he had fulfilled his best man duties so far—including organising a bachelor party last week in Athens—but had he really been there for Christos?

When he thought of the calls Grace shared with Matt and Lizzie, full of warmth and genuine concern and interest, he realised how amiss he had been—both recently and in the past few years. Three days ago he had had no idea that the hopeless romantic he had rescued at the airport would cause him to pause and take stock of his own life.

He deliberately went through a detailed breakdown with Christos, of everything the planner and Grace had done for tomorrow, and then ran through the itinerary for the day again. But as he spoke he got increasingly distracted. A man had approached Grace. He sat down beside her—much too close for Andreas's liking. What was he playing at? And why the hell was she smiling back at him, being so friendly?

Jealous fire raged through his veins. But then Grace turned around and pointed at him. The other man gave him an uncertain smile and backed off. Unbelievably, twice more this happened during the course of his conversation with Christos, before he was able to end the call.

Grace smiled up in relief when Andreas returned. The call had been much longer than she'd expected and she was hungry...for food *and* his company.

His earlier ease was gone, though. His expression was tense, and his eyes barely reached hers.

'Our table is ready in the restaurant.'

She followed him out on to the terrace and then down stone steps to a lower level terrace. Their table was next to a glass balustrade which gave unending views out on to the Aegean and to the lights of the towns to the west. The whole terrace was awash with candles on white tabletops and storm lanterns on the white concrete floors.

Andreas recommended the house special, lobster spaghetti, which they both ordered—along with a bottle of the local *assyrtiko* white wine.

Throughout the ordering process Andreas seemed distracted, and once their waiter had left she asked, 'Is everything okay?'

'Do you usually get so much attention when you're out?'

Perplexed, she sat back into the cushions of her chair. 'What do you mean?'

'When I was on my call several men approached you.'

'So?'

Cold eyes challenged hers. 'Why?'

She recoiled for a moment, at the cynicism in his voice, but then she sat forward and challenged him back. 'Why did they approach me? Oh, come on, Andreas, why are you asking me that? We both know why... They wanted to buy me a drink but I said no, that I was waiting for you.'

He made no response, but kept on staring at her sceptically.

Anger and disappointment collided within her and she said bitterly, 'A few hours ago you said you trusted me. Were you lying?'

He still said nothing, and she knew this night was over.

She placed her napkin on her plate. 'I don't feel hungry any longer. I want to go back to Kasas.'

She went to move, but his hand snapped around her wrist. His eyes were furious, but also shadowed with confusion.

'Why did you refuse their drinks...? It's not as if we are a couple.'

She jerked back in shock. 'Are you angry that I refused? Did you want me to accept?'

He shook his head vigorously. 'Of course not... But there was nothing stopping you, so why didn't you?'

Totally bewildered, she answered, 'Because I'm with *you*. Yes, we might not be a couple, but we *are* out together...why would I accept a drink from another man?'

'To play mind games with me—to make me jealous.'

Frustration surged through her. 'Good God, what do you take me for? I'm not that type of person. I don't play games. I don't hurt other people.'

For a while he stared at her, his jaw flexing. His mouth became a tight grimace. 'I'm sorry. That was uncalled for.'

His remorse looked genuine, but he had some explaining to do and she wasn't going to let him off the hook. 'If you're sorry, prove it to me. Explain what the last fifteen minutes has been about.'

A waiter arrived with their food, but Andreas spoke to him in Greek and the waiter walked away with the plates.

'I told him we weren't ready and that we'd order again when we are.'

She nodded and waited for him to speak.

His hand rubbed against his cheek and then ran up into his hair, messing it up just the way she loved. Oh, why was she so attracted to this man who had *heartbreaker* written all over him?

Andreas felt sick to his stomach. He had behaved abominably. Grace deserved an explanation. But the thought of recounting the past was tearing him apart. His sense of self, his certainty of who he was, felt as unstable as the flickering flames on the candles at the centre of their table.

'Two years ago I received a blackmail threat. A member of the paparazzi had photos of my wife making love to another man on his yacht.'

Grace's hand moved towards his but he pulled away. He didn't want her pity. They sat in silence and eventually he gazed towards her. There wasn't pity in her eyes, but anger. He frowned, and she answered his unspoken question.

'I hope you reported him to the police and told *her* exactly what you thought of her. How could she have done that to you?'

Thrown by her outraged disbelief, he paused, unable to find an answer. Her outrage almost made him want to smile. Grace was a fierce protector; no wonder she'd taken on the task of protecting her siblings.

'How could I have married her, more like.' The exact question his father had shouted at him, accusing him of bringing dishonour into the family.

'What happened between you, Andreas...? Why did she do something so awful?'

'When I confronted her she said she was lonely, that she hated living on Kasas, and the amount of travel I did.'

'It doesn't sound like you believed her.'

'I was away because the recession had taken hold.' Inhaling a deep breath, he arched his neck back and stared briefly up into the night sky; the stars seemed impossibly far away. 'My businesses were struggling in the worldwide property crash, but I knew that, even though it was high risk, it was my opportunity to radically extend my asset base—which would firmly secure the future of the company. I travelled the world, persuading investment firms to finance my property deals. Unfortunately my ex did not agree with my expansion plans, nor the risks involved—and nor the way it curtailed our cash flow. So she had an affair with a man who could provide her with the lifestyle she had expected when we married—a man I had considered a friend.'

Grace considered him nervously and shuffled in her seat before saying, 'You're a shrewd guy...'

'So why didn't I know what she was like when we

married? Because I believed her flattery.' His throat burning, he paused and then admitted, 'I trusted her at a time when I was trying to deal with my uncle's death and the fight with my father that was causing me to lose my family.'

'And you thought *she* could be your new family?'

She spoke so softly and with such emotion he felt the humiliation that had carried him through the conversation to this point evaporate. Only regret remained. 'Yes.'

'And your friend?'

A bitter taste grew in his mouth. 'He knows to stay out of my way.'

Her eyes trailed above his left eyebrow. 'That scar…'

'He came off much worse.'

The flicker of a grimace crossed her face for a moment. 'I'm sorry, Andreas. I'm sorry she caused you so much pain. Your friend too. I can't think of anything worse than being betrayed like that.'

'It taught me a valuable lesson: that I can never again believe I truly know another person.'

She moved forward, passion burning in her eyes. 'No, I don't agree. The timing of your marriage was terrible— you were grieving for your uncle. I think in normal circumstances most of us *can* know another person, even if it's just a gut instinct about them.'

'People wear masks—they tell you what they think you want to hear.'

'Let's put it to the test. How about me? Do you think I would cheat on a partner? On my husband?'

'How would I know?'

'Would I cheat, Andreas? Yes or no?'

Every fibre of his body knew that she wouldn't. But it was hard to admit that his long-held views were wrong—

that in a few short days this woman had turned so many of them upside down.

He inhaled a deep breath and said tersely, 'No.'

'You're right. I wouldn't. Because when I marry it will be for love and because I respect my husband. I want a hundred per cent honesty and trust in a relationship. I will never lie, never play games… My marriage will be too important to me to ever even contemplate compromising it.'

'Your husband will be a very lucky man.'

She gave him a rueful smile. 'I just need to meet him.'

Something hard kicked inside him at the thought of her married to another man. His mind jumped ahead to her leaving Kasas, leaving *him*. 'When are you leaving?'

She tapped a fingernail on the bottom of her fork before she gazed up with a sad smile. 'Monday.'

'Two more days.'

Her smile faded.

His heart began to pound. Could he let her go? Could a brief passionate kiss be all that they ever shared?

CHAPTER SEVEN

LATER THAT NIGHT, back on Kasas, Grace's heart did a funny little jump of delight when Andreas held her hand all the way from the helipad down to the villa.

When they entered the living room, the silence that had been with them for the entire journey home from Santorini continued to bounce between them. It was a silence born from the intensity of the connection they had shared tonight—a connection of emotional honesty.

Andreas opening up about his marriage had changed everything. He had let her into his world, trusted her. He had reached out to her. And she wasn't sure what to do with the emotional chasm that sat in her heart as a result. A chasm full of hunger to connect with him even further. To know him to the depths of his very being. A hunger to express her feelings towards him.

The chasm had her wanting to reach out to him, but she didn't know how. She was scared she would do the wrong thing. Her old self-doubts sat like a cloak on her shoulders.

'Would you like a drink?'

Uncertainty had her dithering for an embarrassing few seconds before she said, 'I think I should go to bed. It's almost two and I have to be up early. Thank you for a lovely night.'

His eyes searched hers for a moment before he nodded. But as she turned away he said, 'Wait. I have something I want to give to you.'

He disappeared upstairs and, intrigued, Grace waited on the edge of the sofa where he had earlier fastened her sandals, a shiver running through her body when she remembered the tender touch of his hands on her ankle.

When he returned, he reached out and said, 'Give me your hand and close your eyes.'

'What are you up to?'

'Just close your eyes. You'll see in a few minutes.'

Grace held out her hand cautiously, and it was just as well that he had told her to close her eyes as she did so anyway, involuntarily, when his fingers held her hand. His thumb stroked down the sensitive skin of her inner wrist. Goosebumps ran the length of her body.

In a low voice that had her jerking forward with a need to close the distance between them he said, 'I was going to give this to you tomorrow, but...'

'But what?'

'We'll probably both be too busy.'

His fingernails lightly grazed against her skin and she giggled. 'That tickles. What *are* you doing?'

'Sit still. You wriggling like that isn't helping.'

Grace inhaled a deep breath and tried to ignore his fingertips stroking her wrist, the way that simple touch was setting her alight, making her yearn for more.

And then her body stilled, although her heart exploded in her chest as a sudden realisation hit home: the empty ache of loneliness that had been her constant companion for so many years was gone. With Andreas she felt whole, somehow. Safe and protected. Understood.

Panic flared inside her. She needed to see him. *Now*. 'I want to open my eyes.'

'In a few seconds.'

His fingers continued to dance on her wrist and she had to squeeze her eyes to stop the burning temptation to fling them open and drink him in. They had so little time left together.

'Now open them.'

On her silver bracelet sat a new charm—an intricate violet flower, its purple-blue design sitting between the miniature flower clippers and the violin that Matt and Lizzie had given her last Christmas. She wore the bracelet as a constant reminder of them; it felt right that Andreas's charm sat with theirs.

She ran a fingertip over the exquisite design. 'It's so pretty…thank you. Why a violet?'

He gazed down at the charm. 'Because it symbolises courage and intelligence.'

She couldn't stifle her giggle. 'You just made that up! And anyway, it symbolises modesty.'

His brows knitted together in consternation. 'Does it?' He gave her a sheepish look. 'I definitely didn't buy it for that reason.'

His expression grew serious and he leaned over to touch the flower charm, his finger briefly brushing against her skin, sending every nerve-ending into a tailspin of desire.

'I bought it to thank you on behalf of my family for everything you've done to make tomorrow special.' His fingers stilled on her wrist. His voice grew deeper. 'And because it's the same incredible colour as your eyes.'

She stood up, her body shaking with the intensity of the emotions surging through her. It couldn't end like this. She couldn't walk away from him without being true to herself.

Her heart raced even faster, and though her stomach

churned she forced herself to speak. 'Stay with me to-night.'

Shock replaced the earlier heat in his eyes. 'What?'

Had she misread this whole situation? But she had seen how he had stared at her all night, felt how he had held her in the bar when they danced.

A deep blush flashed on her cheeks and she went to leave.

He stood in her way. 'Hold on—where are you going?'

She shook her head but kept it dipped down, too mortified to look him in the eye.

'You can't ask a man to stay the night and then run away before he even has the opportunity to reply.'

Humiliation had her answering sharply, 'Your expression was enough of an answer.'

'*Aman*, Grace! The sweetest, sexiest woman I have ever encountered has just asked me to stay the night and we both know that I should say no.'

He thought she was sweet and sexy... But he was saying no. So she was lacking somehow. Was it the gulf between them career and wealth-wise? Their different backgrounds? Or was it that she simply wasn't attractive enough?

Hurt and humiliation twisted in her chest. 'Let's just forget this conversation ever happened.'

He ran a hand through his hair and a groan came from somewhere deep within him. 'Trust me—I would like nothing more than to spend the night with you. But I can't. I'm not what you're looking for, Grace.'

'Not in the long term, no...'

'You're playing with fire.'

She shook her head vigorously. She knew what she was doing. She had never been more certain of anything in all of her life.

'No, for the first time in many years I'm listening to what I really want.'

She paused, wishing she was brave enough to say everything that needed to be said. That she wanted fun and passion. Wanted to feel as physically close to him as she did emotionally. She searched for words, but everything seemed either too brash or needy.

And before she was able to find the right words Andreas stepped aside, his expression sombre.

'*Kalinichta*…goodnight, Grace.'

Grace's footsteps disappeared along the upstairs corridor and Andreas sank onto the sofa, tiredly dragging his hands over his face.

Turning Grace down had been one of the hardest things he had ever done.

What had he even been *thinking*? A gorgeous woman had invited him into her bed and he had said no!

But there were so many compelling reasons for doing so. The future they would share as part of Christos and Sofia's lives. The future Grace wanted. Her tender, soft heart. So many logical and reasonable arguments for staying the hell away from her.

Why, then, was he sitting here with regret storming through his veins, angry at the recognition that the past two years he had been living a lie, pretending he was content in his life?

Three short days with Grace had shown him just how empty his life really was. Three days in which he had developed a bond with this woman such as he had never had before. A bond of understanding and trust.

He raked his hands through his hair. If he had the energy he would get up and pour himself a brandy. But telling Grace about his failed marriage had hollowed him

out, He felt spent. However, it had also brought a light
ness, the lifting of a burden he had carried on his own
all this time. Her anger and understanding had touched
him deeply. It had lifted some of his doubts and guilt. It
had shown him that integrity *did* exist.

He respected everything Grace stood for. With her,
there were none of the dramatics of his marriage, which
had emotionally and physically drained him. Grace instead was intuitive and supportive.

And physically she drove him to despair.

Tonight, when they'd danced, her body had moved
against his like a siren call. Her eyes had held a sexy
promise, her mouth the whisper of endless pleasure.

They were both adults. Deeply attracted to one another. Why *shouldn't* they act on it if they were both clear
on what the future held?

He stood and made for the stairs.

Grace scrubbed at her teeth, her back to the bathroom
mirror. She couldn't bear to see the angry blush that still
marred her cheeks.

How on earth was she going to face Andreas in the
morning?

A knock sounded on her bedroom door and she leapt
in surprise. It could only be one person. She turned and
stared into the mirror. What was she going to do?

Her pride yelled at her to ignore him. He had made his
position clear. She didn't need any further humiliation.

A second knock tapped on the door...slow and patient...like a man confident she would answer.

On the third knock she stalked to the door and yanked
it open. 'Andreas, I'm trying to sleep, to—'

He didn't give her an opportunity to finish her sentence. He marched into the room, shutting the door be-

hind him, and forced her back against the wall. Only inches separated them. He reached out an arm and his palm landed on the wall to the side of her head. He loomed over her, his face taut, his body pulsating with frustrated desire.

His dark eyes devoured hers. 'Did you mean it when you asked me to stay the night with you?'

She tried to answer but his gaze moved down her body and her words were swept away.

'Did you mean it?' His words were a low growl.

'Yes.'

'I can't offer you anything, Grace. We have no future together.'

She ignored the way her stomach flinched at his reminder and looked him solidly in the eye. 'I know.'

His hand reached out and sat on her waist. Slowly he drew her forward until their bodies met. She waited for his kiss, but instead he stayed gazing down at her, his hands following a torturously slow path around her body, sending jolts of pleasure to her core.

He lowered his head and kissed the tender spot at the back of her ear. She gave a low groan.

'You're every man's dream…' He paused to trail kisses along her neck. 'Beautiful, sexy, great legs…' His fingers played with the strings of her pajama vest top for a tantalising moment. 'You smell like a summertime garden in the heat of the midday sun…'

His trail of kisses moved upwards, his stubble dragging lightly across her skin, yet another reminder of his forceful maleness. His mouth hovered over hers.

'And you have the most gorgeous kissable lips.'

With that, he began a slow exploration of her lips that had Grace moaning, her fingers digging into the hard muscle of his shoulders, desperate for him to deepen it.

She was close to tears when he did eventually deepen their kiss, and without warning he lifted her up and wrapped her legs around his waist. Still kissing her, he walked to her bed and together they fell down, Grace crying out in pleasure to feel his weight upon her.

The following morning Andreas woke suddenly, when the bed shuddered hard and banged against the wall.

'Oh, that hurts…ouch…my knee…' At the foot of the bed Grace hobbled on the tiled floor, quietly muttering some low expletives.

'Are you okay?'

She jumped when he spoke, and whispered, 'Sorry, I didn't mean to wake you. I couldn't see in the dark and whacked my knee against the bedpost.'

Andreas sat up further in the bed and switched on the bedside lamp. They both turned away from its glare. A hand over his eyes, he asked, 'Why are you dressed? It's still dark.'

'I need to make a start on the bouquets and finish off the other prep work.'

'What time is it?'

'Five.'

'*Five!* We didn't go to bed until two…to sleep before at least four. You can't function on less than an hour's sleep.'

She reached down and massaged her knee. 'I'll be okay. I have to go.'

The anxiety in her eyes told him that she wasn't going to listen to reason. He would have to resort to other tactics.

'Fine. But not until you come here and give me a kiss.'

She pondered his request with a frown, but then walked over and dropped a quick kiss on to his cheek.

She went to move away but he wrapped his arms

around her and pulled her down onto the bed. He rolled her over him and wrapped his legs around hers, holding her prisoner. She glared at him and he gave a small chortle.

'What are you doing?' Her voice was a breathless low whisper. She pushed against him, but already desire was flooding her eyes.

His fingers dipped beneath her sweatshirt and into the waistband of her jeans. Her body jerked against his.

'Grace Chapman, were you just about to leave without even saying goodbye?'

'No!'

'You're not a very convincing liar.'

'I told you—I have to get to the flowers.'

'And *I* say that you need some sleep. So, whether you want to or not, you're staying here with me.'

She pushed hard against him.

He shook his head. 'You'll have to try harder than that.'

For a moment she considered him. But then she nodded her acceptance and he felt her body relax into him. He gave a low groan when her hand reached round and stroked along his spine. Her mouth, hot and warm, trailed kisses on his chest. Every cell in his body stirred.

His eyes closed of their own volition and he murmured into her hair, 'You're not playing fair. We're supposed to sleep.'

Her hand moved to his belly. His eyes popped open. He inhaled deeply when she gave him a dark, sultry look. He untangled himself from her and flipped onto his back, already lost to her touch. But while he was turning Grace flipped around too—and hopped out of the bed.

He caught her just as she was about to make for the door. He pulled her back into the bed beside him and wrapped his arms around her. 'That was a dirty trick if ever I saw one.'

At first she smiled, with a look of guilty conscience, but then the smile faded, to be replaced by a troubled expression. 'Andreas, please.'

His gut tightened. He ran his fingers lightly against her cheek. 'What's the matter?'

'I'm worried the flowers aren't right. That I've forgotten something.'

'The flowers are perfect. And with your military-style planning you can't possibly have forgotten anything. The most important thing now is that you get some sleep.'

Her breath floated against his skin in broken anxious waves. 'When I woke earlier it suddenly hit me that the wedding is *today*. I don't feel ready.'

He held her tighter to him. A hand gently stroking her hair, he whispered, 'Everything's going to be okay. Sleep until seven. Then I'll come and help you with the prep work.'

She arched back and her violet eyes searched his. 'Are you sure?'

'That I want to be a florist's assistant? No. But I'll do it for you.'

To that she gave a small smile. 'Really?'

'Yes, really.'

They stayed locked together in that position for the longest while, staring into each other's eyes. Her lips lifted into a breathtaking grin and she whispered, 'Thank you.'

A surge of protective desire tore through him, so strong he was momentarily stunned. He kissed her, deeply and intensely, and she responded in turn. They kissed as though their lives depended on it. He ripped her clothes from her. His head spun at the feel of her soft round curves again and he inhaled her scent.

He went to flip her onto her back, but she fought against him. She pushed *him* back onto the bed instead, and when they joined together he stared up into those violet eyes and his heart cracked open at the sight of the honest passion and warmth in her endless gaze.

Grace woke later to the sound of her name being called softly, a hand stroking her hair. She opened her eyes lazily and found Andreas crouched down beside her at the side of the bed. Freshly showered, he wore nothing but a towel wrapped around his waist. He was so delicious she gave him a crooked smile. He smiled back, those green eyes flecked with gold and dancing with…contentment?

'It's six-fifty.'

She gave a lazy nod, her body languid.

'Take a shower and I'll get breakfast ready.'

She swallowed against a dry throat. 'Thanks, but I need to go straight down to the workshop. I won't have anything.'

He raised an eyebrow to that. She thought he was about to argue, but then he gave a small shrug. 'Fine, I'll go and get dressed in my room. I'll join you at the workshop in a little while.'

As he walked towards the door she had a sudden impulse to shout out, to tell him not to go. Not to leave her.

On shaky legs she made her way to the bathroom. Soon afterwards she stood under a scalding shower, her mind racing as her body gave up constant reminders of the intensity of her night with Andreas. A night full of passion and tender moments.

Her head dipped when she remembered that she would be leaving in two days. The hot water battered her neck.

She gritted her teeth and clamped down on all thoughts of the future. It was futile. Sofia and the wedding needed her full attention today.

Ten minutes later she hesitated by the terrace door. She should leave immediately for the workshop, but the rich aroma of coffee and the draw of seeing Andreas again pulled her in the direction of the kitchen instead.

Barefoot, he wore navy shorts and a pale pink polo shirt, his back to her. She hovered at the door, weak with sexual attraction. She longed to go and run her hands through his damp hair, to tousle it, kiss that warm mouth, feel the pulse of his body when he pushed against her.

He turned with a lazy grin and beckoned her over to the breakfast counter. Her legs went weak.

'I should go to the workshop.'

'Come here. Now.'

It was lightly said, but the fire in his eyes told her it was an order—not a request.

When she reached him his hands landed on the waistband of her jeans, just above her hip bones.

'*Kalimera*...good morning.'

Her insides melted at the low, sensual tone of his voice. He lifted her up to sit on the countertop.

As weak as water, her resistance was only a low gasp. 'What are you doing?'

He gave her a wicked smile and, with one hand remaining on her knee, stood between her legs and reached along the countertop. He pulled a bowl towards them. He dipped a spoon into the bowl and brought up a spoonful of sinfully creamy Greek yogurt and glistening golden honey.

'I'm going to feed you. You have a busy day ahead of you...' He paused and a mischievous glint danced in his eyes. 'And you just had an exceptionally intense night.'

His eyes stayed glued to her mouth when she opened it, the tip of her tongue nervously running along her upper lip. She opened her mouth even wider and squirmed on the countertop as an explosion of tart yogurt and sweet honey hit her palette, but a groan of pleasure managed to escape.

'That tastes *so* good.'

Andreas dropped the bowl to the countertop. *'Thee mou!'* He pulled her towards him, wrapping her legs around his waist.

His mouth tasted of freshly ground coffee, warm and safe. His kiss, at first light and playful, deepened as his hands reached under her sweater and moved up along her spine, around to dance on her ribcage and then over the lace of her bra.

He broke away and spoke against her hair. 'This is impossible.'

She could only agree. With him, she lost all sense. Forgot everything she'd said she wanted in life.

'I know...'

He pulled back and traced his thumb along her cheek, his eyes sombre but tender. 'We need to be careful today.'

She moved to the side and hopped off the countertop. 'Of course.'

'We don't want anyone jumping to the wrong conclusion about our relationship.'

He was right—but that didn't stop her heart plummeting to the floor. She busied herself pouring a cup of coffee from the cafetière. 'Absolutely. Last night was a one-off. I think we should just leave it at that.'

When he didn't respond she glanced in his direction. His arms crossed on his chest, he asked, 'Are you saying that you don't want anything else to happen between us?'

'Aren't you?'

'When you leave on Monday where are you travelling to?'

Uncertain as to why their conversation had taken this direction, she frowned before she answered. 'I'm taking a ferry to Chania, in Crete. There's a renowned wedding florist based there; I'm taking a two-day course at his school next week.'

'Crete is a beautiful island...you will have a lovely time there.'

She had to act nonchalant, pretend that this conversation was *not* leaving her floundering as to how Andreas felt about her.

'I was planning on returning to England towards the end of next week, in time for Matt finishing his exams, but I've decided to stay a little while longer.'

She had listened to what he had said about not feeling overly responsible for her siblings. It was time that she started to let them go and began building her own life in earnest.

She sipped some coffee and glanced at him. He was staring at her, deep in thought.

She should go, but an innate reluctance to leave him had her struggling for something else to say.

'How do you feel about today?' He frowned, and she tried to ease the tension between them with a joke. 'Are you *nervous*?'

He inhaled deeply. 'What do you think?'

Of course he was. Her joke backfiring, she gave him a tight smile. Could she have been more insensitive? After everything he'd told her last night.

'Sorry...of course you are.'

He nodded and poured himself some more coffee.

'I'd better go and start on the bouquets, or at this rate Sofia will have none.'

He glanced at her briefly. 'I'll join you in a little while to help.'

His tone was distracted, with no hint that they had spent the night in each other's arms, sharing a connection so deep that her heart had felt as if it was going to explode with the need to blurt out everything he meant to her.

CHAPTER EIGHT

WITH SOFIA SURROUNDED by the make-up and hair team, Grace slipped out of the bedroom they had taken over in the villa, telling Sofia's mum that she needed to do one final check on the flowers.

She ran all the way down to the workshop. Inside, the room was empty except for the centrepieces and the displays for the reception. While the wedding ceremony was taking place the local florists would take care of positioning them. The centrepieces were even more of a success than she had hoped. Andreas's uncle's porcelain vases emphasised the delicate beauty of the peonies and lisianthus.

Back outside, Grace ran towards the chapel, passing alongside the bay trees and lanterns elegantly lining the path. She smiled at the ribbons floating in the light breeze, but then a dart of pain shot through her heart. *Their time alone was over.* She pushed that thought away. The wedding guests would be arriving in less than half an hour. She needed to make sure all the flowers looked perfect.

As she approached the chapel her heart sank. The floral displays lined the red-carpeted aisle, sitting at intervals between the rows of white wooden seats. But the florists were still attaching the garland to the frame of the entrance to the chapel, and the garland for the bell tower still sat to one side of the terrace.

She rushed forward to help them and together they finished the door garland. At the same time Grace ran through with them the checklist of all the other jobs that were to be done. When she came to the corsages and boutonnières, the two women studied her blankly.

Grace closed her eyes for a second. *She had forgotten to arrange for them to be delivered to the bride's and groom's parties.* The guests would be here soon, and Christos and Andreas would need to be down at the jetty to greet them.

She raced back to the workshop, praying that the carefully constructed cascading curls the hairdresser had created, twisted into a half-knot at the base of her neck and topped with a spray of lisianthus, wouldn't fall apart.

In the workshop she grabbed the corsages and boutonnières and sprinted back to the villa. She heard loud voices coming from the formal sitting room. She gave a light knock and entered.

Christos was surrounded by at least ten friends, all larking about as Andreas helped him into his tuxedo jacket. They all turned as she entered, smiling at her curiously. She went to turn away, certain she had made a faux pas in her intrusion on this male domain, but Andreas's mother—beautiful and elegant in a powder-blue knee-length dress—suddenly appeared, and with an exclamation of delight gave Grace a warm hug.

'*Kalosìrthes!* Welcome, Grace! How lovely to see you again.'

Over his mother's shoulder she briefly caught Andreas's eye before he resumed buttoning Christos's jacket. Her throat closed over at the sight of the intimacy between the two brothers, and when she pulled away from the floral cloud of his mother's perfume she bent to rearrange the boutonnières, desperate to hide the tears filming her eyes. What on earth would his mother think if she saw them?

There was a lot of good-natured jostling between Christos and his friends. Despite his mum's welcome Grace hovered on the outside of the group, awkward and unsure. She understood why Andreas was staying removed from her, in his desire to hide the truth of their relationship, but part of her longed for him to show some form of acknowledgement, some warmth towards her.

His father approached, pouring champagne into a flute, which he forcibly handed to her. 'You are just in time. I'm about to make a toast.' He twisted around and held his glass up high. 'To Christos and Sofia. May they have a *long* and happy marriage.'

A loud cheer went up from the other men and they all moved in to hug Christos, their affection and friendship for the groom clear. Her eyes darted to Andreas as he stepped out of the friendly jostling. His tight expression told her that he too had heard his father's heavy emphasis on *long*.

'Aren't these flowers so pretty? Grace, you've done a fantastic job.'

His mother fussed around her, and Grace instantly knew that she was accustomed to deflecting any potential arguments.

A laughing Christos extracted himself from the group long enough to draw her into a hug. 'Yes, thank you for all your work.' His eyes glinting, he asked, 'What did Sofia say when she saw the flowers?'

Earlier Grace had taken Sofia to the workshop to show her the flowers. Sofia had burst into tears, and a horrified Grace had thought it was because she didn't like them, but Sofia had assured her it was because they all were so beautiful. The bridal bouquet—a hand-tied spiral cloud of pale pink Sarah Bernhardt and ivory Duchesse de Nemours peonies, finished off with a long length of silver-grey ribbon—now sat in pride of place on the bridal suite's dressing table, along with her own smaller version made with the Sarah Bernhardt.

Grace had never seen Sofia as worked up as she was today. And the last thing an already nervous-looking Christos needed was to know that his albeit deliriously happy bride had been shaking like a leaf all morning.

'She loved them and she can't wait to see you.'

Christos gave a grin of relief which grew into a wide megawatt beam: the gorgeous smile of a man in love. Grace had to walk away for fear that tears would fill her eyes again at witnessing this real-life romantic tale unfolding before her.

She took a sip of champagne and dared a glance at Andreas, who had come to stand next to Christos. Both he and Christos were wearing beautifully tailored tuxedos, crisp white dress shirts and black silk ties. They both looked gorgeous...but when she glanced at Andreas memories of last night had her weak-kneed with desire.

He was staring in the direction of the other men, who had moved over to a table of food at the opposite side of the room. But her instinct told her he was attuned to everything she was doing—as though he was on tenterhooks about her letting slip the truth about what they had shared over the past few days.

Flustered, and feeling too hot, she placed her champagne flute next to the flowers on the coffee table. 'I'd better get back to Sofia.'

'Stay and help us fix the boutonnières,' his mother

said, picking up one of the sprays. 'When Andreas got married I couldn't get them to sit properly.'

Then, as though realising what she had said, his mother glanced towards Andreas and then his father in alarm. Christos threw a worried glance at Andreas, who stood rigid, still, tight-lipped.

His father bristled and in a low voice said irritably, 'I thought we'd agreed not to discuss that wedding?'

Grace picked up his mother's corsage and turned her back to the men. Much taller than Mrs Petrakis, she fixed the single ivory-white peony backed with two sprigs of lisianthus to her powder-blue dress and gave her a sympathetic smile. She smiled back at Grace gratefully, blinking hard at the tears in her eyes. Eyes the same green burnished with gold as Andreas's... Though finished, Grace deliberately fussed with the corsage a while longer, until Mrs Petrakis touched her arm gently and nodded that she was okay.

Next Grace attached a boutonnière to Christos's lapel. She gave him a cheeky smile. 'You look incredibly handsome today.'

Christos smiled back in delight. And then he lowered his head and said, for her ears only, 'I'll take good care of her.'

Tears instantly filled Grace's eyes at his tender but heartfelt promise, and for a few seconds she wondered if she would ever meet a man who would be so keen and happy to marry *her*.

She busied herself with selecting the next boutonnière, and then steeled herself to approach Andreas's dad. He glanced down at her briefly, and then looked away. Though not quite as tall as Andreas, Mr Petrakis exuded the same power and strength as his oldest son.

Her fingers fumbled with the catch of the pin and she could feel his impatience growing.

To distract him, but also in a bid not to allow herself to be intimidated by him, she stood up tall and looked him in the eye. She pretended to speak to the four of them as a group, but her gaze remained on his father. 'I'm afraid that I've been a nuisance to Andreas over the past few days, but to his credit he has been courteous and generous at all times. You should be incredibly proud of him.'

Mr Petrakis glared at her impatiently. 'Of *course* we're proud of him.'

Behind her she heard Andreas give a disbelieving laugh. And as she picked up the final boutonniere, Christos chortled and said, 'My brother? Courteous? Who knew? You're mellowing in your old age, Andreas!' Christos threw an arm around Andreas's shoulder. 'But you're right, Grace, about him being generous—he always has been.' Christos looked directly at Andreas. 'Thanks for hosting the wedding.'

Behind her, Mr Petrakis cleared his throat noisily. 'I still don't understand why you wanted it *here*. It would have been so much easier in Athens, rather than dragging everyone out into the middle of the Aegean.'

Andreas's jaw tightened. In an instant Grace wanted to stand up for him. 'I think the majority of people would *love* to marry on this island—it has to be the most romantic place I've ever been. I'd happily stay here for the rest of my life.'

Flustered at the eyebrows rising around her, and the prospect of placing a boutonnière on Andreas's lapel, Grace walked towards him and, thoroughly distracted, said to Christos as she passed him by, 'You must be pleased with Andreas's wedding present?'

Christos stared at her, confused. 'What present?'

Panic soared through her veins and she looked at Andreas in alarm. His jaw had tightened even more, and irritation flared in his eyes.

'I'll tell you later. It was to be a surprise.'

Grace hesitated in front of him. She swallowed hard as a deep blush fired on her cheeks. She gazed up at him and mouthed, *I'm sorry.*

He gave an almost imperceptible shake of his head before looking away. The double lilac lisianthus was perfect against the black of his suit, but her fingers trembled so much she was worried that she'd never actually manage to pin it on. Her head spun from embarrassment, and the effect of standing so close to him. It reminded her of how good it had been to have those arms around her, being free to inhale his scent all night long, the way his body had dominated hers, the sensuality of his lips, his mouth...

Behind her, his father said, 'Well, if Grace knows about the present, then I think there can be no reason why *we* shouldn't.'

Grace froze. Beneath her fingers Andreas's chest swelled as he inhaled a deep breath. She pulled away just as he spoke, his tone sharp.

'Later.' He checked his watch and turned to Christos. 'We should go down to the jetty—the first boats will be arriving soon.' As though to punctuate his words, the sound of a helicopter overhead reverberated through the air.

His father walked towards the door. 'I'll go and greet the guests coming by helicopter.'

All the men disappeared from the room. Grace tried to ignore the way his mother was studying her and quickly made her excuses and left the room too.

She climbed the stairs and stood outside the bridal

suite for a while, inhaling some deep breaths. How could the man who had looked at her with such impersonal detachment just now be the same man who had made passionate love to her last night? Had whispered private words of endearment.

He had made her feel as though she was the centre of his universe, but right now she felt as if she had been cast out of his world.

Beside him Christos jigged nervously as they waited for Sofia to arrive. The late-afternoon sun was dipping low behind them, casting shadows on the terrace. In front of them Grace's flowers looked like giant balls of marshmallow—the perfect romantic finishing touch to what even *he* had to admit was an incredible wedding venue.

His skin itched even at the thought.

He took a glance backwards to check for Sofia's arrival and caught his father's eye. Since he had arrived a few hours earlier his father had once again managed to push his every button. The same old grievances about how overworked he was and how lucky his friends were to have sons who gladly took over the family business. A none-too-subtle reminder of how this island should have been his all those years ago. And several digs as to how he hoped *this* marriage would last.

Andreas gave Christos a quick, encouraging clasp of the shoulder. 'She'll be here soon. She can't change her mind and run away too easily on an island.'

He had to forget his father, forget his past, and concentrate on making this day special for Christos.

'Cheers, brother, that's really reassuring.'

The two brothers grinned at each other and then Christos ducked his head down so that no one else could hear their conversation. 'So what's this about a wedding present?'

Emotion thickened Andreas's throat and it was a while before he managed to speak. 'The paperwork is in my office... I'm giving you half of this island.'

Christos studied him, speechless. 'Seriously?' he said at last.

'Yeah, scriously.'

The two men embraced and then stood side by side in silence. Eventually Christos spoke, 'We had great times here as boys, didn't we?'

Andreas nodded. 'And we'll have them again.'

Christos looked as though he was about to say something, but just then the sound of traditional music reached them. The trio of musicians, playing violin, bouzouki and the *toumbi* drum, would have led the bridal party all the way from the villa to the chapel.

Sofia was the first to appear behind the musicians, on the arm of her father, her dark hair covered in a lace veil. Beside him Christos inhaled a deep breath, and Andreas couldn't blame him. Sofia was radiating elegant beauty and happiness, her eyes dancing, her mouth a wide beam. And when her eyes met Christos's a single tear trickled down her cheek and Andreas had to turn away. He felt as though he'd been punched in the gut.

He tried not to look back but was unable to resist doing so. When he did, he knew he should look away, but he couldn't. His breath had been knocked out of his lungs. Her head slightly bowed, a smile playing on her lips, Grace followed Sofia. Her silver-grey dress was made of fine lace on the bodice, and a full-length tulle skirt. Silver sandals were on her feet. Was she wearing the underwear he had unpacked? And was it truly only twelve hours ago that they had lain together, their bodies entwined and damp with perspiration?

He forced himself to turn. Already he had seen his

parents' curiosity as to what was going on between them. His mother constantly searched for any sign that he was in a relationship again, hoping against hope that one day he would have a family of his own. It would be unjust and cruel to mislead her.

He stared at the peonies cascading down from the garland around the chapel bell. He had helped Grace place the peonies in flower tubes this morning. He had thought then that he could trust her. Had thought so last night. But within minutes of meeting his family she had hinted at the personal nature of their relationship by revealing that she knew about his wedding present to Christos. Was she playing him? Trying to back him into a corner?

His stomach twisted at the thought that he might have been duped once again.

When Sofia reached Christos she raised her hands to his and they stared at each other for long moments, before they drew into each other, their noses touching. Together they grinned and turned to the congregation, who broke into spontaneous applause at how infectious their joy was.

The priest eventually managed to draw the wedding party into a semicircle, so that he and Grace were practically facing each other as they flanked Sofia and Christos. While their eyes would briefly meet, and then fly away from one another, in contrast Christos and Sofia never stopped gazing into each other's eyes, lost in one another.

What was Grace thinking? Was she dreaming of her own wedding? When her eyes landed on him did she imagine *him* in the role of her groom? Panic surged through him. Surely not? He had made his thoughts on marriage clear. But last night they had shared an extraordinary intimacy. One that in truth had rocked him to his core. What if she had felt that intensity too? What if he had given her false hope?

When it came to the time for exchanging the rings, he heard Christos's words of reassurance to Sofia, whose fingers were trembling so much he found it hard to slip the ring on her finger. Immediately Sofia stilled, and the couple shared a look intense with understanding and care. Andreas's gaze moved to Grace. She was staring at Sofia and Christos with tears glistening in her eyes. And then she was looking at him, as though asking him a question.

He glanced away. His heart sank. He had no answers for her.

The whoops of joy from the other guests when the newly married couple kissed for the first time transported him back to three years ago, when a similar whoop had echoed in an Athens cathedral. He had been so blind.

He looked back into the congregation. So many of those faces had witnessed his own marriage. How many still speculated as to why his marriage had gone bad so quickly? Why he no longer spoke to one of his closest friends.

His gaze met his mother's. She gave him a sympathetic smile of reassurance. He glanced away and pulled at the collar of his shirt. He needed a drink.

When they followed the bride and groom down the aisle Grace's hand barely touched his arm. They both smiled, but tension kept their bodies rigid as the crowd shouted, *'Na zisetel!'*—Live happily!—while showering the procession with a mixture of confetti and rice.

Before them, Christos and Sofia stopped at the edge of the terrace, where they would greet each of their guests before moving on to the reception. The couple were tied in an intimate embrace and Grace's footsteps faltered.

'I'm sorry about earlier.'

Andreas turned around to see if anyone was close by before he replied. 'I said that we needed to keep our relationship private.'

The volume of the voices around them increased, and Sofia's soft laughter ran through the air at something Christos had whispered to her while in their embrace.

Grace moved closer to him. 'I know. I wasn't thinking.'

It would be so easy to believe her—especially when her eyes pleaded with him to do so. He stepped back. They were standing way too close together. 'My parents are now speculating as to why I told *you* something so personal.'

Grace peered up at him with hurt in her eyes, but didn't respond. He led her over to stand next to the bride and groom, so that they too could greet the guests and be on hand in case they were needed. He felt torn in two.

Unable to stop himself, he leaned down briefly and whispered in her ear, 'You look beautiful.'

She studied him, confounded, and then looked away into the distance, tears in her eyes.

Andreas began to exchange hugs and handshakes. The happiness of everyone else was pulling him apart—along with the guilt of knowing that last night with Grace had been a major mistake.

Out on the Aegean the sun had long disappeared in a spectacular sunset of fiery pinks when the main courses of grilled swordfish and mouthwatering lamb *kleftiko* were finally cleared away. The wedding reception was proving to be a loud and fun affair, with numerous toasts and shouts for the wedding couple to kiss.

In other circumstances Grace would have been able to relax at this point, knowing that the flowers had proved to be a huge success, with many favourable comments. But not only did she have Andreas's father sitting next to her at the top table, as the day progressed she was feeling more and more alienated from Andreas.

The tapping of a knife-edge on a glass had her glancing along the table. Andreas stood and the terrace grew silent. He threw the crowd a devastating smile, but she could see tension in the corners of his eyes. She held her breath as her heart pounded. *Please let this go well for him.*

He spoke first in Greek, and then after a few sentences stopped and translated into English for the guests from England. At first he spoke about the tricks he had played on his younger brother when they were children, with Christos eager to believe everything his older brother and idol said. And then of what Kasas had meant to them both growing up. He told them about their joint adventures, including a failed entrepreneurial attempt to start breeding goats, in which the stubborn animals had proved much too temperamental for the young teenagers. And then, his voice thick with emotion, he said how happy he was to see Christos marry here today.

Beside her, Grace could feel Andreas's father tense.

He went on to compliment Sofia on how radiant she looked today, which drew a large applause from the crowd. And then he faltered. For the longest while he stared down at his notes.

Grace shifted in her seat, her stomach clenching, her heart thundering as she willed him on.

He pushed his notes away. 'I was told that I shouldn't wing my speech, which was probably good advice—but as my father will tell you I'm pretty stubborn when it comes to taking guidance.'

This drew knowing laughter from some of the crowd

and friendly heckling. At first Mr Petrakis sat frozen, but then he gave a nod of acknowledgement and said, 'Whoever hurries stumbles.'

Andreas and Christos shared a look that said they had often heard that expression before, and then Andreas continued. 'Firstly I must compliment Sofia's chief bridesmaid, Grace, who is also the florist for today. Having seen first-hand the work involved, I must admit to a whole new appreciation for the skill and dedication required.' He raised his glass and said, 'To Grace.'

His eyes met hers for the briefest of moments before he turned away. Grace smiled in acknowledgement of the guests toasting her and shared a hug with Sofia. Inside she felt as if she was going to die. She hadn't expected him to say anything about her, and that would have been preferable to the impersonal way he had just done so. As though they were nothing but mere acquaintances. Where had the fun and the friendship between them gone?

'Passion can spark a relationship, but it can't sustain it. Aristotle described love as being a single soul inhabiting two bodies. Christos and Sofia—that is my wish for you: that you share the same dreams, the same values, have a common life vision. These are the things that keep a couple together.'

Grace bent her head and closed her eyes on the emotion in his voice, swallowing against a huge lump in her throat.

'May you for ever be a single soul, living a life of shared dreams that allows your love to take root and blossom with each passing year.' Then, raising his wine glass, he invited the guests to join him in a toast. 'May your love blossom.'

For the rest of the speeches Grace sat trying to listen,

forcing herself to smile and laugh when others did, but feeling numb inside.

As soon as the speeches were over she made her excuses, while the terrace was being cleared of tables for the dancing, and went to check that all the lanterns were lit on the lower terraces and on the path down to the jetty. She tried to stay focused on her work, refusing to think about Andreas's speech and the obvious implications for them as a couple when they didn't share a single dream.

When she eventually returned to the terrace the music had started.

Sofia rushed over to her. 'I was searching for you! It's time to dance the Kalamatiano.'

Sofia pulled her out on to the dance floor, along with her mum and Andreas's mum. They all held hands and were soon encircled by a large group of female wedding guests. The music started and they began circling the dance floor, using small side-steps. The music was infectious, as was Sofia's happiness, and for a while Grace lost herself in the joy of the dancing, in the endless smiles of the women facing her.

But then she spotted Andreas where he stood beside Christos, watching the women dance. The two brothers couldn't have appeared more different in their expressions. Christos was laughing, his eyes glued to Sofia, while Andreas just stared at her for a moment, his expression devoid of any emotion, before he turned away to talk to a group beside him.

He said something to a striking dark-haired woman and stepped closer when she laughed. Something pierced Grace's heart. She felt like doubling over as jealousy and pain punched her stomach with force.

Memories of her father's voice taunted her. *'You need*

to toughen up, Grace. Your looks are fading as quickly as your mother's did.'

As they twisted and circled around the terrace, the high spirits of everyone around her, the beauty of the candlelit terrace bathed in the scent of jasmine, mocked everything in her.

What had she expected? She had known what she was getting into. One night of fun—nothing else. But as she watched his dark head bend, saw him talking to the woman whose eyes were shining at being on the receiving end of his attention, she knew it had never been that simple.

CHAPTER NINE

'COME AND TALK to Giannis.'

Andreas gritted his teeth and turned at his father's call. He reached out to shake Giannis's hand, but was pulled into an enthusiastic hug instead.

'Good to see you, Andreas. I haven't seen you since...' Giannis's voice trailed off.

His father tensed beside him and Andreas answered deliberately, in a casual drawl, 'Since my wedding.'

Giannis gave him an uncomfortable smile and obviously decided to change the subject. 'I've been following your successes in the business pages.' He paused and glanced to Andreas's father. 'You must be enormously proud of Andreas and everything he has achieved.'

His father frowned, as though he wasn't certain either of the comment or how to respond. He eventually brushed off the comment with a dismissive wave of his hand. 'Of course, of course...but now it's time for Andreas to come back to the family business. Like all good sons would do.'

Andreas didn't want to hear any more. He made his excuses and walked away. Out on the dance floor, the party was in full swing. He should be enjoying himself. But in truth he just felt frustrated. Frustrated and angry. He had sat through Christos's speech with pain and regret burning in his gut, knowing he would never have the same dream for the future, the vision of having a partner for life, children, a family of his own.

This wedding was a constant reminder of his own failings. And now his eyes fixed on his greatest frustration of all. *Grace*.

She was out on the dance floor with his cousin Orestis. They were standing much too close to one another. A cut-out section in her dress exposed her upper back. It was the sexiest thing he had ever seen, and images of his mouth running the length of her spine last night almost knocked him sideways.

They had shared so much last night—physically and emotionally. At the time it had felt right, but now he was questioning everything about it. It had left him feeling exposed, and with emotions so conflicting that he couldn't even begin to process them in the madness of the wedding.

His cousin was a charmer and a heartbreaker. He marched right over.

'Whatever Orestis is telling you, don't believe a word of what he's saying.'

Orestis stood back from Grace and raised an eyebrow. 'Well, I *did* learn everything I know from you, cousin.'

Beside him Grace's lips twitched. Andreas didn't like the feeling that it was him against the two of them. Grace was supposed to be on *his* side.

'Not everything Orestis… I'm not a heartbreaker.'

His cousin squared up to him, Greek male pride refusing to back down. 'True, but from what I hear you don't hang around long enough to be one. You don't break hearts—you just steal them.'

Grace looked from Orestis to him and back again.

'Two peas in a pod, I would say.' She walked away into the crowd.

He caught up with her in the centre of the dance floor as the band moved to a slower tempo. 'I've been neglecting my best man's duty to dance with the chief bridesmaid.'

Angry violet eyes damned him. 'Thanks, but I'm not in the mood.'

She went to walk away but he pulled her around and into his arms. His frustration with the whole damn day boiled over and he lowered his head to her ear. 'You weren't so reluctant last night.'

Her foot stamped on his. He held back a groan and tightened his grip. Her body squirmed against him, her heat and scent sending thunderbolts of desire to every sensitive point in his.

He glanced up in time to see some speculative gazes been thrown in their direction. He took a step back but kept a firm grip on her, in case she decided to bolt. With a false smile he warned, 'If we don't dance, people will be even more suspicious of us.'

She gave him a frustrated glare and said through clenched teeth, 'I don't care what people think of us.'

'Really? So the next time we meet you don't care if everyone is wondering about us? Hoping that we get together?'

She hesitated for a moment. 'They won't.'

'Look around you, Grace.'

She gave an indifferent shrug. 'I just see women staring at you and looking as though they would love for *me* to disappear off the face of the earth.'

'And beyond them are my aunts and uncles, my parents, hoping that one day I will marry again.'

'Would that be such a bad thing?'

It was a question he didn't even want to entertain. 'We're not going over that again, are we? You know how I feel.'

The anger in her eyes disappeared. 'I know. I just hate the thought of you going through life on your own.'

Her comment hit a raw nerve and he tried to bite down on the anger coiling in his stomach. 'Not everyone needs a fairy-tale ending to be happy.'

She gave him a long, hard stare. 'As long as you *are* actually happy.'

He wasn't going there.

Inch by inch they moved towards one another. His hand touched the bare skin of her back. He had to swallow a groan as he felt the smoothness of her skin, the delicate ribbon of her spine, the slender span of her waist.

'I haven't seen much of you today.'

He glanced down in order to understand the true meaning of her comment. Her wounded expression had him looking away quickly. A surge of defensiveness followed. 'I've been busy talking to all the guests. I haven't seen many of them in a number of years.'

She didn't respond, which only upped his frustration a notch. Was he messing up *everything* today? He needed to get them back on neutral ground. Grounds of friendship. If that was possible.

'Many guests have spoken to me about how incredible the flowers are; you must be pleased.'

She threw him a dirty glare and said with a note of sarcasm, 'So you said in your speech.'

He'd felt all day as though he was under attack—from memories, from others' expectations, from his own stupid pride. He was sick of it, and his defensiveness surged back at her comment. 'You didn't like my speech?'

For a while she glared at him, and then the fight

seemed to leak out of her. 'No, it was a perfect speech. Funny, heartfelt, kind…just like you.'

He gave a disbelieving laugh. 'That's not how many people would describe me.'

'If you let them into your life they would.'

'Maybe I don't *want* to let them in.'

A small shrug was her only response. Her breasts moved against his shirt and he pulled her a little closer. He was unable to hold back a low groan at the feel of her body pushed against his.

Her voice was unsteady when she spoke. 'Are you enjoying the day?'

He could take no more.

In a low growl he answered, 'Not as much as last night.' His pulse went wild when he pulled back to see the heat in her eyes. 'Let's go somewhere private.'

Grace followed him into the villa, wondering if she was losing her mind. It was as though she was addicted to him and to what he could do to her body.

The villa was empty, and at the bottom of the stairs he took her hand. Upstairs, he pulled her down the corridor and into a dark room. In the moonlight she could see a bed in the far corner.

'Where are we?'

'My bedroom.'

'Is this a good idea?'

'Of course not, but you started it.'

And she had—last night, when she'd asked him to stay the night with her.

In the near darkness his eyes blistered with need, pinning her to the spot. Her body was already on high alert to him, tense with building desire. His head lowered even closer…his hand lightly touched against her neck. She gave an involuntary shiver and a small cry of frustration.

His mouth hovered over hers. 'You do crazy things to me… Do you realise just how beautiful, how sexy you look today?'

She shook her head, unable to speak as her body cried out for his mouth, for the pressure of his weight.

'Are you wearing that lingerie I unpacked?'

He spoke in a low, demanding whisper, his lips agonisingly close to hers, pulling every nerve in her body exquisitely tight.

She was incapable of doing anything other than giving a simple nod.

He gave a primal groan and his mouth landed heavily on hers. His hands clutched the sides of her head, so that he could deepen the kiss even more. His mouth was familiar, but wondrous, hot, seeking, relentless. Her hands ran down the hard thick muscle of his outer chest, over the indentations of his ribs.

She gasped when his hands dropped to work on the buttons of her dress.

She should pull away. But she didn't care. She wanted him. *Now.*

Her dress fell in a puddle to the floor and he stepped back. His eyes devoured her. A powerful jolt of desire rocked her body as she saw his hunger, his ravenous appreciation of her almost naked body. His head dipped to her breasts, his lips running along the curve of exposed flesh cupped by the bustier. His hands trailed along the delicate flesh of her inner legs. With a groan he twisted her around to face the wall and ran his hands over her bottom. The weight of his body pushed against her.

He dropped his head down to her ear. 'I can't get enough of you.'

A tremor went through her at his low tone and suddenly, for some unfathomable reason, she was unable to stop shivering.

Behind her, he stilled. And before she knew what was happening her dress was being pulled back up and he was closing the buttons.

Too confused to speak, she waited, her body a mess of desire and unstoppable tremors. Buttons finished, he twisted her back towards him. He said nothing, but ran a hand through his hair, frustration clear in his expression.

'What's wrong?'

His mouth was a tight grimace. 'We can't do this again. I was wrong to bring you here.'

Just like that, he was shutting her out again. She had no idea what he was really thinking. Why had he suddenly decided to push her away?

Humiliation clawed in her chest. 'Tell me the truth, Andreas. What's going on?'

He gave a frustrated sigh. 'The truth? The truth is we should be downstairs with the others…and I like you too much to hurt you again.'

Confusion built thick and fast in her chest until it ached. His words were bittersweet. She didn't know how to respond. All she knew was that a ball of rejection had been growing inside her all day. For the past little while it had shrunk, whilst they had danced and kissed, but now it was a giant boulder inside her, weighing her down, consuming her.

The last time she had felt so rejected had been when her mum had told her that there was no hope of them ever being a family again.

Feeling lonelier than she had in a long time, Grace walked away, terrified that she was about to start crying in front of him. Downstairs, before she walked back out to the terrace, she glanced backwards to see Andreas following her, his head bent as though in defeat.

Andreas stared out onto the dance floor, knowing he had two choices. He could either walk away from the celebrations now, in an attempt to try to pull his head together. Or he could forget about everything and embrace the wild momentum of the party.

It was an easy choice.

He walked onto the dance floor and was pulled into the dancing.

The pace and communal elation, the sheer goodwill, numbed him to the emptiness inside him. He joined Christos and their mutual male friends. Wasn't this camaraderie and friendship enough?

And then the floor cleared and he was pushed forward to perform the *zembekiko*. He resisted the pushes from the other men. It was a hot-blooded dance that demanded that all emotions, all weaknesses be expressed. To dance the *zembekiko*, the manly dance of improvisation, you had to be unafraid of expressing the true you...and right now he didn't know who he was.

The guests were crowding around the dance floor, some kneeling, others standing, all urging him forward. He still resisted. To do this dance right he would need to expose his feelings of pain, of unfulfilled dreams. The crowd would think of his failed marriage. He would think of the future that had been wiped out the moment he had opened the blackmail letter and seen those photos of his wife.

Sofia was moving through the crowds, pulling Grace behind her, and they dropped to the floor in front of all of the other guests.

The band began the low plaintive music. He glanced

towards Grace. She returned his gaze with eyes heavy with sadness.

He moved to the centre of the room. He would dance for her. It was the only way he could reveal what was in his soul.

Andreas stood in the middle of the dance floor, proud and dignified. He stared into the distance, his broad shoulders tense, his arms flexed. His tux jacket had long disappeared and his shirtsleeves were rolled up.

He started the dance with slow, deliberate movements, his leg bending in a fluid movement upwards so that his hand tapped his heel. He circled the dance floor, assured and noble, ignoring the crowd who were calling out his name and clapping to the beat of the music.

Grace clapped blindly, her heart beating heavily in her chest.

His movements intensified, growing ever quicker, and he dipped and twirled, lost to the rhythm of the music. His movements were strong, but they held sadness, loneliness. He was all alone out on the dance floor, with the world looking in.

Suddenly she wanted to go to him. Wanted to comfort him as his body stamped out a message of despair. But she sat there, her hands clenched, her heart aching, as he spun around, his hand whirling down to slap the floor. The crowd shouted out whoops of approval. Tears filled her eyes. Sofia reached for her hand. Together the best friends watched this powerful man dance with passion, his focus only on expressing the emotions within him. His aloneness.

The dance ended abruptly. Andreas walked straight off the dance floor towards Christos, his gaze never meeting hers. The crowd erupted into loud applause.

Beside her Sofia gave a soft chuckle and exhaled loudly, wiping her eyes. 'Wow, I feel worn out! That was incredibly moving. I've seen the *zembekiko* danced many times before, but never with such raw emotion.'

Grace could only nod, her throat much too tight to utter even a few meaningless words. She stared at Andreas's back as he stood silently amongst a group of friends, wanting to go to him, to place a hand on his arm, on his back. To be with him. To be part of his life. And in that moment she knew that she was in love with him.

She closed her eyes and winced. She couldn't be. He wasn't what she wanted. He didn't want a relationship, or romance in his life.

Beside her Sofia stood and held out her hand to Grace. As Grace stood, Sofia whispered, 'Are you okay?'

She could not burden Sofia with her problems. Anyway, what had happened between her and Andreas was too personal, too private. She doubted she would ever tell another person about what they'd shared. *Ever.* It was a secret she would hold in her heart for the rest of her life.

She forced herself to smile. 'I think it's just culture shock—weddings in England are so much more tame in comparison to this... I hadn't realised Greek weddings were so passionate.' She paused and gestured around her at the dancers back out on the floor, the large groups laughing and hugging, dancing with abandon as though there was no tomorrow. 'And so much fun.'

Sofia tugged her out onto the dance floor, where they joined Sofia's beaming dad. He twisted and twirled them around the floor and Grace tried to forget about the man standing in the crowd behind her, who had stolen her heart.

It was well after midnight when the band leader called Sofia and Christos to the stage. With the encouragement of the crowd Christos knelt down and helped Sofia step out of her shoes. He lifted them up to Sofia and together they inspected the soles.

Earlier that morning Grace had watched Sofia write the names of all the single woman attending the wedding onto the soles, as was tradition. Now it was time to reveal the names that were still visible on the soles—the women whose names still showed would be the next to marry.

Sitting with a group of Andreas's family, Grace watched, bemused, smiling at the hopeful girls and women eagerly waiting for their names to be called out. It seemed she wasn't the only romantic in the world.

A dart of pain shot into her heart and she glanced towards Andreas, who was seated at a table with a group of fellow young and beautiful Athenians. He was engrossed in conversation with another man, oblivious to her. The group seemed so effortlessly chic and full of vitality. Inadequacy crept along her bones. She touched a hand to her hair, fixed her dress, wishing she had taken the time to check her make-up.

Sofia gave a squeal that echoed into the microphone. It hooked everyone's attention and conversations died as they all focused on the stage.

Christos stepped closer to the microphone and spoke first in Greek and then in English. 'There's only one name remaining.' He chuckled when Sofia gave another squeal of excitement, and stepped back to allow her to speak.

Sofia scanned the terrace. When her gaze landed on her, Grace stared back, fearing her heart was about to give way. *Oh, please, would someone tell her that Sofia hadn't included her name. She didn't want attention... this number of eyes on her.*

Sofia held up the shoe. 'The only name remaining is... my bridesmaid, Grace!'

All two hundred guests turned to study her. Her heart leapt with joy for a few insane seconds, but then she pushed it away. Heat fired through her body. What was she supposed to do? Stand up and wave? Make a speech? Protest and say that it had to be a mistake...that she was the most unlikely woman to marry...that she had just fallen in love with a man who didn't want to be in a relationship, never mind marry?

She grimaced at Sofia, silently warning her best friend that she would get her back for this. Sofia responded with a defiant grin. Grace squirmed, and wished that people would stop staring in her direction. Her cheeks burnt brightly. Vulnerability swept through her and she wished she was anywhere but here. She forced herself to smile; to do otherwise would be churlish. She didn't dare peek in Andreas's direction.

His aunts made cooing noises of appreciation around the table, and his mother translated for her. They were saying that it would soon be Grace walking down the aisle, as hers was the only name remaining. His mother watched her curiously and she squirmed even more into her chair.

'That's very unlikely.'

His mother translated her response back to his aunts but it was greeted with frowns and shakes of their heads. His mother didn't need to translate their words contradicting her disbelief and she sat there, dumbfounded, wondering how she had ended up in this surreal mess.

The dancing resumed and she exhaled in relief when her five minutes of attention faded. She took a sip of her white wine and glanced towards Andreas. He was staring directly at her. His expression was impossible to pin down...thoughtful...frustrated...hacked off.

He needed to know that she gave no significance to the shoe tradition. That she thought it was a silly bit of fun.

She approached his table and threw her eyes to heaven. 'Well, *that* was embarrassing.'

'Was it?'

'Lord, yes...your aunts are predicting a wedding before Christmas.' She shrugged and laughed, but clearly Andreas wasn't finding it funny.

He gave her a brief, impersonal smile—the kind of smile that passed between strangers. Then he stood and gestured for her to sit on his chair. He introduced her to the others at the table and said, 'I need to go and speak to some of the other guests.'

He walked away.

Grace sat there, randomly smiling at the people around her, trying to pretend that she didn't feel as if she had just been punched in the chest...trying to convince herself that he hadn't just blown her off.

CHAPTER TEN

GRACE ADJUSTED HER sunglasses against the glare of the afternoon sun as it bounced off the body of the helicopter and forced herself to smile and wave enthusiastically, saying goodbye to Sofia and Christos. Her throat felt as raw as sandpaper and her eyes burnt with tears.

A sharp wind whipped around her as the helicopter blades picked up speed and she backed away, glad to have an excuse to move away from Andreas who had also come to the helipad to say goodbye to the honeymoon couple.

As soon as the helicopter was in the air she gave one final wave and walked away. Andreas caught up with her on the main terrace, now restored to its original state after yesterday's wedding reception. The terrace, as with the rest of the island, both so full of chatter and merriment yesterday, now felt empty and forlorn. All the guests had left over the course of the night and this morning. Only she and Andreas remained.

'Come and have some lunch.'

She turned at the brusque nature of his invitation. Was this the same man she had slept with, shared so much intimacy with, less than two days ago? Not trusting her own voice, she shook her head and went to follow the path back down to the workshops.

In an instant he was at her side and pulling her to a stop. He regarded her curiously. 'Are you okay?'

Even the brief touch of his fingers on her arm made her resolve to stay away from him waver dangerously. 'I'm fine...'

'You obviously aren't. What's the matter?'

'I'm just upset that Sofia's gone. Yesterday went too fast, and this morning...' Grace paused and willed herself not to blush. 'I didn't get to speak to her for more than five minutes.'

They both knew that the reason this had been the case was because the honeymoon couple had been holed up in their bedroom all morning.

Andreas looked unconvinced by her answer. But before he could ask any further questions she turned again for the workshops, where she had already spent the morning tidying away all the floral displays from yesterday, glad to have a reason to avoid Andreas.

Not once had he spoken to her again after the 'name on the sole' debacle last night. In fact he had barely even glanced in her direction.

She had gone to bed long before the party had ended, heart-sore and mentally shattered. At first she had fallen into an exhausted sleep, but had woken with a start to hear a female giggle as the dawn light had crept between the shutter slats. She hadn't dared move when she had heard Andreas's voice. *Was he with another woman?* The voices had quickly moved on and she had resisted the urge to peek out of her window. She was humiliated enough without adding the role of jealous lover to her repertoire.

Back at the workshop, she busied herself removing the peonies from the long length of garlands. She hesitated when Andreas appeared at the door, but forced herself not to react.

'Did you clear away all these flowers yourself?'

She glanced up at the astonished tone of his voice. He gestured to the peonies Grace had brought back to the workshop during the course of the morning, and then pointed down to the jetty.

'And the pots and lanterns? Who brought all of those back to the jetty?'

'I did.'

He glared at her incredulously. 'By yourself? What time did you start working this morning?'

'At seven.'

'The wedding didn't end until sunrise. What's the rush? I could have helped you if you had asked.'

She stared at him pointedly. 'I went to bed at two. I had plenty of sleep until I was woken by voices at dawn.'

His mouth twisted and he folded his arms on his chest.

Memories of last night felt like a red-hot poker sticking into her heart. Hurt swelled inside her. 'I've decided to leave Kasas today, so I needed to start the clean-up early. Ioannis says he can take me over to Naxos for the five o'clock ferry.'

For a moment he looked stunned, but then his eyes narrowed as though he didn't quite believe her. 'You're leaving today? Why?'

'Do you *really* need me to answer that, Andreas?'

He moved closer to the workbench and bent down to meet her eyes, his eyes boring into hers, his jaw working. 'I wouldn't ask unless I needed to.'

She turned to throw some peonies that were shedding their petals into a composting bin. Her chest ached; she could barely draw in enough breath. The composting bin was starting to fill up and she studied the dying peonies with regret. Their time of beauty was much too short.

She turned and faced him with her head held high, determined she would maintain her dignity. 'I'll be blunt. We slept together Friday night and you ignored me all day yesterday.'

'No. I didn't ignore you. I told you we had to be careful that people didn't get the wrong impression.'

'And what other people might believe is more important than hurting me?'

He gave a disbelieving shake of his head. 'I hurt you? How?'

'You shut me out completely.'

He threw his head back and stared down at her with that arrogant expression he sometimes used. 'You're exaggerating.'

His tone reminded her of her father's belittling attitude. Fire burnt through her veins. 'Really? You barely looked at me all day, never mind actually *talked* to me. I thought I meant a little more to you than that... And I deserve a little respect.'

'Maybe if you hadn't blurted out about knowing what my wedding present to Christos was we wouldn't have had my mother watching us like a hawk all day, wondering what was going on between us.'

Grace marched over and grabbed a cardboard box from the floor. At the bench she began to pack her floristry equipment into it. Without glancing up, she said angrily, 'It seems to me like you were looking for an excuse to push me away.'

'Why would I want to do that?'

She knew she should stop—that she was only hurting herself. But a force inside her—an emotional force she didn't fully understand—pushed her to lash out, even though the rational side of her yelled at her to stop, that she was going too far.

'I don't know. Maybe you regretted Friday night? Perhaps revised your opinion of me because I was the one who suggested it? Maybe, facing your family and friends, you suddenly realised that I was lacking? After all, I'm just a florist—which is pitiful compared to your career. And I certainly don't stack up against the women who were only too keen to grab your attention yesterday. Like the dark-haired woman in the white trouser suit. Was it *her* you were with this morning out on the terrace?'

Andreas moved forward and pushed the cardboard box away, so that nothing stood between them other than the table, which he leaned on in order to eyeball her at a closer range. His eyes were dark with fury.

'Yes, it was. Her name is Zeta and she's my cousin. Orestis's sister, in fact.'

'Oh.'

His lips twisted and he growled, 'And I do *not* regret Friday night. Do you?'

She could barely breathe. In a small whisper she admitted, 'No…'

'What do you want from me, Grace?'

She wanted to go back to what they'd had on Friday night, as they had lain in bed together. That emotional and physical connection. A connection so deep and right and secure. She wondered now if it had all been a dream. How could they have gone from that to this so quickly?

'I thought we were friends.'

He exhaled loudly in irritation. 'Friends don't sleep together.'

'Yes, they do…married couples are best friends to one another.'

He stared up towards the ceiling and rubbed a hand

down over his face. 'I forgot what a romantic you are. All of this was such a bad idea. What were we *thinking*?'

He sounded worn out. She should stop. But the force deep inside her was driving her on, wanting to test him. Wanting him to admit what was in his heart. That, yes, he *was* pushing her away. Closing himself off from her and everything that they'd shared.

'I don't know...what were *you* thinking? Was I just another conquest for playboy Andreas Petrakis?'

He walked away from her and stood at the door. His body was rigid, his hands balled at his sides.

It was a while before he turned and said coolly, 'I am not going to dignify that with a response. Why do I feel you're trying to back me into a corner, here? I have always been honest with you. I told you that I could never give you the type of relationship you wanted.'

He was right, in a way. She *was* trying to back him into a corner—but not to try to manipulate him into a relationship with her. No, what she wanted was him to tell her out loud that it was over, that the connection they had shared had been of no consequence to him. That without a backward glance he would walk away from her.

'I know... I just wish I hadn't fallen in love with you.'

He felt as though someone had punched him. Every fibre of muscle in his chest constricted painfully. His ears rang. Nothing made sense.

He looked away from the pain in her eyes. He had to get away before he did something stupid. Something he would regret for ever. Like taking her in his arms and making her promises he could never fulfil.

He sucked in some air. 'I wish you hadn't said that.'

She flinched, but said nothing.

His chest felt as if it was about to explode. He walked closer, his eyes never leaving hers. 'Why did you?'

Her eyes held his for a few moments. She was clearly bewildered by his question. And then they grew wide with shock. 'You think that I'm *lying*?'

'Are you?'

She stood stock-still, only her eyelids blinking, a thousand thoughts flashing in her violet eyes. Eventually he saw a grim determination take hold and she stared at him coldly. 'No, I wasn't lying. But if you can think that I'm capable of doing so, maybe I was wrong.' She paused, her hands gripping the side of the workbench. 'No, I'll rephrase that. Not *maybe*. I *was* wrong. I can't possibly be in love with a man who can think that I would lie about something so important.'

He didn't want her to be in love with him—and yet her words twisted in his gut. 'Your love seems pretty fickle if you can change your mind so rapidly.'

'Maybe you've just revealed your true self to me... Don't blame me for falling for your pretences.'

'What pretences?'

'That you trusted me, respected me enough to show me kindness and consideration. Yesterday just proved that you never truly did trust or respect me.'

'Oh, come on! That's utter rubbish. Yesterday I had responsibilities that needed my attention. I was the host and the best man. I had to speak to the other guests. I'm sorry if that made you feel neglected. Added to that, I had my family breathing down my neck. Why on earth are you blaming me for trying to protect you from years of my family wondering what happened between us and if anything will happen again? Do you honestly want that speculation? That pressure? You heard Christos. He wants us all to meet here in August for a family get-together. Christos sees you as *family* now, Grace.'

Her shoulders sagged. 'I know. And somehow we need to try and get on. Put these days behind us.'

Her voice now held sad resignation. Her anger he could handle; this pain was unbearable to witness.

She reached for some floristry wire and twisted it in her hands. 'We have to put some distance between us. That's why I must go today.'

'I do respect you…and I've always been honest with you.'

'But you're not even honest with *yourself*, Andreas. How can you possibly be honest with me? You've put a barrier up against the world because you were hurt before. You put on this mask of being hard-headed and cynical. But deep inside you are kind and lovely. Or at least I thought you were. Right now I don't know who you really are. Maybe even *you* don't know.'

'Are you suggesting that I *don't* learn from my past? From my mistakes? If you take that path, Grace, you'll be hurt time and time again. Maybe being cynical and tough is the only way to survive this world. Maybe those barriers will help me thrive. And are they any different to the romantic dreams you hold…? Aren't they a barrier in themselves? Will you ever meet your ideal man? Or will you realise we are all made with feet of clay?'

About to drop a spool of wire into the box, Grace paused and peered at him with a distracted expression, deep in thought. Any remaining fight in her seeped away.

'Maybe you're right.'

She went into the adjoining room, returned with a sweeping brush and began to clean the floor. Exasperated, he walked out of the workshop, his fear of ever really trusting a woman battling with the desire in his heart to turn around and take her in his arms and make this mess go away.

Later that afternoon Grace sat on the side of her bed and stared down at the blank page of her notebook. She wanted to write him a note but didn't know where to start. She didn't even know if it was the right thing to do. Maybe she should go and speak to him. But her heart plummeted to her feet even at the thought.

She was in love with him. And it was so wrong. She wasn't supposed to fall in love with a man who was cynical about love, who could shut her out with such ease, with such indifference as he had shown yesterday. Unfortunately she knew that there was another side to him—a man who was fun and attentive, kind-hearted and tender. A seductive, powerful man who made her melt just by looking at her.

But he didn't love her.

In truth she had no idea what he *did* feel for her. Friday night, when they had made love, she'd thought he felt the same strength of connection. In the moonlight he had lain with her, his eyes holding hers, filled with the same happiness and amazement that had flowed through her. She had thought his feelings for her were as deep and profound as hers for him.

How could she have got it so wrong? And why were a hundred different emotions chasing her down? One minute she was in shock, the next close to tears, the next wanting to yell at Andreas and demand to know what those tender words he had whispered to her in Greek when they made love had meant. Because to her they had sounded like declarations of love.

What was she going to do about August? Sofia was

moving to Athens with Christos next month, and had been so excited about inviting Grace to join them here on the island for holidays. Sofia would be hurt if Grace said no. Perhaps she should promise to come next year instead. But then would she just be putting off the inevitable? Would it be even harder to face Andreas next year?

A small voice in her head mocked her, goading her weak resolve, pointing out that she couldn't possibly bear not to see him for another year.

'Ioannis is waiting for you out on the terrace.'

Her head shot up to find Andreas standing at her bedroom doorway, his sombre expression only adding to his unfair good looks. He propped a hand against the door frame, his burnt-orange polo shirt riding up to expose an inch of muscled torso above the band of his faded jeans. Her pulse thundered even faster.

She shut her notebook and stood. 'I'm ready to go.'

His eyes moved to her suitcase and to the weekend bag beside the dressing table. He nodded, but didn't say anything.

She gripped the notebook. So much adrenaline was coursing through her body that despite her legs feeling weak and shaky she was possessed with a burning need to run. To run out of the room, to run away from the gut-wrenching desire to touch him again, to feel his lips on hers.

She placed the notebook and pen into her weekend case. 'I have already told Ioannis, but just so that you know, the florists from Naxos are coming tomorrow to take away the floral supplies, and they will reuse the peonies for a church.'

Again he nodded, but didn't say anything. She grabbed her suitcase and walked towards him. He didn't move. She forced herself to give him a tight smile, her eyes darting over his face quickly, instinctively knowing that to linger would spell trouble.

Tension crackled in the room. Even a few feet away from him she felt the tug of his body. Her eyes blinked rapidly as she tried to ignore the pull of memories: the weight of his body, the overwhelming power and strength of his hold.

In a low voice he said, 'I meant what I said last night. I do like you. A lot. And I never meant to hurt you.'

Distress coiled in her chest, in her throat, blocking off her airways. He went to place a hand on her arm but she stepped back. If he touched her she wouldn't leave here with a shred of self-respect intact.

Though she had never wanted more to run away, she forced herself to speak. 'Thank you for everything you did to make yesterday so special for Sofia.'

'Will you tell Sofia?'

How could he ask her that? Did he know her at *all*? 'Of course not.'

'Why not?'

Now she definitely wanted to yell at him. Yell at him that she wouldn't betray his trust, that she couldn't possibly reveal what they had shared, the awful soul-wrenching beauty of it, even to her best friend. Disappointment invaded every cell in her body.

'Why? Are you going to tell Christos?'

'Of course not…but women like to share these things.'

'Why *wouldn't* you tell Christos? Maybe then he would understand if we were tense when we're together. In fact, maybe we should tell them. And then they might do the sensible thing and keep us apart as much as possible.'

Grace was staring at him with wild eyes, a slash of anger on her cheeks. What was he *doing*? Why did he have such a burning need to prove that he couldn't trust her? It was like a monster inside him, consuming him. He hated himself for it. But it was out of control.

'I'm hoping the next time we meet the heat will be gone out of our relationship.'

She jerked back. The blood drained from her face. 'The heat?' She grabbed her suitcase and made for the door.

If he hadn't stepped out of the way he was certain she would have shoulder-charged him. As it was, the wheels of her suitcase rolled over his toes.

He cursed and ran after her. He yanked the suitcase out of her hand. 'I'll carry it downstairs for you.'

She grabbed it back. 'No. Just back off, Andreas. *I don't need you.*'

Her biting words felt like fingernails clawing into his heart. He followed her down the stairs.

She walked out to Ioannis on the terrace and called to him in a happy voice. Then she turned to him. He'd expected a scowl, but she gave him a bright smile. Only the tremble in her hand when she reached it out to him told of her pretence.

'Thank you...' For a moment she paused, as though uncertain as to how to continue. 'For your help with the flowers.' Affecting a breezy air, she added, 'I'll see you again in August. It will be lovely to spend some time with Sofia.' Her tone was cool and distant.

He needed to let go of her hand, yet he held on to it. He felt her trying to tug it away but his fingers clasped tighter. 'Enjoy your time in Crete.'

Tears shone in her eyes and her smile quivered for a moment. 'I can't wait.'

CHAPTER ELEVEN

FOUR DAYS LATER Grace sat at a waterfront bar on the horseshoe-shaped historic harbour of Chania city. Around her tourists ambled in the early-evening sun, soaking in the architecture and beauty of the Venetian harbour, stopping to inspect the menus at the vibrant restaurants or to step into the craft shops that lined the waterfront. Behind the harbour, on one of the criss-crossing narrow lanes, lay her hotel, one of many boutique hotels located in the restored town houses of the Venetian quarter.

Her floristry workshop had finished an hour earlier, and while part of her had wanted nothing more than to go back to her room and collapse onto her bed, she had forced herself instead to make the most of her time in this pretty city. To ignore how her heart bent in two every time a couple passed her.

This city seemed to do something to people. It was as if its romantic laid-back atmosphere insinuated itself into everyone's mood. Couples held hands and whispered intimacies to one another. Families sat at café tables and chatted for hours on end. And Grace was so lonely she felt physically ill with the pain tearing at her heart, the empty pit in her stomach.

But she could not let it defeat her. For the past few days she had stared that loneliness in the face, and as small chunks of realisation had formed into a larger understanding she had slowly begun to make sense of her past. And why Andreas pushing her away had hurt so much.

A couple passed in front of the bar, bent into one another, laughing and teasing, hands tucked into each other's sides as they tickled one another. She glanced away and grabbed her wine glass. She lifted it to her mouth but put it back down untouched. Blindly, she pulled out some coins from her purse and left them on the table.

On the cobbled street of the waterfront and in the side laneways she kept her head down, navigating the crowds, racing away from memories of how Andreas had pulled her back into bed that Saturday morning and held her hostage with teasing and tickles—a prelude that had quickly led to the most shattering of lovemaking.

Her hotel was tucked along a narrow lane in the middle of a stacked terrace of four-storey town houses. The reception was a simple hallway that daylight only touched early in the morning. In the evenings the owner—Ada, warm and generous—lit a row of candles that beckoned her guests in.

Grace climbed the wooden stairs to her bedroom on the top floor, hearing the now familiar sound of her own footsteps on the worn threads and smelling the scent of furniture polish. The higher she climbed the more sunlight penetrated the windows as the town house crept out of the hold of the neighbouring properties.

On the landing turn of the top floor her eyes met the sight of familiar polished tan shoes. She stumbled against the banister. Shoes she suspected were handmade. Especially for him.

Her heart started. Was she seeing things in her sleep-deprived state?

She saw dark navy trousers, tanned hands gripped

tightly between bent legs as he sat on the top step of the stairs, a pale blue shirt and then his broad shoulders, muscled neck, sharp jawline, the hint of an evening shadow. Her eyes lingered on his mouth and she was assailed by memories of intimate moments, but also afraid to move them upwards. What would she find there?

She gripped the banister and peeked up. Her heart stopped. Deep shadows filled his green-eyed gaze; lines of tension crinkled the corners of his eyes.

'Hi.'

Such a simple word, but said gently and with a small smile it conveyed so much more. But was that just wishful thinking on her part?

The butterflies in her stomach and her leaping heart swooped together to form one mass of confusion in her chest. She stumbled out a stunned, 'Hi…'

His smile slowly died and they stared at each other. The air crackled with the tension of intense attraction and hurt.

He rested his arms more heavily on his legs and leaned towards her. 'How are you?'

She tried not to grimace and met his eyes. 'I'm okay.'

He studied her doubtfully and rolled his neck from side to side, as though trying to rid it of tension. 'For the past few days I've been trying to convince myself that I was okay with you leaving. That you would never be part of my life. But today I flew home to Kasas, after a few days of business in Budapest, and realised just how lonely the island was without you.'

Her heart leapt and hope fired through her. But then reality jumped in and gave her a stern talking-to; he was here because of the sexual attraction between them—nothing more.

A slash of embarrassment coloured her cheeks. 'I'm not interested in a fling.'

His expression hardened. 'Neither am I.'

'So why are you here?'

He twisted around on the stairs and turned back to her holding the messiest bunch of hand-tied Coral Charm peonies she'd ever seen. He held them out to her.

She examined them dubiously. 'Where on earth did you get those from?' The florist who had put the bouquet together should hang her head in shame.

'I went to your floristry school. They told me you had already left. I wanted to bring you some flowers so I bought these there.'

'Somebody in the school created *that*?'

He looked indignant. 'No, *I* put it together—and I thought I did a pretty good job, considering.'

'Why?'

'Because I wanted to show you what you mean to me—if that means faffing around with flowers and embarrassing myself in front of a group of strangers who seemed to find it all very amusing, then so be it.'

Her head spun. This whole conversation was getting more unreal by the moment. 'How did you even know where I was? I didn't tell you the name of the school or what days I would be attending.'

'Sofia told me.'

He was the one who'd wanted to keep their relationship secret. Sofia would definitely suspect something now. 'Didn't she want to know why?'

'Yes, and I told her that I had messed up big-time and needed to find you to apologise.'

'But what about keeping our relationship private?'

'Finding you was more important.'

He spoke with such quiet intensity it left her unable

to draw breath, never mind find an adequate response. She took the bouquet from him and ran her finger and thumb along the fragile petals.

He gestured to the narrow confines of the stairs and the nearby bedroom doors. 'Can we talk somewhere more private? In your bedroom?'

Her budget had only allowed for a single room. Avoiding physical contact with him in such a small space would almost be impossible. She shuffled uncomfortably. 'It's a tiny room—nothing like the hotel rooms you would use. There isn't much space.'

His gaze narrowed. '*Aman!* Do you think I care about what size the room is when we have so much to talk about? Heaven help me, but if we have to have this conversation in a broom cupboard we will.'

Andreas stood and waited for Grace to pass him on the stairs. Beneath the top layer of the delicate fabric of her tea dress she wore a rose-pink slip, the borders covered in a deep pink lace... He was like a teenager around her—staring down her dress at the exposed slopes of her breasts, fantasising about undressing her.

With a tiny huff she flew past him. His hands itched to reach out and grab her. To feel her body against his again, to inhale her summertime scent, to feel her gentle breath on his skin.

She opened her hotel room door with an ancient key and went immediately to the balcony doors at the opposite side of the room and flung them open.

Yes, the room was small, but it was filled with her scent, and for a moment he couldn't move with the sensation that *this* was where he belonged. Surrounded by her scent, by the scattering of jewellery and make-up on the dressing table, the sight of her clothes in the wardrobe, her shoes below, a lone white and crimson bra hanging on a chair back.

How was it possible that he adored every single item that belonged to her? Longed to hear when and why she had bought them? He wanted to bury himself in her, heart and soul. Know everything about her.

His head reeling, but more than ever determined to right the wrongs he had committed, he joined her out on the small balcony, which only had enough space for them both to stand.

'Great view.'

Beside him she leaned on the railing, her back arching. Her loose hair swung down to the sides of her face so that he was unable to see her. He longed to push it back, to be able to see those eyes, that full mouth again.

'You wanted to talk.'

Where would he start? His heart leapt wildly in his chest. Fear balled in his throat. He dragged in some air. Through the neighbouring rooftops the harbour was visible. His eyes ran along the harbour wall to the lighthouse at the end. His stomach rolled. He had to explain. But what if the damage he had done was irreparable?

'When my ex cheated on me it changed me.' He paused as humiliation raged through him.

Grace straightened beside him and studied him fleetingly. 'Because you loved her?'

Her quietly spoken question hit him hard in the gut. He gave an involuntary wince. 'The fact that you have to ask that question again tells me just how much I've messed up.'

She rested against the balcony railing and waited for him to continue, watching him warily.

'I wasn't in love with my ex. My feelings for her never came close to what I feel for you. The pain of my divorce was because of my pride. My father had warned me against marrying my ex and I ignored him.'

Unable to face her while saying what needed to be said, he turned and stared instead at the red clay roof-top of her hotel.

'A year later he was looking at photos of my wife, naked with another man. The paparazzi had sent the photos to him too, in a bid to blackmail him. It tore me apart to see his humiliation and disgust.' His stomach rolled again, and he clenched his hands into tight balls. 'We have our differences, but he didn't deserve that.'

On a soft exhalation, Grace said, 'How awful...' Her hand reached out for a moment to touch his arm, but then she pulled it back, crossing her arms on her chest instead. 'Did you talk about it?'

Boy, had they. He gave a bitter laugh. 'Well, he yelled at me non-stop for an hour, about the disgrace I'd brought to the family. And then all the old arguments resurfaced: how I had walked away from the family business, taken sides with my uncle.'

'But he couldn't blame you for your ex's behaviour?'

'He had warned me about her. After we argued my father and I didn't speak until Christos's engagement.'

'And that hurt you?'

More than he had ever imagined. 'Yes. He's stubborn and pig-headed, but in his own way he loves me. The day he passed that envelope of photos to me he seemed broken. Until he lashed out and spoke of the disgrace it had brought to the family name. My wife had cheated on me. So had a close friend. I felt like a failure. My pride had taken a huge dent. The only way I could cope was to throw myself into work and pretend that I didn't care.'

'What about your mum?'

'She was heartbroken and stuck in the middle, trying

to negotiate peace between us. Family is everything to her. She said nothing, but I could see with my own eyes her upset. I'd made it clear that I would never be in a relationship again. And of course that meant that I would never give her grandchildren.'

'Andreas, why are you telling me this?'

'My refusal to trust others again was because of shame and wounded pride. I refused point-blank to believe that I could ever trust in a woman again. I was convinced of it. It gave me safety and security, I would never be humiliated again. I would never endure the pain of being betrayed. And then *you* walked into my life. Loyal, generous, fun, giving. You. I hated how attracted I was to you. I tried to fight it. But I became more bewitched by you every time we were together.'

She stared at him, clearly confused, before walking back into the bedroom. There she sat on the side of the bed, its vibrant yellow bedspread a golden sun in the otherwise neutral bedroom with its white walls and recycled furniture painted in shades of white. She rubbed a hand along the nape of her neck, her head dipping so that he couldn't read her expression when he sat on the chair opposite.

She brought her hands together on her crossed knees and squeezed so tightly her unvarnished fingernails turned white. 'But you didn't trust me.'

'Before the wedding, as I got to know you, I *did*. It was the only reason I came to you on the eve of the wedding. I trusted in you. With me, with Sofia, with your family, you are supportive and strong. You don't play games. You don't try to manipulate others for your own ends. You're honest and loyal.'

Her hands flew up into the air. 'You didn't think that

on the day of the wedding. It was clear you didn't trust me then.'

He grimaced, but nodded his agreement. 'I'm not proud to admit that I panicked. Our night together, the morning after…it blew me away. It was different to anything I'd experienced before. I was falling for you and it scared me. You wanted love and romance. I couldn't give you either. At least I thought I couldn't.'

'I honestly didn't mention the wedding present deliberately. I'm so sorry that I did.'

'I know you didn't. You said the day after that I was looking for a reason to push you away. And you were right.'

Grace bowed her head and ran a hand over her face. Without seeing her expression, he knew he had hurt her again.

In a rush he continued. 'Not just because I saw that my mother suspected something was happening between us, but because the whole day was bringing back memories I had refused to think about since my divorce and I couldn't cope with them.'

'Why didn't you explain any of this to me?'

'Because I didn't even want to acknowledge it to myself. I just wanted my life to go back to the way it had been before. Comfortable and easy…never risking myself personally. I didn't want to fall in love and risk being hurt, being humiliated again, so I just jumped from date to date. And tried to convince myself that it was enough. But then I met you, and instantly I was falling for you, and it scared me to death.'

'Why were you so scared?'

'Because I once had a future mapped out for me. With a wife and children—my own family. And when that dream turned into a nightmare I decided that love and relationships were for fools. That it wasn't worth the risk of being humiliated, failing again.

'I thought I was against Christos marrying Sofia because they barely knew each other, but the reality was I hated having to face everything I'd lost—my dreams of having a loving marriage, children, a woman who would be my best friend.

'At the wedding Christos and Sofia's happiness mocked everything I had tried to convince myself didn't matter to me. And I was also trying to deal with the intensity of my feelings for you. I couldn't deal with how I was feeling: the pain of remembering a future that had been torn away from me, the memories of shame, my damn pride, and how I—a cynic—was falling in love with a woman who wanted to be swept off her feet.

'I just wanted it all to go away. It was all utter madness. I didn't know what to do, so I pushed you away. But for the past few days I've been the unhappiest I've ever been. You've changed me. You've made me look inside myself and realise just how lonely I was before you came along; how empty my life was with its endless work and partying. I'm tired of living a pretence.

'Seeing how courageous you are in helping your family, in what you said to me on Kasas before you left about not being honest with myself, I realised I needed to let go of my shame and humiliation. That I was letting my pride get in the way of ever loving a woman again.'

Though his stomach was churning, Andreas forced himself to admit it. 'The wedding was like an X-ray of everything that was wrong in my life, and because I didn't like what I saw I messed up. And I'm here to say I'm sorry.'

Andreas's apology had tumbled out in a rush of heartfelt words. It was going to be so hard to say no. Even now, with her heart shattering into smaller and smaller fragments of pain, because she knew the reality was that they could never be together, she wanted him with a desperate ache that was tearing her apart.

'You're not the only one who messed up on the wedding day. For the past few days I've been trying to understand why it hurt me so much that you were so distant, and I've realised it actually had very little to do with you.'

He leaned towards her, those broad shoulders tensing under the cotton of his shirt. 'What do you mean?'

She closed her eyes at the memory of her forehead resting on the solidity of his collarbone, the sensation of his chest rising and falling beneath her cheek. Regret and guilt washed over her.

'I was expecting too much from you. I should have seen that you were struggling and supported you, instead of constantly looking for signs that you were pushing me away. You had told me about the pain of your marriage, about your relationship with your father. I should have stepped back and given you the space you needed, but instead I was almost willing you to push me away because I knew it was inevitable. Deep down I wanted it to happen sooner rather than later... I was already in love with you, and I couldn't bear the thought of falling even more in love with you only for you to end it all.'

'Why was it inevitable?'

'Because you told me time and time again you didn't believe in love and relationships. And, let's face it, you aren't exactly the romance-loving guy I plan on marrying.'

'Maybe I could become a romantic?'

'I suppose miracles do happen.'

For a moment they shared a smile, and she wondered how she would manage to walk away from him.

'But there was another reason why I thought it was inevitable.' An awful, giddy light-headedness came over her and she had to pause to try and right the world, which had tilted for a moment. 'It happened with my mum.'

Her words came out in a bare whisper. It had taken every ounce of strength in her to force them out. It was as though her heart had been clinging to them, afraid it might shatter if she spoke them publically.

'And if she could do it so could you.'

Andreas moved forward in his seat so that their knees were touching. He laid a hand gently on her leg. Those green eyes held hers with a compassion so great she had to glance away in order to speak.

'All through my childhood it was me and my mum against my dad. To me, we were a team, protecting Matt and Lizzie against him. We never spoke about it, but we instinctively worked to take them out of his way when he was about to let loose about something. One year, when it was Lizzie's birthday, he came home at the end of her party and there was a huge argument about the house being a mess. What had been such a fun and happy summer's day instantly became dark and terrifying. He started shouting. He decided Lizzie should be taught a lesson for allowing her friends to mess up the house and lit a bonfire to throw her presents onto it. My mum rushed Lizzie and Matt upstairs, before they knew what was happening, and I hid as many presents as I could before locking myself in my room.'

'How old were you?'

'Eleven.'

'You were too young to be dealing with that.'

'Perhaps, but at the time it just felt like it was part of life—and I had my mum on my side. But then one day I came home from school and she had left us. I couldn't believe it. I was convinced my dad was lying. I thought he had hurt her. He wouldn't tell me where she had gone.

Eventually he told me out of spite, during an argument. She had moved home to Scotland. I spent a whole day travelling to see her. I wanted to make sure she was okay. Check when she was going to come home. But she wasn't ever going to come home. And when I begged her to allow Matt and Lizzie to come and live with her she said no.'

'Grace, I'm sorry.'

He edged a little closer and she took comfort from his nearness and the sincerity in his eyes.

'What did you do?'

'I buried my feelings and tried to forget everything about her—the relationship we'd had, that she even existed. I put all my time and energy into Matt and Lizzie. On the wedding day, because you were so distant, all the fear and pain of my mum walking out on me came rushing back and I couldn't cope. Added to that, I was missing Lizzie and Matt. And with Sofia getting married... I guess I just felt extra vulnerable because the people I love were moving on.'

She dragged in some air, tears of regret filming her eyes.

'I'm sorry I wasn't there for you more. I can understand now why you might have thought I was backing you into a corner.'

He came and sat beside her, his hand skimming against her cheek before tucking a strand of hair behind her ear. 'I promise I'll never leave you. *Ever.*'

What was the point in him saying that? They had no future.

'I want you in my life, Grace. I know I have been far from your ideal man, and that I haven't swept you off your feet, but I want to make up for that now. I want to take you on dates, visit Paris and Vienna with you, watch the Bolshoi Ballet, take you hiking in the Pindus Mountains.'

She could not help but smile. 'That sounds lovely, but I now know that I don't need any of that. Ever since my mum moved out I've built up this idea in my head that a great romance would fill the void she left. I thought that was what love was—grand declarations of love, the heady whirlwind of being swept off your feet, the surface romance that has no roots. Now I know it's something much more profound. It's trusting and respecting one another. It's about feeling secure and loved. In those hours before the wedding we *did* have that together, didn't we? In those hours I stopped feeling alone because of you. And that's all I want from love. Nothing else matters.'

For a moment he said nothing, but then a steely determination entered his eyes. 'Marry me.'

What? Where had that come from? He wasn't playing fair. This was close to torture.

'Marry you?'

'Why not? I don't want to lose you. And what better way can I prove to you that I trust you?'

How could he ask her to marry him when he didn't even love her?

'Andreas, I can't marry you just because you want children, a family of your own. I love you, but I'm not going to compromise. I want a man who's passionately in love with me.'

He regarded her with astonishment. 'Can't you see how in love I am with you?'

Her bottom lip wobbled. 'You *love* me?'

'Of *course* I do. I fell for you the moment Christos sent me that photo of you pulling a silly face. As crazy as it might sound, I looked into your eyes and fell in love with you even before I met you. I love everything about you. Your ambition…your loyalty. The fact that you love Kasas as much as I do. How kind-hearted you are. I've never been so attracted to a woman in my life. And it's killing me to think that I might spend the rest of my life without you, not able to see your smile, hear your voice, touch you. Make love to you. I need you in my life.'

Punch-drunk, she tried to buy time to let everything he said sink in by teasing him. 'Andreas Petrakis—is there a romantic soul lurking behind that tough armour you wear?'

'Yes, and if you agree to be with me I promise to show you every day of our lives how much I adore and cherish you.'

He was in love with her.

She tightened her fingers around his, her heart dancing in her chest. 'I'm sorry about not supporting you, doubting you. I love you so much, and I want to be with you for ever too, but for now I'd like us to spend time together, to have some fun without pressure or expectations. I want to have our first proper date, our first trip to the movies, our first summer together. To simply be girlfriend and boyfriend for a while. What do you think?'

With a single move he lifted her up and sat her on his lap. He began to nuzzle her neck and in an instant she was putty in his hands. Her eyes rolled as his lips moved along her skin, his mouth warm, his teeth playfully nipping.

In a low, sizzling voice he said beneath her ear, 'I'll go with it—for now. But I'm never going to let you go. I need you in my life.' And then, pulling back, those green eyes burning with love, he added, 'My helicopter is waiting at the airport; are you ready to come home to Kasas?'

She cradled his head in her arms and buried her nose in his hair, inhaling the lemon scent of his shampoo.

'What were the words you whispered to me when we made love?'

Love shone in his eyes when he lifted his head. '*Psi-himou*—my soul.' His hand cradled her cheek. 'Through your love and kindness you have freed me to believe in dreams again.'

Her mouth an endless smile, she kissed him.

EPILOGUE

THE PALE LATE-AFTERNOON winter sun warmed Grace as she sat on the step outside her hillside flower shop on Naxos, sketching in her notepad. A month after opening and she still got a thrill every morning when she arrived to open up. *Her shop.* She had done it. She was running her own wedding floral design business and florist. All financed by the money she had earned designing and supplying flowers for weddings throughout the islands during the past summer—thanks to the incredible publicity following Sofia's wedding.

In the large shop window she had placed an old bicycle, its yellow paint fading, the front wicker basket filled with an abundance of vivid orange and yellow gerberas. Overhead hung a mix of pale wooden hearts, crafted locally from driftwood. Behind the window display Grace had kept the shop simple: pale green walls, Andreas's uncle's ceramics positioned in the various nooks and crannies of what had once been a bakery, and simple teak wooden tables and counters for displaying the flowers... roses, calla and oriental lilies, alstroemerias, chrysanthemums, euphorbia, bear grass and bamboo spirals all sitting in a mismatch of flower containers.

The sound of footsteps on the cobblestones had her pausing as excitement tingled through her limbs.

It couldn't be. He wasn't supposed to be home until the end of the week.

She wanted to look up, but the fear of being disappointed had her instead staring blindly down at her sketches. But as the footsteps came nearer and nearer goosebumps erupted on her skin and she held her breath as a sixth sense battled with logic.

It's not him. It's only wishful thinking.

Polished black leather shoes came to a stop in front of her. *Andreas!* Her heart leapt into her throat.

'Yassou, psihimou.'

The widest, daftest grin broke on her mouth at the sound of his low greeting. Her eyes shot upwards, taking in the charcoal trousers, matching suit jacket and light grey shirt, open at the collar. A grin played on his lips, and his eyes held hers with a mischievous delight.

Pleasure and excitement sent waves of heat into her cheeks. 'You're home!'

'Yes, I'm home.'

Her heart tumbled. 'I thought you weren't coming until the end of the week?'

He sat beside her, and though her head spun at being so close to him, inhaling his distinctive addictive scent of spice and lemon, she forced herself not to touch him, enjoying these moments of teasing tension too much.

'I cut my visit to the Caribbean short.' With a playful frown he added, 'I had no choice but to do so as I missed you so much.'

She frowned too, pretending not to understand what he was talking about, when in truth the past five days without him had felt as though she had lost a part of herself. 'But we spoke at least three or four times a day.'

He shifted on the step, so that his knee touched against the cotton of her red trousers. He leaned in towards her.

'Yes, but I couldn't touch you, bury my mouth against your throat, run my hands over your body, make love to you.'

Her toes curled in pleasure at his low, sexy growl. For a moment she closed her eyes as the delicious desire which had been building inside her from the moment his helicopter had left Kasas last weekend almost made her fall apart there and then.

She cleared her throat. 'And I thought you were with me for my stimulating conversation...'

His hand enclosed her knee, and he gave it a squeeze before his thumb began to circle against the much too sensitive skin on the inside of her leg. She inhaled a ragged breath, and he gave a satisfied grin before he replied, 'I'm with you because every morning I wake smiling, knowing that you are in my life.'

Oh, God, she was about to cry.

'I missed you so much.'

'Not as much as I missed you.'

That wasn't possible.

She shook her head. 'I doubt that.'

His eyes challenged hers good-humouredly. 'Oh, really? I could barely concentrate in meetings... I lost my appetite. I couldn't stop talking to people about you or sleep at night, even though I slept with your nightdress.'

She tried not to giggle. 'You slept with my *nightdress*! Which one?'

'The dark raspberry one that drives me crazy every time you wear it.'

'The nightdress you bought for me in Vienna?'

'Yes. I stole it from the side of the bath before I left on Saturday morning.'

They both paused as they remembered how he had dragged a sleepy Grace into the shower with him that morning, peeling her nightdress from her body and tossing it away, and how quickly she had awoken to his touch.

She sat for a minute, drinking in the beauty of his face: the strength and pride of his high cheekbones and arrow-straight nose, that mouth that in an instant could make her forget everything but him, the wonder of his eyes that constantly held her in his grip.

'I love you so much, Andreas. It scares me a little. What if I ever lost you?'

He moved forward and his lips landed on her cheek. It was a light kiss, a tender one. And it was followed by a train of similar kisses of reassurance across her cheek to the shell of her ear. Grace arched her neck as her heart exploded and desire coiled in her belly. His breath was warm, his lips firm.

Against her ear, he whispered, 'I will always be at your side. I would lose everything I own, cut off my right arm, rather than ever be without you. You are part of me now. You give everything in my life meaning.'

She drew her head away and they stared into each other's eyes, making up for all those days apart, before she sought out his ear. She whispered with a smile, 'These past few months have been so magical... I never realised it would feel so incredible to be so loved, so supported, so encouraged. You give me a strength, a sense of security that allows me to take on the world with no fear.'

His arm circled her waist and they sat with her brow resting against his collarbone, neither talking, just drawing strength and pleasure from being together again, breathing as one.

Eventually he pulled back from her, a wariness growing in his eyes. 'I've invited my parents to stay with us for Christmas, along with Christos and Sofia.'

Amazed by the news of the invitation, Grace leaned even further back. 'You have?'

Andreas suddenly seemed nervous. He swallowed hard before he spoke. 'You have shown me the importance of family. And I want us to be surrounded by family. Our children will need their grandparents. Now that Christos and I have agreed to jointly take over the family firm it's time to build bridges for the future.'

Grace opened and closed her mouth a number of times as she tried to process everything he'd said. The invitation was a big step forward in Andreas's rebuilding of his relationship with his father. 'I'm so glad.'

'You must invite Matt and Lizzie to join us too.'

She couldn't think of anything better. 'That's a wonderful idea. Thank you.'

'It's your home too, Grace, there's no need to thank me. In fact I think we should make it official that it belongs to you.'

He moved off the step and knelt down before her. Grace gave a little gasp. His eyes met hers, gently teasing her with tender affection. From his trouser pocket he took out a navy velvet pouch. And from the pouch a solitaire diamond ring. He held it out to her. The huge stone sparkled brightly under the winter sun.

'The past six months have been incredible, but I want the whole world to know how much I love you. I want to introduce you to others as my wife. I want us to start a family. Will you marry me?'

Was this really happening? Was the man she loved with every cell of her body asking her to spend the rest of her life with him? *Did dreams like this actually come true?*

'Are you sure? Even after living with me for six months and knowing now how talkative I am?'

'I'm sure.'

'Even knowing how easily I cry?'

'It just makes me want to hold you in my arms all the more.'

'What about my addiction to the Bee Gees?'

He gave a sigh. 'You might have a point...there's only so much *Saturday Night Fever* a man can take.'

'And then there's my obsession with cheese and marmalade sandwiches.'

'Now, *that* could be a problem—and you haven't even mentioned how you like to steal my clothes.'

'Only a sweater every now and again—and anyway you can't talk...you stole my nightdress.'

He held his hands up and gave a guilty grin. 'True.'

Oh, Lord, when he smiled like that life just felt incredible.

His hand rested on her knee. 'I love you, Grace. I know I can be bad-humoured at times, when I'm under pressure, and that I prefer silence to music, that I'm not the best at talking about my feelings, and I've no interest in television programmes like you... But I'd happily sit and listen to you giggle at some sitcom for the rest of my life. Before you I had no future other than work and the endless pursuit of success. Now I can see a life of happiness and fulfilment with you, and hopefully with our own family.' With a playful wince he added, 'Now, can you please answer me before my knees give way?'

Grace sat dazed. In the past six months Andreas had proved time and time again what a passionate, tender and strong man he was. He supported her unconditionally in her business plans, told her endlessly how beautiful and clever she was. Looked at her as though she was the only woman in the world.

'Andreas Petrakis, I fell in love with you the moment

you passed me your jacket the first night we met. I knew that behind that scowl lay a man with a good heart. I love you so much. Of *course* I'll be your wife.'

Eyes aglow with happiness, Andreas stood and pulled her up and into his arms. First he placed the ring on her finger, and then he tilted her face up to him.

'I promise to honour and treasure you for ever.'

His kiss was deep and passionate, their bodies pressed hard together.

When he eventually pulled away, he tucked her loose hair behind her ear and said, 'Close the shop early tonight. We have a whole week of being apart to make up for.'

Grace nodded but, unable to bear the thought of being without him, dragged him into the shop with her. He held her close from behind, his hands wrapped around her waist, his mouth nuzzling her neck while she shut down the till. Together they pulled down the shutters, and in the near darkness, surrounded by the sweet, heavenly scent of flowers, they smiled into each other's eyes.

A single soul inhabiting two bodies.

* * * * *

HIS HIDDEN AMERICAN BEAUTY

CONNIE COX

CHAPTER ONE

DR. ANNALISE WALCOTT adjusted the two huge cases of medicines on her cart before she made the steep climb up the gangplank of the luxury cruise liner *Neptune's Fantasy*. While she'd had most of the supplies delivered straight to her onboard facilities, she liked to bring along the ones that needed refrigeration herself, just to make sure they stayed at the correct temperature. Not that she'd ever had a problem—Annalise avoided problems as often as she could.

Call her a control freak and she wouldn't deny it. She'd learned a long time ago that the only person she could consistently rely on was herself.

She trailed behind the last-minute stragglers, crewmates eking out the final seconds of shore leave before they boarded for the transatlantic cruise. They would be out at sea for over ten days straight before the first port of call, which meant a lot fewer breaks for the staff. And only a small percentage of crew got shore leave at each port. With rotating days off, most of them wouldn't have a personal day on land for at least four weeks.

One by one, they went through Security, a procedure that took forever but which, she had to admit, was a necessity.

A Gulf breeze made the afternoon pleasant despite the strong subtropical sun heating Annalise's back through her roomy, short-sleeved T-shirt. Thankfully, she'd slathered her arms and legs with sunblock before donning her shorts and sandals so she had no worries about her pale skin turning pink. Not a good example for a doctor to set when she warned others about avoiding sunburn.

"Need some help with those, Doc?" A bartender named Brandy pointed to the cases. Brandy sported a new tattoo, still red and slightly swollen.

Annalise hoped she'd had it done by a reputable shop. Illegal backroom bargains had consequences. She had long-lasting firsthand knowledge of that. If only hers had been as harmless as a tattoo.

"I've got them. Thanks, though." She moved forward another six inches in the queue, wincing as the corner of the cart dug into her ankle.

"Have a nice time on shore?" Bartenders were chatty by nature and Brandy was no exception.

Annalise had never learned the art of making small talk herself, beyond the few stock phrases she used to put her patients at ease.

"Just long enough to realize I'm ready to be back at sea."

Being on land in her home port of New Orleans always made her uneasy, even though all personal threats had long since passed.

"Didn't I see you with a friend on the patio at the Crescent City Brew House this afternoon? A male friend?"

"He was my study partner in medical school." They'd been more than study partners, but the bartender didn't need to know how he'd helped her work through her pain and grief all those years ago. "He's my *platonic* friend."

"Nothing more? Not even a friend with benefits?"

Annalise laughed, inwardly wincing as it sounded brittle and forced in her ears. "He's not my type." Not that she had a type.

"What kind of man do you like, Doc? I'll bet I can fix you up. I'm fairly good at that sort of thing."

Annalise wished it were that easy. "You bartenders are really stupid in disguise, aren't you? But there are rules against that sort of thing, remember?"

"I don't know about you, Doc, but the rule against fraternization gets old when I've been out to sea for a while. It's not natural to go without sex for such long periods of time."

Sex. Shipboard sex meant a shipboard relationship—or at least a shipboard flirtation. No way would she risk her career—or her peace of mind—for a fling.

To forestall the conversation, Annalise pulled the brim of her baseball cap down tight and deliberately looked up.

From where she stood, halfway up the ship's side with the ocean far below her and the top deck far above, Annalise felt the weight of such a huge amount of people, both guests and staff, dependent upon the ship's medical facilities. As usual, she was the sole physician on board, but she had plenty of trained medical professionals to help her, including a new physician's assistant. The P.A. came with great recommendations and Annalise was looking forward to meeting her.

Her only worry was the six-year-old girl on the manifest, Sophie Christopoulos, diagnosed with juvenile diabetes. But her parents had been wise enough to have the girl's endocrinologist consult with Annalise ahead of time and Sophie had an introductory appointment before tonight's first supper seating.

Sophie's insulin was in one of the cases on her cart. With precautions, the young girl should be able to enjoy her trip just fine.

A crepe paper streamer sailed down from the top deck to drape itself across Annalise's shoulders like a boa. The makeshift fashion statement made her smile.

She looked up to see passengers on the foredeck already in full party mode and they hadn't even left dock yet. Cruises had attitudes and she could already tell this one was going to be a wild one. No peaceful, relaxing vibes coming from this crowd.

Brandy looked up, shading her eyes. "It's going to be one of those."

"The kind of cruise I enjoy most." While Annalise didn't partake of the party life herself, she enjoyed the energy.

"As long as they tip well." Brandy pointed to the sky. "Looks like a storm is coming in."

Annalise shrugged. "Typical late afternoon for New Orleans this time of year. It will blow through as fast as it's blowing in."

A thick bank of stormclouds dimmed the sun's brightness while a strong gust of wind brought chill bumps to her exposed legs. Sprigs of reddish-golden hair whipped into her face despite the baseball cap she'd plopped onto her head.

The layered cut had been a whim while she'd been on shore, a consolation prize after visiting her mother and finding her the same.

She'd thought short hair would be easier, but she missed the straightforward care of her ponytail. Now her hair was too short to capture with a rubber band and too long to stay out of her eyes without a lot of styling and primping. And primping had no place in Annalise's life. Why waste the time?

Her life was devoted to patching up people and keeping them healthy so they could enjoy their days under the sun. Stolen time away from the workaday world was precious and she wanted the passengers to be able to make the most of it.

Annalise knew the value of escaping the real world. That's why being the *Fantasy*'s onboard physician was her dream job.

A squeal of tires from the parking lot down below caught her attention.

A sporty black convertible with the top down slid into an empty parking slot and careened to a stop. Annalise squinted to see the dark-haired man behind the sunglasses pop his trunk, grab a suit-sized carry-on, a serious backpack and a large rolling suitcase and make a sprint for the entrance of the cruise ship's land-based check-in facility.

She glanced at her watch. A quarter till five.

When the cruise line said to embark before four o'clock,

they had their reasons—security checks being one of the most important ones.

Brandy shook her head. "There's always one who thinks the rules don't apply to him, isn't there?"

Annalise agreed. "He'll have to do some real sweet-talking to get aboard this ship."

Brandy gazed absently at the head of the line. "Some men are worth breaking the rules for."

Not any man she'd ever met.

Stormclouds moved into position overhead, blocking the sun's intensity but adding a couple of points to the humidity scale, making the moist air heavy to drag into her lungs.

The sooner she was out at sea, the better.

"Next," came the call from the front of the line.

As she moved forward, Annalise looked back at the dark-haired latecomer juggling his luggage to open the door to the check-in office.

She had to admit he had a face and body that could entice a saint to at least bend the rules a little.

He flashed a dimpled smile at her as he caught her staring.

She could feel a blush heating her face as she looked away.

She was no saint, but the man didn't exist who could tempt her. Sadly, she wished there were.

Dr. Niko Christopoulos leaned over the counter past the plastic *Closed* sign, giving the middle-aged receptionist a big dimpled smile. He hoped she liked the rugged, unshaven look. It couldn't be helped.

"I'm so sorry to be such a bother. I've been traveling for the last thirty-two hours straight to get here and my last flight landed late."

The receptionist, who reminded him of his Aunt Phyllis with her polite but no-nonsense attitude, pulled up his information.

"You're responsible for the party of twelve, right? The grandmother who thinks she's won the family cruise?"

Niko gave a quick look around the deserted lobby, as if any of his family might overhear. "That's right. Do you need to verify my credit card?"

"We've already done that. But I do need your passport, please." She held out her hand.

He handed her the well-worn leather folder.

"The Congo, Doctor? And before that Haiti? You're quite a world traveler."

Niko didn't talk about his charity work—ever. But if it got him on this blasted ship before it sailed… "Doctors Without Borders. An adventure every trip."

Her eyes softened and she picked up the phone. "Hold the ship for Dr. Nikos Christopoulos. He was unavoidably delayed and will be heading your way in just a moment."

"Thanks for waiting on me."

She gave him a sly wink. "I'm sure you're worth waiting for."

He returned the wink. "That's what they tell me."

"Do you need help with your bags?"

"Got it all here." He pointed to his military-sized backpack full of shorts and swim trunks and toiletries, his suit bag with his tuxedo and his one rolling bag, glad he'd packed for this trip and stuffed his clothes in his trunk before he'd even left for Haiti, for once planning ahead.

He was more of a go-with-the-flow kind of guy—which came in handy when making split-second decisions in the field. Life or death decisions were enough to worry about without adding the little things to the list. But this week he intended to surrender all decisions and worries and soak in the sunshine.

He needed these three weeks of enforced restful play-time. He had become soul-weary, the kind of tired a good nap couldn't cure.

Physician, heal thyself. He self-prescribed a big dose of fun and he intended to follow doctor's orders.

"Have a wonderful vacation, Dr. Christopoulos."

"I'll do my best." It worked. The charm his grandmother loved him for and his brothers taunted him about had gotten him where he needed to be once again.

Use the gifts you've been given, his grandmother told all of them. His brothers could all cook meals that would please the gods of Olympus. Niko couldn't boil an egg.

An easy way with words and a genetically pleasing appearance had been his gift—he just wondered if a woman would ever care enough to see past the exterior to the man underneath.

But then again, that would mean he would also need to look beneath her surface and that would mean getting up close and personal. A relationship was out of the question with the lifestyle he would soon be living full time. His ex-fiancée had made that perfectly clear to him. But that was yesterday's problem.

He would embrace today. Too many years ago he'd learned the hard way that that's all anyone could really expect to have.

As he headed up the gangplank, the calypso music put a kick in his step. This trip may have originally been planned for his family's benefit, but it was exactly what he needed, too.

Niko breathed in the tangy air and prepared to enjoy himself, no holds barred. And maybe he'd start with that cute little honey-haired woman in the baseball cap with the legs that went on forever. She stood at the end of the line apart from everyone else, looking totally unattached, which meant totally available, right? While long-term relationships were out, shipboard flirtations were definitely in.

"Those are mighty big bags for such a little lady. Prepared to dress for dinner, are we?" Niko jiggled his suit bag for emphasis.

Big drops started to fall from the clouds above. He moved closer to squeeze under the canvas canopy sheltering the ship's entrance.

The long-legged beauty tried to shift away but there was nowhere to go.

Just as Niko was considering stepping out into the rain to put her at ease, the line moved, giving her the space she obviously needed.

Then again, it seemed this woman claimed her own space. She looked down her nose at him as best she could, considering she was several inches shorter than him. "I'm on staff here. I don't do dinner."

Which wasn't quite true. Annalise helped out by rounding out the captain's table on occasion to even out the couples ratio. It was no hardship. Seated next to a partnerless passenger, usually an elderly gentleman or an awkward geek, she'd met some delightful people.

People like this stunning man next to her always had a date, or found one or two while shipboard. The ship's relationship rules definitely didn't apply to passengers like it did to crew.

Since she was a rule-abiding crew member, this man was not a threat. Even so, she found herself leaning away from him and his overpowering personality, even while she regretted the sharpness of her tone. She was definitely too much on edge today.

Brandy reached across her toward the guy with an open hand. "Hi, I'm—"

"Next," the security checker interrupted. He slid Brandy's ship's ID through the scanner. "You know the drill."

The tension between the security checker and Brandy crackled, proof that shipboard break-ups made for an incredibly uncomfortable environment.

Brandy turned to Annalise. "You know, Doc, this ship is large enough that a person could sail for a month without running into everyone on board. But no matter how big it is, when you're trying to avoid someone, no ship is big enough."

Annalise felt trapped, literally being caught between a man and a woman and their conflict. A clammy sweat started down her back as the old terror threatened to overcome her.

"Relationships. Not my thing." she managed to choke out as her throat tightened up on her. She tried to laugh but it sounded strained even to her own ears so she coughed to cover it up. From bad to worse.

Behind her, the late passenger took a step forward, concern in his eyes. "Are you okay?"

His voice was a low deep rumble. Masculinity personified.

She could feel the heat from his body as he crowded her.

Annalise took a deep breath as the unreasonable panic settled. It had been a few years, almost a decade, since she'd had a panic attack. But too many memories in too few hours had taken their toll on the solid, secure world she'd built for herself.

The sooner she put New Orleans behind her, the better off she would be.

"I'm fine. Thanks." She gave a numb nod and thrust her card at the security checker, careful to keep her fingers from brushing his.

The security checker took Annalise's card and slid it through. "Welcome back, Dr. Walcott. Need some help with that load?"

"Got it. Thanks."

The man behind her held his card out for inspection.

"Could you remove the sunglasses, sir?" the security checker asked.

"Of course."

Annalise had the strongest urge to turn around so she could look into his eyes but practicality took over. What she saw there would have no bearing upon her.

As she tugged her cart, it turned sideways, crashing into this man who made her feel things she didn't want to feel.

If she were only as graceful as she was independent. "Sorry." She meant for her gaze to skitter across his face but his eyes ensnared hers.

Tiger eyes. Amber golden with specks of brown, rimmed in

a darker brown. Tiger eyes with a depth of…sorrow, perhaps, behind the brightness.

"No problem." He blinked, breaking their gaze and allowing her to blink as well. When he raised an eyebrow at her, she realized she'd been staring.

Flustered, she yanked her cart, banging into the counter and almost taking out the passenger scanner. He must think her a total klutz.

What did it matter what he thought? Odds were they would never see each other again unless he had a medical emergency. And he certainly looked healthy to her. Well-worn jeans and a wrinkled T-shirt couldn't hide his physical fitness.

She bumped into passengers all the time. None of them elicited a significant response from her.

Annalise overcame the impulse to check him out one more time.

What was it about him that made her feel… What? Aware? Self-conscious? Tingly? That made her feel anything at all?

As she fought the cart into submission, she heard the security checker say, "Welcome aboard, Mr. Christopoulos. Passenger stairway is to your left."

Christopoulos? That was the name of her patient with juvenile diabetes. What were the odds?

Annalise headed toward the staff elevators, grateful for the privacy and breathing room that safe little metal box promised.

"Hold the door, please." A large tanned hand inserted itself between the closing doors. If the man had seemed to tower over her before, he loomed now. "You don't mind if I ride up with you, do you?"

"Passengers are encouraged to take the stairs if they're able." Inwardly, she winced at her brusqueness. She had wanted to establish distance, not convey rudeness. Where was her balance?

"I'm nursing a leg injury." He gave her a lopsided grin, as if he were embarrassed to ask for special treatment.

Annalise wished a hole would open up and swallow her. "Of course, then."

She stared at the floor numbers as the door closed, not trusting herself to engage in polite conversation.

She needn't have worried about the man being chatty. He leaned against the back wall of the elevator, closed his eyes and slumped as if he would fall asleep right then and there. Except there was nothing relaxed in the tightness around his eyes or the brackets around his mouth or the squareness of his jaw.

Annalise took a moment to gather herself the way she'd learned in therapy so many years ago, rationalizing that her edginess had been provoked by too many triggers in quick succession, the worst one brought on by her own need to know that someone in the world cared.

When she'd knocked on her mother's apartment door while she'd been on shore leave, Annalise had half expected, even hoped, to be told that her mother had moved and failed to leave a forwarding address.

But she'd been there. Bright pink lipstick had leaked into the pursed lines around her lips and coated the end of the cigarette stuck into her mouth. Age spots showed on her chest and arms, exposed by her cheap orange tank top.

"Anna?" her mother had smoothed down her over-processed hair. "I hadn't expected…"

Scented candles perfumed the air. Annalise recognized the odor. Her mother had always thought men were turned on by heavy oriental scents. The smell made her stomach turn.

"I was in town and just thought I'd drop by."

The furtive look her mother sent over her shoulder to whoever was waiting in the back bedroom was less than welcoming.

"I don't really have the time to come in and visit," Annalise assured her.

The relief was obvious in her mother's eyes. "Maybe another time."

Her mother had closed the door between them without saying goodbye.

It had been over two years. What was another couple of years between family?

Being in her home city, seeing her mother in the old apartment she herself had once lived in, consulting with the little girl's doctor in the same building where she'd attended those therapy sessions, and then meeting with her friend had been a bit much for one day.

And this man next to her, this man who exuded power and testosterone, this man who she was too aware of being just inches away from her, had her all off balance. Something was different about him.

The elevator bumped, threatening Niko's balance. He shifted his weight. From beneath his half-closed lids, he watched Dr. Walcott do the same.

Something was different about her, something that intrigued him. An air? An attitude? A challenge?

Only problem was, Dr. Walcott didn't seem interested. Could he change her mind? When had he last been challenged?

He rubbed his hand across his heavily stubbled face.

When he saw her eyeing him, he said rather self-consciously, "This boat has plenty of hot water, right?"

"The only reason you'll take a cold shower onboard this *ship* is because you take one voluntarily."

"I don't see that happening." He flashed his dimple.

She responded with the slightest of tight-lipped curves at the corners of her mouth. Polite, but just barely.

So much for winning her over with his innate charm. But, then, he wasn't at his best.

A shower and shave and maybe a nap first. Then he might seek out the good doctor on the grounds of professional curiosity. She'd give him a tour of the facilities. He'd buy her a drink.

They'd have a private meal on his room's veranda and watch the sunset together—and maybe the sunrise, too.

"How is room service?"

"Very serviceable." She bit her lower lip then squared her shoulders and took a breath as if she were about to plunge into the deep end of the pool. "I use room service quite a bit. They are very prompt. You should try the salmon mousse."

"And maybe a bottle of pinot grigio to share with a new friend?" With the shipboard doctor, he wouldn't have to worry about expectations and entanglements.

"I've never tried it that way. But, then, I'm not very good at sharing." She glanced down at his bare finger. "I'm sure your girlfriend would enjoy the romantic gesture, though."

"No girlfriend at the moment."

She nodded her acknowledgement while she adjusted her grip on her cart, pulling it more decisively between them.

He'd gone too far, too fast. Message received.

He leaned back and closed his eyes, giving them both space.

He might be a romantic but he was a lousy long-term lover.

His ex-fiancée would be glad to expound upon that.

Impatient by nature, Niko had known there was some deep-seated, instinctive reason he'd never agreed to a wedding date. When she'd insisted he choose, either her or his work, he'd finally understood what that reason was.

Any woman who couldn't love him for who he was didn't love him at all. Sadly, after they'd both said their goodbyes, he'd realized he hadn't loved her either. He'd just thought he should because his family had insisted they were the perfect couple. And his family always knew what was best for him.

When it should have been a tragedy, breaking off their engagement had been a relief. It had also been the last tie to living the 'normal' life his family wanted him to live.

This trip was his parting gift, his apology for letting them down, his peace offering for following his dream when he knew that was the last thing any of them would want him to do.

But his lifestyle change was tomorrow's problem. Let tomorrow take care of itself.

The elevator jolted to a stop, putting the brakes on Niko's runaway thoughts.

"Your floor?"

Annalise jerked as his voice called her back to the present. She'd gone away in her mind to avoid an awkward situation as she had so often in the past. But she'd never let down her guard like that while in a confined space with a man.

He was still leaning against the wall, but one eye was cocked open. How long had the elevator been stopped with the doors gaping open?

Keep it together, Annalise. With that admonishment, Annalise pulled the tatters of her self-discipline around her, took a deep breath and determined to carry on. She gave him a sheepish smile. "Lost in thought."

"Been there, done that myself." He pushed away from the wall.

She tugged her heavy cart to get the rollers moving over the rough separation between the elevator and the hallway floor.

"Need some help?"

"No. I've got it under control." She was making more of this chance encounter than it really was, wasn't she? No man like that would be interested in a woman like her, would he?

"I'll be seeing you around."

Not if I can avoid it. She wasn't ready. Not now, maybe not ever, to feel an attraction to a man, especially a man as virile as this one.

"Enjoy your cruise."

He raised a suggestive eyebrow. "I already am."

She ignored the shiver that went through her. As she pulled her heavy load toward her clinic, she worked hard at dismissing the man who would forget about her the second the elevator doors blocked her from his sight.

Christopolous. If he was connected to her young patient, she knew all about how to keep her professional self apart from her personal self. *But was that what she really wanted?*

What she wanted was to have a normal reaction to a normal situation.

She couldn't help taking a look back.

He was watching her, appreciation on his face. He gave her a long, slow, deliberate wink.

Almost against her will her mouth quirked up at the corners, acknowledging—and enjoying?—his attention.

As she felt the ship's engines begin to churn far below her, she felt confused. She'd thought she was on an even keel, that nothing and no one could ever rock her boat.

Obviously, she'd been wrong.

Her little half-smile was more intriguing than the Mona Lisa's.

She was perfect. A woman in her profession would understand that any romance Niko allowed himself to indulge in would end when the ship docked.

Niko watched the good doctor walk away on her long, strong legs until the elevator doors closed, blocking her from view. This trip was supposed to be about family, about paying back all the sacrifices they'd made for him—even if they'd never know that part of it. But surely he'd find time for himself, time for a harmless shipboard flirtation, wouldn't he?

And if the good doctor wasn't interested, there were plenty more fish in the sea, right?

A wave of exhaustion overcame him. His long hours and primitive living conditions must be to blame. That sinking feeling certainly couldn't have come from the thought of possible rejection. His ego wasn't that big, was it?

If so, his brothers would soon set it to rights.

Niko opened the door to his home away from home for the next three weeks. While not a huge cabin, it was certainly big-

ger than the tent he'd been sharing with a nurse and an anes-
thetist for the last month.

The private veranda was big enough to dine on—and do
other things on, too. Yes, this cabin would do just fine.

The quick shower he took refreshed his energy as well as
his attitude. The restorative powers of hot water and a bar of
soap were nothing short of miraculous. Fresh underwear was
a close second.

He picked out the least wrinkled casual dress shirt and pants
from his rolling bag, shaking out the mustiness. Not too bad.
Packing was a skill he'd had a lot of practice with.

From the connecting door he heard a hesitant knock.

"Uncle Niko, is that you?"

"Yes, Sophie, it's me."

He finished with the last of his shirt buttons then unlatched
and opened the door between them and immediately gathered up an armful of six-year-old girl. Her bouncy black curls
smelled of baby shampoo and her breath smelled of sugar and
spice. Too much sweetness? A hint of fruitiness? Juvenile diabetes sucked.

"Sophie, when was the last time you checked your blood
sugar?"

Before Sophie could answer, a voice worn with age but sharp
nevertheless, said, "What? Not even a hello first, grandson?"

He looked past Sophie, snuggled on his shoulder, to the
four-foot-ten-inch paragon who ruled the Christopoulos family with an iron skillet in one hand and baklava in the other.

"Hello, Yiayia." He put down Sophie and bent to give a hug
to the one woman who had always been there for him. "I've
missed you."

"There's a way to prevent that. No one is making you stay
away." Despite her prickly words, her hug was warm and comforting. She took a step back to look up into his face, keeping
both her gnarled hands on his arms as if she could hold him
in place. "Wanderlust, like your uncle and your grandfather.

At least you have sense enough to keep yourself from getting killed. If I hadn't won this trip, I don't know when we would have seen you next."

Niko squirmed inside while he kept his smile brightly in place. "Livin' the dream, Yiayia."

His mercy missions meant everything to him. But his family would not be pleased if they knew he put himself in such danger, risking his life in areas where lives were lost in wars over water wells as frequently as they were from malaria. His thigh throbbed in memory.

The life of a an overworked, barely paid medical relief doctor was not the life his family had envisioned for him as they'd all sacrificed to send him to college and on to medical school.

He owed them so much. Could he do it? Could he follow his passion, leaving his family with loans and bills and kids to put through college—like they'd put him through all those years.

Yiayia pointed her bony finger at him. "The Christopoulos men are all lucky in love. Someday soon you will find the perfect woman and give me beautiful great-grandbabies."

"Maybe someday, Yiayia." It was easier to agree with her than to argue. And he certainly didn't want to start off a three week vacation on her bad side.

He was so unlike his three brothers in so many ways. Not being cut out to be a family man was the one that hurt the most. He'd dated his fair share of women and then some but he'd not found one he wanted to spend a week with, much less a lifetime.

He flashed the smile that always worked with her. "You've set my standards too high, Yiayia. No other woman can compare."

Yiayia reached up and pinched his cheek. "How can I stay mad at a face like this?"

Sophie had waited as long as she could. She jumped up and down to get attention. "I'm hungry. Ice cream, Yiayia! Ice cream!"

Yiayia's eyes sparkled as bright as Sophie's. "It's included in the trip, Niko. Did they tell you that? Any time we want some. And fine dining each evening, too. Such a dream come true."

It felt good to give back to the family that had sacrificed so much to give him his dream. They would have never accepted repayment for all the support they'd given him through the years. And they all certainly needed a break after the year and a half they'd just been through. If only he hadn't had to set up such an elaborate ruse...

"All right, little one. Let me get my room key." Yiayia turned to find the key.

Niko stopped his grandmother with a gentle hand on her arm. "Wait, Yiayia. What's Sophie's blood-sugar level?"

Yiayia had always made her little ones feel better through food and didn't understand why it had to be different with Sophie—which was one of the main reasons why Niko had agreed to oversee Sophie's care while onboard ship. All his brothers concurred that he had a way with Yiayia that none of the other three had.

"How do I know, Niko? You're the doctor in the family." She switched to Greek, a language Niko heard rarely and only among his grandmother's contemporaries who had immigrated to the United States when she had. But he understood the gist of it.

Yiayia was resistant to taking the disciplined stance needed to protect Sophie's health, thinking everyone was blowing it all out of proportion when her great-granddaughter looked just fine to her.

Niko gave her a stern look. "Where's her blood-glucose meter?"

"In my luggage. I haven't had a chance to unpack yet. She has to check in with the ship's doctor thirty minutes before supper, anyway."

Niko glanced down at Sophie, who was looking scared behind that pout she was sporting. The kid had been through even more than the rest of them.

In addition to being diagnosed with juvenile diabetes, her mother had lost a baby and almost her life through miscarriage when their restaurant had had the kitchen fire. All the trauma had been straining a marriage that had been made in heaven. Sophie's home life had been tense day in and day out for a long time.

The only reason Niko's oldest brother and sister-in-law had let their daughter come without them was because they were on the verge of emotional exhaustion and Sophie's doctor had insisted it would be better for Sophie to be away from the stress and tension for a while. So they had stayed behind to keep the restaurant open and work on their relationship, knowing Sophie would be surrounded by aunts, uncles, cousins and Yiayia, who would all watch out for her.

"I'll take her, Yiayia." He checked his watch. "We're a bit early but we'll stop in and say hello to the doctor while you look for that meter."

He'd promised his brother he would take care of Sophie. Who could have known his solemn vow would have the side benefit of bringing him together with the good doctor? Niko knew enough about life to make use of good luck when it presented itself.

And now he intended to take full advantage.

CHAPTER TWO

ONCE SAFELY IN her medical suite, Annalise took a deep breath,
the first one she'd managed since that man had crowded her in
the line boarding the ship.

Surrounded by the tools of her trade, she found her inner
balance. If she could relive those brief moments as she boarded
the ship...

But, then, going back in time wasn't possible, no matter
how hard she wished for it.

She dragged her clunking cases in front of the locked refrigerator reserved for medicines and inserted her key.

As Annalise put away the supplies she'd brought on board,
bumping the bottles and boxes into uniform rows, she felt calm
claim her. She pushed away the sheepishness she felt about
overreacting. Emotional incidents happened on occasion, especially after such a trying day. Being ashamed of her reaction
did nothing but undermine her success in coping.

The bell chimed, signaling someone had come into the medical suite. Officially, office hours didn't start until tomorrow
morning, but she had scheduled a visit with her juvenile diabetes patient to make sure they started off on the right foot.
She glanced at her watch. Better early than late.

"But I don't want to get stuck, Uncle Niko."

Annalise heard them before she saw them as they entered
the anteroom of the medical suite.

"Can't be helped, Sophie."

Sophie—it was the Christopoulos child.

That was his voice, wasn't it? The elevator guy was with her little patient. Sometimes luck wasn't in her favor.

Still, she liked it that he didn't trivialize Sophie's fears.

She'd checked the manifest earlier—solely to see where her little patient's cabin would be and to verify that a small refrigerator had been moved into her cabin. She found it had been moved to the cabin next door, Niko Christopoulos' room.

The girl was staying in the cabin next door to the refrigerator with her great-grandmother, Olympia Christopoulos. Twelve people surnamed Christopoulos, all with adjoining cabins or family suites, were on the ship, which had made the odds good she might run into him again.

She thought she'd braced herself for that strange feeling he'd caused in her. But her stomach gave a little flutter, knowing she'd soon be face to face with him again.

Apprehension? More than that.

Fear?

No. Not fear.

Anticipation, maybe?

Before she could sort that one out in her mind she rounded the corner and realized she'd downplayed his good looks in her mind. How could a real flesh-and-blood man be put together so well without magazine airbrushing to lend a hand?

He'd changed. He wore a charcoal-gray boxy button-down made of a silky cotton so fine it slid over his chest when he moved. Even though she wasn't the touchy-feely type, she wanted to rub it between her fingers—purely for curiosity's sake. And his white linen slacks looked loose, comfortable, deceptive. She remembered the shape of him in those jeans.

As he filled her office suite, she felt as if an electric current rode just below the surface of her skin. Unsettling was an understatement. But also energizing? Good? Bad?

She wasn't sure.

Annalise stood a bit taller and smoothed down the lab coat

she'd thrown over the chocolate-brown tailored slacks and matching loose blouse she'd changed into.

She felt acutely aware of herself as a woman, an awareness she always pushed down the list behind physician the minute she donned her lab coat.

What was happening to her?

Why now? Why him—okay, that one was easy. How could any woman not fail to go into immediate estrogen overload with him in such close proximity?

He held a notebook. The masculinity of his hand contrasted drastically with the notebook cover, which was totally overlaid with pink glittery stickers.

"Hi, again." He stuck out his free right hand. "Niko Christopoulos, and this is my niece, Sophie."

Sophie wore a baby-blue sailor dress with a large white collar and red cowgirl boots. Annalise could imagine the conversation between this little girl with the adorable stubborn jaw and the person who had helped her dress.

She took Niko's hand, long-fingered and large enough to engulf hers, and that fluttery feeling intensified to an erratic quivering that grew as the seconds ticked by.

Using all her willpower, she made herself hold tight when she wanted to jerk back.

Then he quirked his eyebrow and glanced at their bonded hands.

How was she going to handle this?

Her fallback answer. Professionalism.

She released his hand and used her best patient care smile she'd practiced so hard to perfect. "Welcome, Sophie. I'm Dr. Walcott."

"Uncle Niko is a doctor, too."

"Really?" That didn't surprise her. With his composure, Annalise was sure Niko Christopoulos could be anything he wanted to be.

Annalise squatted down to eye level with her patient, which

gave her a good view of Niko Christopoulos' expensive shoes. "And what do you want to be when you grow up?"

"A cook, of course. That's what we all are—except for Uncle Niko." She said it as if becoming a doctor instead of a cook was the most rebellious thing a man could do.

Niko shifted, causing Annalise to look up.

His eyes were tense and his mouth bracketed at the corners. "That's not true, Sophie. Your mother is studying to become a nurse."

"And my dad says it's all your fault."

He gave a deep, sad sigh as he held out his hand to help Annalise stand. "Maybe I should start over. Niko Christopoulos, black sheep of the family."

Annalise wanted to make up an excuse to ignore his outstretched hand, but she couldn't bring herself to reject the man even that small bit when he'd obviously been rejected enough by his own family. She knew how that felt.

"Dr. Christopoulos, it's a pleasure to meet you." As she said the niceties, he wrapped his hand around hers again, this time with the slightest of familiar pressure as if they were comrades in arms. Between his strength and his warmth she felt cocooned. Before she could feel trapped, he released her.

"Call me Niko. Professional courtesy, right? And you are…?"

She was a woman who rarely gave out her first name to strangers, liking the barrier titles and surnames erected around her.

"Annalise." Saying her own name aloud felt so intimate, like a secret revealed. Trying to erase the uneasy feeling, she said in her most authoritative voice, "I understand you're in charge of your niece's blood-sugar checks while you're aboard. Do you understand how to balance her food and activity with her insulin? Are you comfortable giving injections? I can give you a refresher course if you like. I know some doctors don't give injections regularly."

"Got it down." His sister-in-law had emailed Sophie's requirements and he had studied them on the plane.

"I don't want a shot. I don't like Uncle Niko being a doctor."

Annalise shouldn't get involved in family relations but she found herself saying, "I think it's awesome your Uncle Niko is a doctor. He helps people feel better."

"Daddy says Uncle Niko makes people's noses smaller and his wallet bigger."

This time Niko grinned, his cat eyes sparkling. "Guilty." He gave Annalise a wink. "Although I can see my services are not needed here as you have a perfect nose. But we need your professional help, Dr. Walcott. We need to check Sophie's blood sugar."

Annalise had a huge moment of doubt. "You don't know how to use her meter?"

Sophie looked down at her red boots. "Yiayia might have forgotten my blood-sugar meter in the car."

Niko kept his smile firmly in place to hide his disappointment with Yiayia. She couldn't seem to understand how important it was to monitor Sophie's condition. Juvenile diabetes could get out of hand in a heartbeat.

"It's hard for some family members to accept their young ones needing such continuous care," Annalise said sympathetically.

Apparently, she saw behind his smile. He must be slipping. He *was* beyond tired. Could he catch a nap on deck after supper? A few moments of solitude would go a long way to preparing him to facing three weeks with his raucous family *en masse*.

Annalise pulled up Sophie's charts on her computer screen. "When's the last time you ate, Sophie?"

Sophie shrugged, uncharacteristically shy, and pointed to the notebook her uncle held.

Niko turned to the last entry and angled it so Annalise could have a look at the meal listed there. Fast food at a burger joint. There were better choices—much better.

Sophie was young, but she would still have to be taught to be aware of what she ate.

Annalise asked in a different way. "What did you have for lunch?"

"French fries."

"Anything else?" Niko prompted.

"Aunt Phoebe made me eat my hamburger meat, but I didn't want to and Yiayia said I shouldn't have to because we were on vacation."

"Aunt Phoebe did the right thing." Annalise opened a cabinet and brought out a glucose meter. "Ready?"

Sophie folded her hands together behind her back and stuck out her chin. "No."

Niko's heart broke for her. Life wasn't fair.

What method of persuasion would work best with her?

Of all his nieces and nephews, Sophie was the most stubborn of the bunch. She'd often been compared to him. What would have worked best for him?

"Sophie Olympia Christopoulos, I'm not going to treat you like a baby. You're too brave for that. Now stick that finger out there and prove it to me."

Niko could see the wheels turning in Sophie's little brain and knew he'd scored. She stood up straighter and held out a finger. Right before Annalise rested the meter against it, Sophie broke. "Hold my hand, Uncle Niko, so it won't go and hide again."

Niko looked up at the ceiling, trying to find the strength before looping his fingers firmly around her tiny wrist. "All right. Let's do this."

"Are you ready?" Annalise moved quickly, pricking in mid-sentence before Sophie had a chance to tense up more. "It's over."

Sophie looked surprised. "That's it?"

"That's it."

"When Daddy does it, it hurts more."

Niko could guess why. His brother probably let the drama build so high that the fear was worse than the prick.

It seemed a family meeting was in order.

The tug o'war that had been pulling at him all these months gave a jerk to his gut. He was the doctor in the family, the one they'd all sacrificed to put through medical school. The one they relied on for explaining these kinds of things. But he'd been out of town and out of touch more often than not.

And, if all went as planned, after this trip, he would be practically unreachable most of the time.

Guilt bowed his shoulders.

Annalise read the numbers then showed them to Niko. He hid his wince then checked his watch.

"We'll eat in fifteen minutes. It's about time for insulin, rapid and long-acting. Let's go with the same amount and I'll make sure she eats better this meal to balance it out."

"Sounds good. Check again a few hours before bedtime to see if she needs a snack. Ask your waiter to bring apples and orange juice to keep in your room's refrigerator."

"Will do."

"Ice cream!" Sophie said. "I want ice cream. Yiayia said I could have—"

Niko cocked his eyebrow, stopping her whine in mid-sentence. "If you eat your meal, you can have a little for dessert."

While Annalise opened up her refrigerator and took out a vial of insulin, Niko paged through the notebook. "Abdomen for breakfast and lunch, thigh for supper, right?"

Annalise double-checked her notes. "Yes. And today is left side, tomorrow is right side."

Sophie's face clouded up as tears formed in the corners of her eyes. She looked so small and delicate.

Niko felt so powerless. Injections and a strict regimen were Sophie's fate for the rest of her life.

He picked her up to sit her on the examining table, giving her a big hug midway. "Sweetie, I would take this for you if I could, but I can't."

"If I don't eat, I don't have to have a shot, right?"

"Not an option, little one."

He took the vials from Annalise and filled the syringe to the proper marking.

"Hold your finger out like a candle, sweetie." He held up his own finger, showing her.

"I'm going to hold your leg still." He put his hand on her thigh. "When I say, 'Now,' pretend you're blowing out the candle. Be sure to blow hard."

She gave him a confused look.

"Trust me." He focused on the injection site. "Now."

While Sophie blew, Niko took advantage of her distraction and injected the insulin.

"Good girl. All over." He jotted down the particulars in Sophie's notebook, taking a moment to appreciate the details his brothers and sisters-in-law were trying so carefully to document.

"You want to dig through the treasure chest, Sophie, and pick out a toy?"

"Okay." Sophie shrugged, not looking very excited. After all these months of doctors' visits she'd probably been rewarded with too many cheap toys in the past to make this one special.

Annalise helped Sophie down from the table then opened a huge plastic tub filled with monster trucks and snorkels and magic wands.

"I think there's a superhero cape in there somewhere. A real one."

Sophie began flinging plastic trucks and coloring books out of the box, digging for the cape. "Really?"

"Absolutely. I save the good stuff for the most courageous girls and boys."

Niko gave Dr. Annalise Walcott a long look. She was a

smart one, reinforcing Niko's challenge to be brave with an enticing reward. Small things made big impressions with little patients. While he had the minimum of pediatrics training, he'd treated enough frightened children to pick up a thing or two. Apparently, Annalise had treated her own fair share of children, too.

"Found it!" Sophie triumphantly held up a bright pink cape along with the sparkling wand attached to it.

Niko quickly yanked off and crumpled up the tag that declared it a fairy costume instead of a superheroine disguise.

As she pointed the wand at him, he obligingly shrank back with as much mock terror on his face as he could muster. "SuperSophie. If I were a nasty villain, I would be quaking in my shoes right now."

"Let me tie it on for you," Annalise offered.

The pleased smile she gave Sophie made Niko think the good doctor really had picked out the cape herself. With her long legs she'd make the perfect bustiered and masked crusader.

Niko rubbed his hand over his eyes, clearing the vision. What was it about this demure doctor that had his imagination running wild? Had he been under so much pressure that he needed to resort to a fantasy life for relief? If so, what did that say for his stamina in the field?

Lack of resilience or desire to make a difference wasn't what sidelined most of the special mission doctors. Coping with the mental stress, knowing they were only making a small dent in the needs of so many was what broke most of them.

Then again, maybe Annalise brought out the creative imagination in him. Nothing wrong with that, was there? This was a fantasy cruise after all.

"You're really good with her, Dr. Christopoulos. I'm impressed." When she smiled, her gaze was honest, her voice sincere. It felt better than good to be appreciated.

"It's Niko." His own voice was huskier than normal.

"Niko." She licked her full lips.

Fascinating and, oh, so sexy with no contrivance or even an awareness of what her mouth could do to a man.

Niko reined himself in. It had been a while. Where he'd been wasn't exactly an environment conducive to lovemaking.

How did he ask the good doctor if she would like to share a drink with him under the stars tonight? How could he make himself stand out in a crowd when he bet every man on board this ship would like to do the same?

I don't do dinner, she'd said.

She'd been offputting on the gangway, but Niko could understand why. She probably had to field invitations and propositions all day, every day from total strangers.

What made him different from them? And why did it matter so much that he was? There were plenty of women aboard this ship looking for a diversion. But he had no interest in pursuing them. Only her.

What made her different?

He didn't know, but he wanted to find out.

He searched for the right pick-up line but came up blank. What was the matter with him? He'd had no trouble knowing what to say to charm the opposite sex since he'd turned twelve.

"What? Do I have something on my face?" Annalise wiped away a non-existent blemish.

"How about sharing a bottle of wine tonight?" Nothing glib or witty or clever there. Just a straightforward request. "I thought, as colleagues, we could discuss medicine aboard ship. Strictly professional curiosity."

She was shaking her head before she even started to turn him down. "I don't really think…"

That's when he heard them coming. No one could ever say a Christopoulos didn't give you fair warning before arriving. From the sound of it, the whole family was in the medical suite's anteroom.

Annalise looked alarmed.

"Not to worry. It's not a mass emergency. Just an invasion of family."

Family. Wasn't that what he'd wanted when he'd planned this elaborate ruse, to spend time with family? Why was he even trying to strike up a shipboard romance with a woman who obviously had no interest in him?

He had to admit, paying attention to a beautiful woman sounded a lot more enticing than paying attention to his brothers as they droned on about the restaurant or to the sisters-in-law as they expounded on the joys and tribulations of parenthood.

As he and Sophie joined them he realized, as he had so many times in the past, that he was a square peg in a family of round holes. Now he understood that no amount of buying anonymous vacations was going to change that.

Seeing his sisters-in-law with children in tow, he also understood that no number of casual relationships would fill that hole of not having someone special to belong to, like his brothers did.

Choices. Live every man's dream or live his own personal dream.

He would never again become involved with a woman who made him feel the pain of having to choose.

Annalise.

The good doctor was safe, right?

At a glance, Annalise recognized the people in her waiting room as family. They looked—and sounded—exactly alike.

Still, while the family resemblance was strong, Niko stood apart.

One of the lanky teenaged boys jostled another, who looked like an identical twin. "Of course we'd find Uncle Niko down here, playing doctor with the nurse."

"I'd expect you to be out by the pool, Uncle Niko, checking out the bikini babes. When we walked by, there was this one..." He raised his hands like he was holding coconuts, or maybe watermelons.

Niko cut them both a harsh look. "Respect," he growled.

At the same time as one of the women gave the twins a sharp look and said, "Boys, behave."

Amidst the chaos of the two women and smaller children throwing themselves into Niko's arms and the two men patting him on the back, Niko made introductions.

"Dr. Walcott, these are my brothers and their wives, with assorted nieces and nephews and my grandmother in the back. Family, meet Dr. Walcott. She will be helping us while we're here."

A tiny older woman, small in stature but big in presence, waded through three waist-high children and elbowed her way past the two tall boys to the front of the crowd. "I am Olympia Christopoulos. Everyone calls me Yiayia. We were all greatly relieved to learn the ship has its own doctor to help us with our little Sophie."

Surprising Annalise, Yiayia wrapped her in a big hug. Annalise flailed her arms, unsure what to do, who to be. Should she pretend to be the type of person who was comfortable with this type of thing? Should she hug back? Finally, the hug was over and Annalise could be herself again.

Too late, she wished she'd wrapped her arms around the old woman, just to see what having a grandmother might feel like.

The woman who belonged to the twin boys turned to Niko and patted her huge Hawaiian print tote bag. "I have the meter. I see you have the notebook. It's time for Sophie's s-h-o-t."

From the stricken look on Sophie's face she clearly knew what word the woman had just spelled out.

Niko gave Sophie a reassuring pat. "Already taken care of, Phoebe."

"You wrote it all down in the notebook, right? The time and the amount and her blood-sugar reading?" She turned to

Annalise. "You know how men are. They don't always think of these things."

Who were these people? They acted as if they didn't even acknowledge that Niko was a doctor in his own right. Or was that a good-natured tease? Maybe this was just a normal give and take of a normal family. Group dynamics wasn't her strong suit.

"Don't worry, sis. I learned how to chart in medical school." Despite Niko's self-deprecating smile, his tone held a hint of bite and his jaw held more than a hint of firmness.

His sister-in-law must have seen the same sparks in Niko's eyes that Annalise saw because she tried to excuse herself by saying, "Of course you did, Niko. It's just that you don't usually have children as patients and you have that big staff to do things for you."

Annalise envisioned a spa-like office suite with customized furniture arranged by a top designer, staff in matching trendy uniforms and coffee and tea with French names available to sip as the clientele discussed lifting brows, firming chins and reshaping cheekbones.

Her own utilitarian facilities would be stark in comparison. Still, her suite and her staff were top of the line, assembled to handle any emergency.

One of the men, older than Niko but definitely related, stepped forward. "Time to eat. Let's see how cruise-ship food stacks up to Christopoulos food."

A twin clapped Niko on the shoulder. "It'll be nice to be served instead of being the server for a change, too. But, then, you never had to do the waiter thing, did you, Uncle Niko?"

The tiny ancient woman reached up and tweaked the boy's ear. "If your grades were as good as Niko's, you wouldn't either."

Phoebe turned to Annalise. "Niko tutored during high school instead of working in the restaurant."

Annalise processed information, trying to fill in the holes

while simultaneously wondering why this family would reveal so much to a total stranger.

"Good thing Niko's so smart since he can't cook worth a flip," the other brother added. "Now, let's go and eat."

En masse, they turned and exited, carrying Sophie along with them but leaving Niko behind.

He raised an eyebrow. "Family. Gotta love 'em, right?"

No. No, you didn't. Annalise knew that first hand. But that was knowledge she had no intention of sharing. Sharing meant intimacy and intimacy was something Annalise didn't do, especially with a man who made her breath skip when he stood this close.

She fell back on her professionalism. "Enjoy your dinner. Bring Sophie back any time you need to."

"Thanks."

Annalise stood by the glass door and watched him walk away.

It wasn't that she didn't like to look at men—she just liked to look from a distance. Now she allowed herself to admire the breadth of his shoulders and tautness of his butt even while her medical training had her noticing the slight hesitation of his left leg as he climbed the short flight of stairs leading to the main hallway. He'd said something about an injury when he boarded the elevator with her, hadn't he?

Not her concern unless he sought out medical attention. She had to remind herself of that daily when she wanted to fix the world.

When her office was empty once again, it felt as if all the energy had been sucked out with the Christopoulos family.

No, not energy. They had taken joyous chaos with them when they'd left. The energy had gone with Niko, along with the impression of stability he projected of keeping that wild bunch under control.

Usually her haven, the atmosphere of the medical suite felt

as cold as the stainless steel of the countertops and she felt
restless, on the verge—but on the verge of what?

Underneath her feet the rumble of the huge engines reverberated as they churned through the waters of the Gulf of
Mexico on their way towards the open water of the Atlantic.

She was being silly. The feel of freedom was all around her.
Why, then, was she missing the anchoring sensation Niko had
taken with him?

CHAPTER THREE

NIKO SAT AT the dining table surrounded by family, knowing he'd turned down his best chance of a family of his own.

His ex-fiancée hadn't asked him for anything extraordinary—only to give up his work, to give up his soul.

She hadn't understood. He hadn't been able to make her understand what Doctors Without Borders meant to him. That he'd never felt more alive as he beat the odds, winning out over a harsh world unlike any his family had ever seen and snatching the downtrodden back from the edge of death. What were the odds he could make his family understand anyway?

Misunderstood. Different. The story of his life. Was there anyone on the planet who could understand?

In walked Annalise Walcott. She'd shed her lab coat, exposing the silk blouse over her trousers. Classy.

She was the total package, wasn't she? Brains and beauty. Such a winning combination.

While he'd appreciated the shorts earlier on the gangway, now he appreciated the way her silky blouse moved across her...

"Uncle Niko, what are you staring at?" His nephew Marcus interrupted as the teen followed Niko's line of sight.

"Just taking in the scenery."

"You mean that brunette at that corner table? She looks like your type."

Niko checked out the voluptuous dark-haired woman sitting

alone. Big hair, big earrings, big bone structure, everything he usually liked in a woman. He even liked her interesting nose, more aquiline than fashionable, but it suited her. "She's okay, I guess."

Beside him, Yiayia was taking a keen interest in the conversation while trying to appear as if she wasn't.

"You're not talking about Dr. Walcott, are you?" Marcus asked.

"Absolutely."

His nephew gave him a quizzical look. "She's not Greek."

"It's not like I'm going to marry her."

Marcus laughed. "Everyone knows you're not the marrying kind, Uncle Niko. We all live through you vicariously, even Dad." Marcus elbowed his father next to him to get his attention.

Niko's brother Stephen gave him a somber frown. "You've got to settle down sometime, Niko. We all liked Melina. Maybe if you talked to her? Apologized for whatever you did. Or even if you didn't do anything—"

"My broken engagement is none of your business, brother."

Stephen narrowed his eyes, but backed down and looked away when Niko continued to glare, using refilling his wife's wine glass as his excuse to turn away.

The eight years that separated them in age also separated them in values. Or maybe they were just too different. His brothers were so much like the father he could barely remember, while he was his own person.

If only he didn't have to keep reminding them of that.

Marcus spoke barely loud enough to hear. "It's true, isn't it, Uncle Niko? The Christopoulos men are destined to be family men, aren't they?"

"You've been listening to Yiayia too much." Niko could see a lifetime of family tradition shackling his nephew, just as it tried to shackle him.

"Every man has to find his own purpose. Family is a very

good purpose just not for everyone." Knowing what he was about to do was tantamount to anarchy, Niko leaned in and pinned his nephew with his stare. "Promise me, Marcus, that you'll take some time to think about what *you* want—not what anyone else expects from you."

Marcus swallowed hard. "Not everyone is as strong-willed as you are, Uncle Niko. I envy that about you. But someday..."

Niko thought of all the trips he took abroad with Doctors Without Borders, the trips his family thought he took for leisure. They thought he was gallivanting to tropical paradises, giving his wild side a long leash before settling down while his partners carried his load.

He encouraged them to think that. What would they think if they knew his partners admired and supported his perilous service work? And how would they feel about him if they knew family wasn't on his radar?

Not providing grandchildren was the second-biggest sin in the Christopoulos family Bible, right under "Don't live dangerously."

It was a rule he wasn't very good at following. Neither had his uncle or his grandfather. But, then, his parents had both been killed in a car wreck while on a trip to the store. Playing it safe didn't mean a person would *be* safe. And following the family rules didn't mean he would be happy like they were.

How did the good doctor juggle her family with her medical practice? Working on a cruise ship, she was separated from her loved ones more often than not, wasn't she?

Because he was staring, and because she turned and caught him at it, he stood and walked toward her to invite her over.

She looked around, as if she were looking to see who he was approaching.

He brightened up his smile a few notches.

She gave him a nervous smile back, shook her head and started to turn away. And his ego took the well-aimed shot to heart. Of all the women in all the world, why did he have to find this one so fascinating?

Then fate worked in Niko's favor. The captain, coming up behind her, helpfully pointed out that a guest was requesting her presence.

"Good evening." As the ship rocked, the captain politely rested his hand on Annalise's back, effectively keeping her still and steady. "Are you in need of our doctor?"

Niko had the strongest urge to push away the captain's hand, replacing it with his own.

Need. Yes, he was in need of her. Just standing next to her made endorphins flood his brain. What was it about her? And what excuse could he use to keep her close to him?

"If you have a few seconds, Dr. Walcott, I could use the reinforcement when I explain once again to Sophie's grandmother why Sophie can't have late-night snacks."

The captain dropped his hand and Annalise took a breath and an automatic step back from Niko, trying to find her comfort zone. But nothing about this man could be described as comfortable. As soon as the captain was out of earshot, she called him on his excuse. "I've seen you with your family, remember? When you speak, they all look at you as if every word was gold. You don't need any help from me, Doctor."

"But I do." His tiger eyes glittered. "You might notice I'm the only unmarried brother left. My family would like to change that. You'll keep me safe from their matchmaking, at least for tonight."

Too aware that everyone at Niko's table intently watched them, Annalise hesitated.

"Please?"

Annalise had never been able to turn down a plea for help—at least, that's what she told herself as she said, "Okay. But don't make a habit of this."

As she wove in and out, past the other diners, she questioned herself but could come up with no reason why she hadn't made her usual polite escape whenever a man took notice of her.

Was it the sincerity in his voice? What about him made her feel ready to respond to the interest in a man's eyes?

All the Christopoulos men stood as Annalise approached their table. Their good manners made her feel self-conscious and very feminine.

With Sophie now cuddled in her Aunt Phoebe's lap, it left an open seat between him and Yiayia.

As Niko pulled out the chair for her, he leaned in and whispered, "You're blushing. Nice."

"I'm not used to such…" She held her hand out to the standing men, speechless.

"A show of good manners," Yiayia finished her sentence. "Take it as your due, dear. You deserve it."

What would it be like to be a part of a large family where she was loved and respected on a daily basis?

A warm glow deep inside vied with the chill of nerves prickling along her skin.

Conflicted. Was she doomed to always be conflicted?

"Wine, Doctor?" A server held the bottle of merlot for her inspection.

Normally, Annalise would say no. While she enjoyed an occasional glass of wine with a good book, she never drank in uncomfortable social situations. But she found herself saying yes instead.

"And you, sir?" the waiter asked Niko.

He started to shake his head, but his brother Stephen was nodding instead.

"Give the man another drink. He's a doctor, you know? Under stress all the time. Look at that strain around his eyes. You need to cut loose every now and then, Niko, or you'll be looking as old as me before your time." Stephen held his glass out. "And pour me another one, too, will you?"

Niko knew his brother's remark was a dig at his supposed

frivolous lifestyle, which Stephen was both jealous of and proud he'd played a part in providing. Niko should have never let the misunderstanding lie between them for so long.

But so much had been happening when he'd left for his first mission. The restaurant fire, the miscarriage that had threatened his sister-in-law's life and Sophie's diagnosis had rocked the foundations of his very strong family.

Leaving his family at their time of need had been the hardest decision he'd ever had to make.

He wasn't good at raw emotion. Just being there for his loved ones had made him feel trapped and helpless—made him remember too much.

He'd had to take action. Do something. Fix something. There had been nothing he could do for his family to make them any better.

But he'd had the medical dossiers of a half-dozen children in his briefcase—children who could die without his medical care. He'd decided he would only be in the way if he stayed around.

He'd reasoned that there was no sense in adding to everyone's worries if Doctors Without Borders wasn't for him. Now that he'd made his decision, he wouldn't put a damper on this trip, but he would tell them at the end that working for Doctors Without Borders would be permanent.

He had already made arrangements to begin the sale of his share of the partnership as soon as he returned home. But for now he would keep pretending, for their sakes.

"Everything okay?" Annalise's hand fluttered over his arm, as if she wanted to touch him but felt he was off limits.

Niko pasted on his brightest smile. "I'm sharing a glass of wine with a brilliant, beautiful woman. What could be better? Except maybe a bit of privacy."

While he didn't know her well, he read her eyes with ease. Concern turned to disappointment. It seemed that's all he did lately, disappoint the women in his life.

But, then, Annalise wasn't in his life, was she? She was a

simple, uncomplicated diversion. In three weeks, walking out of her life would be as easy as walking off this ship.

He'd meant to be flippant, but he tempered it with truth. "I've got a lot going on in my head right now. I guess I haven't quite made the transition to vacation mode yet."

As the waiter made the rounds, Niko held out his glass after all. "To vacations."

The rest of the family held their glasses aloft and echoed his toast before drinking.

When the server would have moved away, Yiayia stopped him, holding out her glass for a refill.

"Just leave the bottle. We'll serve ourselves." Phoebe grinned at the young waiter. "We've had practice."

As Phoebe topped up the adults' glasses, Marcus did the same with the tea and juice pitchers for the children.

"A toast. To my grandson the doctor." Everyone held their glasses high then drank. Even the children downed their glasses in style. Bewildered at first, Annalise looked around and followed suit. Niko had to smile at her quick assimilation into his crazy family. If he were looking for a woman...

But who said anything about finders keepers?

He gave her a wink before saluting the table with his glass. "To my family, who put me through college and medical school."

Annalise raised her eyebrows then drank with him as the rest of the family looked at each other, well satisfied with their sacrifice. His decision would be so much easier if they weren't so proud of him.

"And to my brother and sister-in-law who could not be with us today." Stephen, as second oldest, did the honors to acknowledge them.

As soon as Niko took the obligatory swallow, he leaned over and explained to Annalise, "Family tradition. We'll finish off the bottle this way."

As the young nephews and nieces started to droop, climbing into any available adult lap for a good cuddle, Yiayia began her bragging. "Dr. Walcott, did you know that my grandson has been on national television, on a talk show? Did you know that he operates on all the famous actors and actresses? But he won't tell us who they are. Confidentiality issues. It's all very mysterious. They bring them up through the hospital's loading dock."

"Remember that time you made your cucumber yogurt for that actress when Uncle Niko wired her jaw shut?" Phoebe turned to Annalise. "He still won't tell us her name, even though we've begged. He's very discreet is our Niko."

Under cover of their chatter, Niko said to Annalise, "You're very quiet. Don't wait for a turn to talk. Just jump in anywhere."

"I'd rather listen." She gave him a smug smile. "I'm learning a lot about you this way."

Niko was one part chagrined over his family's bragging and the other part overjoyed that Annalise wanted to know more about him.

"Then it's only fair I get to hear your life story, too."

When Annalise looked around the full table tensely, he quickly reassured her, "When we have time to ourselves. I'll want all your intimate details."

Visibly, Annalise shivered. While Niko would usually regard her reaction as a positive response in anticipation of time together, the way she held herself so tightly told him he'd overstepped the mark.

To break the tension, he refilled her glass even though she'd only been taking the tiniest of sips.

She took the glass, looking into it as if searching for answers. "I'm not much on pillow talk." Her voice was husky, hesitant and, oh, so sexy.

She was so much more intense than the women he usually dated, like the Greek goddess in the corner, laughing loudly and holding court with the ship's captain. Annalise wasn't his usual type at all. Whatever type she was, she'd captured his interest and he couldn't seem to let go.

He would need to go slowly with her, pace himself. It was a novel concept when he usually got what he wanted when he wanted. His brothers would find this strain on his ego amusing. He himself found it challenging.

Marcus leaned over his mother to tell Annalise, "Some big charity wants to auction off a date with Uncle Niko. He did it last year and cameras followed him around all night, even when he kissed her."

Phoebe pushed her son back into place without jiggling the sleeping young nephew on her lap. "It would be good if you could bring your date back to the restaurant this year, Niko. We got a lot of publicity from that and we could certainly use it again."

He would have to tell them. No more celebrity stories. No more TV appearances. No more magazine layouts for the hottest catch in the Crescent City.

"Niko? Are you okay?" Stephen's concern brought him out of his thoughts.

He blinked, back in the game. "Fine. Just tired."

Yiayia was telling the good doctor about her own excitement in front of the media crew—a crew Niko had bought and paid for.

"And then this pretty little blonde girl handed me a huge check, just like on the television, and this man with a video camera asked how I felt." Yiayia told her sweepstakes story to Annalise. "I thought I would have a heart attack right then and there. And, of course, no doctor around."

She patted Niko on the shoulder. "My grandson is never home. Itchy feet, just like my late husband Leo. The places we would go when we were young... We travelled around the world before Leo brought me to America and that's the place that felt like home. Travelling is a good thing to do when you're young." She looked around the luxurious dining room of the cruise ship and smiled. "And good to do when you get old, too,"

That smile made all the planning, all the money and all the subterfuge worth it.

As his brother reached past him for the bread basket, doubt jabbed Niko. If he stayed with his practice, he could give his family many more trips like this one. His brothers could expand the restaurant, hire more employees, spend more time with their children.

Although he tried to stop himself, he couldn't help glancing Annalise's way. What would she think of him giving up all his family had worked so hard for on his behalf? Would she judge him to be as ungrateful as he judged himself?

But, then, this was a woman who called a berth on a ship home. Obviously, she was following her dream.

He couldn't help hoping she'd understand.

After escaping from the enthusiastic Christopoulos family, and one dynamic Christopoulos male in particular, Annalise took some time to recover.

Although she wasn't sure there was enough time in the universe for her to recover from the emotions Niko Christopoulos set off inside her.

Right now, all she could say was that she liked being treated with such respect. He had been attuned to every word, every movement she made. The experience had been nerve-racking but very flattering, too.

But, then, from what she gathered from his family, all women thought the same about him. Smooth talking was not an asset in her book.

It was a lot to think about. She was sure she wouldn't be able to sleep tonight.

With the sun still up this close to the equator, the evening was still warm so she slipped on her shorts and T-shirt from earlier in the day and took a good long stroll around the deck's track, thinking of the love packed into those sincere family toasts. Afterwards, she ducked into one of the onboard kiosks to make herself a cup of hot decaf tea with the hope of swallowing down her envy for a life she could never be a part of.

Now Annalise breathed in the sea air as she took the stairs up to the adults-only top foredeck, carefully carrying her hot cup of tea to keep from spilling in the roughening seas. Although the wind was picking up, the temperature was still balmy.

Pinks and yellows colored the blue sky as the sun neared the horizon. At this time of year it would hang there for a good forty or so minutes before it plunged into the ocean. Watching the sunset was her favorite way to unwind and the tiny top foredeck was the perfect place to do it.

Most passengers found this little deck too tame. There was no pool, no wet T-shirt contests, no band and no elevator access. The three flights of stairs put off most people even if the lack of entertainment didn't.

So she was surprised to see someone sprawled out in her favorite deck chair as she rounded the platform at the top of the stairs.

And not just anyone. Niko.

She recognized him immediately, despite the dark sunglasses covering his eyes. His shirt was off as he reclined with his long legs crossed at the ankles, socks and loafers tucked underneath the deck chair.

That chest. Those pecs. If she didn't know better, she would think he'd been airbrushed. Dr. Christopoulos obviously didn't spend all his time in the operating room, lifting eyebrows and tightening chins. He had to spend a great deal of time at the gym as well.

This was not what she needed tonight. She turned to leave, then stopped herself.

No man was ever going to keep her from going where she wanted to go.

What was it about Niko Christopoulos that stirred up so much confusion inside her head?

When she could tear her focus away from his physique, she noticed his face. While his body looked peaceful in repose, his clenched jaw and compressed lips told a different story.

He looked like a man in internal pain.

Suddenly he half sat up, contracting those magnificent abs, and looked over the top of his sunglasses, straight at her. His features calmed, as if he pulled a mask over his emotions.

Had she made a noise? She didn't think so but she must have.

"Want to join me?" he asked.

As he made to stand up, she swallowed down all but the simplest of emotions and quickly said, "Please, keep your seat." The old-world manners made her feel special, even though she knew she wasn't. She pointed to the stairs behind her. "How's the leg?"

He shrugged. "The climb is worth it for the view."

The way he studied her over his sunglasses, she could almost imagine he was referring to her.

She could say no and probably would have if he had come on strong. There were plenty of empty deck chairs. She could say she just needed a few minutes of alone time. He would understand. Wasn't that what he was doing as well?

But he had invited her and she found herself moving in his direction before she could decline.

She picked out the deck chair next to his and placed her tea next to the water bottle on the table between them. "Catching some rays?"

By the deepness of his tan, she knew it wouldn't be the first time. She couldn't imagine him in a tanning booth. Too artificial.

Hold on there, Annalise, she told herself. *This is a man who does artificial for a living.* Why was she assigning him qualities when she knew nothing about him?

He propped his chair up a few notches and reset his sunglasses on the top of his head.

The intensity in those tiger eyes of his mesmerized her so that she couldn't look away.

His voice was low, like a rumbling purr. "It's the wind. There's something about that unharnessed power, that cleansing force that attracts me." He rubbed his chin. "That sounded strange, didn't it?"

"Poetic." She held up her book, William Cullen Bryant. "I like poetry."

"Me, too." He gave her a grin and a wink.

He was flirting—with her!

There was a whole ship of beautiful women and he was coming on to her. But, then, there was no other woman around, which made her convenient, right?

She raised an eyebrow. "Really?"

Her reply was supposed to be a warning that she knew his game and wasn't playing. Instead, it came out as a tease, as if she was taking up his challenge.

"Yup. Used to write it, too, under the guise of song lyrics."

"So you're a doctor and a musician? What's next? You're going to tell me you were a rock star in a boy band?"

"Only on my own block." He reset his sunglasses over his eyes. "Some friends and I had a garage band all through junior high and high school."

"Lead guitar?"

"Sometimes. Mostly drums. Some bass guitar. We switched around a lot."

"Did you sing?"

"Sometimes."

"I bet you had a motorcycle, too, didn't you?"

"An old Harley. I rebuilt it myself. And a black leather jacket—a hand-me-down from one of my brothers. I was really into the vintage rebel look." His self-deprecating laugh revealed two deep dimples.

"I'll just bet you were." With his dark looks she knew he'd pulled off the attitude perfectly. Surreptitiously, she glanced at his bare chest. He still did.

She winked at him. "From teenage heart throb to successful surgeon. Charmed life?"

She expected a flippant response. Instead, he thought about it for a moment then nodded slowly. "I've got a lot to be thankful for."

She wished she could see behind the shades. The moment hung in time, making an uneasiness spread through her. She shifted away.

While he didn't move a muscle, she felt him pulling back, too. Or was she only imagining it? What did she know of this man, except he was a compassionate doctor with the soul of a poet who, by the looks of things, managed his money well?

As she took a calming sip of tea, determined to treat this evening no differently than any other, he broke her concentration.

"Thanks for coming to my rescue this evening. They mean well, but they also think they know what's best for me."

"They're like those made-for-TV families. Are they always so nice? So genuine?"

"Nice? My family has good company manners. Genuine? Absolutely, even when it hurts. But I can call anyone, anytime, my sisters-in-law as well as my brothers, and they would drop everything to be there for me."

"And you'd do the same for them?"

He rubbed his hand over his face but failed to disguise the tightening around his eyes and mouth. "I always have in the past."

"But not in the future?" Annalise immediately regretted her impulsive question. "I'm sorry. None of my business."

"It's not you. It's me." With a forced grin he shrugged away her apology as he spouted the classic meaningless cliché. "How about you? Judging by how quiet you were at dinner, I'm betting your family is a lot calmer than mine."

"No family. Just me." Her recent visit to her mother made her all too conscious of those bound together because of shared DNA. It wasn't a bond she willingly claimed.

"Here it comes." She pointed at the sun, resting on the horizon.

As if the big ball of flame had become too heavy to hold itself up, it plunged into the sea, taking with it all but a flat line of pinks and yellows and oranges to keep the sky separated from the water. Above that slim line of fading color, the night was dark and starry with nary a moonbeam in sight.

Around them, the deck's automatic twinkle lights began to glow.

Under the vastness of the night Annalise felt at peace with the world. She knew the feeling would be fleeting, with the responsibilities and decisions life would bring her, but she would enjoy that feeling while it lasted.

Next to her, Niko drew in a deep breath, held it then let it out again.

Having him near made her feel less alone than she'd felt in a very long time.

That surprised her. She had expected to feel like he was intruding on her special time. Instead, he made it even more special.

The serene minutes ticked away, giving her a false sense of permanence. When the squeaking and creaking of the pool boy's cart broke the silence, she wasn't surprised. Only sad that the moment was gone.

That's when she noticed the chill of the night air as it rushed over her bare legs. Reality. She'd been lucky to escape it for a few moments. To expect that kind of tranquility to last was unreasonable, wasn't it?

Reluctantly, Niko said a silent goodbye to the moment out of time he'd shared with Annalise.

He sat up and put on his shirt, socks and shoes. Normally, he would ask her to join him for a drink, trying to draw out the situation. But doing so tonight would only place expectations on a moment so rare it couldn't be coerced into lasting.

The good doctor lay with her head back and her eyes closed. The pose should be peaceful. Instead, he saw the tension that made the corners of her eyelids twitch and her involuntary jerk when the pool boy let the lid of his towel hamper slam shut.

He glanced at his watch. While he was certain his sister-in-law was taking care of Sophie as carefully as she took care of her own three children, he would check in on her.

Then maybe he would… He wasn't sure what he would do next. When was the last time he hadn't had a list of things in his head that he needed to do, all marked urgent?

As he climbed down the stairs, ignoring the burning in his thigh, he looked out at the dark, flat vastness of the sea. Three weeks.

Three long weeks with nowhere to be and nothing to do.

Why did he think of Annalise when he thought of how he would fill his time?

CHAPTER FOUR

DREAMS, WONDERFULLY WILDLY erotic dreams had made Annalise twist and turn all night. She knew they were normal, even healthy. While these were not her first, they had never been this vivid before.

Her lover had been faceless, nameless and frustrating since she awoke before he could take her where she wanted to go. If pressed, she was fairly certain she could name the source of those disturbing dreams. As disconcerting as they were, she was thrilled to be having them.

Annalise had put in many hours of therapy and self-assessment making sure she didn't stay a victim.

Those hours had not been in vain. She could fully appreciate sexual magnetism evoked by the sight of a good-looking male. A male like Niko Christopoulos, who was looking mighty fine this morning in his red baggy board shorts, tight sleeveless T-shirt and tennis shoes as he sat on a bench outside the medical suite, waiting for office hours to begin.

Irrationally, she wished she'd spent a little more time picking out her own clothing, which was silly. Her monochrome gray blouse and trousers were perfectly professional and practical, if not the cutting edge of fashion. But now they felt a little mousy.

Niko stared out at the ocean, lost in thought.

She cleared her throat to alert him she was there.

He blinked as he focused on her. "I didn't hear you come up."

"Is Sophie all right?"

"She's fine. Her blood sugar was low this morning when she woke up, but not too low. She barely protested when I checked it and gave her the breakfast insulin shot."

Last night's restless dreaming made her feel edgy when she asked, "Then why are you here?"

She winced when she heard herself. "Sorry. Restless night. Can I start again?"

Her problem was she knew how to rebuff male attention, but she didn't know what to do to encourage it. But maybe that was for the better. There were those ship's rules about fraternization to consider.

Still, a part of her, the wanton part left over from last night no doubt, wondered what would be so wrong with a bit of flirtation. Just to satisfy her curiosity. With an experienced man like Niko it would be all in fun, right?

"No apology necessary. I know all about restless nights."

Much more civilly, she asked, "Do you have a medical problem?"

He rubbed his hand through his dark hair, spiking it out of order. "Actually, yes." He looked sheepish. "I've got something I need you to look at."

"Okay." She glanced at her watch. Her staff wouldn't be in for another half-hour. She usually preferred to have another staff member present when treating male patients. But it shouldn't matter in this case since they were both professionals. "Come on in."

As she unlocked the glass doors to the anteroom, Niko pointed to an envelope that had been slipped under the door. "A woman wearing a bartender's uniform, the one I met when I boarded, dropped that off for you."

"Thanks." Annalise pocketed the note. Concerned curiosity burned a hole in her pocket.

Once inside, Niko hitched himself up on the examination table and rolled up the right leg of his board shorts. A half-healed angry red cut at least five inches long sliced the side of his thigh. The stitches strained against the inflammation.

"What happened?"

He swallowed, then said, "A knife."

She narrowed her eyes. "I did my internship in the emergency departments of New Orleans's charity hospital system. I know a wickedly deliberate cut when I see it. This isn't from a steak knife or the slip of a pocket knife."

"I was caught in the middle of a knife fight over a water well in Haiti. So the infection could be tropical or it could be bacteria-related or—"

She put a thermometer in his mouth, making herself look away so she wouldn't stare at his firm, full lips or the rugged beard stubble on his cheeks. She didn't need any more stimulus to make her feel things—risky things—just because those tiger eyes were so mesmerizing.

And she didn't need to satisfy her curiosity by asking for details of his knife fight. The less she knew about him, the more easily she could convince herself they were just like two ships passing in the night.

When the thermometer beeped, he took it out himself, saving her from feeling his breath on her fingers.

"Ninety-nine and a half," he read.

"What have you been doing for your wound?"

"Topical ointment."

"That's all?"

He shrugged. "Antibiotics are in short supply there. I'm healthy, unlike the people I treat. I figured I could fight it off."

With that clue, Annalise couldn't stop herself from trying to put the pieces together. "You were treating patients when this happened?"

"I do a lot of medical relief work in developing countries." He looked down and away, as if he wasn't quite okay with himself for his charity work.

Annalise thought of the free clinics she visited and the donated supplies she delivered when assigned to various routes. She had been thinking hard about her volunteer service recently. "Any particular organization?"

"Doctors Without Borders."

"They really get into the trenches." She took a cotton swab from a sealed package. "I'm going to take a culture, but I don't want to wait for results so I'm going to give you a broad-spectrum oral antibiotic, too. Tomorrow, when I know what we're looking at, I can refine your treatment. Are you allergic to any medication?"

"Sulpha drugs."

"That limits us. How about penicillin-based drugs?"

"I'm good with those."

"I'll be right back." As Annalise left the exam room for the pharmacy closet, she took a deep breath. Success, brains, looks and heart. Being around so much perfection made her feel... She wasn't sure how she felt.

When she came back, he had rolled down the leg of his shorts and was standing in the open exam-room doorway. She handed him the bottle of antibiotic pills.

His fingers brushing against hers almost made her drop it.

"Two now, one each night and morning. Stay out of the water until we know what this is. Come back tomorrow afternoon for the test results."

"Thanks." He cast her a sideways look, half shy and half pleading. "By the way, my family doesn't know about the Doctors Without Borders gig. Please don't tell them."

"I'm very good at patient confidentiality. In fact, I swore an oath. They won't learn about it from me." Annalise stuck her hands in her pockets, feeling Brandy's note.

"I didn't mean any insult. It's just that..." He stopped and held the pills up between them. "Thanks again."

Secrets. Why on earth would he want something that noble to remain a secret from his family? It wasn't her business, though, was it?

Still, it bothered her. Secrets made her think of lies. Was he lying to her?

Annalise hated secrets more than anything else on earth. How many times had her mother whispered "Don't tell…" as she was juggling men in her life? Then there had been the man who'd whispered "Don't tell" as he'd crept into her bedroom when her mother hadn't been home.

Annalise pulled out the note and read it.

"Doc, I need an appointment, but I'm working during your office hours and I don't want my shift manager to know. Could I come in after hours? Drop by the bar and let me know, okay? Brandy."

Annalise sighed. No doubt her tattoo had become infected.

The bell tinkled, signaling patients in the lobby. She quickly filled out a chart for Niko—Dr. Christopoulos—as she readied herself for the next patient.

As Caribbean music played softly from the overhead speakers, Annalise reminded herself that her life was totally what she'd made it and so far she hadn't done half-bad. Just keep it simple, she reminded herself.

And simple didn't include Niko Christopoulos.

Simple obsession. That's the only reason that could explain why, on a ship carrying several thousand people, Niko caught her attention as she took her afternoon break on deck.

She'd thought about him all day. His playboy image. His love for his family. His compassion with Sophie. His work with Doctors Without Borders. There was nothing simple about Niko and no simple explanation for why her feet were now carrying her straight towards him.

On the first full afternoon afloat, the ship was alive with activity and the Christopoulos family was doing its fair share to add to the frivolity.

Niko stood contemplating the rock wall. His older nephews

had their harnesses strapped on and were waiting. Niko was not one to turn down a challenge.

He felt her before he heard her. Even though they barely knew each other, he knew the warmth by his side was uniquely Annalise.

"It's going to be difficult to keep that wound a secret if you break open the stitches halfway up," she murmured, for his ears only.

"The voice of reason. Where have you been all my life?" He waved is nephews on. "I've found something better to do," he called to them.

Marcus looked pointedly at Annalise then jostled his brother and grinned.

Annalise arched an eyebrow. "Are you being presumptuous by meaning me?"

"Let's not call it presumptuous. Let's call it hopeful." He gave her his best puppy-dog eyes. "Want to watch for dolphins off the starboard bow with me?"

When she hesitated, he appealed to her medical side. "You'll be keeping me from doing something stupidly injurious to my health."

"Are you sure it's not too late? I think you've already fallen on your head one time too many since you've chosen me to flirt with."

"Flirt?" He grabbed at his chest. "You've wounded me. I would never toy with your affections." Yet wasn't that exactly what he was doing?

No. No, it wasn't.

Annalise lived on a cruise ship. No permanence there. She would know the score. There was no serious romance involved, just a casual attraction that would end at their final destination.

"Of course you're not flirting with me. Why would you when there are plenty of toys in this floating toy box?" Although she smiled when she said it, Niko thought he saw a bleakness cross her eyes or maybe it was only a cloud cross-ing the sun.

Before he could decide, she blinked and the fleeting look was gone.

"Ready? The dolphins won't wait." She led the way, weaving in and out of the passengers on deck.

"Thank you for rescuing me from myself. When the twins dared me, I didn't have it in me not to race them up. If you hadn't come along when you did, I would be halfway up the rock wall by now and my thigh wound wouldn't have appreciated my bravado."

"You have a hard time turning down a challenge?"

"Challenges are just another word for thrills for me. And you?"

She stopped at the railing and looked out on the sun-sparkled sea. "Challenges bring out the stubbornness in me."

"I've always thought stubbornness was a very good trait to have."

"Others would disagree." Very subtly, Annalise shifted away from him. Niko doubted she even realized she'd done it.

"Those *others* don't understand how much determination it takes to get through medical school."

"Determination. Scholarships. Student loans. Lots and lots of caffeine." She rubbed her arms. "And, occasionally, the kindness of the few others who do understand."

"Or who support you even when they don't understand." Niko thought of all the sandwiches his brothers had brought him as he'd studied past midnight. Of all the twenty-dollar bills his grandmother had slipped into his pockets after she'd laundered his clothes.

"Like your family?"

"Like my family." The family who wouldn't be at all happy with his new career path. "So where'd you go to medical school?"

"Tulane. I went there for both medical school and under-graduate pre-med."

Niko raise his eyebrows at the mention of the exclusive private college in uptown New Orleans's Audubon Park district. "Wow! I'm impressed.

"Did you grow up in New Orleans? The Crescent City has a thousand accents, but I think I hear a hint of a traditional New Orleans drawl, don't I?"

Her mouth tightened at the corners before she answered, "Yes, I did."

"What part?"

"It doesn't matter. Hurricane Katrina wiped it out." She shuddered, as if she was shaking off memories, before she forced out a smile. "Your turn. Where did you go to medical school?"

"The local state university."

"Ah, home of the Tigers. Did you play sports?"

"No." He grinned. "Even though that's their reputation, not everyone does—but I did drink a lot of beer. And you?"

"Beer or sports?" She smiled back, her face lighting up like sunbeams shone on it.

Niko soaked in her glow. "Either."

"Neither. I was on academic scholarship. No money for beer and no time for sports. I held a couple of part-time jobs, so that kept me busy when I wasn't studying. I was rather boring back then, I'm afraid."

"You, boring? Not possible. More like admirable to make it through Tulane's medical school while working, too." Niko once again realized how much his family had given him. "I worked at the restaurant on occasion and did a few odd jobs here and there, especially during the summers. But generally I had it pretty good."

"One of my jobs was as a dog washer for a local vet. I really liked working with the dogs. It wasn't a bad job—just messy and smelly."

"Did you ever think of switching to veterinary medicine?"

"Nope. I'm allergic to cats."

"Not many cats on a cruise ship."

"Not a single one on this ship."

"There's quite a bit of difference between working in an inner city E.R. and working on a cruise ship, I'd imagine."

Giving him a thoughtful look somewhere between sunshine and shadow, Annalise answered, "I like a bit of challenge, too. New places, new people, a diversity of problems to be solved. The E.R. took care of two out of three, but a cruise ship takes care of all three."

"Itchy feet. I understand all too well that the thrill of adventure gets your adrenaline rushing."

"As far as adrenaline rushes go, I can't say a cruise ship compares to being airlifted into a developing country, but we try." She grinned, showing off a dimple as she shaded her eyes and scanned the water for dolphins. How could she be so unaware of her beauty?

"That's what the brochure said."

"So what thrilling adventures have you had this morning?"

He had spent considerable time watching a very enjoyable wet T-shirt contest with the twins but he decided to tell her about the starfish demonstration he'd attended with his younger nieces and nephews instead.

"I had no idea starfish could regenerate body parts."

"Fascinating." She gave him a wry look. "Anything else?"

"Lunch with the family. Dining with them is always a major event, for us and for everyone around us. My brothers had to have a taste of every kind of bread in the basket to analyze taste and texture. The little ones spilled one glass of milk and one glass of orange juice in quick succession. And Sophie decided she wasn't hungry. Making her eat to balance out her morning insulin shot was a real challenge."

"How did you do it?"

"Yiayia gave her the evil eye. It always works." He'd had a

long talk with Yiayia last night about Sophie's juvenile diabetes. While she didn't understand everything, she finally did understand the importance of working with Sophie's caregivers instead of against them.

"Your grandmother is very special to you, isn't she?"

"She raised me. I owe her and my brothers everything." He rubbed his hand across his eyes. He didn't like to talk about it. So why was he about to tell Annalise?

"My parents died when I was young. The three of us were in a car wreck." He left out the details about being stranded in the car with them for hours while the rescue workers had tried to save them all.

"It's why I hate goodbyes." As if compelled, he found himself confessing, "Before they died, they both told me they loved me. I didn't understand. I had the chance but didn't take it. I thought, if I didn't say goodbye to them, they would live."

"How old were you?"

"Eight." He stared out at the vast ocean all around. "My brothers were sixteen, fourteen and thirteen then. They buried their grief, trying to help me recover from mine. They had to grow up so fast for me. Along with Yiayia, they've been taking care of me ever since. They've never once complained about their lot in life."

"Your family finds strength in each other. I saw that last night at the dinner table."

He gave her a wry look. "And then there's me."

"You're different?"

He nodded confirmation. "I'm different."

"How?"

"I love my family but I often feel trapped, smothered. Uncomfortable in my own skin." He'd never said any of this out loud. Not even to himself in the dark of night. Why now? Why Annalise?

Was it because they were complete strangers and would never see each other after this trip ended?

He'd had so much on his mind and in his heart for so many years. Recently, since he'd started to consider selling his portion of the practice, the pressure had been building more and more until he thought he would come apart at the seams.

"They've sacrificed so much to give me a comfortable lifestyle they'd never even dream of having themselves."

And he had been determined to succeed for them. To give back to them. To show his appreciation by being all they wanted him to be.

"They're very proud of you. Even when your brothers tease you, they do it with pride in their voices. And your grandmother told me at least a dozen times how you have big-time celebrities for clientele." Realization dawned. "You're afraid of disappointing them. How could you? You've become everything they sacrificed for. You've fulfilled their expectations. They get to be in the limelight through you, and I think they're perfectly happy that way."

"But that's not me." He struggled with being that man they imagined him to be. The one who strutted onto talk shows to talk about celebrity makeovers or who attended black-tie affairs with a model on his arm. The whole time he sipped champagne and waved away expensive hors d'oeuvres he thought of those who didn't have the basics of clean water to drink or food to eat.

"The sparkle in Yiayia's eyes when she brags about my photos on the society pages of the newspapers can't erase the bleakness in the eyes of the mothers whose children suffer from cleft palates. Doctors Without Borders. That's where I belong. No fanfare. No glory."

No family. That part was too painful to say aloud. Giving up the happiness his brothers had found in the arms of the women they loved had been a decision he'd willfully made but he still couldn't stop wishing he could have it all.

But his wandering ways didn't make for permanent relationships. A woman needed things. A house full of knick-knacks and baubles, a steady group of friends, children. Permanence. All the things he couldn't promise her.

"You've chosen a tough path."

He nodded. "But I need it. I'm never more alive than when I'm cheating death. I need the deeply satisfying buzz of seeing blank eyes start to sparkle, of seeing hope come alive in environments and conditions that make living from day to day a challenge."

His world was not one where he would voluntarily raise a family.

"I can see that in you. I hear the passion in your voice." Her own voice quavered, as if she was hesitant to offer that much up to him. "Why medicine? There are a lot of professions you could have chosen."

He shrugged. "Most of my memories of the wreck are fuzzy, just a lot of hazy pain, emotional more than physical, I think. I broke my jaw but I don't remember it hurting all that much right then. They sent a helicopter. There were flashing lights and rain and loud voices over the police cars' speaker systems.

"But through it all there was this doctor who crawled into the wreckage and held my hand while they cut my parents out. He promised me he wouldn't let go until I was free and he talked to me the whole time. He was calm and sure when my world was in total chaos. He was my hero. I wanted to be just like him."

Niko wiped at his eyes with the back of his hand. "I've never told anyone—no one's ever asked before."

The silence stretched awkwardly as he looked out at the ocean, feeling the loss of his parents, remembering the hours he'd waited alone for rescue. Knowing how he often felt alone even now, despite the love of his family throughout the years.

Annalise startled him when she covered his hand with her own. She didn't say anything. She didn't even look at him. She just stared out at the ocean, too. But with her hand on his, he didn't feel so alone.

A movement against the waves caught his attention.

"There they are." With his free hand, he pointed at the magnificent mammals playing in the waves.

Annalise shielded her eyes with her free hand. "Four of them."

Two small dolphins played among the larger ones. "A family."

"Their families are called pods. It's a matriarchal structure." Annalise smiled as one of the dolphins broke away from the group and started twisting itself above the waves.

"I'm very familiar with that structure." Niko watched the baby dolphin jump and spin. "There's always one that's got to be different."

She squeezed his hand. "That's not a bad thing."

When the dolphin had done a half dozen jumping twists, he swam back to his pod, where the other dolphins bumped noses in greeting.

The wind blew Annalise's hair into her face. He reached up to brush it back, but something in her eyes made him hesitate and he wrapped his fingers around the railing instead.

She released his hand to push the errant strands away herself. "That must be the dolphin version of a family hug."

She had given him the perfect opening. "How about your family?"

Her lips took on a wry twist. "In some animal species, the mothers eat their young."

She brushed off the hair on her cheek as she lost the brightness in her face. Her eyes looked bruised and sad.

Niko would do anything to wipe that sadness from her soul. But he had a feeling that would take a lot of time and patience and he only had a few weeks.

Then her eyes went blank, making him doubt what he'd seen just seconds before. She took a quick step away from him, glancing at her watch and clearly backing away from the intimacy they had shared. "I've got to go—"

"Back to work?" He said it for her, saving her the indignity of uttering the time-worn excuse. When he'd picked up Sophie's new insulin vial after lunch, he'd already been told the doctor had taken the early shift and was off for the rest of the day.

Obviously, he had mistaken the good doctor's compassion for something more. He wasn't sure what he'd wanted that "more" to be.

Even though she hadn't moved a muscle, he could feel her pulling away. "Niko, this is supposed to be your vacation, a time for fun and recharging."

"Not a soul-searching expedition." He felt rebuffed and more than a little embarrassed. Spilling his guts wasn't something he usually did with a woman—especially a woman he just met and had no intention of getting to know beyond these three weeks out of time. Just because he felt a pull toward her didn't mean she felt it too, or that she had to respond even if she did.

Her forced smile was so very different from her natural one. "Make sure your fun doesn't stress your wound."

This *was* a time for fun, not a time for deep reflection—most particularly about a woman he'd just met and would never see again after his fun was over.

His perspective restored, he nodded. "Sure thing, Doc. I've used work as an excuse myself a few times. I didn't mean to keep you from your patients. And I've got umbrella drinks to try. Maybe I'll catch you later."

Walking away was the right thing to do. Why was it so hard?

Because he never backed down from a challenge, right? That had to be the reason. But maybe this time he should. Life was too short…

From now on, when a woman flirted with him on deck, he would flirt back, buy her a drink, enjoy her company with the understanding they were both stealing a moment in a fantasy world that would come to an end when the cruise ended. He would take advantage of this time that had nothing to do with his reality and enjoy himself.

Then, during those long nights under mosquito nets, he would pull out the memories, have a smile, and find the energy to get back to work in the morning.

As he headed toward the big-haired brunette, the one that was supposed to be his type, he could feel Annalise's eyes on him, watching him.

When he looked back to be sure, he kept his sunglasses securely in place as he flashed her a cocky grin, deliberately hiding his reaction to a woman who moved him like no woman ever had before.

"Is this seat taken?" he asked the brunette.

She had more than enough appreciation in her eyes to soothe his ego, right?

She greeted him with a sweep of her hand to indicate the empty chair. "I've been saving it for you."

Niko let out a deep breath. This woman knew the game. Now to have some fun.

"What are we drinking?"

"I recommend the rum punch." She welcomed him with a raised glass and a gleamingly bright smile. "I'm Helena. Your grandmother said we should meet." Her Greek accent verified her heritage.

She was everything he should want in a woman, especially one who was only temporary.

If only he could be less aware of the reluctant little honey-haired blonde walking away from him and more interested in the eager brunette right in front of him, he would make a lot of people very happy—including himself.

The waiter brought over a tray holding huge glasses filled with enough fruit to host a luau. The paper umbrellas wilted against the condensation on the glasses. Definitely not his kind of drink. He thought about asking for a beer instead, but that would mean he'd have to stay around and wait for it to be delivered and he wasn't sure he wanted to stay that long.

"Your grandmother tells me you're single?"

Niko nodded confirmation.

"I'm divorced." Helen took a deep sip from the new glass and shrugged, as if it didn't matter, but her eyes said it really did.

Niko sipped his too-sweet drink and tried to look sympathetic. He'd heard so many domestic tales of woe that all he got from the conversation was validation that he was not made for marriage. "Sorry it didn't work out."

"Me, too. My ex-husband was a Texas oil tycoon. Sadly, after I turned thirty-five, he became more interested in drilling holes than in me."

"So you're going back home?"

"To visit. Maybe to stay. I'm not sure yet." The way she said it, she sounded like staying wasn't her first choice.

"We're on a family vacation. My grandmother is going to show us her homeland."

"I know. I met your Yiayia. She tells me you're a very successful cosmetic surgeon who's been on television and works on celebrities."

"Maxiofacial surgeon." He gave her his best smoldering look. Somehow, it felt more manipulative than usual. "I can see you don't need my services."

But Helen knew the game. She batted her eyelashes at him. "And here I was thinking you'd be good at popping a champagne bottle cork. Tonight? My balcony?"

It was the kind of invitation he'd hoped to get when he'd boarded the ship. But now all he could think of was sharing a sunset beer or cup of tea with Annalise on the foredeck again.

When he didn't answer right away, she gave him a hard look. "Not interested?"

"As much as I'd like to, I'm here for my family this trip."

"Sure." Her smile was bitter. "I guess my ex was right."

Yes, she knew the game well, fishing for a compliment to negate the ex-husband's harshness. He had a list of phrases he used in situations like this. Why couldn't he think of an appropriate one?

"I hope your homecoming is everything you expect it to be."

He left the drink on a tray, excused himself and determined to be anywhere she wasn't.

It wasn't Helena, who appeared to be perfectly perfect. It was him. He was so tired of playing the game.

Annalise didn't even know there was a game, much less how to play.

Niko suddenly felt very good about his decision. Helena was the kind of trouble he didn't need.

But, then, all women came with a certain amount of trouble, didn't they?

Why did Annalise seem worth it when all the other women didn't?

While he didn't believe in love at first sight, he now had first-hand knowledge that obsession at first sight was a very real phenomenon.

CHAPTER FIVE

ANNALISE DUCKED INTO an elevator and hit the button to close the door just as she began to shake. The intensity of emotion Niko had shared with her had caught her off balance. She'd wanted to reach out and hold him tight, to take away the pain in his heart, to make him all better.

But all she'd managed to do had been to touch his hand then make a hasty retreat before the conversation turned deep again. Sharing secrets about her own family would have been more than she could have handled.

As always, she hid behind her work, just like Niko had accused her of doing. It was all she had.

Annalise spent the rest of her afternoon off in the office, helping her new physician's assistant get settled into the ship's routine.

The work was familiar. Safe. Unexciting.

Unlike the way she felt around Niko.

As she worked, she couldn't keep herself from thinking of all she was missing, keeping herself apart and safe. And unexciting.

In fact, she would have to describe her life as downright boring.

For the first time ever, she craved a thrill down her spine, the kind of thrill she got when Niko was near. She wasn't sure what she should do about it but she was certain her lack of ability to handle her emotions had come across to Niko as disinterest.

That buxom brunette certainly had no problem projecting her interest, had she?

As she and her P.A. documented inventory and filed their charts, she was glad that the P.A was either in too chatty a frame of mind or was discreet enough to pretend not to notice her mercurial mood.

With only a fraction of her attention Annalise listened to her talk about leaving her fiancé at the altar.

"I figure I'll do this for a while, maybe a year. Then, when all the fuss dies down, I'll go back home."

While some did it for the adventure, the P.A. was one of many who had chosen to work on a cruise ship to run from bad history. She and Annalise had that in common.

Annalise responded, to be nice. "Better to break up before the marriage than after, right?"

She didn't add that it was even better to break up before the preacher and congregation were seated, waiting for the bride to walk down the aisle, like her new P.A. had done. That was an opinion better kept to herself.

But her P.A. seemed to be competent in her work. The way she managed her love life was none of Annalise's concern.

Then, again, with Annalise's lack of experience she really didn't have much basis on which to judge these matters of the heart.

Was Niko a love-'em-and-leave-'em kind of guy? From what his family said about him, she'd just bet he was.

"So what's your story, Doc? The contract office said you'd been sailing longer than any other doctor they had signed up."

This was not a conversation Annalise wanted to have. Her dread must have shown on her face because the P.A quickly followed up with, "They said it in a good way. That you were the best to learn from. But you've been doing this for a while, haven't you?"

"Yes, I have." The normal explanation would be that she was still running away, and maybe that was correct, but she had no intention of discussing her personal hang-ups with anyone other than her therapist. Hopefully, her tone would discourage any further conversation along this line.

Her contract was up when they made port in Malaga, Spain. She had an option to extend her tour of service to cover the extra week the ship would be looping through the Greek isles, but was thinking hard about whether she wanted to sign another contract at the end of this trip.

Regardless of her reasons, putting down roots in her home town of New Orleans, or in any one particular place in the world, held no appeal for her.

She'd been thinking about Niko and his charity work ever since she'd examined his knife wound. Maybe she'd find a private moment to ask more. It would be a legitimate reason to see him again instead of a trumped-up excuse.

And just maybe he wouldn't reject her like she had rejected him.

Tonight? On the foredeck? Annalise didn't believe in happenstance, but maybe this once she could allow herself to believe that if it was meant to be, it would happen.

Niko and his brothers and sisters-in-law had been hitting the "golf balls" made of fish food off the back of the ship for over an hour now. Watching the fish school to eat the "golf balls" made Yiayia and the children smile.

He teed up the fish-food golf ball and concentrated on swinging the club. Or at least he tried to concentrate on his swing. Even though he'd vowed to put Annalise from his mind, he hadn't been able to do it.

As he shanked his shot, he realized what had been nagging at him. That blank expression on her face when he'd asked about her family. He'd seen that look before—from victims trying to cope.

The thought of anyone anywhere hurting Annalise sent a burst of rage through him.

He teed up another fish ball and swung, hooking this one but sending it further than any of his previous hits.

Stephen put his hand on Niko's shoulder.

"Don't frown, little brother. I'll show you how it's done."

Marcus teed up his own ball. "Because we've been taking lessons. Right, Dad?"

Hearing his brothers' hearty laughter emphasized how much he had in his family.

And how much Annalise didn't have. As she had comforted him, he wanted to comfort her, give her a shoulder, let her know...

Know what? That he would always be there for her?

He couldn't promise that to any woman. The places he went, the things he did made commitment to a woman impossible. He was actually grateful to his ex for showing him the futility of trying to have it all.

"It's only fair that I pass on what I've learned." Stephen looked Niko in the eye, more serious than usual. "After all, thanks to my baby brother buying into the restaurant, we've been able to hire another manager so I can take the occasional afternoon off now and spend more time with my sons. I can never thank you enough for that, little brother."

"After all you've done for me, it's me that is in your debt." Niko grinned. "But I bet you a beer I can hit this next one farther than you can."

"I'll take a side bet on Niko." Phoebe grinned at them both. "Don't you know that doctors know how to play golf? It comes with the diploma. I'll bet you play at all those fancy resorts you keep running off to."

"I'll take that side bet, Mom. I'll bet Uncle Niko doesn't play a lot of golf when he's out of town." Marcus gave Niko a strong stare. "Ask his ex-fiancée. He's not like most doctors."

What had his ex told Marcus now? Had she broken her promise to keep his charity work secret?

Phoebe patted Niko on the shoulder in case he needed comforting. "It will take a strong woman to keep our Niko's attention.

Annalise. Why did he think of her when he thought of a strong woman? He didn't even know her.

Could she live on canned beans and peaches for ten days straight because the supply truck had been hijacked? Could she sleep on the ground under a mosquito net because the wind was too strong to pitch a tent with a hurricane blowing in off the coast? Could she complete surgery as rebel gunfire threatened to overrun an encampment?

That's the kind of superwoman that would fit into Niko's life.

He had to grin as he thought of Annalise draping the superhero cape around Sophie's shoulders. Going from cruise ship to jungle boat would take a superhuman leap—a leap he could never expect anyone to take on his behalf.

He squared up to hit the last fish-food golf ball into the ocean.

Sophie jumped up and down and pointed at the splash he'd made. "Hey, look how far Uncle Niko hit it! He just beat everybody."

As one, his family turned and applauded him. That's what the Christopoulos family did when you met expectations. They cheered you on.

He'd never let them down yet. What would happen when he did?

As Annalise was unlocking the etched-glass doors leading into the medical suite to accommodate Brandy's off-hours request, the bartender rushed up to her.

"Doc, you're here." Her face showed panic and her voice was on the edge of hysteria.

Annalise pushed open the doors. "Come in. What's wrong?"

"How could I forget? And now…" Brandy bit her knuckle. "Now I think I'm pregnant."

"You were fine when we boarded. What happened between then and now?" Annalise tried to put the pieces together. "Did you have unprotected sex recently?"

"No. Yes. Well, not within the last day or so, anyway." Brandy wrapped her arms around herself. "I can't have a baby, not the way I live. What will I do with it?"

A sympathetic knot formed in Annalise's stomach. She squelched it down, intellectually keeping her own personal experience safely dissociated from her patient's. Emotionally keeping her distance was more of a challenge. But overlying Brandy's circumstances with her own personal trauma wouldn't be good for either of them.

"Let's talk about it back here." Annalise ushered her back to an examination room, seated her in a chair and took out her clipboard with a fresh chart. "How many days has it been since your last period?"

"I don't know. I don't keep up with it, really, since I use the kind of birth control that keeps you from having one very often. But I've been feeling a little tired and my roommate says she's noticed I've put on weight." Brandy patted her gently rounded stomach. "I feel puffy and my breasts are really tender. Once my roommate pointed it out to me, it was obvious. All the signs are there."

"What type of birth control do you use?"

"The patch." Brandy looked down at the floor. "But I think I forgot to change it."

She looked up, desperation in her eyes. "What am I going to do, Doc?"

Annalise hated that question. She was duty-bound to discuss options, but she knew all too well all the choices would have life-changing consequences.

Annalise stared down at the blank form, using her analytical training to compose herself. "The first thing to do is take a pregnancy test. Test your urine first thing in the morning when the hormones will be more concentrated. If the test comes back positive, we'll do an ultrasound to try to determine how long you've been pregnant."

She took a pregnancy testing kit from an overhead cabinet and handed it to Brandy. Brandy hugged it to her chest like a lifeline.

"And then?"

"And then I'll give you some information and you can make some decisions." Three weeks. They would be out at sea for three weeks. So many things hung in the balance.

The wild look in Brandy's eyes worried Annalise. Even though she wasn't keen on personal touching, she felt compelled to cover the bartender's hand with her own.

"A strong support system will help you through this, Brandy. Your parents? Siblings? I can set you up with a ship-to-shore line and you can give them a call."

Brandy shook her head. "We're not that kind of a family."

"We can't all be that lucky, can we?" Annalise thought of the Christopoulos clan. Even though she'd only seen them in action a few times, she knew they would rally round one of their own, giving comfort and security.

Hesitantly, she asked, "What about the father? Would he be supportive of you?" When she thought about support, why did Niko come to mind? She'd barely met the man. Why did she cast him in the role of protector?

Brandy looked up at the ceiling, hugging herself tight and rocking back and forth. "I'm still thinking about that one."

"Promise me you won't do anything rash or stupid."

Brandy flushed as if Annalise had caught her in the act. She stood, hugging the pregnancy test box to her chest. "I promise, Doc."

"See you in the morning, then. Have me paged if you need me before that."

With a nod Brandy was gone, leaving Annalise with a quiet, sterile room and too many painful memories.

* * *

Needing alone time, Niko rushed through supper with his family. He loved them, each and every one of them. But they were so—so *there* all the time, like a litter of puppies, rolling over each other, playfully nipping at each other, never letting a littermate out of sight.

He settled into the lounge chair he'd claimed the night before. Board shorts, barefoot, beer in hand, now he could breathe deeply. He toasted the ocean, thinking of all the toasts his family had just saluted each other with. Too many of those toasts had to do with him finding the perfect woman, settling down, starting a family. They had drunk *to his future happiness!*

And to theirs, he'd toasted back, his lemon-twisted water standing out in stark contrast against his brothers' rich merlots.

He'd had enough wine the night before to last him a while. Unlike his family's preference, wine wasn't his favorite. Just like attending tomorrow's tour of the cruise-ship kitchens was a field trip he'd opted to skip.

Only a few days out and he was already prowling the decks. This low level of activity wasn't good for him, tying him up in knots instead of letting him relax.

That sixth sense that had kept him safe innumerable times in the past told him she was approaching. Annalise.

"Is this seat taken?" Something in her eyes looked vulnerable, hopeful. Anxious. "Can I sit here?"

Something in his heart couldn't say no.

Waves of emotion surged through him. What he was feeling for her was more than the foam that short-term flings were made from.

He could so easily drown in the deep blue depths of her eyes.

The smart thing to do would be to explain his need for privacy. It was a valid answer. But he found himself saying, "I was saving it for you."

And he found himself realizing that's exactly what he had been doing.

She looked at him, looked hard enough he felt compelled to push his sunglasses to the top of his head.

"Hard day?" she asked.

He flashed her his celebrity smile. "I'm on a cruise ship. Is there such a thing as a hard day?"

Her eyes said it all. She was disappointed in him for skirting her question. He wanted to redeem himself very badly.

"I'm not used to doing nothing. It feels so…trivial."

"Tell me about Doctors Without Borders." Gracefully, she sank into the lounge chair without spilling a drop from the cup of hot tea she balanced on her saucer.

"What do you want to know?"

She leaned forward, as if she wanted to catch each word before the wind tore it away. As if what he said held great import. As if *he* were of great import. "Where was your first mission?"

So he told her about the trauma care facility in Northern Afghanistan and about how hours of operating made a person numb to the dangers around them.

"The real danger is becoming numb to the people around you. But there was always someone—a father or sister or friend—who reminded you that your patients weren't just bodies that needed medical attention but loved ones who needed medical care."

He couldn't imagine trying to explain this to anyone else, but with Annalise he could see the understanding in her eyes.

Her hands clenched and unclenched around her tea cup. "I was in my first semester of rotation in the E.R. during Hurricane Katrina. In my mind, everything runs together after those first forty-eight hours."

She took a sip of her tea. "What was your first assignment?"

"The tsunami."

"Tell me about it."

He talked for hours, longer than he'd ever spoken about his work before. And she listened, asked questions, nodded sympathetically and laughed at the humorous stories the human psyche needed to break up the horror of it all.

He fell asleep sometime during the evening and when he awoke with the stars gleaming overhead she'd covered him with a blanket against the night air.

CHAPTER SIX

SADLY, ANNALISE HAD had no erotic dreams during the night but she had fallen asleep with Niko on her mind and woken up thinking of him, too. She certainly wouldn't call her night restful. Who would have guessed such a heroic heart beat beneath that pretty boy rebel exterior?

Annalise went down to the medical suite as soon as the early morning yoga class on deck was dismissed. Brandy was usually in that class, but today she was a no-show.

It must have been one of the longest nights of Brandy's life. Annalise's heart went out to her.

When Annalise had realized she was pregnant she'd been almost as frightened as when—

The bell signaling patients arriving kept Annalise from going down a path she'd rather never travel again.

Like it always did, helping others took her mind off her own concerns. Annalise had a steady stream of patients with sunburn from strong tropical rays that took them by surprise and acid reflux from overindulging, both typical complaints at this point in a cruise.

Halfway through her shift one of her receptionists delivered a note, sealed and addressed to her, that had been left at the front counter.

Annalise opened the note. "Not pregnant. Relieved, but kind of sad, too. Am putting on a new patch this morning. Brandy."

Simply apply a patch and go on with life. It was an uncomplicated way to handle a shipboard romance.

So why did Niko and complications pop into her head just as she was confirming her desire for the simple life?

After an hour of wandering around the ship, trying to accidently bump into Niko, Annalise finally spotted him wandering aimlessly around the main pool area. Instead of rushing up to him, she stayed back and observed him for a while. What was it about him that compelled her to watch him? Was it his natural good looks? Or the way his black wavy hair fell onto his forehead in that perfectly casual way? Or the way his T-shirt stretched across his muscled shoulders? Or was it the way he moved, strong and lethal like the tiger she saw in his eyes?

Or maybe it was the way those eyes lit up when he talked about fixing a cleft palate on a little girl and seeing her smile years later when he was reassigned to the same area.

She tried not to notice as she stood next to a high table near her favorite kiosk and dunked her tea bag into her cup of hot water. But as she stirred sugar into her afternoon tea her attention kept returning to him.

He sat at the bar for a while, ordered a beer, then moved toward the lounge chairs, but decided to look over the railing instead.

She had expected to see a playboy on the prowl. Instead, she saw a man alone who didn't know what to do with himself. She had the strongest urge to offer suggestions—suggestions that included her company.

As if he could hear her thoughts, he turned from the rail, scanned the crowd and found her.

"Annalise."

Through the noisy crowd she couldn't hear him, but she could read his lips. In the past, if a passenger wanted to get friendly, she would wave him off and move on, but she couldn't put Niko into the same class as just another passenger. So when he walked towards her, she stood still and waited for him.

"Hey, you." He pushed his sunglasses to the top of his head and gave her a movie-star grin that almost made her swoon. She barely stopped herself from looking around to see who he was really talking to.

If she had been diagnosing herself, she would have had to say her palpitations were the results a developmentally delayed teenage crush.

"Hey you back," she managed to say, pleased that she didn't sound at all bedazzled. "Just hanging out at the pool?"

"I threw a penny in the wishing well a moment ago. That thing really works."

"You got your wish already?"

"Yup. I wished a beautiful woman would come up and talk to me and here you are."

Self-consciously Annalise pulled down the hem of her new orange tank top, which she'd layered over her new bright yellow one, and wiggled her newly painted toenails exposed by her new beaded leather sandals. It was silly to feel self-conscious amongst all the string bikinis on deck.

"Thanks." She didn't need the glance in the glass doors that separated the cruise ship's interior from its exterior to remind her that she was showing a lot more skin than she normally did. She usually only wore tank tops under shirts or thin blouses. But something—or, if she was honest, someone—had inspired a shopping spree.

She might not be as sophisticated as that Greek woman but, still, she'd not done too badly, if she did say so herself.

He kept staring into her eyes. She realized she'd been staring back and blinked.

"So, what did you do today?"

He took a deep sip from the drink he carried. "I played bingo with Yiayia for a while this morning. I won a T-shirt and she won a key chain. Then I went to the kids Underwater

Explorers' activity, where we learned about submarines. The twins are on the water slides, but my doctor grounded me from that. And the rest of the family is attending a pastry-making school. Can you believe it? They all cook for a living, but they go on vacation and now they're cooking again."

"I guess they love what they do."

"I guess so." He shrugged, giving her a crooked grin. "If the ship offered a seminar on reconstructing sinus cavities, I'd probably be in the front row."

The wry expression on his face made her laugh. "You should drop off that suggestion at Guest Services. They're always open to new ideas."

The smile he flashed reached all the way to his eyes. She hadn't realized how brilliant those eyes could be. They took her breath away.

But the sparkle didn't last long. "I was just wondering what to do next. Any suggestions?"

She consulted the flyer listing the day's activities, which she'd picked up after her pedicure, and picked the first thing on the list. "I'm going to the gourmet coffee tasting. Want to come?"

He leaned in close to read the paper she held. "I'll go any-where with you."

The way he said it, so low and intimate, sent shivers through her. Practically, she wondered how many women he'd practiced on before he'd got that timbre just right.

He gave her a quizzical look. "What?"

"Just you and your pick-up lines."

"You don't like them?"

"I didn't say that." She looked up into those glistening eyes. "They just aren't necessary. I like you fine without all the swagger."

He pulled his sunglasses over his eyes. "But without the swagger, what do I have?"

Apparently, she'd hit a sore spot. This man-woman interplay wasn't her forte. She started walking toward the coffee shop.

The silence between them felt awkward and needed filling. Annalise said what was on her mind, hoping her honesty didn't get her into worse trouble. "If you're fishing for a compliment, I can give you several. You're talented, according to your prestigious client list. You're generous. Brave. Good with children. Should I go on?"

She didn't know someone so deeply tanned—or so cocky—could blush as deeply as he did.

"If you keep it up, I'll have to hire you as my publicist."

"Do you have one?"

He gave her a sideways glance. "Uh—no. I'm a serious working doctor, no matter what you've heard from my grandmother."

"She's very proud of you."

"She's proud of all of us."

"I didn't hear her bragging about your brothers at supper the other night."

"Magazine covers and TV interviews impress her." He stopped outside the café's entrance. "It was all to build the practice. Thankfully, it worked. I keep telling my brothers they need to do the same to build up the restaurant, but they've resisted so far."

"Where's your family's restaurant?"

"In the city on Audubon Place. It's called Olympia's, for obvious reasons."

"I'll put that on my list of places to eat next time I'm in New Orleans."

"Just tell them you know me and they'll cut you a good deal."

"They'll probably charge me double, thinking that if I'm a friend of yours, I'll be trouble," Annalise teased.

Niko gave her a genuine smile. "Minx."

This was fun! In the past, when a man had flirted with her,

she'd often thought of amusing retorts in kind but she'd never just blurted them out like this. She'd been too shy.

But with Niko she felt bold and confident. It was a good feeling.

"Want to sit here?" She gestured to a nearby table.

"Sure." Niko offered Annalise a hand to help her sit on the bar stool fronting the coffee bar. He probably did it without even realizing how chivalrous he was being. But Annalise didn't take the courtesy for granted.

His hand was big. Strong. Probably very nice. Still, she pretended not to notice as she climbed onto the bar stool.

As soon as he withdrew his hand she regretted not taking it. Maybe this time would have been different. After all, Niko was different.

He gave her a thoughtful look as he took the seat next to her, obviously not knowing what his personal touch would do to her. How could he know?

She'd never told anyone why she usually kept her distance. She'd never wanted to explain herself, never wanted a man to understand, until now. Maybe she should give him just enough clues that he'd know it wasn't him but her.

She swallowed. "Niko, I—"

The barista interrupted the moment and Annalise didn't know whether to feel relieved or disappointed.

She gave them the coffee-house spiel as she lined up six small cups of coffee in front of them.

"I recommend trying the samples from light roast to dark roast. Lighter is less acidic. Darker has more body." She put an icy-cold silver creamer and sugar bowl on a silver tray on the table. "Let me know if you want to try anything else on the board or if you have any questions."

Niko had lots of questions, but not for the barista. He wanted to know everything about the fascinating woman across from him. He especially wanted to know about the pain in her eyes and how to make it go away.

But by the way Annalise was avoiding looking at him, he knew this wasn't the time or the place.

He would enjoy the moment for what it was and do his best to make sure Annalise enjoyed it, too. There would be other opportunities. He would make sure of that.

After making generous use of the sugar bowl, he took his first sip and hid his wince. Coffee wasn't his favorite drink, but he would have agreed to share a bottle of absinthe if he'd had to, rather than turn down Annalise's invitation.

Annalise took a sip of first cup and grimaced.

"Not to your taste?"

"Not this one." She dumped cream and sugar into her next cup and gave it try. "Too much more of this and I'll have another restless night."

"Another?" Niko added cream to his cup, too, but hesitated before giving it another try.

"You know, Niko, I don't really like coffee. And I'm thinking you don't either. Would you rather have a nice umbrella drink instead?"

"To tell you the truth, Annalise, I'm not very fond of those either." He leaned forward, knowing he was about to either breach a barrier or end this barely budding relationship at one go. "Instead of getting ourselves into something neither of us want, let's make a pact. Truth between us and nothing less."

By the wary expression on Annalise's face Niko knew he had his answer.

"All right." She laughed—a genuine laugh from deep inside. "You were expecting a different answer, weren't you?"

"Sadly, yes. Bad past experiences."

"About that—experiences, I mean. I'll be truthful, but I also reserve the right to not answer."

"Deal." He thought of the sweepstakes ploy he'd engineered for his family and, of course, his Doctors Without Borders gig. "Everyone has a few secrets they don't want revealed."

Niko caught the barista's attention and they placed their

orders—a beer for Niko and a fresh cup of tea for Annalise because she had to check back in with her P.A. before the end of office hours.

"So…" Annalise licked her lips, making Niko yearn for a taste "…want to play Twenty Questions?"

"Sure." He couldn't have refused if his life had depended on it.

"Favorite color."

"I would have said blue before I saw you today. Now it's orange. Most definitely orange."

A rosy blush crept up her face even as her eyes sparkled. She ducked her head. "Thanks."

"What's yours?"

"Mine?"

"Your favorite color?"

She grinned. "Amber. Like your eyes."

Women had complimented his eyes before, but it had never mattered. Now it mattered. *Keep it casual, Christopoulos*

He pushed the flattering remark away. "So you want to play that way, huh? Game on, girl. What do you want in a man?"

Annalise bit her lip as she tilted her head to the side and considered. Worry made Niko's heart pound faster.

From her expression, she was taking this game way too seriously.

"Kindness. Compassion. Strength enough to stand up for those weaker than him. Enough intelligence to hold up his end of the conversation." Very deliberately, she studied him. "And muscles in all the right places."

He spread his arms wide. "You might need to check me out for that last one, Doc. A physical exam would be so much more thorough than a mere visual inspection."

As she took a sip of her tea she looked up from under her lashes. So coy yet so direct. He couldn't stop staring at how she seemed to glow from deep inside when she was happy.

"And you, Dr. Christopoulos. What makes a ladies' man like

you choose one woman over another? Give me a comparison chart, no names necessary."

"Comparison chart? Right now, you're the only woman I can even bring to mind."

"You're a glib one, aren't you?"

He put his hand over his heart. "Only truth between us."

"In that case, how long have you experienced this selective amnesia, Doctor?"

"Ever since I stood behind you when we were boarding."

"What about a certain buxom Greek heiress who needed sunscreen rubbed on her back?"

Helena hadn't even entered his mind. "Merely being polite. Are you jealous?"

"Nothing to be jealous about."

"You're right. You have nothing to be jealous about." He reached over to take Annalise's hand, but she checked her watch before his fingers could graze hers.

"I need to check in with my P.A." She looked down at her activities list and pointed to the next one on the list. "Look. They've got an origami towel-folding class starting in a few minutes. Would you like to try that?"

"Towel origami? Was it something I said?"

She looked at him, long and hard. "Duty before pleasure. You know the score."

"All too well." But something in her eyes didn't ring true. He was pretty certain he was getting the brush-off.

Still, he held out his hand to help her off the bar stool.

When she took it, giving his fingers an apologetic squeeze, he felt a zing go straight to his gut. This woman was different. Special.

And he loved a challenge.

"See you tonight on top?" he called after her.

She stopped and gave him a sexy look over her shoulder. "If you're lucky."

* * *

Annalise didn't show.

Niko waited until past midnight, tensing in anticipation each time he heard footsteps coming up the metal stairs, but he was disappointed each time.

He went over and over the conversation in his head. Had he come on too strong? Shy had never been his type before Annalise. But she had seemed to enjoy their banter.

And why did it mean so much to him? Why did he feel so at a loss? Feel such rejection?

As he unlocked his cabin door, he saw the blinking light on his cabin phone. Impatiently, he followed the lengthy button-pushing instructions to retrieve the text message that scrolled across the phone's display.

Medical emergency. How about tomorrow? Ice skating after breakfast? A.

Short. Cryptic. Exactly the kind of note he'd texted his ex when he had been running late. Now he understood why she hadn't always been satisfied with his terse communication.

Niko spent too many hours staring at the ceiling, thinking about relationships old and new, telling himself he should back away from this one before he fell too deep. Then, finally, admitting to himself he might have already fallen.

As he fell asleep he made the firm, sensible decision to skip the skating date, skip the moonlight trysts, skip all further encounters with Dr. Annalise Walcott. There was no future in it. He had enough goodbyes to say at the end of this trip. No sense in adding one more.

CHAPTER SEVEN

ANNALISE STUDIED THE contents of her closet and clothes drawers. While the ice rink wasn't too cold, her body was acclimated to the tropics. Usually, for ice skating she wore thick sweats, but she opted for her slimmer-fitting yoga pants this morning. Being a little chilled was worth the fashion trade-off.

She contemplated her oversized sweatshirt advertising the cruise line. Her other option was a T-shirt, which would be too thin no matter how much better it showed off her assets.

As she pulled the sweatshirt over her head, Annalise was not oblivious to the change Niko was making on her daily habits.

They definitely had chemistry together, but it wasn't only sexual attraction but also intellectual attraction.

Annalise's mother had often told her that she was too smart for her own good. That she intimidated men and she should try to tone down the brains. While she would have if she could have, she hadn't managed to do that. But with Niko she had no need to. He challenged her mind just as she did his.

Was he the right man? Or was this simply the right time? Even before she'd met him, she had been feeling the need for a change, thus her reluctance to renew her contract and her growing interest in medical relief missions. Even her unsuccessful visit to her mother could be seen as a sign that she was ready to move on from her status quo.

The right man at the right time.

Was she ready? How long was she going to let her past hold her back?

Dark secrets. Was she prepared to look at them in the light of day? It would take a very special man to help her breach the darkness and come into the light.

Did she want Niko to be that man? Would he even want to be that man once he found out about her past?

Secrets.

Niko watched Annalise walk toward him as he stood by the skate counter, fully aware how his pulse sped up at the sight of her.

So much for all his late-night contemplation.

He had no idea where this was going, but if it was leading to something serious… He surprised himself by wishing it could. But he would never be ready for a serious relationship. He'd made his decision.

Thankfully, Annalise was safe. She had her career, too. A career that harbored no expectations of a home and children and a husband who came home every night.

"Hey," he said as she came within earshot.

"Hey back at ya."

Niko grinned at how they had fallen into sync so quickly. He could get used to this. Warning bells went off in his head. Less than three weeks. No sense in getting used to anything about her.

Still, he could enjoy her company, couldn't he? She didn't just pretend to listen when he talked. She really *did* listen. They had well-informed conversations, give and take, back and forth. Yin and yang.

How often had he been misunderstood in the past? A parade of beautiful women flashed through his mind. He had to admit he had not always based his date choice on compatibility.

But with Annalise he had both beauty and brains in one package.

The only problem was—he didn't have her at all. She was her own woman with her own life that he only got to be a part of for the next two weeks and a few days.

This trip was supposed to be about relaxing, not about feeling the pressure of the clock ticking. Why did he do this to himself?

"Ready?" She raised an eyebrow at him in challenge.

Because he couldn't resist, he answered, "Ready."

As Niko bent to lace his skates, he rubbed his thigh, an absent gesture Annalise was certain he wasn't even aware of.

"How's the leg?"

"Fine."

Although she wanted to probe deeper, she practiced great restraint and let it drop. He was entitled to his privacy, just as she was.

"I'm ready to get rid of these stitches."

"I'll take a look tomorrow."

She watched him stand on the rubber map, his ankles wobbling. As soon as she stood, he grabbed her shoulder to steady himself.

Normally, she would shy away from such contact. But this was Niko. Instead, she reached out a hand to steady him.

"You really meant it when you said you wanted me to teach you to skate. You've never done this before?"

"Nope. Never."

"Keep your ankles firm."

"And then?"

"Then the first thing you need to learn is how to fall."

His grip tightened on her as he wobbled back and forth. "I'm thinking that lesson will come to me naturally in a very short time."

"Falling isn't inevitable."

"Except for falling in love," he quipped. Then he became very still. "At least, that's what Yiayia would say."

She was all too aware that they were avoiding each other's eyes. "That L-word can ruin a lot of friendships."

He nodded. "Then we won't let that happen, will we?"

Abruptly he sat on the bench behind him, craning up to look at her.

She sat next to him, putting them at the same height.

"Annalise?"

"Yes?"

"We can be friends, can't we? Even after this is over?"

She drew in a big breath. "Long distance? We can try. No promises, though."

He nodded. "No promises."

A group of teens rushed by, laughing and playing and reminding Annalise that life was full of fun as well as drama.

"Are we going to skate today, or hold down this bench for the rest of the morning?" she dared him.

"Let's skate." This time when he stood up he planted his feet firmly, not needing her for support.

"If you start to fall, lean back, tuck your chin in to protect your head and fall on your butt."

"Sage advice for life as well as for ice skating." He reached for her, brushing a strand of hair from her eyes. His finger lingered on the rim of her ear as he pushed the strand behind it.

The thrill made Annalise jerk away.

His lips were so close to hers she could almost taste them when he asked, "Ticklish?"

She took a step backwards, her skate catching on the rubber mat. As she windmilled her arms, he reached out to catch her.

They both lost their balance and he ended up sitting down hard on the bench with her in his lap.

Annalise jumped up.

"Sorry," she said, even though he should be the one apologizing. She hadn't been expecting that sizzling touch. She certainly hadn't asked for it either.

"I'm not."

Take it in stride, Annalise, she reminded herself. *This is flirting. This is fun. Nothing else. And nothing more.*

"Watch me." She walked in front of him. "See how I'm walking a bit forward and bending my knees?"

"Yes. I see."

The teasingly licentious tone of his voice made her grin but she didn't turn around and return it. Not this time. Too much had passed between them that needed some space.

She heard a scrape of blades once he came onto the ice, but no *kerplump.*

Turning, she skated backwards and instructed, "Just lean forward and bend your knees, like you're a superhero if you have to exaggerate it, until you get your balance."

Niko's black hair fell forward into his eyes, making Annalise think about how he could be her Clark Kent any day. Just not today. Too much, too soon.

Then again, this trip wasn't going to last forever.

Niko closed his eyes and took a breath, apparently finding his balance because when he opened them he said, "I'm ready."

And then he skated like he'd been born on the ice, taking long, sure strides and handling the corners with no problems for several laps.

He ran into the wall of the rink to stop.

He looked back over his shoulder at her. "Not graceful but effective."

Showing off a little, she demonstrated a hockey-style stop.

He raised an eyebrow. "Isn't there an easier way?"

"See the cleats on the blade? Drag your toe. They'll catch and slow you down until you stop."

He tried stopping a few times and then said, "Now I'm ready to do that thing you did when you turned around to skate backwards."

"Okay. Changing direction is best done while you're moving, not standing still."

She skated away from him, then crossed her feet and executed a smooth turn so that she faced him, skating backwards. It had taken her many hours of practice to be able to change direction so smoothly.

"Be patient with yourself if you don't get it right the first time."

"I'm not big on patience."

She skated towards him, turning again when she drew even with him. "I've sensed that about you."

Niko took a couple of strides, then crossed his feet, doing a complete circle instead of a half-one.

"It takes practice." Annalise turned back and forth a half dozen times in as many strides, enjoying what she was doing as much as flaunting her skills.

Niko frowned down at her feet, then nodded and gave it a try. Of course, he picked up the technique on the second pass. Was there anything this man couldn't do?

He dragged a toe, ending up a few inches from her, close enough she could see the golden flecks in his eyes. "Now that I've done it, I don't understand the appeal of going round in circles. Maybe speed skating or doing those dangerous moves and jumps they do on television would make it more exciting." He skated backwards to Annalise's forwards.

"Always the extremes for you, isn't it, Niko?"

He looked sad. "It's when I feel most alive."

But that wasn't precisely true. Not anymore. He felt the same thrilling awareness of existence whenever he was with Annalise.

It wasn't a revelation he was happy to discover.

But he couldn't make a clean break of it. Finding an excuse to prolong this, he scratched at his thigh through his shorts. "No office hours today, huh?"

"Impatient man." Her smile was strained as she sat on the bench to unlace her skates.

Niko sat next to her, though not as close as he had before.

Was there something more behind her bantering exasperation? He shouldn't want there to be more.

"Come by tomorrow morning and I'll take a look."

Tomorrow morning. Niko wanted to ask about tonight.

"Maybe I could just borrow a pair of scissors and tweezers." He gave her a practiced grin as he kicked off his skate. "I'm ready to try the water slides."

"You can always stop in and visit my P.A."

Niko thought about that, thought about how that was a very sound solution, then thought about how he yearned to feel Annalise's warm hand on his leg, gently tending to him. He decided he could put off the water slides until tomorrow.

He lined up his skates, one next to the other, and slipped into his tennis shoes, wiggling his toes at the familiar comfortable fit.

"See you then—if not tonight?"

"Tomorrow, for sure. Tonight?" She bent to unlace her second skate, effectively hiding her face behind her hair. "Maybe."

He wanted to ask what he could to do convince her, to insist. To make her commit.

Which would call for commitment on his part, too.

He checked his watch. "Family calls. I need to check on Sophie."

"Okay."

"See you then," Niko said again, restraining himself from clearing up the ambiguity. These things happened in their own time. If only he had that much time.

He grabbed both pairs of skates and headed for the counter to turn them in.

He couldn't help watching her as she walked away, her bottom perfectly defined in those form-fitting yoga pants beneath that huge sweatshirt. He'd bet each of those perfect butt cheeks would fit perfectly in his hands. How wise was he to want to prove himself right?

* * *

After filling the rest of her morning with grueling, hot yoga then a long swim in the pool after lunch, along with a trip to the video arcade to play a big-screen version of tennis, and a couple of miles on the treadmill instead of supper, Annalise should have been dropping from exhaustion. Instead, she found herself climbing the three sets of stairs to the top deck, a cup of hot decaf tea in her hand, anticipation in her heart.

The deck was deserted.

Annalise almost turned around and left but stopped herself in mid-step. What was she doing? A cup of tea on the top deck had been her habit ever since she'd started sailing on this ship. After all the cruises she'd worked, why would she let one man on one cruise change a tradition that gave her so much pleasure?

Hazy memories of the pleasures her dream lover had almost given her had her sloshing tea over the rim of her cup. It was a dream she would welcome again.

As she would welcome the man behind the dream?

Today, for the first time since she'd signed her first contract, the huge ship seemed too small. Like her P.A. had said, Annalise was a legend in the cruise line's history for her longevity of employment. Most people got tired of running from whatever it was, or found what they were running towards, after a few seasons of ship work. But she'd always been slow to make a change, hanging onto stability, to security.

Her yoga instructor would say that without change there was no growth. And without growth, death. At least in spirit.

Wasn't that what had happened to her own mother so many years ago?

Annalise was not like her mother. But, then, flirting with a man didn't mean selling her soul to him. That's not what a relationship, or even a casual encounter, had to be.

She had established her professional life on her own terms. She could certainly establish her love life on her own terms, too.

Right before the sun made its nightly plunge into the ocean, she heard Niko running up the steps.

"I didn't miss it, did I?"

"Even the sunset waits on Niko Christopoulos."

She'd expected that to elicit a smile or even a laugh from him. Instead, he settled down next to her, twisted the top off one of the two beers he held and saluted the pink and yellow horizon.

"To peace of mind." Although the strangle hold he had on the neck of his beer bottle told a different story.

She raised her tea cup in solidarity. "To peace of mind."

Niko lay back on the lounger with the last of the sun's rays casting shadows over his face, making him look tired.

She wanted to make it all better but they didn't have that kind of relationship. Silence was the best she could do.

As they lay within arm's reach of each other, attraction snapping between them like heat lightning, Annalise wondered how this would end.

CHAPTER EIGHT

NIKO WAS THE first one in her office. It was easy to do since he'd been up since before dawn. In fact, he wasn't sure he'd slept at all.

Annalise had been too much on his mind.

He hadn't spent a sleepless night over a woman in…in longer than he could remember.

Annalise bit her bottom lip, a worried line appearing between her eyebrows. "That knife could have sliced across your throat as easily as it cut into your thigh."

"Lots of things could happen that never do."

"You're one of the lucky ones. You have a family that cares. You could have died and they wouldn't have even known why. Closure heals a lot of hurts."

But acknowledging that something fatal could happen meant dealing with the emotions associated with that nebulous something. He didn't do family drama very well. "I'm going to tell them as soon as the time is right."

Niko felt Annalise's hand burning on his thigh. Her touch set him on fire. He couldn't deny it.

Just as he couldn't deny that he was a man of flesh and blood. If this had been more serious, if he had died, his family would never have understood. He would never have had the opportunity to explain. He owed them more than that.

Annalise was right. Soon. As soon as the opportunity presented itself.

Like that was ever going to happen.

Niko pushed that thought away, determined to squeeze every ounce of enjoyment out of this trip. He had almost two weeks left and he would make the most of them.

After Annalise confirmed that Niko's knife wound was healing well enough, he sat on the exam table and picked out his own stitches, using the tweezers and scissors Annalise lent him as she stood, propped against the wall, watching him.

She'd offered. He could have accepted. But her hand on his thigh would have led to an embarrassing situation that his baggy board shorts couldn't have hidden.

He looked up at her from under thick, dark lashes. "Are you as good at climbing the rock wall as you are at ice skating?"

She arched a brow at him. "Better."

"As soon as I'm done here, then, want to race?"

"I don't know. I might be taking unfair advantage." Annalise frowned as Niko tugged on one of the stitches to get it loose. "Living on this ship, I've climbed that wall a thousand times at least. And I've scaled real rocks, too."

"Yeah? When?"

"Before I was hired by the cruise line, I signed up for the emergency medicine residency swap program. So I gave New Mexico's emergency medicine program a try. I learned to climb there."

"You're just full of surprises."

She shrugged. "In New Orleans, I'd always lived around three feet below sea level in the inner city. I thought I'd try different terrain for a while."

"What did you think of it?" Field medicine wasn't for most doctors.

"I loved everything about it. The mountains. The desert. It was like the elements dared me and I was determined to win."

"Sweet Annalise in those rugged conditions. I've noticed you've got a competitive edge." The need to beat the odds was the attitude it took to be a good field doctor. More and more, he was learning there was more to Annalise than he'd thought at first glance. Although the first glance had been rather thrilling, too.

"You're doing it again." She rubbed at her cheek. "You're staring at me like I've got something on my face."

"Sorry. I must be losing my touch. That's supposed to be my intensely interested look. Obviously, I need to work on it."

"Honesty?"

"Honesty." He crossed his heart and held up his fingers like a scout. "When you smile like that, I can't help but stare."

She laughed, shaking her head at his compliment, not taking him seriously. "You and your flattery."

While he'd totally meant the compliment, he liked it that she wasn't too taken in by it. Annalise definitely stood on her own two feet.

"But a beautiful woman deserves beautiful compliments."

"Pretty is as pretty does." She gave him a sideways look. "You're good looking. Does that make you a better person?"

Her question, delivered quick and solid, caught Niko by surprise. "Of course not."

"Remember that next time you're throwing around random compliments."

Niko thought of the sinking feeling he always got when he thought a woman was more interested in his appeal as an arm ornament than as a person. "Yes, ma'am, I will."

He flexed his leg, watching the healed skin hold true. "If you were in the emergency response residency program, I'm guessing you specialized in emergency medicine. So how did you end up here?"

"I applied for a couple of positions that would have set me up for emergency rescue work." She swept her arm around the exam room. "I was seduced by the glamour of all this."

He looked around in appreciation, catching a glimpse of the ocean out the high transom window. "It's a nice gig."

"I've had it for a while. And it puts me in the position of being an excellent rock-wall climber. Ready to lose to a girl?"

"Winner gets a back rub!" Niko didn't know why he'd said that. When he saw the shocked look in Annalise's eyes, he almost awkwardly retracted the prize.

But then she blinked and said, "You're on," and he was glad after all. Regardless of who made it to the top first, he was a winner.

And that's exactly what he was feeling, clinging to the wall as he looked up and over at Annalise's ankle, up to her calf, to her thigh and her wonderfully perfect butt.

"Hey, Uncle Niko, are you going to let a girl beat you?"

Why had he thought he was going to do this without an audience of family members?

The harness straps cut him in places where he'd rather not feel that kind of pain. To get some relief, Niko found the next toehold and pushed upwards. Because he was taller than she was, now he was even with her.

She looked over and met his eyes. "You haven't won yet, Christopoulos."

His fingers touched a plastic thing bolted onto the fake rock and he dug the tips of his fingers around the edge to pull himself up.

At the same time Annalise reached for the same plastic thing, covering his hand with hers.

"Oh!" She jerked her hand back. So he wasn't the only one that felt the heat when they touched.

Her eyes went wide as she swung her arm wildly, off balance. Then down she went on her guide rope. She fell at least halfway before the rope latch stopped her.

By the surprised but happy grin on her face she was fine.

Niko thought for a moment. He could slide down now, too, but that would mean no winner. And no winner would mean no back rub.

He gave her a wry look. "I like my massages with warm oil," he said, just loud enough for her to hear.

"You haven't made it yet." She swung back to face the wall, scrambled for a plastic thing and began climbing much faster than she'd climbed earlier, making him realize she'd been holding back and pacing herself to him.

The competitive spirit kicked in full force. Niko felt around with his foot, reached outside his comfort zone and found the toehold he was looking for. His healing leg quivered from fatigue as he willed muscle and sinew to lift.

It was a stretch but he could almost reach the next—

And then he was falling, falling, with his stomach flipping until the harness jerked him to a halt.

"Ow." The harness did unkind things to him. Good thing he hadn't planned on having kids.

Annalise paused her climb to look down at him as he dangled a few feet from the floor.

"You okay?"

"Just singing soprano now."

She gave him a wink then covered the last four feet of wall as if she were a spider. With great aplomb she rang the bell at the top.

"For form's sake," she called down to him as she planted her feet and descended in graceful hops as if she'd been born on the mountains instead of on the flat, soggy soil of New Orleans.

Niko worked at setting his own feet and pushing against the wall, descending until he finally touched the deck.

Annalise was only two hops ahead of him. By the time he'd unbuckled his harness, she had hers off, too.

Before the Christopoulos clan could totally engulf them, he leaned over close. With any other woman, he would be suggesting his room, but that didn't feel right with Annalise. She needed more finesse. And he was pleased to be the one to give her what she needed. Instead, he asked, "Tonight on deck?"

She nodded, adding, "I like my oil to smell like lavender."

And then she was gone, wading through his brothers and nephews and sisters-in-law and nieces as they gathered around to snap pictures and pat him on the back and tease him as only a brother could about his loss to a girl.

As he anticipated the evening activities, he couldn't help but grin. This was no loss. In fact, it was a pretty big win in his book.

Annalise made her way up to the top deck with equal parts of anticipation and trepidation. Maybe she should have let him win? Then she would have been more in control, touching him instead of him touching her.

Stop it, Annalise. It's just a back rub in public.

She wore her swimsuit underneath her shirt and shorts. She'd thought long and hard about what to wear, giving it much more consideration than the situation merited.

Should he really go through the trouble of finding lavender oil, the modest one-piece exposed her shoulders and back and was easily washable.

If this back-rub thing started to become more than fun and games… Every time she imagined how his hands would feel, her mind skittered away.

As she rounded the corner, she saw he was already there on his favorite chair.

"Hey." His voice reached that place deep within her that her mind had been avoiding thinking about.

She rubbed her hands down her arms to rub away the prickles that danced along her skin.

She swallowed. "Hey back at ya." It was throaty, husky and entirely not what she had intended.

He had her chair decked out with a couple of thick towels and a bottle of oil with an expensive label she recognized from the spa on deck three.

He stood and indicated the lounge chair. "Madam, your

masseur awaits your pleasure." With an exaggerated leer he rubbed his hands together then cracked his knuckles.

Before she could lose her nerve, she whipped off her top. "Just remember, you're a cabana boy tonight, not a chiropractor."

She thought about lying prone, but that seemed too intimate so she straddled the lounger instead. "So I can watch the sunset," she explained. *So I won't feel so vulnerable,* she admitted to herself.

"Okay." He swung his leg over to straddle the lounger behind her, thigh to thigh. "I like exploring new positions."

Annalise was too busy reacting to the sizzle along her nerve endings to think of a retort. *I want this,* she reminded herself.

At the first touch of his palms on her shoulders, her apprehension made her shiver.

"Relax," he crooned into her ear, which made her feel anything but relaxed.

His hands, slick with fragrant oil, slid along her shoulders until this thumbs found the knot at the base of her neck. With the right amount of firmness and gentleness, he made circular motions to get her shoulders to loosen.

Annalise tried to concentrate on the sunset instead of the man who sat inches behind her.

His hands stilled. "Okay?"

She wanted to be okay. With every cell of her body she wanted to want this, to enjoy this, to want more.

"Annalise?" It was a question wrapped in a worry.

A noisy crowd of five people scrambled onto the deck she'd foolishly begun to think of as their private nirvana.

She had a sinking feeling at the relief she felt to be interrupted.

"I— We…" What should she say? Sorry? Maybe next time? I wish things could be different?

"Look at me!" One of the intruders stood at the rail and held out her arms. "It's like I'm flying."

The others gave it a try, cackling with laughter and spilling drinks in the process.

Niko dropped his hands and blew out a sigh as Annalise leaned forward to grab for her shirt.

She pulled it on, grimacing when the back stuck to the oil on her skin.

Niko sat motionless behind her. She couldn't even feel him breathe.

Without a glance she got up and headed downstairs, down to her cabin with no windows, down to her dark little hidey-hole that kept the world locked out—but kept her locked in.

For the first time in years she cried into her pillow. Long, ragged, ugly sobs for all that had happened to her and who she wanted to be.

With her throat too swollen and sore to cry anymore, she made up her mind. She would not be a victim for the rest of her life.

Many hours later, as she lay in bed, reliving the scene over and over again, she kept up her litany, praying it wasn't falling on deaf ears. *Please. Another chance.*

CHAPTER NINE

NOT ALL PRAYERS were answered.

Her patient load was extraordinarily heavy with barely breathing room. Between shifts, Annalise tried to casually run into Niko but could never find him. She even made a point to look for the Christopoulos clan at their family dinner, even though she dreaded facing the lot of them. All that family happiness only contrasted with her own sad situation, reminding her how different she and Niko were. But her need for Niko overcame her unease.

She found out from their waiter that her courage was for naught. Apparently, they'd all decided to forgo formal dining in favor of an early picnic by the wave pool.

That evening, she sat alone on the top deck, watching a sunset obscured by stormclouds. Today was only the beginning of much rougher seas ahead.

Was Niko avoiding her? Of course he was. She couldn't blame him. He must think her the most fickle female on the planet.

But the next evening found her on the top deck once again, hoping. Praying.

After all, what better did she have do to and where better did she have to go?

Niko called himself all kinds of a fool as he climbed the stairs to the top deck. Some things just weren't meant to be so why was he trying so hard?

Because he couldn't get her out of his head.

He clenched his fists, remembering the feel of her skin under his palms. The energy that radiated through her into him made him feel so buzzed, so alive.

But she could turn it off faster than any woman he'd ever met. Maybe it was his imagination, but when she looked at him he thought he saw a wistfulness in her eyes. And he wanted to—had to—give her whatever it was she wanted. *Because he wouldn't be complete until she was.*

Niko rubbed at his eyes, trying to rub away that fanciful thought. With any other woman he would have walked away by now. But there was something—something that had him coming back to her.

He didn't know if that something was in her or in him. All he knew was that he was climbing these stairs because he couldn't think of any other place he would be okay about being in right now.

"Hey," she offered cautiously.

"Hey back at you." He set down between them the two cups of hot tea he'd brought up.

"Busy morning?" he asked.

"And booked until late afternoon, too. They come in—"

"Waves." He finished her sentence for her. "It happens that way, doesn't it? Biorhythms or something."

"I always blame it on moon phases." The conversation felt stilted, but at least they were talking.

She watched him add three packets of sugar to his tea. "Not sweet enough?"

He held up the cup. "Bitter. It steeped too long. But enough sweetener can fix anything."

Could she be fixed with enough sweetener? She hoped so. "I heard the Christopoulos boys closed the bar down last night." She'd heard it from Brandy at yoga that morning. She'd also heard Niko had turned down quite a few offers of female company before moving to the sports section of the bar to watch football with his brothers instead.

"We won." He hoisted his cup. "Go, Tigers. But, then, I think I cheered them on one too many times last night."

She grinned at his hesitant hurrah. "You're on vacation. You're supposed to be having fun."

Vacation. The fun wouldn't last for ever. And hers might be over before it even began if she didn't take action.

"I've had fun. I've especially enjoyed the ship's medical services. The cruise line employs a very fine doctor."

"Compliment accepted." She sipped her tea.

"I have to admit, though, while I've enjoyed my time aboard ship, I'll be glad to make our first port. I didn't realize these transatlantic cruises had so much sea time up front." Niko took a sip of tea and winced. "Only two more days, right?"

"Yes. Two more days until our first port of call, Isle de Paridisio."

"You've been there?"

"A few times."

He took a sip of tea. "At least I've got it drinkable."

"You could have always got another cup."

"I like this one just fine." He stared out at the ocean. "I know my family is a handful, but we would love to have you join us."

This was the opportunity she'd asked for. The one she'd prayed for. A second chance for her. She needed this so much. Such a double-edged sword.

"I'm sorry. I can't." Turning him down was one of the hardest decisions she'd ever made.

The ill and injured of Isle de Paridisio needed her more.

The cruise line fully supported staff volunteering at the various ports of call, often matching private donations and giving away tons of food to the shelters.

Annalise always offered her assistance to any of the medical clinics along the cruise ship's routes. So many of these tropical paradises had beautiful tourist resorts as a thin veneer over the destitution of the rest of the island.

During their stopover at Isle de Paradisio, the youth directors would visit a local orphanage to donate books and clothing and the kitchen chefs would donate food. Other staff would help, too.

Annalise would head to the refugee camp. So many refugees traversed the Mediterranean, making it only this far, with nothing but their lives to call their own.

She had medicine to deliver, donated by New Orleans charities, and she would lend a hand where she could while she was on the island.

The beeper on her hip buzzed. She squinted in the failing light to read the code, seeing that it signaled an immediate emergency.

"I've got to go."

"Of course. Duty calls. Been there. Done that." His mouth twisted into a wry smile. "Maybe later."

"Wake up, sweetie. Wake up for Yiayia." Hearing those ominous words float down the hallway of the medical suite, Annalise's heart sank like a stone and she picked up her fast walk to an all-out run.

There was Sophie, lying limp in her Uncle Stephen's arms.

Her other uncle, all her aunts and her cousins surrounded her. If love could fix her, she would be the healthiest little girl on the planet. Sadly, juvenile diabetes had no cure.

Her clothes were urine-soaked. Her little arm felt cold and clammy and her breathing was so slow as to be barely detectable.

"Did she vomit?"

The whole family started talking at once, but the general gist was that they didn't think so.

Annalise spotted Marcus. "Get your Uncle Niko. He's on the upper foredeck."

She would need him to run interference with his family as she helped the little girl.

"Bring her in," she directed Stephen, and pointed to the nearest exam table. "Where's her meter?"

Phoebe pulled it from her tote along with the notebook.

Annalise pricked Sophie's finger and the meter evaluated Sophie's blood-sugar level.

It was dangerously high.

Sophie's endocrinologist had warned Annalise that trying to balance blood sugar was more of a gut feeling than an exact formula. Drawing on her healer's instinct, Annalise grabbed a vial of fast-acting insulin and checked the charts. She filled a syringe conservatively and gave Sophie the injection. Now the wait.

Meanwhile, she wrapped a rubber tourniquet around Sophie's arm, trying to find a vein so she could draw a blood sample from her dehydrated little body.

Vaguely, she was aware of Niko herding out his well-meaning family members.

"Find out what happened," Annalise threw over her shoulder as she prepared to prick the vein.

Sophie fluttered her eyelids and feebly tried to move her arm away. "No. Don't."

It was a sleepy response, but still a response.

"Be brave, little one," Annalise murmured. Niko's big, strong hand came into view, gently holding Sophie's tiny arm still.

Sophie opened her eyes. "Uncle Niko?"

"I'm here for you, Sophie."

"I'm taking this to the lab. Stay with her, okay?" Annalise put the sample in the analyzer then rejoined them while the machine did its work.

Sophie's spark of defiance had been short-lived as she now lay still once again.

"What's the scoop, Niko?"

"Her aunt had given her permission to get a banana from the fruit bar. Apparently, Sophie figured out how to use the ice-cream machine next to it by herself. A helpful passenger boosted her up when she was too short to reach it. That inspired a binge. One of her cousins tattled and they found Sophie hiding under a dining-room table with a tray full of cookies and donuts and brownies. By the time they found her, it was too late to prevent this."

She handed Niko a water bottle. "Get her to drink as much as you can."

Annalise checked her watch. Almost twenty minutes.

This time Sophie protested the meter prick, which was as good a sign of her recovery as the blood-sugar level, which was slowly edging downwards. She gave Sophie and Niko a reassuring smile. "We're getting there."

The lab analyzer beeped and Annalise read the results.

Showing them to Niko, she pointed to the potassium levels. "Looks like we're okay here."

"Thank God." Niko bent down and placed a kiss on his niece's forehead. "I should have been there. I promised my brother I would watch over her."

"No, Niko. Stop it." Annalise hesitated, then touched his shoulder. "Your family is saying the same thing. But they're only human. Do you blame them?"

"Of course not."

"Then don't blame yourself either."

He scrubbed his hand through his hair. "Little kids should be able to sneak an occasional ice-cream cone. They shouldn't have to get injections three times a day the rest of their lives. It's not fair."

"You, of all people, with all you've seen, all you've done, know that life's not fair and bad things happen. We do what we can to pick up the pieces and go on."

Niko looked into her eyes, searching—for what? Sincerity? Truth? She had that in spades.

Acceptance that they had to make peace with the unfairness of the world? No. She couldn't give him that.

"You understand, don't you?" He ran his finger down her cheek. "You understand the frustration of not being able to make everything all right."

She nodded. "I understand."

On the table, Sophie stirred. Her face screwed up in a scowl. "I'm wet. Who threw water on me?" She sniffed. "Somebody peed on me."

Niko shook his head. "You had an uh-oh, little one."

"I'm not a baby. I don't wet my pants." But the embarrassment in her face showed she understood that she had. To cover up, she pawed at the bandage taped to her arm, where Annalise had taken her blood sample. "This hurts."

Niko and Annalise both grinned at her irritability, a good sign of her recovery.

Niko raised an eyebrow at her. "This happened because of the ice cream and the cookies and the donuts, Sophie." He said it gently but firmly.

Annalise knew him well enough to know it was breaking his heart to deliver this lesson.

"But Phillip got some."

"You have to be more careful than Phillip. He doesn't get sick when he eats too much sugary food but you do."

"It's not fair."

Niko shrugged, a studied, calculated movement by the stiffness of his shoulders. "But that's the way it is."

Annalise did one more blood-sugar test, pricking Sophie's finger with the meter before she could protest. As Sophie glared at her, Annalise read the meter and found the level becoming more satisfactory.

She documented everything in Sophie's notebook and then wrote down her instructions. "We should be seeing normal readings in about another hour and a half. If not, call me. I'd do a check every hour for the next three hours or so. Then every two hours so both of you can get some sleep. Watch for it to swing. Going too low can look like sleep and be a coma instead. But, then, you know that, right?"

"It's different when the patient is family." Niko rubbed his hand across his face. "I appreciate your instructions. They help me keep my head on straight."

Not having family to speak of, Annalise wouldn't know that. "Call me if the levels are out of this range."

She wrote down the numbers in the notebook. "I can't recommend sleeping in. Keep her on her morning schedule of insulin and breakfast. Maybe a nap during the day. Come and see me tomorrow afternoon and we'll do a blood test to double-check that potassium level. Until then, no bananas and no tomatoes." She made herself look into Sophie's sad, angry eyes. "And no ice cream or cookies or brownies."

As tears welled in Sophie's eyes, Annalise steeled herself to keep from joining her. Niko put his hand on Annalise's shoulder and squeezed, comforting her.

Life was unfair but she would do what she could when she could. Perhaps someday she would learn to be content with that.

Until then it was nice to know that someone in the world understood.

CHAPTER TEN

IT HAD BEEN a long, sleepless night.

After assuring himself that Sophie's blood sugar had stabilized and that she had more than enough family members surrounding her, Niko spent the morning drifting in and out of sleep on deck.

Helena kept him company. Or rather she used him to keep a would-be paparazzo at bay. Somehow the man had figured out who Helena's rich ex-husband was and had been trying to interview her about their divorce ever since last night.

Niko didn't mind. Helena was comfortable with long silences. When they did converse, she was intelligent and well read. Her ex was a fool and he told her so.

And when the waves picked up, the nosy man, along with most of the passengers, retired to the interior of the ship, where the rocking didn't seem as pronounced if they couldn't see the splash.

Which left Niko pleasantly alone except for Helena but left Annalise incredibly busy. Which might be just as well.

They had shared moments, special moments that came from deep inside him, when she'd asked about his work with Doctors Without Borders, when they'd talked of his childhood and how important his family was to him, when they'd taken care of Sophie.

But maybe those moments had only been precious to him. Looking back, Niko realized that Annalise had dodged any questions about her own life before she'd become a cruise ship doctor. Had he forgotten his own rule? The one about shipboard romances?

When this cruise was over, so would be their relationship. Serious relationship and career choice didn't fit in the same sentence for him. Yet Annalise was not a woman to be taken lightly.

"You are frowning, *filo mu*." Helena adjusted her hat brim against the sun.

Filo mu. My friend. He knew for certain Helena would be his friend only until they docked and he was fine with that. Many people passed in and out of his life. Many more would come and go in the future.

But the thought of never seeing Annalise again—that was giving him a bit of heartburn and he wasn't sure what medicine to take that would offer relief.

Annalise had checked on Sophie throughout the day as often as she could. The child was resilient, as most children were. It helped that her young cousins treated her no differently than each other, even though the older family members tended to hover into the late afternoon.

If only the other passengers were so hardy. The waves and swells had picked up that afternoon as a storm moved in. Annalise and her colleagues had been handing out motion-sickness patches as fast as they could complete the examination. The patches took a while to work, though. Too little too late for most of the passengers.

The invitation to the captain's table tonight didn't surprise her. With this weather, he had probably received several cancellations.

Annalise wondered who she would be dining with this evening. In the mood she was in, anything was better than eating alone. She was having a hard time keeping her mind off Niko and that Greek woman he'd glued himself to all afternoon.

Jealousy, especially unjust jealousy, was an ugly lump in her stomach she had never expected to experience.

In front of the mirror, she braced to keep from swaying with the rocking of the ship as she tried to arrange her hair. Ponytails swirled into ballerina buns were so much easier than this layered cut.

After twenty minutes of failure, she gave up on pinning the loose strands that drifted down and let them wisp around her neckline *au naturel*. She swiped on another coat of lip gloss since she'd eaten off her earlier application while trying to style her hair.

Mentally she reviewed the cases that had come through her office that day. The Christopoulos family seemed to be of robust stock, Sophie's diabetes notwithstanding. Not one family member had come to see her for seasickness.

A man like Niko wouldn't let a little thing like ocean motion interfere with his game plan. When she'd taken a quick break on deck to breathe in the fresh air, she'd seen him cozied up to that Greek heiress from Texas looking like he was her personal bodyguard.

Or maybe she had that backwards. The woman certainly looked like she wanted to guard Niko's body, keeping it all for herself. And Niko didn't appear to mind at all.

Annalise thought they'd shared something special—something unique just between the two of them all those evenings on deck. Then, the second she'd had to work, Niko had found another woman to tell his soulful tales to. Would any woman do for him or had that big-bosomed Greek goddess been able to give him something more than she could?

In the mirror, her cheeks were blotchy red. Time to take a reality check. The truth was, even though Niko had trusted her with his most precious secrets, she'd backed away whenever he'd tried to understand her. She'd shut down, just like she always did whenever anyone wanted to get close.

Annalise added more powder to her flushed cheeks then

adjusted her cleavage, plumping it up to make more of it. She might not have as much going for her as the goddess, but she would make the most of what she had. And if she happened to run into Niko tonight…

What? What would she do if she happened to run into him? Promise not to leave so abruptly when the talk turned personal? Promise…?

That was the kicker. She could make no promises.

To the empty room, she said, "Who said anything about promises, Annalise? What's wrong with a little fun? No commitment required?"

Saying it aloud sounded bold and brave and beautiful, all the things she wanted to be, right? She would *not* continue to be haunted by a past that had been out of her control. She *would* live a normal life, a life that included a healthy relationship with a man.

She would look for opportunities. If not with Niko then with someone else.

That affirmation felt flat and uneasy. Try as she may, Annalise couldn't envision anyone other than Niko in her bed.

She looked at herself in the full-length mirror, reached up to adjust her halter-topped emerald-green dress for better coverage, then made herself drop her hand.

She was no more exposed than any other woman. She would hold up her head and be proud.

Niko twitched in his tuxedo as he was seated next to Helena at the captain's table. He'd dressed up for Yiayia but there she sat, across the room at a table for two. He would have to check out the little old man she was leaning so close to as they laughed together.

But now he apparently had a rich Greek heiress from Texas to entertain. He'd bet his passport his grandmother had had something to do with it.

The captain made the introductions. Mr. and Mrs. Smith,

who were celebrating Mrs. Smith's seventy-fifth birthday. The ship's entertainment director. And Helena Grubbs.

"It's Artino now," she gracefully corrected him. "I'm going back to my maiden name."

"Helena. Always a pleasure." Niko murmured the polite response but ignored the hopeful question in her eyes. No. He wasn't interested.

The twins were right. She was his type. So why wasn't he more enamored of her when her big brown eyes freely offered so many possibilities? Because there was no spark. Only one woman on this ship held his interest. If only the feeling had been mutual.

"We keep running into each other," she said. "Destiny?"

He'd thought she knew where he stood. He hadn't been sending mixed messages, had he? Looking her straight in the eye, he made his intentions as clear as he could. "Maybe you're the sister I never had."

By the dimming of her expression, he saw that she finally understood.

"How about being my friend? A girl can't have too many of them, can she?" Clearly disappointed, she turned away to focus her attention on Mr. Smith.

Niko glared at his grandmother, who had put them in this awkward position, but she was too intent on the man across from her to notice.

"Is anything wrong, Mr. Christopoulos?" the captain asked.

"Nothing. I've just never seen my grandmother dine with another gentleman before."

"Don't worry. He's one of our regulars, a widower. He makes trips with us several times a year," the entertainment director reassured him.

Mrs. Smith nodded knowingly from across the table set for seven. "Running from loneliness." She patted the arm of a man seated next to her. "Thankfully, I ran into the arms of a man who promises me I'll never be lonely again."

Niko felt the emptiness of the unoccupied chair next to him.

Then he saw her heading toward them. Immediately, he stood. How could he not in the presence of such beauty?

The captain made the introductions. "Dr. Niko Christopoulos, I think you might know our ship's doctor, Annalise Walcott."

"I've had the pleasure." On impulse, he reached for her hand. Surprisingly, she held it out to him.

He carried it to his lips, breathing in the scent of lavender lotion and Annalise.

As he pulled out her chair for her he had the strongest urge to whisper in her ear and tell her how stunning she looked but he wasn't sure how she'd take it, especially in front of the captain.

"Sorry to be late," she apologized to the captain and the table at large.

"Nonsense. I know your afternoon has been busy." The captain introduced her to the couple across from her. Mr. Smith might be elderly, but he wasn't too old to appreciate Annalise's cleavage.

Niko wanted to cover her with his coat or maybe the tablecloth.

"What?" Under cover of passing the bread, Annalise asked him, "Is something wrong?"

Rein it in, Christopoulos, he told himself. "No. Nothing." He forced a smile that strained his jaw muscles.

She lifted her eyebrow, not taken in by his pseudo-civility. "Where is your family?"

"I had expected to meet them here." He nodded toward this grandmother's table. "Yiayia tells me that Stephen and Phoebe are dining alone in their room while the twins watch over the little ones in the family suite. My other brother and his wife had a casual supper earlier and are on the deck, counting stars."

The no longer lonely Mrs. Smith leaned toward them. "Such a romantic set of brothers. Does it run in the family?"

Niko could feel himself blushing under her scrutiny.

"Yes, it does." Annalise answered for him. "I've seen him in action."

"And perhaps benefitted from his seductive side?" Mrs. Smith teased.

Annalise busied herself with buttering her bread instead of answering.

Thankfully, the captain chose that moment to make a toast—most probably to save his ship's doctor from the awkward moment. "To those who love the sea!"

Obediently, they all raised their glasses. The waiters followed up the toast by presenting plates of steak and stuffed crab for each guest.

Helena, seated next to the captain, had become incredibly chatty with him, requiring no conversation from him. Besides, they'd run out of things to say early in the afternoon. Funny, thought Niko, how he and Annalise had never run out of things to talk about, even though they'd spent hours together over the last few days.

For some reason, though, the discussions they usually shared seem too intimate to have at a table full of people. Not the subject matter, although the kind of medical discussion they had would probably bore the rest of the guests, but the conversations themselves.

The entertainment director was gifted in small talk, keeping the Smiths amused with funny tales of previous cruises, while they countered with narratives of their grandchildren. All parties involved seemed to be pleased to have new ears to listen to their old stories.

Conversation flowed around Niko and Annalise, leaving them in a cocoon of silence.

Annalise seemed to be lost in thought and he respected her enough to leave her to it as she picked at her food. Was it too much to hope she felt the same way he did about their private conversations? Or had she just had a long day and needed some down time? Either way, he was content enough to sit beside her. He didn't need any other stimulation. Not that he would turn it down if more were offered.

As they were served dessert, the entertainment director interrupted their quiet contemplation.

"Annalise, I hate to ask it of you, but the weather forecast doesn't look great tomorrow. Calm seas but rain. We'll need to have more activities below deck. Do you think you could participate in a staff talent show?"

It was an activity Annalise had never minded helping with before. Dressing up in costume, being someone else for a little while, was always a kick. But sitting next to Niko, she felt shy.

Taking a big bite of strawberry pie bought her some time.

"What's your talent, dear?" Mrs. Smith asked.

"I sing a little."

"She's got a voice that will rival any rock goddess," the captain bragged. "We've got outstanding talent on this ship."

She wiped her mouth with her napkin. Hadn't she learned a long time ago that the best way to face her fear was head on? "I'll be glad to, Captain. Dr. Christopoulos used to sing in a rock band. Want to join in, Niko?"

Before he even thought about it, Niko agreed. What was it about Annalise that called forth in him the need to make her smile at him?

Not only did she smile with those luscious lips, she smiled with her eyes. Sparkling in the way they were, those green eyes made him feel like he'd just fulfilled her greatest fantasy. Or maybe that's what he read in them because that's what he wanted to see.

Because as soon as the spark had come, it went out, leaving her eyes smoky and obscure.

And leaving Niko feeling chilled. What was it about this woman who blew hot and cold? Was it him?

He turned to Helena on his other side and flashed her a

questioning smile. She flashed back, reassuring him she was okay—then put her hand on his shoulder.

"I think I'll skip dessert. It's not good to rumba on a full stomach and the captain has promised me he's quite an enthusiastic dancer."

The captain pushed back his chair, almost knocking it over. "Ladies. Gentlemen. It was a pleasure."

He pulled out Helena's chair. "Madam."

"It's mademoiselle." She took his hand and they were gone.

What would Annalise feel like in his arms? Niko wondered. "Do you rumba?"

"No. But thank you." She gave him a sideways glance. "Do you?"

He took a breath. "I'm not too bad at it. I could teach you. Or if you prefer ballroom dancing, isn't there a big band playing somewhere?"

Mrs Smith nodded. "Yes, on the aft deck."

Annalise gave him a probing look. "You ballroom dance?"

"One of my part-time jobs during high school and college. Classes always have more women than men. One of my grandmother's friends owned a dance studio. She hired two of us. Quite coincidentally, the other guy became a doctor, too."

By her eyes, he could tell she'd gone somewhere else in her head again. Curiosity burned within him. This woman intrigued him like no other. Such complex intricacy. So many levels.

"I've always wanted to learn to waltz."

Niko had the strongest urge to hold her in his arms right then and there. But he reached deep and found the gentleman his grandmother had instilled in him. "Dessert first?"

She cast her eyes down. "If you want."

He wanted. But not food. "You're all the dessert I need."

There it was again. The sparkle as Annalise looked around the table at the other guests. "If you'll excuse us."

Niko tried to read the message behind the look the entertainment director gave him. He wasn't sure what exactly the man was trying to say but he had a feeling it had something to do with being very protective of his ship's doctor.

The director needn't worry. Niko would cut off his right hand before he harmed Annalise. He'd never felt like that with any other woman. Why did he feel that way now?

He had to remember that in a few short days anything between them would have to be over.

"Ready?" Annalise looked expectantly at him.

Ready? He wasn't quite sure what he was ready for. He only knew that if she was involved then yes. He was ready for anything.

CHAPTER ELEVEN

"Look up," Niko whispered in her ear.

Annalise looked up, away from her feet, to drown in those tiger eyes. She missed a step.

"Sorry."

"Don't be sorry. Everybody has to learn." As his breath warmed her ear, raising shivers along her nape, his big hand guided her in the right direction.

The deck was dark enough that the few couples on the make-shift dance floor were nothing but faceless shadows. The band was good—as was all the entertainment the cruise line provided.

The vastness of the night sky fell into the ocean, wrapping them in velvet darkness. Stars came and went overhead as clouds floated by. The moon was a gray crescent sliver overhead. The sea breeze was just enough to make Niko's body next to hers pleasurably warm.

She was acutely aware of his hand on her bare back as the pressure of his palm suggested a backward step.

"One, two, three," he counted for her. "Turn, two, three."

His words were like a litany that went beyond hearing, moving her body beyond her conscious control.

She felt like quicksilver, an extension of the music, part of the night.

"Exquisite," he murmured.

Annalise knew he wasn't talking about her waltz.

She was floating, floating with no concept of space and time. All she knew was Niko's body next to hers, floating, floating in perfect rhythm.

A lovely surreal mist surrounded her reality as she let her essence free.

As the ocean's waves and swells picked up, Niko held her closer, making their steps smaller and smaller until they were barely swaying.

"Look up," he murmured.

She did.

His mouth covered hers and she parted her lips, tasting, inhaling the scent of him, moving closer at the pressure of his hand on her back. She could read it through the energy he surrounded her with. He needed her.

She understood. She needed him. She answered his need, giving, taking, asking, demanding until she lost herself in his kiss.

Her world spun around her as she held onto Niko, secure in his steadiness. Right now, at this moment, he was the center of her universe, directing the moon and the stars. Directing each beat of her heart.

Annalise gasped, realizing she'd forgotten to breathe, realizing the music was now only in her head.

His voice rumbled through her. "Want to continue this in my suite?"

She blinked as if coming out from under hypnosis. The part of her that had ceased to think and could only feel said, "Yes." She sounded dreamy, drugged.

Then panic began to thin out the haze of her fantasy world. Old panic that should have long since been put to bed.

No. She wouldn't let that lovely floating feeling go that easily.

"Yes," she said again, wincing at the way her voice quivered, regretting that she was now anticipating the clamminess that would soon be rising up in her, the way it always did, wishing away a past that kept following her long after her assailant had been locked away.

No, she would not be a prisoner to another man's crime.

Niko placed the gentlest of kisses along her nape. One long finger traced down her spine and his hand splayed across her bare back, supporting her as she leaned away enough to look into his face.

Deliberately, she met his eyes. "Yes."

She sounded firm this time, sure of herself, bold and daring.

Intense desire swept through Niko, making his palms sweat and his heart race. Triumph!

He'd felt her hesitate. Then he'd poured on the charm, following his gut instincts to know what she needed from him, and it had worked.

Annalise. He would soon be running his hands over her, tasting her, feeling her respond—feeling himself respond.

And that's where the apprehension surfaced. Apprehension that this would mean more to her than...

No. That this would mean more to *him* than he was prepared for it to mean.

Logically, he knew he was being unreasonable. They had only met a handful of days ago under circumstances that were totally out of the norm for him. Circumstances that weren't made for anything deep or serious.

Hell, *he* wasn't made for anything deep or serious, no matter what the circumstances.

This was not a time for a game of cat and mouse with a mouse who didn't understand he would be letting her loose as soon as he'd caught her.

That he'd sensed her pulling away was solid proof that this shouldn't be happening like this. Not without the full truth revealed between them.

He was a fool for asking her to join him in his suite. He was a fool for continuing to hold her in his arms when he should be putting distance between them.

Annalise did it for him. Putting her hands on his chest, she pushed him away. "What? I wasn't supposed to agree?"

Niko looked up at the night sky that only seconds before had been comforting in its cocooning darkness.

Now the vastness looked daunting, imposing and desolate.

He looked into her eyes, wanting her to see what he didn't know how to say. "I wasn't supposed to ask."

She darted a quick glance at his ring finger, then back up to his face. "You're not married, are you?"

"No." A raw, self-deprecating laugh worked its way through his chest. "No, I'm not the marrying kind."

"I don't understand." Tears welled, although Niko knew she was trying to hold them back. She was wounded, rejected, hurt. Her pain caused him misery.

"You're not the kind of woman to love and leave. You deserve someone who will stay."

Fire erased the tears in her eyes. "Who are you to say what kind of woman I am?"

"I'm the man who desires you with a want greater than any need I've ever felt before. But I can't take the guilt of feeling I might be coercing you into something you'd regret tomorrow morning."

"Coerce? As in force?" She gave him a wry smile. "Seduce maybe, but not coerce."

"Seduce then." He rubbed his hand through his hair. "I'm sorr—"

She held a finger up to his lips, not touching him by scant millimeters. "No. Don't say it."

He breathed in her lavender lotion, clenching his fists to keep from pulling her to him and kissing her until the shreds of his own good sense floated away on an ocean of pheromones.

Not trusting himself to speak, he gave her a parting nod and turned away.

But she caught his arm. Her hand on his sleeve held him still better than any pair of handcuffs ever made.

"What would it take—?" She stopped. Licked her lips and swallowed, then continued. "What would it take to convince you that a shipboard romance would be enough for me?"

"In the state I'm in right now? Not much." His mouth quirked up as he said it. Humor instead of hurt. It was what he did.

But then he pressed his lips together tightly and thought, respecting that she'd asked a serious question. "Come to me. No stars. No wine. No music. No romance." Niko knew his conditions would drive her away. She was too practical, too guarded, too astute to fall for a guy like him. "Come to me and tell me you want me. Then I'll know."

He turned his back on her and walked away.

With each step he took away from her, Niko felt he was going in the wrong direction. If he'd known it would be this hard, he would have never set foot on this ship.

Perspective, Christopoulos, he reminded himself. This trip was a slice of fantasy out of real time. Annalise would make a nice memory, maybe even a what-if memory. But she could never be his reality. He knew what was important to him and it couldn't include a cruise-ship doctor he would never see again once he disembarked.

What would it feel like when he walked away for good?

Reality made his head ache.

With a sigh Niko headed towards the neon-lit bar with music loud enough to drive throbbing thoughts from his mind.

Through sheer willpower, he kept putting one foot in front of the other until he ended up in a bar so overly loud, so neon flashy and so anonymous he could finally drop the mask of firm decision he'd donned to keep her safe—to keep them both safe—from foolish passion.

Instead, he dropped his head into his hands, not even looking up when he ordered a double Scotch, neat.

CHAPTER TWELVE

ANNALISE SWAM LAPS in the empty adults-only pool until Brandy, who was working the poolside bar, insisted she would grow a mermaid's tail if she didn't come out soon.

Reluctantly, she admitted that going back and forth without getting anywhere was not making progress, only making her exhausted.

How dared he? She scrubbed the excess water from her body then threw the towel into the poolside bin.

How dared he see through her bravado to the insecurities lying underneath?

Her legs quivered as she made her way back to her cabin. But her physical exhaustion did nothing to diminish her mental anguish or her sexual frustration.

Her body burned for Niko. For that nebulous release she'd heard about, read about, but had never experienced.

Finally, hours after she had pushed her alarm clock to the floor to hide the mocking numbers, she fell asleep.

Some time during the night she'd had fevered dreams that had left her soaked in sweat. When had that happened? When she had felt like her body was on fire?

She stripped off the oversized T-shirt and gym shorts she usually slept in, avoiding the mirror as she headed for the shower. But then she stopped herself as she realized her nudity, even in the privacy of her own cabin, made her feel uncomfortable.

Annalise gave herself a stern mental shake. If she wasn't comfortable with her own naked body, how could she be okay with Niko's?

Experimentally, shyly, she ran her hands down her curves.

Unknowingly, he'd dared her to explore her own femininity, to explore her own sexuality, to explore him.

And she *would* explore him, every nook and cranny.

Annalise realized she was standing in front of the mirror, her hands propped on her hips. After too many years of glancing away, she took a good, long look.

"Annalise Walcott, you are a fine-looking woman. A strong woman. A sexy woman—more than sexy enough for Niko Christopoulos. Now, prove it to yourself."

Her beeper startled her with a beep as it displayed the texted reminder, 'Talent show practice in thirty minutes.'

She had forgotten. Niko and she were to perform in tonight's talent show.

Annalise grinned. She knew exactly what song they would sing together.

Niko's late night and the predicted rain splattering on his cabin window lulled him into sleeping late. He awoke with a start, panic over needing to check Sophie's blood-sugar level sending his adrenal glands going into overdrive until he discovered that Phoebe had already taken care of the whole routine.

He was definitely off balance.

Headachy from his overindulgences at the neon bar, Niko looked over the lyrics he'd just been handed as he arrived at the theater two hours late to practice for the talent show.

You ain't no saint, I ain't your angel.

He knew the song. The melody was simple, the chords basic. Still, it had lots of room for drama. It was a good choice for a quick performance.

Apparently, Annalise had already come and gone. He would practice with a recording and hope they hit their cues right tonight. Thankfully, this selection had a lot of wiggle room to improvise and recover from mistakes.

After an hour and a half of getting comfortable with the finger progressions on his borrowed guitar and singing his part with a throat that needed a spoonful of honey to ease last night's excesses, he decided to spend a quiet couple of hours in the ship's library, reading and napping.

Before he could reach the literary refuge, his twin nephews found him.

Marcus gave him a speculative stare. "Uncle Niko, we were going to rent a couple of video games to play in the video-game room but the desk person said it wasn't authorized. They said we had to have your permission. What's the deal with that?"

"I'll take care of it."

"Or we could just ask Dad for his credit card."

That's all Niko needed this morning, to have to deal with his sweepstakes deception being discovered.

"Where's your dad?"

"He and Mom are hanging out in the adults-only pool area. Something about a hot tub and remembering their youth." Marcus shuddered. "I don't want to think about it."

"And everyone else?"

"Yiayia has the little kids in the kiddie theater, watching a movie. I think Uncle Theo and Aunt Chloe were going back to bed after breakfast." Marcus shrugged. "That's all I know."

"Which game did you want to rent?"

They told him and he promised to join them in the games room as soon as he had it arranged. Maybe blasting a few brain-sucking aliens and saving the planet was what he needed to clear his head.

Distracting himself in the games room was a good plan. It might have even worked if Annalise hadn't had the same idea.

Who would have known Dr. Annalise Walcott had a yen to be a kickboxer?

She barely gave him a nod as she kicked and punched, making the video version of herself teach a harsh lesson to the thugs and muggers of the unreal gamester underworld.

He wished he could be so focused as alien after alien blasted his video avatar into smithereens. Instead, he couldn't take his attention from Annalise, clad in a sports bra and bicycle shorts, virtually fighting her way through the underbelly of society.

To his nephews' exasperation, he wasn't nearly as successful in demolishing the invading aliens as Annalise was in dispatching society's scumbags. But the activity did make the time go quicker.

By mid-afternoon he realized he hadn't eaten all day. It was a good, if not quite valid excuse for his irritability. In the dining room he scarfed down a quick sandwich and a fruit plate then hurried off to costuming, hoping Annalise hadn't picked something totally ludicrous for him to wear.

A large crowd had been driven into the theater by the rain that was continuing to fall throughout the late afternoon. They had already sat through a half dozen acts of dubious quality and were getting restless.

In her white choir robe and feathery angel wings Annalise waited for her cue. Despite her nerves, she was ready to sing the opening bars.

While she could never have stood in front of a room full of people to deliver a speech, this was different. She was singing someone else's words, being someone else, being someone bold and brave and beautiful.

Niko would be entering from the opposite side of the stage. She could hardly wait to see how he carried off the costume she'd arranged for him—or to see his reaction to hers.

When she whipped off her angelic robe, she would be revealing a side of herself no one had ever seen. That made her extremely apprehensive. But she was no longer going to let fear stop her from going after the life she wanted.

And that life was quite a bit different than the one she'd been living. This life, this cruise-ship venue, had nurtured her when she'd needed it most but now she had grown past that need.

Doctors Without Borders. She'd been thinking about it for quite a while. She'd been delivering donated medicines and doing volunteer work for the poor of the islands whenever the ship dropped anchor ever since she'd started working for the cruise line, a practice she'd learned from her predecessor. The charity work had been the most rewarding part of her trips. After hearing the passion in Niko's voice when he'd talked about it, she was ready to make it her full-time work.

Since she would be leaving the ship at the end of this run, she would leave them with something to remember her by.

As the captain's personal stewards finished up their shaky barbershop quartet to politely enthusiastic applause, Annalise let out a sigh of relief. They wouldn't be a hard act to follow.

The curtain fell and the production manager gave her a nod along with a thumbs-up.

She hurried out to take her place next to the Styrofoam column that temporarily hid Niko's borrowed guitar. For some reason she'd never doubted he'd be up to the task of pulling off this act. He was the kind of man who inspired confidence.

As the curtain rose, her confidence fell. All those people clapping, waiting, listening for her.

With the floodlights in her eyes, she couldn't make out details, but she saw a movement at the edge of the stage. Niko.

She was not alone in this.

He strode out, tight jeans, black T-shirt and black leather jacket. His tiger eyes gleamed as he ignored the crowd and gave her his full attention.

He stood so close her wings brushed his midnight hair.

"Ready?" He grabbed his microphone from the stand.

She left hers in the stand, clasping her hands angelically instead. "Ready."

As the pianist played the intro lines, Annalise took a deep breath, held it, then belted out the notes right on key.

You say someday the right man will come along,
The man who will see my angel wings and hear my angel
song.
But I say to you, you're wrong.
Because that day has already come and gone.
And it looks like you're here to stay.

He leaned in close, so close she see the sparks in his eyes as he glanced her way then focused on the audience.

I may be here today, but I won't stay.
I'm the kind of man that plays then goes away.
You deserve a man who will never stray.

Niko grabbed the guitar and did a screaming instrumental of angry chords before cueing back to the lyrics.

I've got a wandering soul
And I'm not made to grow old
In one place, even if that place is heaven.

This was the moment Annalise had been planning for. As Niko performed the next guitar break, she unzipped the heavy, shapeless robe and wings and let them fall to the floor, stretching her arms wide to revel in the form and freedom of the tiny, shiny gold spandex dress.

Vaguely, Annalise heard the roar of the onlookers, but nothing spoke as loudly to her as the look in Niko's eyes.

If his tiger eyes were anything to go by, he was definitely feeling carnivorous.

She struck a pose, leaning in close and daring to look straight into those mesmerizing eyes as a dangerous thrill energized her like a bolt of lightning.

Plucking her microphone from the stand, she sang.

You ain't no saint. I ain't your angel.
I'm the woman who can match you, play for play.
Day by day.

She grinned, growling the words out.

And night by night.

Niko missed a beat as he swallowed. Then caught up with her.

Night by night
Day by day
You're the woman who can match me
Play by play.
And I'm the man that can match you, too.
Because I love you.

Together they sang,

Because I love you.

Annalise didn't even realize the curtain had fallen until it started to open again. From the dazed look on Niko's face he hadn't realized it either.

Amazingly, he looked away first, a bashful casting down of his eyes.

"Good job," she whispered as they took their bows.

He nodded, still not looking at her. "And you."

She grabbed his hand and almost dropped it again as heat travelled up her arm and throughout her body. Remembering who she wanted to be, she clasped it tighter as they took another bow and then she led him offstage.

Once alone backstage, he turned to her, searching her face. "Wow."

"Wow back at you."

And then the Christopoulos family interrupted, whooping and laughing and complimenting them.

How could she resent the intrusion when it was all too easy to breathe in the love, the cherishing and solidarity they gave Niko and, by extension, her, too?

What would it be like to be part of a family like this?

But they would expect more than she could give.

Niko lifted her chin. "What's wrong?"

"I need to change before these shoes start to pinch."

He eyed the high-heeled sexy shoes that made her legs look miles long. "That's a shame."

"Life's not fair." She shrugged, trying to smile through the truth. But the twisted feel of her lips told her she had failed.

When one of the twins said he was hungry, Annalise checked the clock. The show had run overtime and it was time for supper. Niko's brother Stephen nodded toward Sophie and said, "My turn," as the family gravitated toward the door.

Annalise knew that supper would be filled with joyous noise, kudos for Niko and endless toasts offered with unconditional love.

Niko called back to them, "Don't wait for me."

Annalise would not be the one to keep him from his family. "No, Niko. Go with them. I may join you later."

Sophie crossed her arms and planted her feet. "I want Uncle Niko to give me my shot. You hurt, Uncle Stephen."

Stephen sent Niko an apologetic look. "Maybe you can show me again."

Niko looked at Annalise as if he were seeking her permission. She nodded, releasing him.

"Sure, brother." He reached down and took Sophie's hand. "Let's show Uncle Stephen how brave girls do this, okay?"

Annalise watched the Christopoulos family troop out, looking and sounding so much like each other that anyone would know they were family. What would it be like to look into a child's face and see your own reflected there?

She could usually stave off her utter aloneness, the lack of a legacy to prove she'd left her mark on the world.

But today her future was harder to accept. One hand drifted to her damaged womb, which could never carry a child, and the other hand covered her damaged heart, which could never carry the love of a man.

She waited for the anger to well up within her, to burn through the melancholy that always followed her reminder of reality. Waited to feel the remembered fear when her mother's boyfriend had loomed over her and she had shut her eyes tight no matter how loudly he'd shouted at her to open them.

She took a breath. Anger and fear and despair were ugly scars she didn't have to wear.

Instead, she thought about Niko. About being held in his arms as they swayed to the music under the stars. About feeling admired and respected whenever he looked at her. About how she would let her passion build and grow when they made love.

And they would make love.

She hung up the leather jacket Niko had worn. It was the only thing he'd needed from the costume wardrobe. The rest of the outfit had been all his.

With measured steps she trod onto the curtained stage.

Carefully, in the tight dress and high heels that she was so unaccustomed to, she stooped to pick up the heavy robe and angel wings from where they had fallen.

She'd tried to have a relationship before with her medical school study partner. They had become great platonic friends, with an easy way between them. When she'd asked, pleaded, for his help, he had agreed.

They'd both tried to make it work—she'd wanted it to work so badly. She'd wanted to prove to herself that her rapist wouldn't win in the end. He'd been kind, gentle and mercifully quick.

But all she'd managed had been distant numbness. Would it be the same with Niko? Would that fire in his touch, that tingling warmth that penetrated her thickest barriers, flame out when it reached her icy core?

Or would he be the one to unthaw her, heart and soul? She could walk away now. Never know. Never fail. Always think it might have worked out, while sanctimoniously congratulating herself on following the rules.

No shipboard romance. No knowing to what heights and depths this chemistry between them could take her. No having to say goodbye when this trip came to its end.

No guts, no glory.

Now was the time. Niko was the man. Tonight she would learn what it was to glory in being a woman, body and soul.

CHAPTER THIRTEEN

NIKO STOOD ON his veranda, his hands gripping the rail as he looked out onto the starlit ocean going past. He'd thought about spending another evening at the bar but muddling his thinking by drinking too many glasses of forgetful juice wouldn't solve his problem. Neither would going up to the top deck.

Would she come to him? So much depended on it.

He'd had it all mapped out, even to the point of accepting that his family wouldn't be happy with his decisions. He'd been so sure of what he wanted. But now...

Now he wanted more than he could have.

What if he loved her?

He shook his head. There was no *what-if.*

He couldn't imagine getting off this ship and never seeing her again.

What was he going to do?

Annalise knocked. Once. Sharply. Then turned away to flee back to the safety of her own berth.

The door opened and Niko reached out, catching her hand and pulling her to him. He bent his lips to her ear. "Annalise. You came." He breathed it like she was an answer to his prayers.

She inhaled his scent, wanting to hold it deep within her forever.

"About your rules, Niko. No stars. No wine. No music. No

romance." She paused. "I've decided you don't get to make all the rules."

She set an ice-filled wine bucket on the counter then went to the wall of windows, looking out at the night sky where the last of the rainclouds were skittering away, exposing a handful of twinkling stars. "What's sex without romance?"

As he walked up behind her, she willed herself to stay relaxed.

Still, he noticed. "Problem?"

What should she tell him? "I don't usually…"

He moved a footstep away. "This isn't your first time, is it?"

Her laugh was much too harsh, much too revealing. "My previous experiences haven't been that great."

"Want to tell me about it?"

"Maybe another time." She closed her eyes. "Tonight I want something more than talk."

"Are you sure you want to do this?" He took another step away. "With me?"

"Yes." She didn't dare turn around, afraid she might show him something with her eyes that she would rather keep to herself.

He was silent for so long that a dozen stars had time to make their appearance. Annalise raised her palm to the glass, anchoring herself.

Ever so lightly, he rested his fingers on the nape of her neck.

She couldn't stop her instinct to hunch her shoulders and shrink away.

He dropped his hand.

"I can't—we can't do this with you being frightened." He backed away, sitting on the bed. "Annalise, you need to tell me what is scaring you."

For the longest time Annalise stood as still as a statue, staring out at the stars. Finally, she sighed deeply, looked at him, avoiding his eyes, then looked at the door.

Just when Niko thought she would go, she sat down next to him, her thigh touching his.

In the dark, in the silence, Annalise said, "I was sixteen when I was raped by my mother's boyfriend. I was afraid to tell her. Afraid she'd say it was my fault. Afraid she'd kick me out of our apartment. That happened to a girl who lived down the hall from us. She didn't even make it a week on the streets before they found her body. I figured one rape was better than a gang rape."

Niko felt such rage race through him he had to use all his concentration to keep his hand from squeezing hers.

"He got me pregnant. I tried to hide it from her but she figured it out when I was sick every morning for two weeks. She took me to this place above a bar and a stinky, greasy woman... she did things to me and I bled."

Bile rose in Niko's throat. He couldn't imagine what the sixteen-year-old Annalise had overcome. Few people, especially teens, would have had the mental strength. She had not only survived but thrived.

"She said the bleeding would stop after a while, but it didn't. Finally, my mother drove me to the hospital and dropped me off at the emergency-room door. She didn't come back for me."

Annalise was squeezing his hand so tightly his fingers tingled.

Niko had to swallow hard to ask, "Afterwards, where did you go?"

"At first I was in a home for wayward teens, repeat offenders in trouble with the law—not that I was one. It was the only place they had to put me." Her laugh was like sandpaper. "And I'd thought I was pretty tough."

"Then what happened?"

"The social worker from the hospital kept looking for a better place for me. She finally got a church-sponsored boarding school with an attached private high school to take me in. I was one of their charity cases. It wasn't bad and the education

I received was outstanding. I was able to earn scholarships that paid for a lot of my college and medical-school expenses."

"Annalise, I don't know what to say." Niko wanted to hold her and protect her from all the bad things in life. But he was too late.

She brushed the tears from his face that he hadn't realized he'd shed.

"Hold me, Niko. Keep me safe tonight."

Could he do this?

His throat closed so that he could only nod. For the first time in his life he understood the healing power of being there. A gentle touch was all the action desired or required.

Annalise curled up in his bed and he curled up around her, cocooning her.

And they slept.

In the morning, she was gone.

Annalise hurried down the gangway, pulling her cart of donated medicines behind her. The island's refugee camp would be anxiously awaiting her delivery of supplies as well as her skills as a physician. Her charity work was one of the reasons she loved her job so much.

That's why, when she'd dropped her application for Doctors Without Borders in the outgoing mail packet early that morning, she'd been certain she'd made the right career-change decision.

She hurried, very aware that the camp would have been expecting her much earlier.

They'd docked sometime during the night and she'd planned to be off the ship at daybreak, but she'd overslept. She was certain she'd never slept so deeply in her life as when she'd been wrapped in Niko's arms.

If only every night's sleep could be as restful.

A wave of sadness threatened to swamp her but Annalise refused to dwell on what couldn't be.

A shipboard relationship, by its nature, was impermanent. With Niko, there were no expectations and no disappointments. She would just be sure to make the most of the little time they had left together.

Niko Christopoulos would always have a special place in her healing heart. Because of him there was a profound difference very deep down within her, like cleansing light had been shone into the dark corners of her psyche.

But it was better that way. Even if Niko was an adventurer now, she'd seen how much he loved his nieces and nephews and how much he admired his sisters-in-law. He would want a family of his own someday. And that was something she could never give him. The thought of being separated from him made her feet feel heavy.

"Annalise, wait up." Niko's deep voice startled her from her thoughts.

She slowed her pace and looked behind her to see him trotting toward her, concern on his face.

"Niko, what's wrong?"

"What's wrong?" He rubbed his hand across his eyes. "I woke up and found you gone. That's what's wrong."

She grinned, both relieved and flattered. "Not everyone is on vacation, Niko Christopoulos."

"You're working?"

"Volunteer work. This island has several refugee camps. People try to navigate the Mediterranean Sea and this is as far as they get sometimes. Different charity organizations have set up clinics. I do what I can when we come through this way." She started pulling the cart toward shore again, carefully concentrating to keep it from rolling out of control.

"I'll go with you."

"What about your family?"

"We've all had quite a bit of togetherness lately. I think we're ready to have some apart time." He commandeered the cart from her, easily keeping the pace steady.

"But you'll miss the tourist attractions."

"What I miss is practicing medicine. I'm not made to be idle this long."

"I understand. The few times I've tried to give myself a break from seeing patients between cruises, I've wound up being irritated with the world and itching to go back to my work. Being a doctor isn't just what I do, it's who I am."

Niko flashed her a brilliant smile. "You do understand."

"This one is not as advanced as some of the other free clinics on the Caribbean islands where we call," she warned him. "But working with Doctors Without Borders, you're used to a lot worse conditions, I'll bet."

"I've seen some primitive environments," he agreed.

Annalise thought about mentioning her recent decision and asking if he would mind if she requested to be assigned with him but now she was thinking that might be a bit presumptuous. If Niko could get tired of his awesome family, what would he think of being saddled with her, a virtual stranger?

Only Niko didn't feel like a stranger. He felt like someone she'd been waiting to meet her whole life.

Which meant that if they were assigned together, the arrangement could get complicated.

She should probably let fate take care of that little issue.

As Niko dragged the cart through the streets, past the brightly colored tourist shops and the clapboard houses with their white-picket-fenced yards, he asked, "What am I hauling?"

"Supplies. Donations from different charity groups. We have a nice collection of used eyeglasses. So many children and adults can't learn to read because they don't see well enough to make out the letters. The glasses are always a welcome donation."

Niko nodded. "Glasses are one of the sought-out donations on missions I've been a part of, too."

They weaved in and out of streets and alleys. The paint

on the buildings became older and sparser until there were no buildings at all. A tent city sat on a span of vacant lots in front of them. Little more than a few strands of sparse weedy grass separated the tarps and quilts and stitched-together rags from each other.

For some, the hodgepodge temporary living quarters didn't appear to be so temporary but rather looked like journey's end. People of all ages sat outside their tents or walked aimlessly from place to place.

Annalise led the way toward the center of the encampment, where four sturdy canvas tents stood with their side walls rolled up.

"That one." She pointed to the tent on the far left.

And that's when they got busy. For the rest of the day, far into the late afternoon, Annalise and Niko saw patient after patient.

As Niko carefully lanced an eardrum, fluid-filled almost to bursting, on a toddler, Annalise said her goodbyes to the staff. Most she had never met before as they changed so frequently. But a few she had known for quite a while. She explained that she wouldn't be back, but her new physician's assistant would come next trip if possible.

The staff took her departure in their stride. They had never known consistency. They just did the best they could with what they had.

As soon as Niko was done, she pointed to her watch. "We've got to get back to the ship. It's getting dark."

They walked in silence for the most part. Leaving behind such squalor for the luxury of the cruise liner, it always took Annalise a moment to adjust.

At the bottom of the gangway, Niko stopped.

"You were great today."

"You, too."

"Especially with the children. You'll make a great mother, Annalise."

No. She wouldn't. She couldn't. The botched abortion had taken away any possibility of her bearing children. "Not in the plan." It came out flippantly to hide her sorrow.

Niko gave her a long look. "I owe you an apology. I underestimated you."

"Most people do." Annalise shrugged it off then blatantly inspected Niko. "Good looks, expensive watch, attitude of nonchalance. I'll bet most people underestimate you, too."

"A man can be more than one thing."

"Like a good lover as well as a good doctor?"

He stopped walking. "What are you saying, Annalise?"

"I'd like to try it again." She licked her bottom lip. "If you're willing."

"With you, I'm always willing." The words were right but the tone was hesitant.

She put her hand on his arm. "Niko, please. Don't. Don't treat me like I'm fragile. I don't break."

"Tell me what you want, Annalise."

"I want to feel like a real woman, a woman who can make a man's blood run hot. I want you to make love to me because you think I'm sexy, not because you feel sorry for me."

"You trust me, don't you, Annalise?"

"I do trust you, Niko."

"Then believe me when I say I don't do pity sex."

"I'm trying."

"What can I do to prove it to you?"

"Make love to me like I was any other woman."

"Oh, no, Annalise. I can't do that. You're not any other woman."

"Because I'm different."

"Because you're special."

Outside his cabin door, he asked her once more. "Are you sure?"

"Yes, Niko, I want to make love to you more than I've ever wanted anything in my whole life."

He opened the door for her and followed her in.

Very quietly, he whispered in her ear, "Let's make this the first-time experience it should have been."

Annalise swallowed past the lump in her throat. "I would like that."

Slowly, gently, he reached up and touched her hair. She breathed in the scent of him as he ran his fingertips across her shoulders. Then he glided his fingers along the edge of her bra, barely brushing the side of her breast.

"Yes?" he asked, his voice throaty, needy, full of want for her.

"Yes." She turned in his arms, putting them chest to chest.

His hand traced her back through her thin T-shirt, leaving a trail of flame sizzling down her spine.

She lifted her mouth, needing to taste him. He met her lips with his own, teasing her mouth until she opened for him. Her knees weakened as the world around her began to blur, soft and hazy and out of focus. Niko was all that mattered.

His big hands brushed over her shoulders and down her arms, capturing her. A distant part of her mind waited for the flinch that would bring disappointment to his eyes. That's when the numbness would begin.

But she didn't flinch, didn't step back, didn't squeeze her eyes closed. Instead, her body leaned in as her instincts trusted Niko to bear her weight.

He carried her to the bed, gracefully sitting her in his lap as he leaned against the headboard.

"Niko." She said his name, soft and husky with an underlying plea for more.

"I'm yours for the taking." He'd heard her and was willing to give her what she needed. He spread his arms wide, giving her total access.

The moonlight through the open window gave the room a feeling of a black and white movie. He made a hell of a leading man.

The look of desire in his eyes emboldened her so she felt like his femme fatale.

Starting with his top button, her clumsy fingers pushed it free of the buttonhole. With her index finger she traced inside the open V. Under her fingertip his chest hair felt coarse while his skin was smooth.

He groaned, deep and long and soulful. "What sweet agony from my exquisite Annalise."

"Should I go faster?"

"No. Please." He kissed the tips of her fingers. "I want this to last forever."

She worked the next button free but couldn't stop herself from going for the next and the one after that until his shirt lay open, exposing his chest and abs. She splayed her hands across his chest, feeling the twin peaks of his flat pecs respond to her touch. Experimentally, she rubbed them. He sucked in his breath like he'd been sucker punched.

She'd done that. She'd taken his breath away. A feeling of power rolled through her.

"Are you okay?" She couldn't keep the provocative pride from her voice when she asked any more than she could keep herself from flicking those sensitive peaks again.

"Vixen." The amusement in his voice caressed her while goading her to continue.

But her own body ached for his exploring touch.

"Tell me, Annalise. Tell me what you want."

"Take my top off." That had sounded demanding, hadn't it? "Please," she added.

"Absolutely." He reached for the hook at the nape of her neck. He pulled her T-shirt over her head.

The appreciated groan he gave her made the heat rise deep down inside that place that had never felt warm before.

She revelled in the way his eyes went dark when she reached back to unhook her bra.

So much appreciation. So much awe. So much desire.

Bare to the night air, her nipples peaked, aching for his attention. "Kiss me."

Obediently, he reverently suckled first one taut tip, then the other. The moan that escaped sounded like it came from the depths of her.

"Thank you." She sounded wispy, breathless.

"My pleasure." His voice was a deeply sincere growl.

"The panties match. Want to see?"

"Yes, oh, please, yes."

Smiling, she shimmied out of her shorts, revealing her newest purchase. No granny panties for her tonight.

In the gray moonlight, her black panties contrasted with the paleness of her skin, making her feel naughty and so very sexy.

She pushed Niko backwards until his knees hit the back of her bed. Fluidly, he lay back on the bed and she climbed on top of him.

Under her, Niko grimaced and shifted his weight.

Immediately, she lifted herself so she straddled him without holding him down. "Your leg?"

He grinned up at her. "No."

"Then what?"

"These jeans are getting a bit tight."

"Oh." Her own naïveté made her blush.

"Do you think you might want to take them off soon? Or at least unzip them?" Her hand hovered over the zipper as the intimacy of what she was about to do made her hesitate.

He grinned at her, his dimples deep as a cloud shifted and a moonbeam splashed across his face. "Please?"

Shyness won out. "You do it."

"Cover my hand." He waited until her hand rested on his before he unbuttoned and unzipped.

"Better?" she asked, even though she could see his jeans restricted him.

"Not quite." He lifted his hips, putting his rough jeans in

contact with the sensitive ache that only the thin silk of her panties protected.

Beneath her, he pushed his jeans off his hips and thighs then kicked them free, all the while bucking underneath her, making her want... Oh, how she wanted.

She marveled at the throbbing that needed fulfillment. She had been sure such passion was only a myth made up for movies and books.

Niko drew in a deep breath. "You are so beautiful."

She stilled, realizing what a silhouette they made in the moonlight.

Quickly, she pushed down her panties. Just as quickly, Niko grabbed protection from the nightstand. His tip nudged her bud and she guided him inside her. They fit together as if they were made for each other. And somewhere in the joyous center of her soul she knew they had been.

She rode him, with her back arched and her hands braced against his chest. His lean body under hers responded to her pace and rhythm, faster and faster until they were both gasping for breath.

A throaty, wordless note of ecstasy came from her throat. Niko answered with his own deep roar of celebration. Together they pulsed in time with the universe.

After an eternity of bliss Annalise lay spent on Niko's chest as he brushed his hand along her back.

"Annalise?"

"Hmm?"

"Tomorrow morning we make port in Malaga. Whatever you have planned, I want to be part of it."

"No plans for Malaga." Annalise thought hard about what she was about to offer. Would it be more painful to experience what being a part of a family was like or more lonely to forgo the whole experience?

Better to have loved and lost than never to have loved at

all. Poets were supposed to be experts at this sort of thing, weren't they?

"I've got the perfect idea for your whole family. Do you think—?"

"I think I want you all to myself."

"This is supposed to be your family vacation."

He grinned at her. "Now you sound like one of the Christopoulos women."

"If only you could be so lucky." Too late, Annalise realized what she'd implied.

Niko lost his grin. "If only…"

He said it low, but Annalise was too tuned in to his every breath to have missed it.

Only what would she do with it?

"Your idea?" Niko prompted.

"Malaga has some great bike tours. They even rent bikes with carriages on the back for Yiayia and the little ones. There's one tour in particular I've heard great things about that I think your family will enjoy."

Looking deceptively like a tame house cat, Niko turned those tiger eyes on her. But she'd seen them blaze with hunger only a short time earlier and was not deceived. "I'm sure my family will enjoy it, but what's in it for me and you?"

"I don't know about you, Niko Christopoulos, but I would love to spend a day with your family." Had Niko heard her yearning to experience being a part of a family underneath her light and breezy tone? She turned away in case her expression gave her away.

Niko came up behind her, giving her the lightest of kisses along her nape. "My family will love spending the day with you as well." Those kisses deepened as they travelled across her throat and down her breasts.

"How about room service tonight?"

"Your family—"

"Will have me all day tomorrow. Tonight I'm yours." He

stopped kissing her a lip's width from the tip of her breast. "If you want me."

His breath on her sensitive skin made her ache so deeply she groaned her answer.

And Annalise found new pleasures she would never have imagined on her own. Much, much later, as she lay in his arms while he slept, she thought about all she had learned from Niko. The stuff that dreams are made of...

But who could go back to living on dreams of the heavens when she'd touched those glorious heights themselves?

Some time in the wee hours of the morning Niko felt Annalise shift, tidying up the bedcovers as if she were tidying up their relationship.

"Annalise?"

She laced her fingers through his. "The way you say my name makes me feel like the most special woman on earth."

"Then you've caught my meaning exactly right."

"Tell me what to do to make you feel special, too."

Niko had never felt so honored. "That you want me to feel that way does the trick for me."

She unlaced her fingers and sat up, letting the sheets fall to her waist. Moonlight showed her beautiful breasts full and perfect for his hands. He gave in to desire and reached toward her, cupping one, savoring the weight in his palm.

"So beautiful."

She reached up and brushed his hair from his eyes. "So are you."

"Tell me what you want, Annalise. Tell me what I can give to you."

"I want you," she said, shifting under him. "I want to feel your touch on every inch of me. I want to be so feverish with needing to feel you in me that I scream with desire."

"Should I start here?" Niko traced her ear then nibbled on the sensitive rim. "And should I taste you as well?"

"Y-e-s." She drew the word out, like she never wanted to let it go.

"And then move to here?" He trailed kisses down her neck, smiling when she grabbed his shoulders and pulled him closer.

"Now. I want you now." She wrapped her legs around him to pull him closer still.

As a gentleman, Niko complied.

And when they came together, each shouting the other's name, Niko had never had a more special moment in his life.

CHAPTER FOURTEEN

ANNALISE HAD BEEN to Malaga many times before, but seeing it through Niko's eyes made all the difference. When she'd recommended the tapas and wine bike tour for the family, they had insisted she come too.

For the first time in her life Annalise felt like she could understand the enormity of being accepted. Along with the whole Christopoulos clan, Annalise cycled along the tapas and wine tour route, eating, drinking and laughing. The younger nieces and nephews took turns riding with Yiayia in a carriage behind a bicycle, which the two older nephews were coerced into manning, while all the Christopoulos men opted for bicycles built for two with their women.

No one blinked an eyelash when Annalise paired up with Niko although she did catch a few winks behind her back.

It was a tour after the Christopoulos family's heart.

At their first stop Stephen raised his glass in a toast to Annalise, with great thanks for the suggestion of the bike tour. When Annalise followed it up with a toast to the strong backs and legs of the Christopoulos twins, the hardy laughs and cheers made her felt like one of their own.

Soon she was stuffed with olives and cheese and fried squid and was giddy from a bit more vino dulce than she was accustomed to drinking.

"This looks interesting. Want to try it?" She held a tapas up to Niko to taste.

He nibbled it from her fingers. "Mmm."

Stephen leaned forward and watched him chew.

"He swallowed it." Stephen high-fived his wife. "Annalise, you are some special lady."

Phoebe explained. "Niko is our picky eater. He won't put anything in his mouth without knowing exactly what it is first."

Niko smiled. "I'll eat anything from the hands of a goddess."

At every stop Yiayia charmed the chefs into giving her inside information, showing such appreciation for their skills that they were bringing the family their specialties to taste.

Cooking meant so much to them, especially to Yiayia and Stephen. It was a part of who they were even more than what they did.

Like medicine was to Niko and to Annalise.

Annalise rubbed her full stomach. The tapas bars of Malaga would not soon forget the Christopoulos family.

Annalise understood. A Christopoulos was not an easy person to forget. She was certain that, no matter what happened, she would remember Niko throughout eternity.

By the time they all reached their last stop, the beach at the fishing village of El Palo, the children were happy to build sandcastles while the adults and teens rested and watched.

The Christopoulos men procured beach towels and spread them on the sand, each trying to be more gallant than the others as they extended a helping hand to their women.

Annalise couldn't help pretending she was a part of this great loving family. She was so full of food and wine she could be excused for letting the line between fantasy and reality blur a bit, couldn't she?

Sitting on the beach, leaning back against Niko, Annalise had never felt more content.

Niko leaned forward and whispered in her ear, "I think this is the happiest day I have ever lived."

While he didn't say it, Annalise took liberties in thinking

that his happiness was in some small part because she was there.

She knew he was the source of *her* bliss.

"Me, too," she said.

Her voice did things to him deep down that he would never have imagined were possible. His heart beat faster, his breathing deepened, and his hands itched to run along her arms and feel her silky-smooth skin.

He gave a quick look around to see if they had an audience, but his brothers were giving all their attention to their wives while Yiayia and the twins watched the little ones.

As shy as Annalise was in public, he took a chance and dropped a kiss on her neck simply because he couldn't help himself. Annalise leaned her head, giving him better access to drop a second one on top of the first.

Apparently he wasn't quick enough because Marcus gave him a thumbs-up. Thankfully, Annalise didn't notice or if she did, she no longer cared that his family saw their public displays of affection.

He was hoping it was the latter. All day he'd fought the urge to kiss her in front of strangers, which only made his anticipation of their time alone tonight much more intense.

He would have stayed there forever if not for the children becoming too cold and wet from the spray of the ocean.

Reluctantly they headed back to the ship. The only thought that made leaving the beach bearable was the thought of Annalise in his bed.

His anticipation was rewarded.

Still shy with him, she asked permission to touch him here and there. Knowing what she was about to do then feeling her gentle, hesitant exploration touched him in ways beyond the physical.

Lying with his hands laced behind his head, he encouraged Annalise to explore. Whatever made her happy made him ecstatic.

She coasted her hands and then her mouth over him, eliciting the most wonderful pleasure he had ever known.

While the night started out for her benefit, her tender explorations quickly turned the tables, making it the most memorable night he'd ever had.

He had a strong feeling that each night with Annalise would be more memorable than the last.

As he was about to grasp a bigger concept, Annalise straddled him. Any logical thought patterns he'd been about to form completely fled his brain while a more primeval part of his body took over.

Softly, sweetly, she mounted him and they came together, swirling, swirling in a haze so rich with the rhythm of love Niko felt her whole body throb in tune with his.

As she lay collapsed on him, he ran his finger down her backside, loving the femininity of her curves.

Annalise soaked up the attention Niko gave her. She'd never had a man want to please her before. All too easily she could become accustomed to feeling cherished. Was it real? Or was it the Christopoulos charm Niko showed all his women?

Happiest day of my life, he'd said. She wanted to believe him. It had certainly been true for her.

But, then, the truth didn't matter, did it? This chance crossing of paths would soon come to an end.

Annalise thought of the enquiry she'd sent to the board of Doctors Without Borders. Maybe, if fate was kind, she and Niko would cross paths again. But Annalise couldn't count on fate.

It was time to practice some self-preservation, time to pull away before Niko left.

On the bedside table Annalise's watch beeped a warning.

Reality. Annalise reached over and checked the time. "I've got to go."

"Go?"

"I've got to dine at the captain's table tonight."

Naked, he stood behind her and turned her to the mirror. He ran his hands over her shoulders. "What can I say..." he gave her a sultry look "...or do to convince you not to go?"

What could he say? *I love you* would work. But he'd given no indication of that.

Lust. Tenderness. Gallantry. Niko had given her all that in spades. But love? There was a good reason for the rule against shipboard romances.

"Say no to the captain. Tell him you have plans with me." He flashed her his best practiced smile.

"Don't do that."

"Don't do what?"

"Don't get all plastic playboy on me because I can't stay and play. Respect me more than that." She had put in too many years of loyal service to want to leave on a bad note. And she needed a clean recommendation.

Plus—and it was a big plus—Niko had taught her to expect respect. Before she'd met him, before she'd seen how much he and his brothers respected all women, including her, she wouldn't have demanded it.

Niko blinked, as if he had been caught looking through her instead of at her. He backed off, leaving her to face the mirror alone. "Sorry. I've started thinking I have you all to myself. Forgive me?"

She turned to look at him, to read his expression. His face was like an open book. No smooth artifice. No practiced smile. Simply sincerity.

He could put more emotion into those tiger eyes of his than anyone she'd ever met. And she had to admit, his possessiveness *was* on the flattering side.

"Forgiven."

"Thanks." He dropped a chaste kiss on her head that left

her wishing for more despite her resolve to put distance between them.

"Tomorrow in port?"

She shook her head. "It's my P.A.'s turn for shore leave. I've got to stay on board and handle the medical suite."

He blew out a breath, looking like a little boy who'd dropped his popsicle in the dirt. "Is it something I did?"

"I'm not on vacation, remember?"

"We're having a private birthday party for Yiayia tomorrow evening. I want you to come." His eyes sharpened, daring her to say no.

Annalise felt honored to be invited but, "It's for family. I don't want to intrude."

"Are you kidding? My family loves you." He looked into the mirror to shave off his five o'clock shadow. Annalise had suspected that with those dark looks he was a twice a day man.

He kept his attention focused on her reflection as she watched his. Seeing those eyes in the mirror gave her no reprieve.

She swallowed, determined to treat this lightly. "You've got a great family. Everyone meshes so well together, brothers and sisters-in-law and all the children."

He lifted his chin to shave but still didn't break eye contact as if he wanted to judge her reaction. "They're a handful. Especially the nieces and nephews. But being the favorite uncle is the perfect deal. I get to cuddle and spoil them when I'm around, then leave them to their parents when one of us gets cranky."

Annalise had resigned herself to never having babies of her own, but being around the Christopoulos children made her wonder what her life might have been like if she could have been stronger and said no when her mother had marched her up to that filthy back room above the stripper bar and ordered the greasy haired woman there to "get rid of it". But at sixteen, with no means of support and her mother threatening to throw her out of her home, she'd been better at hysterical crying than rational action.

When she saw herself in the mirror, she looked incredibly sad. "They'll expect you to have babies one day."

"They have great expectations." Niko broke eye contact, looking at himself instead of her. That same expression he'd had the first day they'd met, the day he'd called himself the black sheep of the family, resurfaced. "They are destined to be disappointed."

"When you tell them about Doctors Without Borders? How can they be?" She reached out to touch him then dropped her hand as if the barriers going up around him were razor sharp. "Niko, you're a hero. A man to be proud of. The work you do is so important to so many."

She thought about telling him how he inspired her and that she was sending in her own application, but this moment wasn't about her.

He pulled a pair of linen pants from his closet. "The price of these pants would feed a family of five for several months in some of the places I've been."

Annalise waited, knowing there was more.

"Sadly, improving lives isn't all about money. There's a lot of generous people out there. If all it took was throwing money at the problem, poverty would have been stamped out a long time ago. Education, health and developing strong leadership skills in the right people is the answer."

"And that takes time." Wrapped in a towel, Annalise inspected her clothes, wincing at the dirt and sweat from a day of bicycling.

He nodded. His time, his skills, his determination to make a difference were the most valuable contributions he had to give. "The cycle of poverty is so entrenched it all seems hopeless sometimes."

"I've read that burnout among the health-care specialists is a big problem."

He'd seen those who had given their all. War and disease took their toll on the workers, but burnout was a huge hazard, too. That's why trips like this were so important.

"Yes. Burnout is a big deal. I've given a lot of thought on how to deal with it. Vacations like this help."

He needed to remember the joys in life so he could deal with the tragedies. And right now one of those joys was joining his family, listening to the prattle of the little ones, seeing the hope for the future in his older nephews' eyes and knowing that love held the universe together as he watched his brothers and their wives make the world a better place just by being their happy selves and raising their happy families.

What didn't work for him was having a wife and kids at home who waited for the infrequent visits of a husband and father too involved in his work to give enough attention to his family.

Which was why there could never be anything between Annalise and himself beyond what they had now.

"What's wrong? Are you in pain?" Annalise scanned him, making him wish he was still naked. Making him wish for things he could never have, for the woman he could never have.

"I'm fine."

"You groaned and pushed your fist into your stomach."

He used his distracting smile. "It must have been that green stuff you made me eat."

Annalise narrowed her eyes. "If you don't want to tell me what's wrong, that's your business." Then her face went blank. "You're entitled to your privacy."

After being so intimate, the concept of keeping anything from each other seemed to make a mockery of their time together.

But how could he tell her his gut clenched at the idea of leaving her when he left the ship?

Niko turned away to give himself a moment.

Where he had been, what he had done, he had learned to

live with loss, only it had never been so personal. And personal made the pain of loss excruciating.

He took another shaky breath, careful to keep his face hidden from Annalise. She could read him like no other.

When he had gathered his composure, he dug through his clothes and handed her one of his T-shirts and a pair of gym shorts. The T-shirt fit her like a dress. The shorts bunched around her waist when she tightened the drawstring enough to keep them from falling off her hips.

"You like?" She held out her hands and turned to model.

Niko caught his breath as he saw the hint of unfettered breasts under the shirt. The woman was breathtaking. "I like—and it has nothing to do with the unique style."

Her laugh brightened his world better than sunshine. "They'll get me back to my room."

"See you at the party tomorrow night?" He saw the hesitation in her eyes. "Please?"

She reached up and ran a finger over his lips. "Has anyone ever said *no to you*?"

"I've heard *no* on occasion and survived. But from you, it would be devastating."

"What would you say if I said the same thing to you?"

"Please, Annalise. It will be our last night on the ship." The implication laid heavy between them.

What could he do? What could he say? The reality of the moment ripped into him. "We can't leave it like this between us."

"Like this?"

"Unfinished." He refused to meet her eyes, afraid of what he might read in them. Which would hurt worse? Resignation or loss?

She nodded. "Closure is a good thing."

No. Closure meant the end. Inside, he screamed it, but he couldn't seem to say it. "Annalise..."

She reached up and cupped his cheek. "I won't go without saying goodbye."

She slipped away before he could answer.

CHAPTER FIFTEEN

ONCE THE DOOR closed behind her, Annalise had to run before all the pent-up emotion made her explode. With tears streaming down her face, she ran down the stairs to her floor. It wasn't that she didn't care who might see her, it was that she couldn't help herself. Running was the only way to keep the pain from overwhelming her. So she ran until her side ached and her lungs burned, her vision so blurry she could barely see.

But, no matter how fast she ran, she couldn't outrun the pain of knowing this had to end.

Then she had to stop. Standing before the door of her room, Annalise had to stop and face herself. Like too many times before, she had nowhere else to go.

She hugged herself, feeling Niko's encompassing shirt around her, smelling his scent rise from her own warm body. Remembering the depth of his eyes when he'd looked at her.

She'd been running away from looking inside herself ever since she'd knocked on Niko's door the first time. But now she'd run into a dead end and the nights spent together had caught up with her.

She had thought making love to Niko would change her inside. And it had, but not the way she had expected.

She had expected to feel braver, more secure, free from her past. Instead, she felt invisible ties binding her to Niko—a man who lived his life without boundaries. What did ties mean to him? She only had to look at his brothers to know.

While she couldn't have children, maybe she could try to be a mother, for Niko's sake?

But what kind of a mother would she be when she really didn't want to be one? The kind of mother *her* mother was, she was afraid.

As much as she wanted it to work, she couldn't be the little woman, barefoot and pregnant, waiting for her man to return.

She couldn't be the woman for him. She couldn't give him what he needed. Family, children, stability to anchor him between missions, to refresh him and send him out again.

Annalise couldn't be that stability for him. Her restlessness was the equal of his. She had her own limits to push. As much as she wanted to be, she was not the home-and-hearth kind.

Niko, with his big heart, would forgo his own needs and accept what she could give, trying to make it work.

But she would know that she couldn't give him what he needed. Niko would always have a place in his heart for children to carry on his legacy, a hole only his perfect partner could fill. With her, that place would always be empty. She could never do that to the man she loved.

Tomorrow they would dock in Barcelona. While half the passengers would disembark then, the other half, including the Christopoulos family, would continue their trip for another week, touring the Greek isles before flying back home.

For the reduced passenger list, the cruise line didn't need both her and the P.A., though the captain and the cruise line had offered to let her stay on for the extra week without duties as a bonus for her long service. She had thought about staying, but now...

Now she thought about going. She had no future with Niko. More time together would only make leaving harder.

The only thing she knew for sure was that she would survive this. She would put her life back together, learn from the experience and go forward. That's what she did.

She was a survivor.

* * *

After a long hard night dining and then sleeping without Annalise, Niko had endured a long, hard day without her, too. If he couldn't get through eighteen hours without her, how could he live the rest of his life without her?

He now understood what his brothers meant. Love for the right woman made a man feel whole. Without it, he had an aloneness that not even his family could fill. In Barcelona, he had accompanied his family to a cooking school presented by one of the area's famous restaurants, had chaperoned the youngest nieces and nephews through the children's museum and had people-watched with the twins, which was usually one of his favorite pastimes but today felt boring beyond measure.

Niko knew the problem wasn't with his activities but with his lack of a partner. If Annalise had been with him, it could have been one of his favorite days of all time. That's what being with Annalise did. It made every day his favorite day.

Niko kept glancing at the door to the party suite, even when he willed himself not to.

Marcus elbowed him. "Looking for someone, Uncle Niko? Someone special?"

He elbowed Marcus back. "Always."

Marcus cocked an eyebrow. "That's a different Niko Christopoulos than the one I've known all my life."

"Just wait, nephew. Your time will come, sooner or later."

"In your case later."

Niko guessed he did seem old to a seventeen-year-old. "Better late than never."

That's what he'd tell Annalise when she finally arrived at Yiayia's party. And what he'd tell his family when he announced she was the one.

He glanced toward the door for the thousandth time in a minute. Where was she?

Niko hadn't caught a glimpse of her since last night at the late dinner seating when he'd sat with the family and she'd sat at the captain's table next to a computer nerd, smiling and nodding as if the twenty-five-year-old millionaire was the smartest man on the ship. Niko had to admit the kid probably was. Not that he had a right to be jealous, but…

If he only had that right…

Soon. Soon he would ask for that right.

Not that he would be the jealous type.

Had she really made a special effort to avoid looking at him, or had that been his ego aching, wanting her attention as she'd chatted the evening away with the computer nerd?

He would make sure Annalise never felt lonely enough to even want to talk to another guy *in that special way* a woman talked to a man.

But he couldn't be there for her, couldn't watch sunsets with her, if he was in some field operation with no way to communicate except by short-wave radio carried to the highest local mountaintop. Could he ask her to wait for him?

That's why he'd never intended to fall in love. But life didn't always turn out the way a man planned it, did it?

She wasn't going to show. Despair followed on the heels of the devastating thought he kept trying to push away. What if it was one-sided? What if this was only a shipboard romance? And if it was more—it had to be more—where did they go with it from here?

What if she didn't show? What if she didn't care? She did, though, didn't she? Hadn't he seen it in her eyes? Felt it in her touch?

Niko caught himself staring at the door as he remembered how her eyes had flashed then squeezed tight in ecstasy the first time they'd come together.

It wasn't only sex. Not for him. Not for her either. All those times together, all those sunsets had to mean more than a vacation fling. He was as certain of that as he was that he was going to take another breath.

As he desperately tried to keep his attention on his excited six-year-old niece telling her rambling version of feeding a talking parrot, Niko felt a tingle in the back of his neck. Without turning, he knew she was there.

Suddenly, all the pieces fit into place inside him.

Yiayia confirmed it when she called out, "Dr. Annalise, welcome to my party. Let me get you some cake."

Her sundress with oversized orange and pink and purple flowers fit her better than his T-shirt but he missed seeing her wrapped in something that belonged to him.

Yiayia gave her one of the prized corner pieces of cake topped with an icing rose.

"For our special friend." Yiayia added a hug with the cake.

Over Yiayia's shoulder Annalise caught his glance. Shadows colored her eyes the same shade of sadness he was feeling.

"Thanks." Annalise's smile, even clouded, lit the darkest corners of his soul.

Before she could take a bite, Sophie demanded her attention. "Dr. Annalise, look at my picture. I'm feeding a parrot."

Niko watched her with Sophie, giving the child a lot more focused attention than he'd been able to. Annalise blended into his family as if she'd always been a part of them.

She was so good with children. He'd seen that at the refugee camp as well as with his own nieces and nephews.

She deserved a husband who could give her a house full of them.

Something very ugly inside him cringed at the thought of Annalise with another man. But it didn't have to be that way.

He could be that man who gave her babies.

He hadn't finalized the papers to sell his part of the practice. He could give her whatever she wanted.

Could he give up his dream, his calling to be a part of Doctors Without Borders, for her?

Or his other option—could he get up every morning, knowing he'd never see her again?

And the biggest question of them all. Did she love him like he loved her?

"To Yiayia!" His brother Stephen began the toasting. "May she have another great eight decades."

"To my grandson Stephen, who had the good sense to marry Phoebe!" Yiayia toasted back.

"To all the fine Christopoulos children, that they may be as wise and gracious and noble as their great-grandmother someday."

The older kids saluted Yiayia and the younger ones quickly followed suit with a little coaching.

"That's how it is in our family," Niko overheard Marcus explain to Annalise. "Like the Musketeers. All for one and one for all."

"To Dr. Annalise, who has graced us with her wisdom and compassion," Phoebe announced.

That was a toast Niko was pleased to drink to.

The toasting went on for almost an hour until every single family member had been covered, except for him.

He cringed, dreading the toast that was sure to come.

His brother Stephen was the one to deliver it.

"To Niko, the slow one of the family." Stephen held his glass high. "May he recognize love when it bites him on the butt then marry the woman and give her a household full of children before she figures out he's so much trouble."

Under the guise of saluting them all with his glass, he noticed Annalise fail to drink. What did it mean? Anything? Everything?

Annalise couldn't do it. She couldn't wish Niko into the arms of another woman. Thankfully, no one seemed to notice.

Phoebe splashed more wine into Annalise's glass as Yiayia toasted her late husband, gone but not forgotten.

She made sure Annalise knew about his heroic exploits.

"My Leo, he was a brave and adventurous man. We travelled many places until we found the one that fit."

"Leo started the restaurant?"

"Oh, no, child. Leo couldn't cook any better than our Niko. He could never sit still either. Just like our Niko. Leo was a fireman. He died saving a pregnant woman. They called me to the hospital. He wasn't burned, at least not that we could tell, but the doctor said his lungs were too full of toxins. They didn't have all the fancy machines they have nowadays to save people. Two lives for one, he said, just before he died. Two lives for one." She looked sad but resigned and proud. "That woman's husband was a banker. He lent me the money to start the restaurant. My boys, Theo and Nicolos, they helped me after school. But then Nicolos became a policeman. We lost him in a bank robbery."

Yiayia glared at the Christopoulos men around her. "Until my grandsons, every generation has had a daredevil as far back as I can remember. But it stopped with my grandsons. I raised them to raise their own families, not to go and get themselves killed. It's a family tradition I'm proud to break."

Over Yiayia's head, Annalise shared a look with Niko, undertanding too well his reluctance to tell her about Doctors Without Borders. What would it do to Yiayia when she found out about his work?

Yiayia waved away the conversation. "Enough of the sad talk. This is a party. Niko, bring Annalise a plate of grapes and cheese and crackers. She will need some meat on her bones when she settles down to have her own children."

Niko loaded up a plate as directed, bringing it to her with a blank expression on his face. She could imagine the turmoil under the surface and her heart went out to him.

When Niko spoke of Doctors Without Borders, the resonance of his voice as well as the passion in his words told her how much it meant to him. When he described the work by saying it was the only time he felt like he was truly fulfilling his purpose for being alive, she easily believed him.

She also knew how much he loved his family. If she had such a wonderful family, it would wound her beyond healing to know she had to disappoint them to live the life that meant so much to her.

While Annalise regretted not having a family to speak of, at least she had the freedom to make her own choices, guilt-free.

Annalise picked at the plate of food until Sophie called her to come look at how she could jump higher than her cousins.

Before the evening ended, Annalise was treated to at least one family story for each member of the Christopoulos clan, from the story about Stephen getting his tongue stuck on a block of dry ice to the one about how Niko hadn't told anyone about his motorcycle and how he'd been grounded for a week until he'd talked Yiayia into taking a ride on the back of it with him. Of course, she'd then forgiven everything and let him keep it.

Finally, Yiayia declared the party over when half the little ones were asleep on the chairs and the other half were running around in circles from being overtired.

All the brothers and sisters-in-law and their little ones hugged her goodnight, just like she was family. Annalise soaked it up. It would all be over too soon.

When they were the only ones left, Annalise asked Niko, "Want to go up top with me?"

"I'll follow you to the ends of the earth." While he'd meant it to be a teasing flirt, Niko had meant it from the bottom of his heart.

She grinned at him. "Tonight, the top deck will do for me."

"For me, too." Those moments alone with her each night gave him a calm serenity he'd never known before.

Tonight he needed that serenity to ease his angst. Niko had some deep thinking to do. If there was any other way…

But he'd heard it himself, verifying what he already knew.

Every woman wanted babies, a home, a husband she could count on.

His grandmother had survived the tragedy of having to bury both a husband and a son. She'd raised her sons and then her grandsons alone. It had been a burden he could never ask any woman to carry.

With the work he did, the risk was always high that he wouldn't make it back home. He was willing to accept the odds for himself but he couldn't accept them for the woman he loved.

Giving up Doctors Without Borders would be like giving up his right arm. But giving up Annalise would be like giving up his heart.

CHAPTER SIXTEEN

MARCUS WAYLAID THEM before they got very far. "Uncle Niko, could I talk to you? In private?"

Marcus looked serious, old beyond his years. Dread made Niko's gut feel heavy. Whatever this was about, it wasn't going to be good.

Niko put on his professional stoicism. Teenagers could be spooked easily so he intended to play this as nonchalantly as possible. "Let's see if the library is deserted."

Annalise gave Marcus an encouraging smile. "You two go ahead. I'll catch up with you later, Niko."

"Dr. Annalise, I was hoping you'd weigh in on this, too. I could use a woman's opinion on how to deal with the females in the family."

Annalise looked confused but reluctantly agreed. "I'm not sure how much help I'll be but I'll give it a try."

Marcus sent a surreptitious glance toward his parents, got a thumbs-up from his twin, who had obviously been assigned to keep them busy, and grabbed a folder of papers from under a chair cushion.

He led the way to a secluded alcove half-obscured by a big potted palm. Niko and he straddled a lounge chair each and Niko had to grin at how much he and his nephew were alike.

But the grin didn't last long. Marcus pulled out a magazine and plopped it in Niko's lap.

On the front cover was a coastguard helicopter, hovering to pick up patients on a sinking home-made raft.

Niko remembered that day well. He identified the sleeve of his own jacket. He'd been just out of camera range for the shot. The photographer had caught the anxiety in the coastguard officer's eyes as he'd checked the straps on the carrier before the patient had been lifted up into the helicopter.

Niko was all too aware of Annalise studying the photograph. Did she understand the danger involved? By the seriousness in her eyes he thought she might.

"That's what I want to do, Uncle Niko."

"Be a doctor?"

"No. A coastguard pilot." He handed Niko a sheaf of papers. "The recruitment office sent me this paperwork. I can sign up now while I'm still in high school and get preferential consideration for the coastguard academy when I graduate. But there's a problem."

Without Marcus having to explain, Niko understood fully what the problem was. Stephen and Phoebe. They would be adamantly opposed to their son choosing such a dangerous career.

"Your parents won't like it at first but they love you, Marcus. There is nothing that will make them stop loving you."

"But Mom and Yiayia… What do you think, Dr. Annalise?"

"The women in your life are a lot stronger than you give them credit for."

Niko glanced down at the magazine cover's headline. "*U.S. Coastguard Teams with Doctors Without Borders to Make Daring Rescue*". "You want me to talk to them?"

"No. I don't need their permission. I'll be eighteen by the time I graduate. I won't need their signatures. But I need to get on the list now to take advantage of early enlistment." He handed Niko a blank form. "I want you to recommend me."

Niko blew out a breath. "Marcus, you know you've got my support in anything you want to pursue and I think you'll make a great coastguard pilot. But I won't go behind your parents' backs. Hiding things from your family is the wrong thing to do."

He was all too aware of the sideways glance Annalise shot at him.

With the way Marcus stared at him, apparently she wasn't the only one who knew he had something to hide.

"You mean like paying for this trip and saying Yiayia won it?" Marcus flipped open the magazine to a photo of Niko precariously balanced on the disintegrating raft as he started an IV in the arm of a child. "Or like being part of Doctors Without Borders?"

Niko looked away from his nephew's eyes and swallowed. "The wrong thing for the right reasons."

Marcus nodded. "You gave us this trip because it's something Yiayia always dreamed of doing but we couldn't have afforded it. You figured everyone's pride would be too great and they wouldn't have accepted it as a gift."

Niko nodded. "That's about the size of it."

"And keeping this a secret?" Marcus pointed to the magazine. "Because you didn't want to worry anyone?"

The dread of family drama built in Niko's stomach. He felt as helpless as a child—as an eight-year-old, to be exact. After all these years Niko realized he associated family turmoil with that time of tears and hysteria he'd barely survived.

Annalise put her hand on his shoulder, anchoring him and giving him strength.

Niko leaned into her touch as he looked into the eyes of the nephew who looked up to him. "It's time we came clean, both of us."

"You first?" Marcus challenged him.

"Me first." Niko threaded his fingers through Annalise's. "Come with me?"

"This is a family matter. They won't appreciate an outsider hearing about your financial ploy." Annalise unthreaded her fingers from his, leaving Niko feeling alone.

Usually she would be right, but his family had taken her in as one of their own.

"You're not an outsider anymore."

"Then what am I?" She crossed her arms, hugging herself. "No. I don't do families."

The guarded look in her eyes stopped him from saying more.

"Náste kalá." She reached up and kissed him on the cheek. *"Antio."*

As the two of them walked towards the party room, Marcus said, "You're going to tell them about paying for this trip and about Doctors Without Borders, right?"

"I'll tell them about the trip." Niko said aloud the decision he'd not wanted to face. "I'm resigning from the field."

"Why?"

"I want a—" Niko almost said *family.* But that was the easy answer, the answer he was programmed to give and Marcus was programmed to accept.

In the face of Marcus's honesty, Niko could do no less. "I can't ask a woman to take on my passion and travel with me or to stay at home and accept a part-time man in her life. So I'm giving up what I love most for who I love most."

"You're in love, Uncle Niko? With Dr. Annalise?"

Niko nodded.

Marcus cocked an eyebrow, looking so much like a typical Christopoulos male it made Niko smile. "The women in our lives *are* a lot stronger than we give them credit for. You should talk to her about it before you decide."

"Maybe I will, Marcus." Niko had to look away because he knew he wouldn't. Annalise would feel honor-bound to set him free. He would never put her in that position.

She would either tell him to go and she would wait for him at home—or she would just tell him to go. The first would wound her but he was certain the latter would kill him. While

Marcus made arrangements with his brother to watch the little ones, Niko roused the adults and herded them into one of the family suites amid much confusion and speculation.

Once they were gathered, Niko tinged a half-full wine bottle with a fork to get everyone's attention.

"Marcus and I have some things to tell you." Niko took a deep breath, wishing he'd drunk the rest of the wine first. "I'll go first. Yiayia, the lady who delivered your sweepstakes check was an actress who owed me for medical work. I paid for this trip."

Thankfully, the suites on either side of his family's suite were no longer occupied as they all got uncivilly loud.

He told them everything—how much they meant to him for raising him and putting him through medical school, how he would be forever in their debt, how he deeply regretted disappointing them, but he had to be his own man. Everything had all tumbled out, as if the words couldn't escape him fast enough.

In the confusion and the turmoil Niko wasn't quite sure how his confession came out so ungracefully. All he knew was that no matter how angry his family was with him, they still loved him, even if he insulted them by thinking he owed them anything. They did what they did for love—not for paybacks.

"Because that's what families do," Phoebe yelled at him when he tried to defend why he'd hidden his financial gift.

"Anything else you need to confess, Niko?" Yiayia asked. At his hesitation, his sisters-in-law added their own questions. Who could withstand the interrogation of the Christopoulos women *en masse*?

How he wished Annalise had been there to protect him when he said, "About those trips I've been taking…"

He made a full confession about Doctors Without Borders, even though he planned to resign for Annalise's sake.

Yes, Chistopoulos women were stronger than they looked. They still weren't on board with Marcus's plan to make early application to the coastguard training academy. But when Stephen told Phoebe that at least Marcus was showing self motivation and they wouldn't have to keep on him about keeping up his grades, Niko know they would eventually come round.

As always, his brothers forgave him everything, even expressing admiration, despite their wives' frowns.

Yiayia wasn't so kind about his involvement in Doctors Without Borders and his apparent bad influence on his nephew.

She wasn't speaking to him. In solidarity, neither were the other women. From past experience he knew their silent treatment wouldn't last beyond the night, and in the morning they'd be just as vocal as ever—which would not be a good thing if they were all still angry at him.

Yet he knew, when all was said and done, they were family—his family—and they loved him as much as he loved them. That's how the Christopoulos women were.

It was a comforting feeling.

But he had another woman on his mind who was giving him heartache.

Niko took the stairs two at a time, needing to see Annalise, to touch her, to hear her voice. Needing to reassure himself he was making the right decision.

As he made his nightly climb, he heard voices from above.

The top deck was filled with passengers watching Barcelona grow smaller and smaller as they pulled away from shore.

But it felt completely empty without Annalise.

What was that she'd said when she'd kissed him on the cheek? *"Náste kalá. Antío."*

Be well and goodbye.

She hadn't meant…she couldn't have meant…

There was still too much unsaid between them.

Packing had gone quickly. Everything Annalise wanted to take with her fit in a single suitcase. The rest she left for the crew, as was the custom.

She now stood on the dock at Barcelona's main port, watching the ship sail without her. The single suitcase made travelling easier as she caught a taxi to the airport.

Her last-minute decision meant she'd be flying to Athens for her interview with the local office of Doctors Without Borders tomorrow afternoon, instead of arriving by ship. Otherwise, everything was going as planned.

Except she hadn't expected her heart to be shattering into a million pieces.

How had she fallen in love so hard, so quickly?

Saying goodbye had been the hardest thing she'd ever done.

But it had been the right thing to do.

Annalise had left the medical suite in good hands.

Should an emergency occur, Annalise had total confidence in her P.A. and the ship would be in port each day with easy access to the best of medical care. And Sophie was surrounded by her loved ones, who would take very good care of her, just as they would if she were at home, while the Christopoulos family spent the week among the Greek isles. The thought made her smile. Those islands would never be the same again after they left.

After meeting them—after meeting Niko—she would never be the same again.

The further the ship sailed from shore, taking Niko away from her, the deeper she felt the pain from the shards of her broken heart. How could loving someone hurt so intensely?

A tour bus pulled up and Annalise realized she was standing under their sign.

"You want a ticket for the Night Lights of Barcelona tour, lady? Special admission into the museums and other tourist attractions."

"Sure. Why not?" Anything was better than wishing for what could never be.

Touring the galleries of Barcelona by herself, Annalise had

never felt so lonely. Before Niko, she'd preferred to explore alone, taking her time to enjoy what she liked most.

But a thousand times during the evening she wanted to turn to Niko and say, "Look. What do you think?" and see his tiger eyes, hear his deep voice as they shared something of awe or beauty.

Could she ever share anything with anyone again?

Checking into the hotel, she saw a father with his two children, a daughter and a son, and it made her smile.

The son had a dimple that flashed like Niko's. She bet the boy got whatever he wanted when he turned on the charm.

Niko was perfect father material.

That's the future Niko's family wished for him. That's the future he should have. The future she could never give him. Reality tore her in two.

She loved Niko with every cell in her body. She loved him enough to let him go.

In her hotel room she wrapped herself in blankets and tried to warm her cold soul with memories. She closed her eyes, remembering the heat of his hands on her, the healing fire he'd built in her heart and in her body.

Niko had forever changed her for the better.

Logically she should be grateful for that and move on.

Her heart clenched in agony. As hard as she tried to be practical, her emotions kept seeping through.

One breath at a time. That's how she survived.

Annalise knew that about herself. She was a survivor.

And she could help others be survivors, too.

She had skills to give the world and for that she would continue to move forward in her life. She would do it in honor of the man who had shown her what love was.

She wished she would have told Niko about her plans. Wished she could have told him how much he meant to her. Wished there had been a better way than simply walking away.

But she might have found the limit to her strength. Saying anything more than goodbye to Niko might have destroyed her.

Finally, as dawn broke through the darkness, she boarded the plane that would take her to her new future.

Niko was not in a good mood. Not being able to find the woman you loved did that to a guy. He'd stayed awake long after midnight, thinking, hoping, wishing she'd come knocking on his door. It hadn't happened.

As soon as morning had broken, he'd searched the ship—their favorite kiosk by the hot tubs, the video arcade and the skating rink, their place on the top deck, everywhere he could think to look.

It was a big ship but he'd always been able to find her when he looked for her before.

Where was she?

They hadn't made plans to meet, but he'd taken for granted—

He'd taken *her* for granted, assuming she would be there when he wanted her.

Fighting down panic, he found her P.A. in the medical suite.

"I don't know where she went, Dr. Christopoulos. She didn't tell me."

The P.A. said Dr. Walcott was done with her duties, had finished her contract. No, she couldn't give out Dr. Walcott's private cellphone number. No, she couldn't give out her cabin number either.

The P.A. gave him a sympathetic shrug. "If she's still on the ship, I'm sure she'll show up."

Niko turned away from the medical suite, stunned. Confused. Lost.

He wandered the ship, bow to stern, for hours.

Desolate, with no appetite, he joined his family for lunch. The smaller passenger list meant only one sitting. He would see her there. It would all be a bad coincidence that they hadn't connected. They would laugh about it. He would propose on the top deck. They would watch the sunset together. And his life would have meaning again.

But when he scanned the dining room, Annalise wasn't there.

The captain said he could give Niko no information. Then Helena took pity on Niko. She batted her eyelashes at the captain and asked sweetly on Niko's behalf. The captain agreed to have someone check the manifest to see if Annalise was still on the ship.

For now, all Niko could do was wait.

The meal with his family was as raucous as ever, reminding Niko what a misfit he was. While Niko barely mustered the will to swallow his soup, the rest of the family chattered around him.

As the wine began to flow, a steward came up to him, giving him a folded note.

Her contract with the ship is over. She vacated her quarters last night and disembarked in Barcelona. She's gone. I'm sorry, Helena

Niko waited impatiently for the ship to dock. His first stop in Athens would be the office of Doctors Without Borders. He would hand in his resignation and then search for Annalise.

He'd spend the rest of his life looking for her if he had to. And when he found her, he would do whatever he needed to do, be whoever he needed to be, to stay by her side.

Niko hurt deep down to the center of his soul. The ache was constant, like a thud on a hollow drum. He knew what it really was. It was the empty place where his heart used to be. Wherever Annaslise had gone, she had taken it with her.

Not that he hadn't given it to her freely. Only she had to be near him for it to go on beating, otherwise his life was just one day after the other with no heart in it.

* * *

Packets in hand, Annalise caught a taxi for her interview. If all went well, she would have a new job with Doctors Without Borders by the time she left Athens.

Once at their offices, Annalise signed the documents pledging herself for the coming year. The administrator gave her a genuinely grateful smile.

"You're perfect, Dr. Walcott. You've got emergency response training and emergency medical experience. You're used to making independent decisions and directing an ever-changing staff. You've even got all your shots."

Annalise gave her a rueful grin, remembering all the inoculations she'd had with the cruise line. "Sounds like I'm your woman, then."

"As soon as we finish all our background checks, we'll have your assignment for you. Not to worry, we'll put you with an experienced team leader until you're comfortable enough to be a team leader yourself."

Niko was a team leader. She had to grip her hands and bite her tongue to keep from requesting him. The wisest answer would be to specifically not ask for him.

It was a large, spread-out operation. What were the odds she would run into Niko on occasion? Would fate be cruel or kind?

In the end, she only nodded her understanding. "I'll be ready."

Emotion swamped Niko as he walked toward the Athens offices of Doctors Without Borders. Impatience overshadowed them all.

The sooner he got this excruciating decision behind him, the sooner he could begin his search for Annalise.

The doors opened and he blinked twice, sure his overwrought brain was playing tricks on him.

"Annalise?"

"Niko?" All blood drained from her face.

If he stood still, she would come to him, right?

After standing frozen, giving her space, giving her time that seemed to draw out for an eternity, he could stand still no longer.

He took three long, quick strides, bringing him next to her. He wanted to reach out and grab her, hold her and never let her go.

But she stood there looking so brittle, he thought if he touched her she might break into a thousand pieces.

"Hey." His throat was so dry from nerves, his voice almost cracked.

"Hey."

"I told them. Told them all about paying for the cruise, about my work, everything."

"And?"

"And it's okay. They're my family."

"You're a lucky man."

"Yes." He thought about how he had been ready to search to the ends of the earth for her and here she was. "Yes, I am."

She swallowed. "What are you doing here?"

"Remember all those toasts my family gave, the ones about me and babies?"

"How could I forget?" She wrapped her arms around herself and stared straight up into the cloudless blue sky. "Go on."

By the way Annalise barely breathed her words, Niko knew how crucial this was to her.

"I'm leaving Doctors Without Borders. Trying to have a family life, expecting my wife to raise the children while I'm gone for months at a time, it wouldn't be fair."

"Your family will be pleased."

Niko expected to see joy and maybe even appreciation for his sacrifice in Annalise's eyes. Instead, her jaw was set in determination as if she was about to swallow a dose of bad medicine.

"And you, Annalise? Aren't you pleased?" He waved his

hands at the building behind them. "I'm doing this for you, for us. For our children."

"No. Not for us. There can be no *us*." Pain made the words cut like glass in her throat. "I've joined Doctors Without Borders. I'll be leaving as soon as I receive my assignment."

"Annalise, I can't let you do that. It's too dangerous."

"You can't let me? Niko, you have no choice in this."

"I can't lose you."

"You never had me," she lied. A piece of her soul would always belong to him. But it was better this way.

"What are you saying?" Niko stared at her as anger tumbled with sorrow and churned with disbelief. "With all that has been between us, I mean nothing to you?"

She pressed her lips together and shook her head. "No."

Her eyes, brimming with tears, and her voice, shaking and thick, said otherwise.

"Only honesty between us, remember?" He reached out for her. If her body said the same thing her lips said, he would know.

Gently, as if she would break at his touch, he cupped her chin. The energy was there. That connection he shared with no other person on earth pulsed under his fingertips. "You say I mean nothing to you. Then why the tears?"

"There was damage. I can't carry a child to term." She blew out a breath. "I've never said that out loud before."

"Annalise—"

She reached out to touch him, but dropped her hand before she made contact. "I've got to go."

"No." He was fierce in his answer, frowning at her, blocking her way.

"You would be such a good father but I'm not cut out to be a mother." She took two steps back and wrapped her arms around herself. "Please, Niko. I'm breaking into pieces here. Don't make this any harder."

"I don't want children." He frowned. "I thought you did."

She wiped at her eyes with the back of her hand. "Why did you think that?"

He seemed genuinely puzzled. "All women do, right?"

Through her tears, she gave him a watery smile. "Has anyone told you that you sometimes have a chauvinistic streak?"

"So you were just going to walk away from me? Without a discussion?"

"I couldn't ask you to choose, babies or me."

"You couldn't ask me? What about my right to choose?" He wiped at his own eyes. "But, then, you just said the same thing to me about Doctors Without Borders, didn't you? We're two of a pair, aren't we? Except for me, there is no choice. Without you, there is no me."

She stopped him with a finger over his lips. "Someday you'll want babies, Niko. You deserve babies. I can't give them to you."

He kissed her finger before clasping her hand, keeping her at his side. "If that day ever comes, there's more than one way to have children. We could adopt."

"You would do that for me?"

"Don't you understand, Annalise? I would do anything for you. Even resign from Doctors Without Borders. Anything."

She put her palm over his heart. "You were going to give up what you loved most for me?"

He covered her hand with his, feeling it warm under his touch as he held it tight against his chest. "I love you, Annalise. What I love most is whatever makes you happiest."

"What makes me happiest is being with you." She gave a nod back to the building. "Think they'll assign us together?"

"They will if they want to keep two very good doctors on staff." He looked down into her eyes. "Is this what you want? I'll give it up for you."

"I would never want you to cut out a part of yourself for I love you, Niko. The whole package."

"The whole package. No more holding back. No more secrets—even if it is to protect the other person."

Annalise held out her free hand to him. When he wrapped his long, strong fingers around her delicate ones, she felt his strength surge through her. This was how it had always been between them. This was how it always would be.

"I'll make you a deal, Niko. I'll work on my communication skills if you'll work on yours."

He cocked an eyebrow at her. "It's going to take a lot of practice. A lot of togetherness."

She nodded. "A lot of patience and compromise."

"Sounds like a marriage to me."

"Are you asking?"

"No, I'm begging. Marry me, Annalise. Make my life whole."

"Yes, Niko. We'll be whole together."

* * * * *

LET'S TALK
Romance

For exclusive extracts, competitions
and special offers, find us online:

f facebook.com/millsandboon

🐦 @MillsandBoon

📷 @MillsandBoonUK

Get in touch on 01413 063232

For all the latest titles coming soon, visit
millsandboon.co.uk/nextmonth

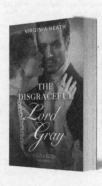